Also By

DI Matt
A REAS
LETHAL INTENT
A NEED TO KILL
CHOSEN TO KILL
A PASSION TO KILL

The Joe Logan Series
AFTERMATH
ATONEMENT
ABSOLUTION
ALLEGIANCE

Other Crime Thrillers
DEADLY REPRISAL
DEADLY REQUITAL
BLACK ROCK BAY
A HUNGER WITHIN
THE SNAKE PIT
A DEADLY STATE OF MIND
TAKEN BY FORCE
DARK NEEDS AND EVIL DEEDS

Science Fiction / Horror
WAITING
CLOSE ENCOUNTERS OF THE STRANGE KIND
RE-EMERGENCE

Children's Fiction
Adventures in Otherworld
PART ONE – THE CHALICE OF HOPE
PART TWO – THE FAIRY CROWN

A
DEADLY
COMPULSION

A DEADLY COMPULSION

By

Michael Kerr

ISBN 978-1530032099

For Joan, Lorraine, Sarah and Matt.

Monsters are not always
recognised for what they are.
Some walk among us and the
apparent normality they
present is no more than a skin-deep
layer of deception,
employed to mask their deadly
compulsions.

~ MK

"Even when she was dead she was
still bitching at me.
I couldn't get her to shut up."

~ Edmund Kemper
(Serial killer)

CHAPTER ONE

TIME and tide...as the saying goes. He had to be on his way, about his business. And although Sharon looked absolutely stunning, staring up at him with such a beguiling and beseeching expression in her cornflower-blue eyes, he needed to be somewhere else.

He pulled the plastic shower cap down at a jaunty angle over her forehead, so that it covered the top of her right ear. It looked like a beret. She could have been mimicking a French onion seller. Just wearing that one item of attire made her even more sensual and provocative, if that were possible.

Leaning over, he kissed her shoulder, neck and mouth, and then said goodbye and hurried away before he could be tempted to weaken, strip off and climb in the tub with her.

Driving home, he savoured the thought of all that he and Sharon had done together. She was one foxy young lady. He could still smell the mellow hint of apple blossom that had wafted from her thick, sun-kissed, flaxen hair. And in his mind's eye he could see her pert breasts, flat stomach, and the downy triangular patch, that to his fingers had felt as soft as a rabbit's scut.

His pulse was racing. He could hear it beating in his ears, almost loud enough to drown out the nondescript voice of Kylie, Jaylo, or whoever the hell it was whining over the airwaves. It was a distraction. He turned off the radio and made plans. Life was so sublime. No one had the slightest idea who he really was. The world truly was his oyster...or oysters, which equated to women. They were his to collect; to prise open and extract the exquisite pearls from within their warm centres. There was nothing that he could not do. He was a hunter, picking off his human prey with the same expertise as a wolf singles out a weak, old or wounded member of a herd. Though *he* harvested the fit, young and strong; those that conformed specifically to his particular needs.

Back at the house, he showered, went through to the bedroom and spent a long time admiring his muscular body in the full-length wardrobe mirror, before slipping on a robe and going down to the kitchen. He was ravenous, and although it was late, he felt wide awake. His stomach was growling. Sex always gave him an enormous appetite. It would be impossible to sleep just yet. Not until he had come down from the natural high he was on. Had he not to be at work so early, then he would probably have stayed up to greet the dawn.

He ate a stack of ham sandwiches with lashings of mustard and drank a pint of milk, straight from the container. He still felt excited as he stealthily climbed the stairs again, stepping over the ninth tread, which had creaked for as long as he could remember. Silence was golden, as his mother would always preach. He tiptoed into the bedroom like a thief in the night. He needed to crash out and get some well-earned rest.

With thoughts of the lovely Sharon, and the mental picture of her pouting mouth, firm rosebud-tipped breasts and shapely legs parted, he fell into a deep slumber.

Laura shuffled papers together, tapped and squared them on the desktop and sank back on the swivel chair, yawning and stretching, closing her eyes momentarily against the harsh glare from the fluorescent tube that hummed overhead. As the breeze from the blades of the fan hit her she felt cold and so lowered her arms, conscious of the patches of perspiration at her armpits. She picked up the Styrofoam cup and winced at the bitter taste of now lukewarm, machine-brewed coffee, and then opened the top drawer of her desk and fumbled a cigarette from the pack hidden there; firing up with a cheap throwaway lighter, silently promising to quit the habit, yet again, once this present mess was sorted.

"We've got another one, boss," Detective Sergeant Hugh Parfitt said, rapping his knuckles on the frosted glass partition of the door and sauntering in.

"Shit!" Laura said, frowning, crushing the now empty cup and tossing it into the waste bin next to her desk. "You sure?"

"Identical MO. It has to be the same guy."

"Well, don't just stand there, Hugh," she said, nodding to the only other chair in the office. "Take the weight off, for Christ's sake."

Detective Inspector Laura Scott was having a terrible month. This was the third gruesome murder in as many weeks. Not just three unrelated random killings, which would have been bad enough, but the work of the same sick individual, who had now butchered three young women and left their bodies in plain sight at various locations around the city. The media were having a field day with it, and as

OIC – Officer in Charge – of the case, she was being showered with the brown stuff, as it hit the fan and flew off in her direction.

Laura had been in post at York for almost two years. And up until this had started she had felt like the cat that'd got the cream, having escaped the Met and moved up to Yorkshire. She had said good-bye to riots, murders by the bucketful and the general feeling that life was just a conveyer belt of violent crime; much of it drug related. The move had also got her away from London, which had been a constant reminder of personal tragedy. The relocation was a much needed fresh start. Now, in the Vale of York, amid country pubs, beautiful scenery and village life, she had the makings of another fucking 'Ripper' on her doorstep. Whoever had passed this case down to her was far from stupid. It could make or break her. If the team made a swift arrest, then she would come out smelling of roses. If not, she would be a handy scapegoat, and would more than likely end up demoted, probably back down to DC for the rest of her career. Sexism was still alive and well, but practised far more surreptitiously these days.

Laura hated the term 'serial killer', but that was what they appeared to be dealing with. It was obvious that some psycho out there had short circuited and was getting his rocks off by slaughtering teenage girls in a ritualistic and barbaric manner. It made her physically shiver. She felt as if the temperature in the office nose-dived ten degrees as her sergeant gave a thumbnail sketch of the latest atrocity.

"So let's go, Hugh. Bring me up to speed on the way," Laura said, rising and pulling on her jacket, almost reaching the door before turning back to collect her cigarettes and lighter from the drawer. Smoking was verboten in the station, but rules were made to be broken.

"Two lads found the body," Hugh said as he drove out of the city heading north towards Strensall. "They were tooled-up with air rifles, shooting rats at a landfill site. She, er, the body was in an old plastic bath. The bastard had even put a shower cap on her head. He left her handbag complete with contents so that we could identify her."

Laura lit a cigarette, unfazed by Hugh's quick look of annoyance as he hit the button and lowered his side window six inches.

"When did they find her?" Laura said as she exhaled twin columns of blue smoke through her nostrils.

"About an hour ago. They went to the site office and reported it to the old guy that oversees the place. He rang us. The forensic team should already be there, and the area is sealed off."

There was a uniform stationed at the gate. He checked their IDs and waved them through, past the bottle banks and skips that were for public use; out through a second set of gates reserved for council trucks to access the large landfill site beyond.

Hugh drove along the rutted track and parked on a large area of compacted earth, next to one of several police vehicles.

Climbing out of the car, Laura could see the fluttering blue and white tape that cordoned off the now tented crime scene. Gulls screeched and whirled overhead as she picked her way carefully across the rubbish-strewn ground, ducked under the tape and entered the Incitent with Hugh at her heels.

Sharon Holder had been sixteen, an intelligent and good looking blue-eyed blonde. She had been a devoted 1D (One Direction) fan, a vegetarian, and had still attended high school. She was like most other girls of her age. But unlike most other girls, Sharon had not made it home from a night out. Her mother, Lisa, was divorced and had only the vaguest Scotch-fogged idea of what Sharon and her elder brother, Paul, did, or where either of them happened to be at any particular time, day or night. Sharon had been a latchkey kid for years, ever since her dad had waltzed off with a tart half his age, never to be heard from again. At the time her body was found, Sharon had not even been missed. If she had ever needed her mother urgently, she had always known which city pubs to phone.

"Jesus!" Hugh said, turning away from the tub, hand over his nose and mouth.

"It's the heat," said Brian Morris, the Home Office pathologist, as he examined the corpse amid the hustle and bustle of the forensic team as they photographed, dusted, and carried out a fingertip search of the scene. "And the rats," he added, nodding to Laura in greeting as he spoke. "The tip is teeming with them. They've been feeding off her for a while."

The body had been badly bitten. The stomach gnawed open to reveal a coil of chewed, purplish-grey intestine, which had been dragged out to hang down between her legs like a surreal Giger-like painting. Her eyes had also been taken, and the hand that Laura could see was missing the ends of at least three fingers.

"How long has she been dead, Brian?" Laura asked, hunkering down next to him, ignoring the stench. "Just a guesstimate," she added as he raised an eyebrow in reply.

"At least seventy-two hours. Rigor has passed. The cause of death appears to be the same as the other two. Her throat has been cut, just deep enough to open the right carotid and jugular. She was bled out at another location, then cleaned up and dumped here."

"Thanks, Brian," Laura said, unable to avert her eyes from the corpse. The girl's mouth was stapled shut, and two blue-rimmed craters topped the small breasts where her nipples should have been. They too had been bitten off, but not by rats.

"I'll know more when I get her on the table," Brian said, straightening up with a grunt as his left hip complained.

Laura also rose, turned and hurried out of the tent as Hugh held the flap aside for her. They walked back across the littered and uneven ground towards the car, noting the large white van – an outside broadcast unit – that was being held at bay by a harried constable. Laura thought of the media as jackals and vultures; scavengers drawn by the smell of blood to a recent kill. A metallic-blue Scorpio appeared and parked up next to the van, and one of Laura's least favourite people climbed out and strode purposefully up to the policeman manning the gate; her attendant camera and sound crew trotting along in her wake. The imperious blonde bitch was Trish Pearson, one of the anchors of a local TV news show. She had latched on to this case and was taking a personal interest in it. It was high profile. The sort of fodder that hit her spot and turned the cool cow on.

"I'll be in the car, Hugh. You can give her the standard brush off. I think if she stuck that microphone in front of my face at this minute, I'd have to tell her where to ram it...sideways."

The mortuary was a cold and soulless place. An old, time-weathered building that had, in Victorian times, been an orphanage.

"Anything new?" Laura said to Brian, watching him walk over to the sink, peel off his stained latex gloves and deposit them into a custard-yellow biohazard bin.

The pathologist liked Laura, or maybe fancied her would be a more honest description of his feelings towards the slim, good looking DI with short dark hair, umber come-to-bed eyes and slightly melancholy smile.

Brian was a stocky fifty-six-year-old, with thinning grey hair and matching goatee beard. His gold rimmed glasses perched precariously on the end of his snub nose, and he jabbed them up absently and habitually, only for them to immediately slip back down again. He was married with three adult children, but that didn't stop him lusting, and the object of his covert lust was Laura Scott. Whereas most other case officers were given short thrift and gruffly advised to wait for a written report, Laura was an exception to the rule. She enjoyed special consideration, and knew it.

"Same as the other two," he said, scrubbing his arms and hands under hot water at the large double sink; the smell of antiseptic and lye soap failing to mask the stink of corruption. Behind him on one of the aluminium tables, the dissected body of Sharon Holder leaked its fluids into the collecting pan beneath. She was now an even more disfigured and hollow vessel with her organs removed, weighed and sectioned; just so much offal. Laura clenched her teeth as she experienced a heartfelt surge of sympathy for the poor girl, who had suffered so much violation, albeit that this particular procedure had been post mortem and carried out to confirm the cause of death.

"The hypostasis in her feet and legs show—"

"Hold it, Brian. Give it to me in layman's terms," Laura said, dragging her eyes away from the cadaver. "Remember, I'm just a copper, not a medical student."

"Uh, sorry. I tend to forget that everyone isn't a pathologist. The bottom line is, that this girl died hard. She was initially struck across the right temple with enough force to probably daze or render her unconscious. Her mouth – as you saw at the scene – was stapled shut. And she had been raped and sodomised. Her nipples were removed by human bite, which will give odontology a good chance of coming up with an impression of the offender's teeth. It's the first useful forensic evidence we've had.

"All this was done ante mortem, before he cut her. The serotonin and free histamine levels will bear that out. He then hung her up. There are rope burns to the neck. She bled out and was left hanging for several hours, which explains the hypost...er, the blood settling to her lower legs and feet. There is also a residue of adhesive around her mouth, wrists and ankles, which I have no doubt will prove to be from insulation tape, the same as with the others. If it runs true to form, we won't get much more. He wore a condom previously, and he meticulously cleans the bodies before he transports them to the location he leaves them to be found. Oh, and the throat was cut from right to left again. He's a lefty, unless he uses his left hand just to try and throw us."

"So he sticks to the same pattern?" Laura said.

"Apart from, in this case, the nipples, yes. He's methodical. He leaves no prints or DNA, so is aware of what forensics can do. The only foreign matter that we've found is a small fragment of plastic material that was snagged under a toenail. I won't be surprised if it turns out to be from a sack of some sort. Once he's cleaned them with surgical spirit, he doesn't risk contamination. He knows what can be obtained from carpet fibres and hairs. He may be a lot of things, but stupid isn't one of them."

"He's a fucking maniac, Brian, that's what he is," Laura said, taking a last look at the forlorn and desecrated remains of the girl, whose head was slightly raised on a wooden block, giving the impression that she was looking down with empty eye sockets at her eviscerated torso.

Thanking the pathologist, Laura left. The paperwork with all the mind-boggling medical jargon would follow.

CHAPTER TWO

IT was a little past midnight when Laura finally arrived home. She kicked off her shoes in the hall, went through to the kitchen and poured a large brandy, needing a jolt of alcohol to help her to unwind and clear her mind a little before even contemplating sleep. The brandy was both French and expensive; one of the few extravagances she allowed herself. The smooth, mellow liquor warmed her, and went a long way to relaxing and unfrazzling nerves that felt frayed and raw from the tension and horror of all that had filled her long day. She draped her jacket over the back of a chair, then unzipped her skirt and let it fall to the floor, now too creased to wear again without being washed and ironed. A pleasure almost as gratifying as the brandy, was the shedding of her clinging black tights. Surely no snake or lizard could know the same joy in sloughing its skin as she experienced by ridding herself of the hot, encompassing denier, which she had been sheathed in for almost seventeen hours.

Feeling unrestricted in just blouse, bra and panties, Laura went into the lounge and curled up on the settee, feet tucked under her, glass in one hand and cigarette in the other. She closed her eyes and let her brain put the events of the day into perspective, mentally filing them away.

Damn! Another five hours and she would be up and getting ready to face another barrage of slings and arrows.

The cottage was her bolt hole; a refuge from the turmoil and frantic pace of her work of late. Situated in splendid isolation on the outskirts of Sand Hutton, – a village east of the Scarborough road – it stood alone, its backdrop thick forest, which was a perfect foil to the city.

The small dwelling had been a tied cottage for the first century of its existence, tenanted by workers of the estate that it had belonged to. Now, it was a cosy home, sympathetically modernised yet still retaining many of the original beams that were, as the house, over two hundred years old. The ground floor comprised a breakfast kitchen and lounge, with a black wrought iron spiral staircase that led up to a landing with two small bedrooms and a bathroom off it.

Laura found the compact accommodation ideal, and valued its peaceful charm.

Now thirty-nine, Laura had married at twenty-two, and was divorced by the time she was thirty. There was no animosity or bitterness between herself and Douglas, her ex. In fact, the break-up had been a time of acute sadness, leaving a sorrow that in weak moments could still choke her with emotion and bring a lump to her throat that felt as though a piece of rock was lodged there.

Douglas had been worn down by her commitment to the force. He'd often said that if her affair had been with another man, then he may have been able to cope, fight; maybe win her back. But he could not battle against her obsession for police work. Laura admitted, much later and only to herself, that he had been right. She was dedicated to the job, at the expense of all else. Work had always seemed to come between them. She had reached a point where she could face the fact that she had loved her husband, but was not *in* love with him. There was a difference, though she had not really worked out what it was. After parting, they had put Kara first, not looking to score points off each other, only wanting what was best for their daughter. But that bond between them had come to an end after the accident three years ago.

Laura set the alarm for six a.m., and fell into a deep yet troubled sleep within two minutes of her head hitting the pillow, as the cogs in her tired brain seemed to whir to a stop like the workings of a pre quartz clock in need of winding up. In her dark dreams she saw the Holder girl, who metamorphosed, her face becoming elastic and reshaping itself into Kara's. Now it was her daughter stretched out on the autopsy table; chest and stomach gaping open, her head shaking slowly from side to side as she tutted in annoyance at the mutilation that had been visited both on and in her body.

Laura was awake and in the shower before the strident blare of the alarm clock had chance to rouse her.

"We've spoken to the Holder girl's mother and brother," Hugh said as Laura slipped off her jacket and settled behind the desk with a cup of gritty, dark vending machine coffee in hand; a glutton for punishment and caffeine.

"And don't tell me," she said, lighting her first cigarette of the day (as per usual totally ignoring the no smoking policy that drove addicts outside the building to snatch a few furtive drags in the rear car park, or on the street). "You drew a blank. No psycho boyfriend or a father with a history of abuse. Nothing, eh?"

Hugh thumbed through the flimsy file that held a potted biography of the dead girl's life and circumstances of her death on just a few sheets of A4 copy paper.

"I don't think that our killer knew any of his victims," Hugh said. "There's nothing to tie them together, apart from the fact that they all had blonde hair and blue eyes." He passed a recent school photograph across the desk as he spoke, and Laura took it and studied the sweet, unblemished face of the girl whom she had seen the day before, eyeless and with her Colgate-white teeth hidden behind seeping, bruised, stapled lips.

"I don't even want to think that there's no other connection, Hugh," she said, frowning and letting her gaze drift through the begrimed second floor window to the tiles, chimney pots, and the shuffling line of pigeons that perched along the old cast-iron guttering of the building opposite. "There must be something else. We just have to find it."

Hugh shrugged, almost apologetically. "They at no time attended the same schools or had mutual friends that we can find. So far, the only remote link is that all three visited the same city night-clubs at one time or another. But that goes for a large percentage of teenagers in the area."

Laura shook her head. "Then it's our worst nightmare. Random killings, no witnesses, and no known motive. He could kill another three or thirty girls without us getting lucky and nailing the bastard."

"You want some more coffee, boss?" Hugh said, rising from the chair. "You're empty."

"Please," Laura said, nodding to the top of a grey metal file cabinet in the corner of the small office. "But use the kettle and my gear. That machine crap is worse than British Rail's."

"What we need," Hugh said, stirring two heaped spoonfuls of sugar into his mug, "is a lead on his vehicle. He attacks them outdoors, before taking them to what he considers is a safe location to...er, do his thing. Then afterwards, sometimes days later, he transports them to where he wants them to be found. This creep takes the girls home and does them at his leisure."

"That's better," Laura said, taking the mug from him and sipping the Nescafe, relishing the strong roasted flavour. "Okay, Hugh. The other two girls were almost certainly abducted from outside their homes. The first one, Cheryl Blake, had been fooling around with her boyfriend in his car at the end of the street where she lived. She set off walking from the car and didn't make it to her front door, which was only fifty yards away. The second victim, Gillian Bentley, was dropped off at the top of a cul-de-sac just four doors from her house, and was lifted. I want you to have all the neighbours interviewed again. Let's really rattle their cages this time. Someone must have noticed a van or car, or a stranger hanging about."

Two weeks passed with no further killings. What became a daily slagging from 'Barbie Doll' Pearson on the TV was beginning to piss Laura and her team off, big-time. But the investigation was getting nowhere fast. They had talked to everyone that had known the three girls, but had no leads. Odontology had come back with graphics and a computer model that gave them heart. The killer had apparently bitten down hard on Sharon Holder's breasts, and then shook his head like a Jack Russell with a rat in its mouth, ripping the nipples free with a scything action. The initial deep bites had left enough impression of individual teeth to almost guarantee a match, if they ever picked up a suspect. It was a step in the right direction, and showed that their quarry was not infallible. He had left a clue as definitive as a fingerprint or DNA.

It was on the third of July that number four turned up.

Heather Cullen had been missing from home for five days. Her parents had made an official report, and had been phoning and calling in at the station incessantly. The beleaguered desk sergeant had become sick of both the sight and sound of them. Truth was, Heather was not considered a priority to anyone but her family and friends, who knew beyond doubt that she would not just go missing without a word. She had been happy at home, and had taken no extra clothing or personal items. The people who knew her best were almost ignored as they tried to impress on the authorities that foul play or an accident was the only possible, rational explanation for her sudden disappearance.

Heather was twenty-one, which did not give her the same status that a missing minor would rate. She was an adult; just one of a vast number whose whereabouts were unknown. The fact that she was a blue-eyed blonde would have sounded alarm bells, had any of the officers dealing with the 'Tacker' murders – as they had become informally tagged – been aware of the details. Unfortunately, the attention was focused exclusively on teenagers. It had been wrongly assumed that they were the killer's targeted section of the community. The sad truth was, that even had they been suspicious, it would not have saved Heather, or prevented the further considerable and undeserved lampooning of the police, especially from Trish Pearson, who seemed to take a perverse delight in twisting the knife.

Eric Yates was nothing if not a man of habit. Just shy of eighty, and retired for nearly twenty years, he had fallen into a way of life that kept him as active and fit as most men many years his junior. He had no intention of just sitting back and fading away, as the majority of his peers had done. His wife, Audrey, had passed on sixteen years ago. She had made them both a cup of tea on that warm summer morning, then sitting in her favourite armchair, sighed once and closed her eyes. It had been that sudden and simple. One second she was there with him, as she had been throughout forty years of marriage. And then in the blink of an eye she was gone, taken stealthily and with no warning. The week after the funeral, Eric's middle-aged daughter had given him Jess.

"This will keep you busy and stop you moping about, Dad," Patricia Yates had said, thrusting the cardboard box at him. The pup inside – now an ageing and arthritic cocker spaniel – had indeed kept him busy, probably adding years to his life with its need for exercise, and constant demand for his attention and affection.

Every morning at six-thirty, come rain or shine, Eric still walked Jess the mile into Milford, stopping at the small Norman church to sit on the bench beneath the thatched roof of its lychgate, where he would hand-roll a cigarette and rest for ten or fifteen minutes before making the return journey.

Eric knew that lychgates' had once been where coffins would be laid to await the clergyman's arrival; a now defunct practise. But that knowledge in no way prepared him for the presence of the young woman who occupied the bench that July morning. She was naked, with wide tape around her body just below her breasts to the back of the seat, presumably to prevent her from slipping down to the ground. She was a ghostly blue-white, staring down with sightless eyes at the bible that had been placed open in her lifeless hands.

Needless to say, Eric and Jess found a different path to tread from that day forth, turning left outside his gate to head towards Len Crowther's farm, instead of right to Milford and the site of his morbid find.

"That's north, south, east and west," Hugh said as they waited for the Scene of Crime Officers to finish up.

"Uh. What did you say?" Laura said, taking a long draw on her Superking light, tempted to tear the filter tip from it; not getting a lot of satisfaction from the weaker cigarettes that she was enduring in an attempt to reduce her dependence on nicotine.

"Compass points. He's now left a body at each principal point, all approximately six miles from the city centre. This guy is precise."

"That's a new one on me," the SOCO said, easing the seated corpse slightly to one side.

"What's new?" Laura said.

"A driving licence."

Laura moved closer in the crowded space that was enclosed by tarpaulin sheets to hide the atrocity from the press and public. Sure enough, it was a driving licence, still in its transparent plastic wallet, stapled to the right cheek of the dead girl's bottom.

"He's gone out of his way to give us instant identification, again," Hugh said.

"Yes, he's involving us on purpose. He's treating us as fellow players; adversaries in his sick game." Laura stated.

"It's almost a carbon copy of the last one, Laura," the pathologist said over the phone the next day. "He kept this one alive for a longer period, and raped her repeatedly. The tissue damage is extensive. She had only been dead for a few hours when she was found. Rigor hadn't fully set in. All other injuries and procedures fit the pattern. It's definitely your serial killer. Sorry."

"Thanks, Brian," Laura said, and rang off.

Heather's father came in to identify the body. He was in uniform, having come straight from Long Hutton; the dispersal prison twelve miles west of the city, where he worked. He looked the part, fiftyish, about five-eleven, a solid fourteen stone, with crew-cut steel-grey hair and a face all hard planes, from which flinty eyes stared in stony circumspection. He didn't speak or even blink when the sheet was pulled back to reveal his late daughter's face, just reached out slowly and ran a blocky index finger over the punctured lips, then nodded and turned away, his emotions locked behind a granite expression.

Hugh Parfitt didn't like the prison officer's reactions. Most people broke down when faced with irrefutable proof that someone near and dear to them was dead. Under such horrific circumstances, Hugh had expected the man to be on the point of collapse, or to at least show some sign of anger or grief. But this guy was implacable. The DS had seen the same purposeful resolve before, though not often. He decided that Ron Cullen was not the type to blithely accept what fate dealt out. He was a man who would do whatever he deemed necessary to exact rough justice for his daughter's murder, and not give a toss if his actions were lawful or otherwise. Hugh made a mental note to ensure that the man was monitored. His interview with him had also been a negative experience, consisting of monosyllabic answers, grunts, and much head shaking. The bottom line was, that the screw claimed to have no idea who could or would have committed the callous crime, although Hugh felt that if he had, he would have said nothing; just gone off and dealt with it in the manner that Charles Bronson the late actor, in his role as Paul Kearsey in the *Death Wish* movies had.

Laura and Hugh attended the funeral. They had been present at those of the other girls. There was also an officer secretly videoing the proceedings from behind the tinted windows of an unmarked Ford Transit van. It was a fact that some murderers would attend the funeral of their victims, taking perverse pleasure in seeing first hand the aftermath of misery and suffering that they had been the direct cause of.

Walking back to the car, Laura decided that she would call Jim Elliott. It would be unofficial, unethical, and completely at odds with her superiors, should they find out. *Tough shit!* What they didn't know wouldn't harm them. She had not seen Jim in over a year, and only spoken to him on the phone infrequently. But they were soul mates, who had fleetingly been bed mates. He would not be happy at what she would ask of him, and may even just hang up on her. That as may be, it was worth a try. She needed the assistance of someone with a special kind of ability; an expertise that the average copper, however good, did not possess. She needed the insight of a rare breed of man; one who could look into the minds of human monsters with a propensity to understand what motivated repeat, ritual killers; a man who could see...*feel* the crimes from the offender's twisted viewpoint. Jim Elliott was such an individual.

CHAPTER THREE

JIM stared out from the balcony of his top floor flat towards the large, round tower of Windsor Castle. It was bathed in warm light, as though etched from sandstone in relief against a Levi-blue, cloudless sky. He was sitting on a white-enamelled, cast-iron chair, sipping black coffee and savouring both the taste and aroma of the strong brew. Luxuriating in the mild summer breeze, that teased the scent from the ornamental, red-flowered japonica that grew in a large terracotta pot against the waist-high balustrade, Jim welcomed the new day.

A glint of sunlight on steel took his gaze higher, to settle on and follow the slow descent of a distant jet as it drifted into Heathrow in the manner of a raptor gliding down to its nest. Mug now empty, Jim rose and walked back into the lounge, pausing for the umpteenth time to look at the poster-size photograph of the castle, which was a stunning monochrome shot of the ninety-two fire; a greasy, black column of smoke rising above the royal residence. He had added the caption: 'Shit Happens!' in his own neat copperplate on a label at the bottom right corner of the gold-leafed frame. The old photo of the burning castle constantly reminded him not to take anything for granted. However seemingly permanent, anything could go up in smoke without warning.

Jim enjoyed every day now, relishing each as it unrolled before him like a rich, multicoloured and complex-patterned Persian carpet. He had just reached forty the previous week, and his thick black hair was shot through with grey, and collar length. He stood six-two, and felt as fit as he looked. His face was even-featured, craggy, and was considered handsome by most people, especially women. His eyes were a striking grey, almost hypnotic in their intensity, to a degree that caused many to look away, unable to meet his direct gaze, feeling disconcerted by it, as though their very souls were being examined. They had every right to feel that way. Jim used his formidable stare to peel back the layers of insincerity and flimflam with the precision of a surgical laser.

Jim Elliott had been with the FBI, and had risen from field agent in his home state of Arizona – based at the Phoenix office – to the behavioural science unit at Quantico, where he had soon become recognised as being one of the most gifted and ingenious profilers in the bureau. His work had led directly to the capture of a dozen serial murderers, and his input had been the undoing of a great many more. Jim had a unique perception of repeat killers, which defied logic. He could somehow see past the reports and forensic evidence, to think himself into their minds. His gift, if that was what it was, had cost him dearly. He had lost the woman he loved, his sanity had been threatened, and ultimately his life had been drastically modified. At the time, he had thought that it had been the last case he had worked on that put him over the edge. But on reflection, later...much later, he had decided that it was the accumulation. The sickness he had steeped himself in finally backed up like effluent in a blocked sewer pipe, overflowing to envelop him, impregnating him with the stink of evil that he had willingly and voluntarily immersed himself in. Every time he looked in a mirror, he saw the thin, white line across his throat; the scar of a wound that had almost killed him and had made him question his motives. He was no paladin-style knight errant with a need to joust at windmills in quixotic fashion. In the end, he had been more practical and selfish than to put false honour and devotion to duty above his own life.

It was in therapy – after he had walked away from it all – that he had been able to look in from the outside and detach himself from that dark place. He found that he could talk through the pain and grief that his ability had brought knocking at the door, and eventually make the first faltering steps towards rehabilitation and a new beginning. The despair had slowly dispersed like a tropical depression moving on, its fury spent and clear skies brightening the horizon. With the light, he had started to care if he took another breath; had stopped relying on booze and sleeping pills, to become less fragile and insecure. But the years of trying to think himself into the minds of homicidal psychopaths and sociopaths had taken its toll; chased out the optimism and light-hearted spirit of youth to leave an open sore of fatalism that ulcerated in the depths of his psyche, stubborn to heal, but now dormant; no longer active. To his chagrin, he found a part of him, that he despised, still missed the hunt and the ultimate satisfaction of closing in and shutting down the operations of crazed human beings, whose mission was to snuff out members of the society that they lived among. Jim now had the same kind of problem as an alcoholic, who would always be one, even though not drinking. He knew that it would only take a single shot to put him back to square one; just a tempting cocktail of files, photographs and the methods employed by a killer to be placed in front of him, and he would slip into the mode that had almost fused his mind.

He had fought the urge, and his depression. With time, and from the ashes of indifference had risen a faltering flame of hope; one that he wanted to nurture, not extinguish.

After recovering from what he had come to accept as being a minor breakdown, friends in London had cajoled Jim into flying across the pond for a change of scene. The intended short break in the UK had not only been an aid to his convalescence, but had also given him new direction and purpose. Over a decade later, he was still in Britain, which he now considered to be his home. How he had fallen into his current line of work was just pure luck. But he was making big bucks, or pounds, so wasn't complaining.

Jim was now a PR man, spin doctor and image-maker all rolled into one. He stayed anonymous, consciously avoiding the rub-off celebrity status, not courting fame as other guys like Max Clifford had , and seemed to thrive on, until they themselves were put under the microscope and found wanting. He turned individuals and companies around, finding the edge that they needed to realise a greater success in their respective areas of endeavour, over the competition. It was a shallow but safe harbour, in which he had established an outlet for his unique powers of understanding the human condition.

The trill of the phone snapped him from his reverie. He stared at it as though it was road kill, but did not move, content to let the answering machine take the call: *'Hi, this is Jim Elliott. I'm tied up at the moment, but if you leave your name and number, or a message, I'll get back to you'*, his recorded voice said to the caller.

"Jim, it's Laura…Laura Scott. I need to talk to you. You have my York number. It's important. Please call me. Bye."

"Laura," Jim whispered, now looking at the phone as if it was a work of art; a rendering that might have been fashioned by Da Vinci.

Ten minutes later, with a freshly brewed mug of coffee to hand, Jim was next to the phone, replaying the message for a fourth time. Laura's voice was tense, with a raw edge cutting through the controlled cadence. Its rhythm and intonation was slightly clipped, guarded, and holding a note of desperation and urgency that was either measured for effect, or an unconscious but nonetheless compelling ploy to get his attention. She had implied nothing and yet everything, and he knew that when, not if he called her back, he would regret it. The icy tendrils that snaked through his mind and tightened around his brain were a warning that contacting her might lead him into a place he did not want to go. He reached for the phone, rested his hand on it, then pulled back, to stand up again and walk barefoot across to the open door and out once more onto the balcony. The warm breeze caught the bottom of the silk dressing gown he wore, flapping it up against his muscular thighs. And the sun's heat on the concrete was now almost too hot on the soles of his feet. He squinted across at the castellated rim of the tower, sipping absently at the coffee, running through his options.

Laura's call was business. And it didn't take Sherlock Holmes to know what that business was. There had been speculation in the media of a serial killer on the rampage up in Yorkshire, but he had avoided the details, hit the remote and switched channels if it was mentioned on the news. He had no intention of allowing his profiler's thought processes to kick in and begin to overwhelm him again. Goddammit to hell! There were no options to mull over. Laura was going to ask him to help, and he couldn't...wouldn't. She had no right to expect anything of him. Anger swept through him briefly like a bush fire, but was almost instantly smothered as Laura's face – with winsome smile and magnetic brown eyes – materialised in his mind. He stared into his cooling coffee and recalled the nearness of her; the sweet smell of her hair, and the alluring scent of the perfume she wore.

"I'll put you through, sir," a slightly bored sounding female voice said. He waited, ten, then twenty seconds, his stomach in freefall mode.

"Hi, Jim," Laura's voice said, breaking through a background thrum of static. "Thanks for calling. I thought you might not."

He absorbed each syllable greedily, one at a time. Their texture was crushed velvet, and he realised just how much he missed Laura Scott.

"It's been too long," he replied. "How're you keeping, Laura?"

"I'm fine. You?"

"I *was* okay. Why the call?"

He heard the intake of breath and knew that her mind was racing, searching for the right words to broach what she knew would be a taboo subject.

"This isn't easy, Jim," she began. "But I need your help, advice...anything you can give me."

So there it was, as he had expected. This had been what had stopped their relationship from blossoming into more than just a six month fling. Jim had loved her, and maybe he still did. But the police work came between them, chafing his still raw nerves. He had recoiled from the sordid side of life that he had run away from; the side that Laura still embraced and was seemingly so passionately involved with.

"I know what you want, Laura. You have a big problem up there. But it's your problem. It goes with the patch."

"I know that, Jim. I haven't forgotten how you feel, believe me. But I want to save lives. If I don't get a handle on this killer...well, we'll be up to our ears in dead teenage girls, and you know it."

"Don't try sending me on a guilt trip, Laura. You have good people of your own. Why don't you go through the official list of capable criminal psychologists who will be available to consult and work up a profile for you?"

"Because they're not Jim Elliott."

"I'm sorry, Laura, but that life's behind me, and flattery will get you nowhere. You know it never ends. At the present time there are maybe a couple of hundred active serial killers in the States, probably treble that, who knows? If I wanted to be involved, I would have all the work I could handle back there."

"Just advice, Jim, for Christ's sake, that's all I'm asking for. Let me send you some stuff to look at. Give me your thoughts on it off the record, will you?"

"You are one pushy broad, but the answer is still no."

"Have you still got that old fax machine?"

"Yeah, but—"

"I'll fax it anyway. Nothing ventured, eh? And don't let's leave it so long next time. If I remember rightly you owe me a meal."

She hung up before he could reply, and the short conversation had not been enough. It had been an appetiser that left him unfulfilled, hungry for an entrée.

The 'meet' and round of golf at Wentworth was rewarding. Jim bonded immediately with his prospective client. The guy was a fading pop star, only remembered because of a handful of minor hits from the late eighties and early nineties. And then only by the middle-aged, who were reminded of him by the odd 'golden oldie' that got aired once in a blue moon on Radio 2, and the release of his now dated hits, available at cut-price on CD. He needed reinventing.

20

Jim gave him an outline of what he would try to do. He explained that it would be more than a makeover; that it would be the whole nine yards. The singer needed to shed two stone, his present manager, and his habit. Jim assessed the old rocker as still being hungry, and wanting to be back in the limelight. He had been performing in second-rate venues for over twenty years, tooting coke as he spiralled ever downward into obscurity. Unbeknown to the singer, Jim had caught his act at a pub in Hounslow, and had been impressed. He could still hold a tune, and play an audience, and so deserved to be doing better.

Golf is a good yardstick of character and personality. Jim blew the guy off the course, and admired the grit and determination that his opponent displayed, fighting all the way to the eighteenth, even when he knew that he could not win. He had control, composure, and most importantly, hated defeat. He still had the potential to make it happen, with Jim's help, and was taken on as a client as they left the course and headed for the locker room.

Jim did not consider himself a PR supremo. He didn't like labels. He was just good at recognising what was needed to boost a client's fortunes. His last major success had been with an MP of outward mediocrity. All that had been needed was a change of hairstyle, a new tailor, and good press over a fortuitous incident during which the politician had given roadside assistance to a badly injured teenager who'd managed to steer his motorcycle into an oncoming lorry. That the youngster was black and survived the accident, was a bonus. It made good copy. The MP was now a junior cabinet minister, and would probably rise even higher. All he had needed was a push in the right direction, and Jim had given it to him.

Returning to the flat, Jim stashed his golf clubs in the hall and walked through to the lounge. Good as her word, Laura had faxed him a sheaf of stuff, which he ignored as he passed it by and headed for the bedroom. He stripped off his sweaty clothes and slid a Joe Cocker CD into the player, cranking up the volume so that he would be able to hear it in the shower. As Cocker croaked out *Delta Lady*, Jim decided that he would not even look at the information that lay taunting him in the fax tray. At some point he would feed it to the shredder and then bin it. He was not going to be sucked in, and that was cut-and-dried.

It was past midnight when he finally hit the sack. He had been out for an Italian meal at Luigi's on the Staines road with an ex-client who was now fronting a popular TV quiz show, and had become a household name. He had also become one of Jim's best friends.

At two a.m., Jim was still awake. And it wasn't the muggy heat that held sleep at bay. It was the fucking faxes that Laura had sent, calling out to him, chiselling at his mind, demanding him to be aware of their horrific content and of the patterns and motives that would be woven into the fabric of the details. A part of him wanted, *craved* the challenge. The old electrical charge that used to surge through his veins was back with a vengeance.

It was three a.m. when his resolve broke and deserted him like rats from a sinking ship. He had no clear recollection of getting out of bed, or of walking through to the lounge to take the stack of paper across to the table at which he was now sitting. He began reading, and after just two pages was suddenly pushing the chair back, rising, running to the bathroom to throw-up in the toilet bowl. He was shaking, felt faint, and his heart was spiked by a sharp, freezing icicle of unbridled fear. It was a reaction to facing a situation that his subconscious rebelled against. It reminded him of exactly how he had felt on boarding a plane at Dulles airport, west of Washington D.C., back in the winter of two thousand and three. Eight weeks prior to that flight, he had been involved in a crash landing that resulted in over half of the passengers being cremated in the fire that ensued. The chartered DC-10 had fallen the final few feet like a shot goose, crumpling the landing gear, tilting and spinning out of control as one wing struck the ground before merging with the unforgiving runway and exploding. Amid the choking black smoke and the screaming of injured and frightened passengers, he had somehow helped an attendant to open a door, and assisted dozens of survivors to escape down the billowing yellow slide to safety. Only when a blinding ball of flame streaked through the fuselage, did he throw himself down the chute, in no doubt that he would be the last living person to reach the tarmac.

Facing the beginning of Laura's reports had caused the same reaction as when he had flown again for the first time after that incident. It was not an irrational fear. Planes *did* crash. There was no guarantee that you would survive a flight. The odds were heavily on the side of safe arrival at your destination, but after one close call the statistics and percentages had lost a lot of their power to boost Jim's confidence.

It was fifteen minutes later, after rinsing his face with cold water and having poured himself a large measure of Jack Daniel's that Jim tentatively returned to the table. The printed words drew him with the power of a siren luring a seafarer onto an accursed, rocky shore with enchanting song that could not be ignored or resisted.

He started reading, opening and entering a door in his mind that he had kept firmly locked for years.

Laura had been reluctant to contact Jim. She knew how much he had been affected by his years with the bureau, and of the events that had ended his career. She didn't want to hurt him; still cared for him, and was scared that approaching him with this would ruin their friendship. But as per usual she had suppressed personal concerns by reminding herself that the body count was rising, and that a sick individual was on the loose, out of control: a killer who would not stop until he was hunted down and captured. Jim Elliott was – or had been – the most successful profiler on the planet. That was a fact. He had a unique gift; one that could not be matched. If she was able to prise even a few pointers from him, then she would, and to hell with the consequences. That he had refused to even discuss the case was, to say the least, disappointing. She wanted to respect his decision, but was gutted by his lack of altruism. Faxing the files, including crime scene and autopsy photographs, was a blatant transgression. But if she knew Jim at all, then he would not be able to resist looking at them, and if he did, then who knew? He might just get interested.

CHAPTER FOUR

HE remembered. Was back there with clarity of mind that imbued an aura of reality. All his senses combined to recreate the events. He was a young boy again and…

…This was a moment that he always dreaded with a fear that was irrational, but no less real for knowing that he was in no danger and would survive the ordeal. His fingers were cold, stiff and painful with cramp as he clutched the bolt that held the door tightly closed in its jamb; a barrier between him and them. He continued to stand transfixed, heart thudding in his narrow chest with the ferocity of how he imagined a wild animal may slam against the bars of its cage in a futile bid to escape captivity.

The sullen, leaden sky was full of boiling thunderheads that promised rain. And the chill wind cut through his cotton shirt and jeans. Still, he hesitated, putting off what had to be done. With bated breath he finally eased the steel bolt from its staple and pulled back the rough, planked door, pausing as several earwigs dropped writhing from the inside of the frame to scurry into the straw that covered the shed's floor. He stepped over the threshold into the gloomy interior, almost gagging as the acidic smell of fresh droppings and the stale heat from confined bodies combined to sear his nostrils. Wings stretched, unfurled and flapped about him as the two dozen chickens became restless on their perches and in the laying boxes that were fitted to the sides of the hen house. With a trembling hand, he started to collect the eggs, placing each carefully in the large wicker basket that he cradled in the crook of his right arm. He hurried to complete the task as the fowl began to mill about, pecking at his legs and pulling at the laces of his Nikes with their blunted, stabbing, darting beaks.

He hated chickens with a passion that was only equalled by his fear of them. Each morning he hoped that a fox might have successfully gained entry and torn the bony, feathered, brainless creatures apart. But the defences were formidable. His father had dug a three-foot deep trench around the structure, and then sunk galvanised wire mesh into it, before back-filling, packing down the soil and nailing the top of the vermin-proof net to the shed under wooden batons. Then of course there was Duke, their Staffordshire bull terrier; his night quarters a kennel in sight of the mangy birds' shelter. No, his hope of the hens becoming fox food was no more than a pipe-dream.

Halfway back to the house, he stopped, the basket of eggs still held tightly but forgotten in his hands. With his head cocked slightly to one side, he listened to the distant racing of a tractor's engine, and knew that something was wrong.

The west field dropped away steeply. It had to be negotiated with extreme caution and at the right angles. Cutting corners and trying to turn too sharply could result in machinery tipping over; it had happened before.

The oily blue smoke was being blown towards him as he began walking down the partly ploughed field. He didn't rush, being more curious than concerned as he topped the brow and saw the green John Deere on its side, bellowing mechanically, analogous in his mind to a giant Jurassic beast lying mortally injured, unable to regain its feet.

His father was at the far side of the tractor, pinned by it, with only his head and shoulders protruding from under the cab. He appeared to be flattened into the soft ruts of earth; just a partly buried alabaster bust, covered in a mixture of damp soil and blood.

"Don't ju…just fucking stand there, boy, get help," his father wheezed, bright crimson bubbles popping from his grey lips with every rasping word.

He looked down at the eggs. They were a uniform light coffee-brown. Some had pieces of straw stuck to them. Others were smeared with specks of blood, and small downy feathers that curled and quivered in the wind; a few escaping to spiral up fleetingly into the light rain, only to be beaten back down, sodden and limp.

"Die…Die…Please die!" he murmured, keeping his eyes on the eggs, as though they might magically disappear if he let his gaze drift away from them for even a second. He tuned out his father's frantic, weakening, pleading voice, which had at first held anger, but was now a begging, sobbing whine that both amused and pleased him. The droning voice began to sound like the television in the house did, as he lay in his bed at night. It was just an unintelligible and faraway background noise.

A furtive glance showed that his dad – who now seemed a stranger to him – was turning blue in the face. He was no longer making demands. His eyes had rolled back in their sockets and were oblivious to the raindrops that bounced off their red-veined surfaces.

25

He waited until the liquid breathing finally stopped, and then walked slowly across and knelt down beside the still figure, satisfying himself that it was lifeless before directing a gob of spittle onto the corpse's forehead.

Humming tunelessly, he walked back up the hill to the house, around to the rear, where he removed his clay-caked trainers at the kitchen door, entered and placed the eggs in boxes and then filled the kettle. He was suddenly very thirsty, in need of a cup of tea. This, he mused, was without any question or doubt at all the very best day of his life. The fat, no-good, foul-smelling drunkard would never lay into him with his belt again, or strike his mother, or pull her by her corn-blonde hair, to cause her china-blue eyes to shed tears of fear and pain. The old bastard would never do anything ever again, apart from rot under and contaminate the earth, where his now cooling body belonged.

He was almost thirteen, and his mother was not yet thirty, having had him when she was just sixteen. He recalled that there had been little love or even affection between his parents. His father had been many years older than his mother, and treated her as almost a slave on the farm. All her love had been directed towards him.

As he sat at the kitchen table, he brought to mind the first time that their love had transcended normal boundaries. His mother had been bathing him in the old, discoloured cast-iron bath, sponging his back with hot, soapy water. It was then that his penis broke the surface, bigger and stiffer than he had ever seen it before; a pink periscope rising from a submerged submarine.

"Let me see, sweetheart," his mother had said as, too late, he tried to cover it with his hands and a thick drift of suds. He was eleven, and she touched and caressed him in a way that made him feel as weak as jelly; boneless and yet wonderfully excited. She kissed him...down there; put her mouth over him and caused almost unbearable sensations that made him moan aloud with pleasure. And just when he thought he might explode, she stopped, undressed and climbed into the tub with him.

Since that bath time baptism, he and his mum had enjoyed sex regularly. It was their secret, she had said, and no one else – especially his father – must ever know about it.

What had been a dislike for his ageing father quickly turned to smouldering hatred. When the old man was drunk, which was more often than not, he would beat his wife for the smallest imagined indiscretion, then aroused by the violence, take her to his bed.

Lying in the next room, in the darkness, there was no way to blot out the shriek of rusted bedsprings rhythmically scraping together. He would cry himself to sleep, pillow over his head to dampen the noise, knowing exactly what was taking place and picturing his mother pinned to the mattress, enduring all that was being done to her. The loathing for his father had blossomed and grown like a black, thorny bush within him.

After his father's death, up until he was eighteen, everything was absolutely perfect. And then his mother met Tom Brannon – a local councillor – and brought their long-standing incestuous relationship to an abrupt end. He was devastated. He pleaded with her, threatened her, and even raped her. It broke his heart that she would want to abandon him. But what had been between them was over. She was infatuated with Brannon, his money and his shiny silver BMW.

The crash had made the front pages of the local newspapers. Not least because the councillor had been driving with his trousers and underpants down to his thighs, and that the blonde who was with him was a local widow, not his wife. The car had left the road at speed and hit an unyielding brick wall, killing both occupants instantly as the engine block was pushed back to meld steel and flesh in uneasy union.

Due to the fact that both driver and passenger had been drinking, and were believed to have been engaged in some lewd sexual act at the time of impact, the vehicle was only given a cursory check. Had it been inspected more thoroughly, then the loose coupling on the steering rack may have instigated further and more rigorous investigation.

The coroner's verdict of death by misadventure closed the door on what should have been a murder inquiry.

He missed her so much, even though she had betrayed him and forsaken him for another. He loved her and hated her with equal zeal; his confused emotions torturing him and psychologically ripping him apart. He had killed her body and mind, destroyed her for spurning him, but still needed and wanted her. Somehow she must be made to pay an even higher price for the suffering that he had to endure because of her actions.

With the untenable, gnawing need came the will. And with the will came the way to ease the crushing pain, and the ability to recreate her again...and again.

Now, many years later, he sat in the gloom with just the flickering light from the television illuminating his naked body in stuttering, strobe-like relief. He stared at the screen, unblinking, glaring at the image of the presenter, hating the smug bitch as she spouted verbal diarrhoea through a mouth that could shift from flashing, pearly smile of insincerity to tight-lipped pseudo grief faster than a chameleon could change its colour. She, Trish Pearson, was showing photographs of the sluts he had disposed of. Photos of them smiling, fresh-faced and carefree. Photos that had been garnered from the walls, mantelpieces and sideboards of what had been their homes, to show uncaring viewers, who would forget the images as soon as the next item whisked them off to the latest act of terrorism, famine in some barren African cesspool, or bombarded them with the news of a six-year-old who was, thanks to sponsored walks and parachute jumps, now undergoing lifesaving surgery in Pittsburgh or Katmanfuckingdu. *He* had photographs; Polaroid's of the bitches which were scattered at his feet. Frozen moments in time that showed how they had looked at various stages of his ministrations, and in the final poses he had left them in to be reclaimed.

Pressing the mute button on the hand set, he watched the blonde talking head mime for a few seconds, then closed his eyes and replayed his latest exploit through his mind with more clarity than if it had been on DVD with surround sound. He was reliving it with perfect recall. Every moment flooding back as though it was just taking place.

He had been standing in the recessed doorway, hidden by the night, black-on-black, hands thrust deep in pockets as he watched the teenagers entering and leaving The Wired Warehouse, a night-club adjacent to the silky, grey ribbon of the River Ouse. The water shimmered under reflected light from buildings that crowded both sides of its concrete and brick banks. Groups and couples came and went on foot and by taxi.

He stiffened and pressed farther back as a lone figure clipped up the ill-lit side street that led to the brighter and more populated main thoroughfares. As she neared him, he relaxed. She was a scrawny brunette, unsuitable and repugnant to him, not conforming to any of the strict requirements that he adhered to when selecting prey.

It was almost midnight when the blonde appeared from the glowing rectangle of the club's doorway, alone, to hurry along the pavement towards him, unsuspecting. As she passed, he stepped out and followed, overtaking her in three strides, to turn and stand in front of her. She stopped abruptly, startled, unknowingly only three feet away from his black Mondeo, which was parked at the kerb beside her. She looked at him quizzically, her blue eyes wide with apprehension. He smiled at her, before lashing out with his fist to hit her on the temple with enough force to stun and knock her to the ground. Moving quickly, he gripped her under the armpits and dragged her to the rear of the car. Within seconds he had bundled her into the boot and wrapped two-inch-wide duct tape around her head, covering her mouth but being careful not to obscure her nostrils and asphyxiate her. He also bound her wrists behind her back and her ankles together with the tape, before closing the lid and looking up and down the deserted street to ensure that no one had witnessed the abduction in progress.

Back at the farmhouse, he carried her from the car to the barn, placed her on the ground and showed her the knife. He also held a piece of card in front of her to read. He had never spoken to any of his victims. Talk would individualise them and ruin the illusion. COMPLY OR DIE, the simple message in large block capital letters stated. It always worked, giving them false hope that made them more user-friendly. He preferred them to be compliant and malleable, not animated and rebellious.

He cut the clothes from her, apart from the panties, which he removed carefully and put to one side after freeing her ankles. She watched him as he then undressed, her eyes following his every move. And then he began, working under the soft glow of a single hurricane lamp that hung from a nail driven into a sturdy oak post. He caressed her trembling body, exploring every curve and crevice, running his fingers through the shiny tresses of her hair, after first checking her pubic curls to confirm that she was a natural blonde.

The only equipment that he needed lay on the earthen floor beside him: a Polaroid camera, pack of condoms, industrial staple gun and his knife, its long blade narrow from years of being honed to razor sharpness.

It was over an hour later when he left the barn, walking back to the house with the coating of blood on his body a black sheen in the moonlight. Behind him, the girl swung gently from a rope in the darkness, bleeding out on to the soil that lay six inches beneath her still twitching body.

Issuing a low moan, his consciousness snapped back to the present. He reached for the box of Kleenex on the arm of the chair, pulled a tissue free and wiped the warm, pooling liquid from his stomach, before collecting up the photographs and going upstairs to his bedroom. He placed the Polaroids in a drawer, on top of many pairs of panties, which were his treasured souvenirs of good times had. In the bathroom, he turned on the shower, whistling as he looked forward to the next hunt. His mother would keep paying for her sins. The grave had not saved her from his wrath. Each time he raped, mutilated and killed, it was her face, her shining fair hair, and her beseeching lapis lazuli eyes that were beneath him. It was her body that shook with fear, and her nasal screams that rewarded his efforts to make her suffer repeatedly for beguiling him with her charms, using him, and then fornicating with another.

CHAPTER FIVE

AT Heather Cullen's funeral, the late girl's mother was in a state of near collapse and had to be supported by her husband to stop her from actually falling down. Her red-rimmed eyes were riveted to the coffin that held her daughter's body. Only now did she begin to accept that Heather was gone, and that her mortal remains were lying in the pitch-black confines of the polished wooden box that pallbearers were now lowering into the ground. Denial dissipated as the pine lid with its shiny brass plate and fittings vanished into the dank hole in the earth.

Brenda Cullen was now a desolate husk, unrecognisable as the cheerful, outgoing woman she had been up until this travesty of all her dreams and expectations had so swiftly and forever blighted her existence. She still loved Ron, and felt a burden of guilt – on some inconsequential level – for drawing away from him and everything else that had seemed to matter so much. But now, like a sufferer of autism, she was somehow trapped in a world that she could not break free of; locked into a morbid state of mind that inhibited and prevented her from responding normally to her environment. The constant waves of grief that pounded her mind with relentless, increasing force had eroded her sanity with the same inevitability that the coastline acquiesced to the constant pummelling of the ocean. Brenda could not come to terms with the loss of her daughter. It was somehow wrong and unnatural that she should still be here, alive, when her little girl, who she had given birth to and nurtured, was gone. It was unacceptable to outlive her offspring; an abomination of all that was wholesome and normal. Heather had had so much to live for. She had been taking a degree in anthropology, and had been invited to join a team that were flying out to Brazil in just three weeks time to study the cultural contamination of an Indian tribe, who were only just emerging from hermetic jungle seclusion, to undoubtedly be transformed into westernised caricatures of their former selves.

Brenda did not want to be alive and have to adjust to a world from which her child had been ripped from her so brutally. She could not contemplate a future now, and was incapable of and lacking the fibre necessary to overcome the all consuming anguish, and move forward. Her heartbreak was beyond reconciliation, as terminal as if she had been riddled with malignant tumours that could not be excised and did not respond to therapy.

Ron functioned. He went through the motions and dealt with the loss in his own stolid way. Standing at the graveside, his lined face as impassive as scored concrete, he held his wife close and stared straight ahead, not once casting an eye on the gleaming casket; his remoteness somehow unhealthy and disconcerting.

"Cold fish, eh, boss?" Hugh said, eyeing the bereaved prison officer with a calculating look, as though the man's hard exterior somehow implied guilt.

"No, Hugh," Laura said, studying the man's face and admiring his strength, knowing to a degree through personal experience how he must be feeling. "He's just holding it all in, smothering it. If he didn't, he would fall apart at the seams."

"He's still a suspect though, isn't he?" Hugh said.

"Officially, yes. But he didn't do it. I'd put my pension on it. He's a casualty, Hugh. He didn't torture, rape and kill his own daughter."

Ron was back on duty less than a week after Heather's funeral. Brenda's widowed sister, Margaret, had moved in for awhile and was running the house and trying to break through Brenda's wall of grief, with no discernible success.

Now, back on the landings, Ron had become monosyllabic. His colleagues were nervous around him, and had no idea what to say, knowing that platitudes were of no help. Most of them just let him know that if there was anything that they could do, he only had to ask.

Ron was of the old school. He had joined the Prison Service back when many screws had been ex-forces and had swapped one uniform for another. It was a job that had provided quarters to live in, and a way of life that was still, to their minds, apart from Civvie Street. It had been a good service, with ranks, and a code of conduct and discipline for both cons and staff. In those days, the job had been clear-cut, black and white. Cons were not molly-coddled. They were expected to do as they were told, obey orders and do their 'bird'. Being inside was rough, tough, and not for the faint-hearted. Prison was a world apart from a society that lived in comparative freedom outside the walls. The life was, in essence, fair but firm. If a con didn't rock the boat, then he had nothing to worry about, from the staff. There was an invisible line that the majority of screws and cons did not cross. When they did, violence often resulted.

Nowadays, Ron was a dinosaur; one of a dwindling number of older screws that were nearing retirement and just counting down the months by way of pay days. Ron still believed in saying no, when it was called for, and did not back down to cons' demands. The system had become one of escalating prisoners' rights, and committees of inmates that met with management to discuss all conditions and restrictions, chipping away at the rules and regulations, continually hedging for more privileges. No one at the top seemed to realise that eventually you still had to say no, and that could, and in many instances did result in the cons reverting to type and kicking off. With lower manning levels and a more relaxed system, a lot of the younger screws, sadly, turned a blind eye to many breaches of acceptable behaviour.

Ron remembered an old screw – back when he had first joined up and was under training at Armley Jail in Leeds – who gave him advice that had served him well throughout his career.

"Listen lad," George Parker had said. "Most cons are shit. They're not in here for being honest, upright citizens. They're in here doing bird because they cheat, rob, rape and kill people on the out. Most of them are recidivists who look on doing time as an acceptable risk. They might appear reasonable, but if they do it's because they're after something. Don't ever start believing that they like you, because they don't, they hate your fuckin guts. If you stand up to them they think that you're a no good fuckin screw, and if you back down to them you're a soft twat. Remember that some might be better than others, but they're still just shit. Give them all they're entitled to; no more, no less. And be fair but firm. Start off right or you'll just make a rod for your own back. And leave the job at the gate, lad, don't take it home with you, or you'll end up divorced, an alcoholic, or both."

Ron had thought that George had been a cynical old bastard. But now, so many years later, he knew that the long dead screw had been a shrewd judge of human nature. He could still fondly picture him, cap askew on his balding head, overweight and never smart; the front of his ill-fitting uniform jacket and trousers covered with cigarette ash. Smoking had not been allowed on the landings even in those days. But George, he remembered, always had a cigarette hanging from his bottom lip as he slopped them out. That was when cells had no toilets, and pots and buckets had to be emptied in a recess every morning at unlock. The stench of human waste was a little more bearable if you were exhaling tobacco smoke out of your nostrils. Putting flush toilets back into cells during the eighties and nineties – an amenity that had been standard in the nineteenth century – was proof that the Victorians had developed a system that should probably have been left well alone in many areas. The old adage, 'If it ain't broke, don't fix it', was still sound advice, though usually fell on deaf ears.

At fifty-eight, Ron was disenchanted with cutbacks, piss-poor management and what seemed like monthly changes to routines and shift patterns, which were aimed at saving money, but were continually presented as progress and the way forward, into chaos, by a department that had lost the plot.

Now, Ron had a plot; a plan of his own. He was starting a week of nights the following Tuesday, and had decided – in cold rage and a disturbed state of mind – that the same kind of scum who had taken his daughter's life would not continue to be guest's of her Majesty at the taxpayers' expense. They would no longer demand escalating rights, watch TV and DVDs, play pool and snooker, and learn computer skills in the education department. He thought it fitting to mete out the sort of justice that they could have expected in bygone years, up until the abolition of topping. Fuck the do-gooders and prissy-arsed liberals that spouted off about the death penalty not being a deterrent. He had seen convicted murderers released to kill again, but had never heard of a hanged man re-offending.

On the first evening of his scheduled nights, Ron packed his holdall, placing inside it his sandwich box, thermos flask of coffee, a Wilbur Smith novel that he intended to finish, two boxes of heavy-load cartridges, and last but far from least, his over and under Browning Medallist 12 gauge shotgun, shortened into a sawn-off weapon that fitted into the bag without having to be dismantled.

"Look after her, Margaret," Ron said, leaning over the back of the settee and kissing Brenda on her cold forehead; the skin of her face now drum-tight over cheekbones that threatened to pierce the taut parchment it had become.

"Don't worry, Ron, we'll be fine. You have a good night," Margaret said, smiling, but not with her eyes.

"Oh, I will, I will," Ron said, picking up his bag and his car keys from the telephone table in the hall, before leaving the house and closing the front door behind him for the last time.

CHAPTER SIX

SITTING under the hot lights, Laura could feel the perspiration prickling her scalp and dampening her armpits. Her blouse was stuck to her lower back. Opposite her, looking cool, fresh and smug was Trish Pearson, wearing a navy-blue power suit and silver Versace top, probably purchased from a discount designer outlet.

Laura needed this interview like a hole in the head, especially with this supercilious bitch conducting it. Unfortunately it had to be done. This wasn't *Crimewatch*, but it would have to do for now. It was a chance to appeal for witnesses, and to warn young women of the threat that was out there, via what was a popular regional news show.

An anonymous voice counted down from five, and a red light blinked on, its ruby glow signalling that they were on air.

"Chief Inspector Scott," Trish started, shooting from the hip after first greeting her viewers. "Is it correct that a serial killer known within your department as The Tacker is on the loose, preying on young women in the York area? And is it also true that the police...you, have no clues as yet to his identity?"

Laura cleared her throat and somehow resisted the overwhelming temptation to push 'Barbie' off her chair.

"It's Detective Inspector," she began, outwardly composed, fighting the urge to allow her temper out of its kennel like a rabid dog to attack the interviewer. "And yes, it is true that four murders have been committed, that we are attributing to being the work of the same individual. There is no apparent rational motive for the killings, and our investigation is ongoing."

"Is it fair to say that you have *no* leads, and that we can expect more deaths?" Trish asked, shaking her head ever so slightly in a disdainful Thatcheresque manner that she had deliberately copied in part from the late Iron Lady, and also from Jeremy Paxman, whose sometimes derogatory and haughty manner she had admired when he had fronted *Newsnight*.

Laura kept it together, concealing the blaze of anger that rose in her gorge, as magma might in a soon to erupt volcano, and said, "I think that any criticism you have, Ms Pearson, is unlikely to be of any practical help. I just want the viewers to be aware of the fact that we have a repeat killer active in the area; a twisted coward who is preying on girls and young women. All females need to realise the danger that he represents to them. It is a fact that so far he has shown a penchant for blondes with blue eyes, but that does not guarantee immunity from him. His warped mind could fixate on anyone." Pausing, Laura looked directly into the camera's lens and continued. "Do not go out alone, especially at night. And do not put yourself in a position that could result in you being abducted, raped and murdered.

"While we are hunting this maniac down, you must be alert and take all practical measures to ensure that you do not become a victim. If you are suspicious of a stranger, or think that you know who this man is, call us. We need your help to capture him. I'm sure that this psycho thinks he is too smart to be caught...but he isn't. He is just a very sick little man, who we *will* apprehend."

"And do you really—"

"That's all, Ms Pearson," Laura said, unclipping the chest mike from her lapel and flipping it across the news desk. With that gesture, she pushed the chair back, stood up, nodded at the now harassed-looking presenter, gave her a small, game, set and match smile and walked off, out of the studio.

"Jesus, boss!" Hugh said as Laura pushed through the swing doors. "That was a bit over the top, wasn't it?"

"No, Hugh. We need to hassle the son of a bitch and put him off balance."

"You might just redirect him towards yourself, boss, with all that shit you just threw at him."

"If I couldn't swim, Hugh, I'd stay out of the water."

He watched a repeat of the interview on the late night update, and hurled the remote control handset at the TV as he jumped up, his bare feet ploughing through the pile of Polaroids on the carpet as he ran to the set, hawked up a mouthful of phlegm and spat at the screen.

"Fucking bitch!" he shouted at the image of the split arse copper as he pounded the top of the TV with white-knuckled fists. "I'll make you eat those words, you whore." His body shook with fury and his vision red-misted as he emitted a long, high-pitched whining that sounded inhuman. After almost a minute, he went up to the bathroom and turned the shower on. It was a long time before he calmed down under the ice-cold spray. Shivering, he used a thick, fluffy towel to dry off. He would show Detective Inspector Laura fucking Scott. He dressed in T-shirt, blue jeans and Timberland boots, and then splashed aramis over his clean-shaven face. His fair hair was medium length, swept back from his forehead above metallic-blue eyes that showed no hint of the madness that festered behind their enigmatic surfaces. Putting on a black leather jacket, he left the house, determined to vent his fury against not only his mother, but also against the female copper. This one would be dedicated to Laura Scott, and immolated to appease his now wounded ego.

He drove west through the city, out onto the A59 Harrogate road. He had already chosen his next victim; had first seen her over a month ago in Yates's Wine Lodge on Church Lane, then followed her home and added her to his list of potential targets, which now boasted five names and addresses; enough to be going on with.

Parking the car half a mile from the Stroud household, he went into a phone box.

"Hello." A male voice, presumably her father.

"Hello. May I speak to Shelley, please?" he said.

"Who's calling?" A wary father's concerned, protective question.

"Oh, sorry, it's Mark...Mark Chapman. I promised to phone Shelley...about a party on Saturday night."

"I'm afraid Shelley's out this evening. Can I give her a message?"

"Sure. Ask her to give me a call. She has my number."

"Will do, er, Mark. Good night."

"Good night, Mr Stroud," he said, hanging up and quickly exiting the stinking booth, stuffing the bunched tissues he had held the germ-ridden receiver with into his pocket. *There should be a government health warning outside phone boxes. Christ knows what diseases you could catch from the fucking things!*

He got back in the car and drove off, stopping again next to the kerb behind a late model Astra and switching off the lights and engine. He was just forty yards from the house, in the murk, midway between the sodium-yellow glare of two street lights. All the properties along this upper middle-class road were detached, fronted by trees or tall hedges and set well back in gardens so large that the owners probably referred to them as 'the grounds'. These were carefully differentiated dwellings, each insulated from its neighbours' by high fencing, walls, or stands of trees; mainly conifers. The privacy that these residents had created for themselves had rendered them vulnerable, as it also afforded cover for undesirable, uninvited trespassers, and worse, someone like him.

He had driven down this road and passed the house several times, noting the long drive that curved away from wrought-iron gates that were set between brick pillars topped by pre-cast cement lions, whose role as guardians to the entrance was purely symbolic. The drive was bordered by laurel, holly, and other lush evergreens.

It was close to midnight. He left the car, checking both ways to satisfy himself that the coast was clear before vaulting over the low wall and pushing his way into the thick foliage. He squatted down on his haunches, slipping an eighteen-inch-long piece of steel rod from his sleeve, to grip in his left hand. He flexed his forearm, tightened his fingers and felt the satisfying weight of the weapon as he settled with his back against the trunk of a lofty fir to wait.

In his mind he replayed the interview and saw Scott, and heard her words, rich and self righteous as she had called him a maniac and sick pervert. She would regret every insult. The bitch would apologise for each offensive name that she had called him. Not that it would help the Stroud girl. But the copper *would* apologise, when he showed her that getting personal and badmouthing him was not acceptable, and would not be tolerated. He wasn't a maniac or insane. How many countless innocents had been tortured and put to death by the church in the name of God? And were the governments of the world, who used war to gain power, resources and political clout, sane? Could the inventors of nuclear missiles, bombs, land mines and biological weapons be well-balanced? Thousands of guiltless men, women, children and babies were regularly considered expendable, listed as collateral damage; not even addressed as human beings when inadvertently slaughtered during pointless conflict. No, he was not mad. His motives were far more honest and noble. In fact, they were pure and untainted. He did not kill to benefit materially or to promote some dumbfuck doctrine. He killed as a release from personal torment that demanded satisfaction. It was a nonnegotiable affliction, far stronger than any addiction to the most potent drugs. Christ, more people died in road accidents in a week on British roads alone, than he would kill in a lifetime. Had he been an IRA terrorist, who had bombed the civilian population, killing scores, then, for political expediency, with no mind to real justice, he would have been released back into society as part of that blatantly inequitable Good Friday agreement. The authorities were too besmirched by their own mercenary deeds; their hands stained with far too much blood to have any right to judge him. Monday's friend was Tuesday's enemy in their cockamamie world.

The fragmented splash of headlight beams shone through the leaves; myriad points of brightness signalling the arrival of a car. He withdrew further back into the darkness and gripped the cold steel cudgel even more tightly as adrenaline flooded his system.

Shelley paid the driver, and then walked across the pavement to the gates as the cab pulled away. She had just had one of those evenings that would eternally stand out as a landmark in her life. Darren, her boyfriend had, unbeknown to her parents, just moved into a flat of his own off the Selby road. Instead of going to the multiplex to indulge in necking and groping awkwardly, sitting well back from the flickering screen, they had spent the evening at Darren's, christening his new bed. Shelley had been a virgin up until three hours ago, having contented herself – and frustrating Darren – with heavy petting, up to and including oral sex...until tonight.

She had watched enthralled as Darren ripped open the small packet and removed the lubricated ring of rubber. He had passed it to her, as though it was a delicate and precious gift that might be damaged if not handled with all due care and attention. He had lain back, and she had rolled the condom down over his erect member, her fingers trembling with excitement and apprehension at the thought of what she intended to do.

It had hurt, fleetingly. She had felt too tight for him when he entered her. Then there had been a sudden tearing sensation, like a paper cut as her hymen ruptured. What followed was over in seconds, leaving her disappointed; the act resulting in a quick climax for Darren, but an anticlimax for her, both mentally and physically. He was soon hard again, though, and with a fresh sheath, – which with more confidence she slipped on with a deftness that belied her inexperience – he once more entered her and began thrusting slowly and with less urgency. She had gripped his buttocks and raised her bottom to meet each jabbing, plunging stroke. Even now her knees were trembling, and she felt as though her secret act was somehow visible, rubber-stamped on her forehead for all to see. She was sure that everyone would know that she was changed, had moved on from being a girl; a virgin, unspoilt and whole. Her feelings were mixed and confused. There was a certain sadness that she had lost something irretrievable. And yet a door had opened, literally, giving access to a new level of experience. Her face burned in the darkness as she recalled how she had screamed out, 'Yes Darren, yeesss!' at the top of her voice as waves of pleasure engulfed her, spreading up, back into her stomach, stiffening her limbs in ecstasy.

A fleeting movement from the bushes at the side of the gravel drive caught Shelley's attention and brought her to a halt, to peer into the darkness. Even as she thought that it might be a cat, or maybe even a fox, a sudden explosion in her head lit up the night sky with bright petals of gold, yellow, red and orange. For just a fraction of a second she was transported back to a night in Disney World two years previously, standing with her parents to watch the firework display over the castle in the Magic Kingdom, before an inky blackness rushed in to replace the scene, stealing her awareness of anything.

Back at the farm, he lifted the limp body from the boot, slung it over his shoulder as though it weighed no more than a feather pillow, and walked across to the front of the barn and unlocked the large padlock, allowing the thick chain to snake through the hasp with the rattle of an anchor chain rushing from a ship's deck toward the surface of the sea. He entered the building, pulled the solid doors closed behind him and made his way to the centre of the dark interior, shrugging the still form from his shoulder, for it to land in a crumpled heap before him, illuminated by a bright shaft of moonlight that penetrated through the grimed skylight set into the corrugated-iron roof high above, and many smaller rays that shone like pale laser beams through narrow gaps between the wood plank walls.

He had not just stunned this one. He had hit her too hard with the steel rod as an excess of hormonal stimulation added extra force to his pumped-up muscles. He pulled the tape from her mouth and was relieved to see that she was still breathing, albeit shallow and laboured. He wanted this one to last. Had she been dead, he would have just buried her deep under the earth of the barn's floor, where another fourteen bodies were entombed. Corpses were no fun. He needed his 'mother' alive and alert to begin with, to appreciate the exquisite pain that he would inflict on her as continued retribution for the trauma and grief she had caused him to suffer.

Cutting the tape from her wrists and ankles, he undressed her, putting all but her skimpy panties into a plastic bin bag to burn later. He crushed the panties to his nose and mouth, savouring the warm dampness and musky odour; noticing the spots of blood and presuming that they were a residue from menstruation. The only identification that he could find in her handbag was a library card, which he tucked into his jeans pocket, along with the panties. He then prepared her for later, before leaving again and locking the doors, to walk across to the house to light the fire and burn the clothing and handbag, which would be of no further use to their owner.

Pouring himself a large Scotch, he took it upstairs, where he added the lacy panties to the others in the top drawer of his trophy chest. Undressed, he went back downstairs, turned on the radio and made himself a stack of ham and cheese and pickle sandwiches. As usual, the hunt and abduction had given him a voracious appetite. It was a humid night, and he ate standing in front of the open fridge door, allowing the icy air to drift out and cool his sweat-sheened body.

At first, Shelley thought that she must have fallen and cracked her head. It took a while for her numbed mind to become aware of the situation that she was in. Her skull pounded, causing her to grimace and screw her eyelids tightly shut. By degrees she forced her eyes open. She was naked, her arms stretched above her, aching. Her wrists were handcuffed to a large steel ring that was set into a concrete block; the cuffs' chain through the ring. She was cold, very scared, and felt sick from the splitting pain at her temple. Her vision was slightly blurred, but she could read the large writing on the card that lay on the ground in front of her: COMPLY OR DIE.

This had to be a nightmare. She must be safe at home in bed, and this horrific scene was no more than a product of her sleeping mind. Yet it felt so real; a solid, conscious experience. She concentrated on her last memory. She had taken a taxi from Darren's, then begun to walk up the drive to the house...and then...nothing! It was a total blank from that moment.

He had returned to the barn to stand silently in deep shadow and watch her for a long time. She was bathed in the ambient glow from the window above, her contours highlighted, picked out in light and shadow; a blue and white vision of loveliness that he was about to defile and make ready for a higher state of being.

Shelley jerked her head sideways, the pain forgotten as the naked man emerged from the gloom and walked toward her. He was tall, slim, well-muscled. In one hand he held what appeared to be a large pair of nutcrackers, or some kind of pliers. In the other, the unmistakable shape of a large knife. Her bladder rebelled and voided onto the already damp earth beneath her, as a bombshell of sudden realisation burst and overwhelmed her. Jesus, no! *It was him*, The Tacker; the killer that the public was being warned about on TV and in the newspapers.

He knelt next to her and fed greedily from the fear in her eyes, before setting to work with the stapler, ensuring that she would not compound her sins by trying to deny her true identity, or demean herself by begging for mercy.

"You got personal mail, boss," Hugh said, placing a small package on Laura's desk.

She crushed a half-smoked cigarette out in the ashtray that nestled covertly in the open top drawer, before reaching for the packet, to pick it up and turn it over in her hands to examine. It was rectangular in shape, approximately five inches long, four wide, two deep and hardly any weight at all. It was wrapped in brown paper, well sealed with Sellotape. A York postmark showed that it had been mailed the previous day. A small white adhesive label was affixed to the top, addressed to Laura. It was printed in bold type. On the back, hand-written in blue ballpoint was the sender's name and address, which read: From Mr M Chapman, 287 Westfield Way, Strensall, York.

Call it sixth sense, but Laura came out in goosebumps. A cold feeling of dire dread ran through her. She reached for her paperknife and slid the point under the edge of the tape, slicing carefully around the full package before pulling back the wrapping to disclose a blue cardboard box; the type of which a high street jeweller might employ to place a bracelet or neck chain in. She flicked the lid back with the knife and studied the wad of cotton wool beneath, again using the blade as a tool to slowly raise the white pad, only to jerk backwards in her chair as if she had suffered an electric shock.

"Oh, Christ!" Laura said, standing up and walking across to the window, hugging herself as though the room temperature had suddenly dipped twenty degrees.

"What?" Hugh said, moving forward to approach the desk.

Laura turned to him. She could feel herself shaking. "You'd better take a look for yourself. It's not pretty."

Using the tips of his index finger and thumb, Hugh eased the cotton wool back and stared at the blood-smeared ear that had been pinned – like a moth or beetle – to the royal-blue velvet covered display board beneath it.

Laura rummaged in the bottom drawer of a filing cabinet and found a box of cellophane gloves. "Here, wear these," she said, handing a pair to Hugh. "I doubt that there are any worthwhile latents, but we'd better not taint the evidence."

The ear was a bluish-white. It looked unreal, more like a spare part for a waxwork head. A gold stud gleamed in the pierced lobe; the simple adornment making the severed organ appear even more grotesque.

Laura lifted the velvet cushion without touching the ear, and underneath it was a folded sheet of paper and a cut-down Polaroid photograph. Hugh and Laura gazed transfixed at the image of the naked girl. Her mouth appeared to be stapled shut, but her bulging eyes intimated a bridled scream. The corneas were bright red, spotted by the flash from the camera, but Laura knew that they would be blue, just like the others. The girl's blonde hair was soaked crimson at the right side, where the ear had been cut from, and a dark stain pooling between her legs illustrated the terror she was enduring…if she was still alive.

With trembling fingers, Laura unfolded the single sheet of Basildon Bond writing paper. It read:

Laura...Laura...Laura. You *really* pissed me off

with the offensive remarks that you levelled at

me on that slut's news programme. I found

your outburst very unprofessional, but then

realised that you were just attempting to goad

me...upset me.

Well, sweetlips, it worked. Please find

enclosed one ear, complete with a yellow-metal

stud; this item having had only one previous

but less than careful owner. I removed the

organ with a very sharp knife. But as you can

see from the photo, Miss. Stroud was, to say the
least, rather traumatised by the procedure.

She is still alive, but alas, not for too much
longer. You will be in receipt of the rest of her
within a few days.

This one is for YOU, Laura. I was going to
ease up for a month or two and take a summer
break, but your insults prompted me to give
you something to feel rightfully guilty about.

DO NOT BADMOUTH ME AGAIN, YOU
FUCKING WHORE!!

Shelley is going to suffer so much because of
YOU.

Sleep well,

MARK

Laura felt as though hot lead had cooled and set in her veins. She
had only felt this stupefied and sick at heart once before, and had not
thought that she was capable of feeling so bad ever again. She had
got it wrong, screwed-up big time and triggered a response that she
had not foreseen. Shelley Stroud had been missing for four days.
And it was almost certain that when next seen, she would be a
mutilated corpse.

"Get it to the lab," Laura whispered to Hugh, reaching for a
cigarette as she wondered how she would cope with the knowledge

that she had been, in part, responsible for the abduction, mutilation, and imminent murder of a young woman.

CHAPTER SEVEN

ONCE he had broken through the long-standing mental barrier and made the decision to at least look at the paperwork, the floodgates were opened to a torrent of long suppressed patterns of thought that he had developed as a profiler. Jim was at once engrossed and lost in morbid fascination, back in the groove, journeying through a hellish labyrinth as he searched for clues and absorbed himself in the puzzle that was before him.

It was a little after eight a.m. when he rose, unable to ignore his full, pounding bladder any longer. He took a leak, showered, then brewed coffee and sat out on the balcony for awhile, letting what he had read settle and separate out in his mind before going back inside to open a new file on his laptop, pausing for a second before punching in a title: Tacker-1. He then listed the victims' names, ages, height, hair and eye colour; every physical detail, however small. Next, the injuries that they had sustained, and the method adopted and materials used to both bind and torture them with, followed by the locations and positions they were found in. After a further two hours of contemplation, Jim began to assemble a preliminary outline of the murderer. Every single serial killer he'd profiled had had an agenda, however warped. They were incited and driven by deep-rooted trauma that was in almost every case born out of childhood mistreatment or neglect. Some of their ilk ticked away like time-bombs until they detonated later in life, usually in their late teens or early twenties. It was a fact that the vast majority of pattern murderers had a blueprint in their damaged minds, and would keep repeating their acts, continually striving – even if unconsciously – to mete out a punishment on whomever had originally maltreated them. The usual cause for their condition was long-term abuse; mental, physical or a combination of both. They would continue to kill until they were caught, or took their own lives. And not many in his experience had offed themselves. It wasn't in their nature.

After two days, Jim had a feasible picture of the killer. Profiling was not as big a deal as the books and movies made out. Nine tenths of it was just commonsense police work, with studious attention to detail in minutia, sifting through what others might overlook or consider as trivial or irrelevant. His method was to put all information that was known to appertain to the same offender under a logical mental microscope and attempt to focus in and flush out the dross; to see more clearly any ambiguous patterns and connections. It was always a jigsaw with a piece missing, that would, when found, complete the picture; a cryptic code that could be broken and made sense of. What had put Jim in a class of his own in this field had been his uncanny ability to understand what motivated a particular killer; to almost be in his head and be able to enter his sick world of fantasy and depravity.

It had been stop-go work. After a positive start, his brain had started to rebel against the sickening input; kept trying to shut off from the loathsome details. For a while he had thought that he may have lost the ability to make the jumps and feel his way into a case. It had been impersonal at the outset, just printed words and images of total strangers. And then he had started to see beyond the evidence, extrapolate and enter the psychopath's mind, to think his way into the maniac's way of reasoning.

Tossing a holdall into the rear and placing his briefcase on the passenger seat of his Jeep Cherokee, Jim set off. He had not let Laura know that he had studied the faxes she had sent, or forewarned her of his intention to just turn up on her doorstep. He felt exactly as he had done at fourteen; the memory of his first real date popping out of the mists of time as he remembered taking Cindy Lopez to the movies on a sultry summer evening in Glendale, back in Arizona. He had spent over an hour plucking up the courage to put his arm around her shoulders, and followed up that triumph by kissing her lightly on the lips, just once and only minutes before the show ended and they were once more back outside, where further inroads could not be made. The sensation of the thousand gossamer butterfly wings that had fluttered around his stomach in that dark movie theatre was with him now as he envisioned being face to face with Laura again. He had cleared his appointments for four days. If anything crucial came up, then his secretary, Diane, could reach him on his mobile.

He drove the few minutes north from Windsor to the M4, then headed east to pick up the M25. It was six a.m., and the traffic was relatively light as he left what Chris Rea had christened *The Road to Hell*, to join the M1. Keeping up a steady seventy, he anticipated being in York a little after nine o'clock.

As he sped north, Jim reflected on the night, now so long ago, that in part had changed his life. It had been as leader of an armed assault team that he had entered a brownstone house in Georgetown to take down Gary Meeker, who to their knowledge had ritually murdered at least ten young men, and probably twice that number.

Meeker had preyed on the homosexual community, frequenting many of the gay clubs and bars in and around Washington D.C. His victims had all been young males aged between eighteen and twenty-five. His killing spree had lasted for over two years, up until they got a lead, due to his last intended target surviving.

Meeker used Rohypnol, a strong sedative that in the right dosage produced a compliant, almost hypnotic state in those who it was administered to. This was one of the many drugs used by date rapists, though in Gary's case it went beyond that, and was date murder.

Gary Meeker was a slim, good looking thirty-five year old with an engaging personality and the clothes, money and top of the range Porsche that could not fail to impress. He would select a lone punter and strike up a conversation, buying drinks and making it blatantly apparent that he was not only interested in, but was happy to pay handsomely for discreet sex. At a point later in the evening, usually having settled in a booth or at a secluded table, he would introduce the sedative to the mark's drink, and as it began to take effect, would suggest going back to his house, stroking the guy's thigh and crotch under the table as he made the invitation. Once in the safety of his home – and the sacrificial temple that was his bedroom – he sated his craving, and then in disgust at his weakness, bludgeoned to death the living tool he had needed and employed for gratification.

On what would prove to be the last occasion he would ever attempt to ensnare an unsuspecting potential victim, Gary was rising to leave the Shangri-La Bar on Massachusetts Avenue with his chosen and suitably doped-up prey when two things happened that were to bring about his downfall. A work colleague of the now spaced-out young man came over to them and struck up a conversation, and the intended mark, unsteady from the effects of three screwdrivers and the drug, fell on his ass, hitting his head on the corner of the table, which resulted in a deep gash to his forehead that bled profusely.

A small crowd gathered around the trio, and Gary slipped through their ranks and left the bar. Later, in ER, Kenny Tighe's wound was found to be superficial, requiring just four sutures. But the symptoms of the powerful hypnotic sedative prompted a call to the DCPD. Subsequent results of his blood works showed that he had ingested a formidable amount of Rohypnol, a drug flagged with the police department and FBI as being that which the killer who had been tagged the Hypnotist habitually used on his victims. This had been the breakthrough that they'd needed.

Kenny had been a veritable gold mine of information. Once sufficiently compos mentis, he had given agents a comprehensive description of the man who had solicited and then drugged him.

"He told me his name was Gary," Kenny said, "and that he had a brownstone in Georgetown, and drove a red Porsche."

To have freely given Kenny those facts in conversation was a sign of arrogance and overconfidence. Meeker had assumed that Kenny would not survive the evening to repeat anything he was told. The printout from the Department of Motor Vehicles listed all red Porsches in the District of Columbia, and only one was registered to an owner with the Christian name Gary. The address was in Georgetown, and the fax of the drivers licence photograph was shown to Kenny, who immediately and with no doubt or hesitation identified it as being of the man who had accosted him in the bar.

They surrounded Meeker's house. Armed agents covered the front and rear, while an assault team wearing body armour and led by Jim broke in the front door and swept the premises with the aid of flashlights, due to the power having been cut by Meeker, who had removed the fuses from the box in the basement.

In the master bedroom, Special Agent Ed Shelton, followed closely by Jim, checked the recesses and then stooped to look under the bed. Nothing. Ed walked over to the built-in closet that ran the length of the wall and slid open a mirrored door.

The knife blade was driven into Ed's throat, twisted, and withdrawn in an instant. Ed dropped both his handgun and flashlight as his legs buckled. He collapsed onto the floor with blood jetting from his left carotid artery, appearing as black as tar in the low light.

Not immediately sure of what had happened, Jim searched for a target. The stainless steel Colt Python suddenly weighed heavy in his sweating palm. It was cocked, the six-inch barrel following the beam of his flashlight. In the darkness to his left, a more solid, Delphic form overshadowed the gloom and flew at him, emitting a cry of rage that sounded guttural and less than human. Jim swung the pistol, fired, and the blinding muzzle-flash burned into his retinas as a stinging sensation lanced his throat. He staggered backwards, lost his balance and fell, coming to rest with his back up against the foot of the bed.

A break in the night cloud cover allowed a pale shaft of moonlight to pierce the window and reflect off the raised knife's blade, giving Jim a target. He fired again, once...twice, and heard a wet, gurgling moan, just before a body thudded to the floor over his outstretched legs.

Cones of light danced around the bedroom as assistance arrived. One beam found and steadied upon the upper body of Gary Meeker. He was dressed in black, his eyes staring unblinking into the brightness. He was now no longer a dangerous killer, just a harmless corpse, whose death had saved the countless tax dollars which would have been wasted, first on a show trial, then on keeping him caged for years while he undoubtedly lodged appeals from a cell on death row. Not allowing the police to take him alive was a bonus to the authorities.

The blade had opened Jim's throat from just below his left ear to his larynx. He had instinctively pulled back from certain death, escaping with a sewn up neck, tetanus and antibiotic shots, and the promise of a permanent scar to remind him of that night's work. He had fared far better than his fellow agent and good friend, Ed Shelton, though, who was now reposing in a mortuary drawer.

That episode in itself had not been the last straw. The last of the bundle that would break him had come three months later, when the world turned completely pear-shaped and lost much of its meaning. He had got too close to another psycho, who had a predilection for disembowelling hookers and dumping them in the Potomac River. The killer was also a police informant, who knew of Jim's reputation, and of his involvement in the case, and decided to take him out of the picture.

Jim and his then fiancée, Pamela, had just left a concert at the Kennedy Center and were driving over the river to Arlington, planning on more than just a nightcap at her apartment...when it happened.

The dark Plymouth followed them across the bridge, tyres churning through the silvered puddles of rainwater that the storm overhead had released on the city for the past hour. Veins of lightning snaked through the dark flesh of the sky, and thunder rolled and cracked with the sound of cannon-fire across a battlefield.

The wipers thrashed across the windscreen, and the rain drummed on the Honda's roof and hood. Pamela was laughing at Jim's obvious relief to be out and away from the concert, which he had been unable to feign any measure of pleasure in attending.

"Call me a pleb," Jim said, grinning back at her. "But my idea of a concert is Willie Nelson or maybe Eric Clapton, not Bach's Mass in B minor, although the broad playing the penny whistle had a nice pair of jugs."

"That was a flute, you moron," Pamela said through a fresh snort of laughter at his comments. "And she was old enough to be your mother."

Jim leant his head back, smiling, happy to be with Pamela, looking forward to opening a bottle of Californian red when they reached her place, then maybe showering together before making love, and...

...The front side window imploded, resulting in a shower of glass cubes peppering Jim's face and neck. He turned, squinted out into the night and saw the Plymouth; a grinning face at the open window, and the flash of another bullet leaving the muzzle of a gun that was aimed at him.

Pamela had spun the wheel and braked hard, over-steering, losing control, causing the car to leave the concrete roadway and smash into the wall of a furniture store. The Honda stalled, and only the insistent pattering of raindrops on metal broke the otherwise sudden silence.

Jim saw the spray of water at either side of the assailant's car as it accelerated away from them; the Plymouth's speeding, whitewall tyres parting the dark pools as it raced off into the night.

Pamela had slid down as far as her seat belt would allow. She was slumped forward with her head resting on the steering wheel. The second slug had also missed its intended mark, but had found Pamela, entering her temple, to blow bone, brains and blood out of a fist-sized exit wound.

Jim had left the bureau with a scarred throat, damaged mind, and a small invalidity pension as souvenirs of his career as a federal agent. And now he was allowing himself to be sucked in again, back into the quagmire that he had crawled out from. He had taken a giant step backwards, into the domain of what was a race apart from humanity; the serial killer. *Couldn't live with it, can't live without it*, he thought. Some dark part of him – that scared and sickened him – needed the rush and the challenge; was happiest existing between a rock and a hard place.

After Pamela's death, Jim had been trapped in a strange time warp, in a state of almost suspended animation, unable to function in the present or contemplate a future, but also unable to go back to the past, to a time before his life was broken and twisted to leave him empty and with no sense of meaning left to the chaos of existence. Eventually, he had found the strength to move forward and once more participate in life; to not dwell on the certainty of death, which reaped at random with no preferential treatment afforded to the talented or good above the inept or wicked. His short time with Laura had refurbished his spirit and given him a new-found quality of appreciation for all things great and small. Parting with her had to an extent extinguished that.

Shaking off the doleful state of reverie as he neared York, his pulse quickened and he became agitated. He was impatient to see Laura again, with every second now stretching interminably before him, and each mile a seemingly endless journey to a far-off horizon. More than one door had been flung wide open before him with Laura's phone call, and he imagined the trip would take him away from the doldrums of his safe harbour, out to a stormy, raging sea. He was entering yet another new chapter of life, and it both petrified and exhilarated him. A side of him, like the cricket that had been a puppet's conscience, berated him: *'You were doing just fine without this shit'*, it chided. *'Why couldn't you just leave it the hell alone? Laura metaphorically clicks her fingers and you jump like a dumb mutt cosying up to a bitch in heat. It's not too late to bail out, pal. Just turn around and go back home, for Chrissake! Send her what you've worked up and close that fucking door again. Slam it shut and save your sanity'.*

Too late was the cry, he thought as he ran his thumb along the thin white line on his throat. He had known madness and folly, but could not employ the hard-earned wisdom that it had given him to good effect. He didn't like his motives. Didn't like who he was much, either, but knew that he couldn't run away from his personal demon. Time had not banished it, and now the little imp was back on his shoulder, alive and well, urging and prodding him ever nearer the edge of the pit. What was it about touching evil that fuelled him? Did he need to be associated with the unthinkable to realise a modicum of fulfilment? They were questions that, as always, he pushed back into the murky depths from which they had risen. His rationale bit back, happier to keep things simple. His motives were far less honourable than they had been when he was young and full of noble notions and grandiose intentions. Truth being, he *was* a dumb mutt, and *did* want to cosy up to Laura. He had been in a morass, wallowing, entangled and using avoidance techniques that left him feeling little more than an empty vessel. His dark side would not be denied, and Laura was the catalyst that had liberated it. Maybe it all came down to an unfinished affair of the heart. Everyone had needs. His were just a lot more complex than he cared to even try and comprehend. It didn't do to look too deeply into yourself. You might not like what you find.

CHAPTER EIGHT

LAURA was back in her office at the station, sifting through the files that were scattered across her desktop. She was becoming more dispirited by the second as she searched in vain for a clue that had been overlooked. No revelation was forthcoming, and she discounted the possibility of one occurring any time soon. What she needed was a bloody miracle; a golden finger of fate to appear from above and enlighten her by pointing out a key piece of information that she and the team had, up until now, been blind to. At the moment she had far more chance of winning the lottery, which would be impossible, due to the fact that she had never bought a ticket. The facts were that they had been through every word and detail of every report furnished on the murders with a fine-tooth comb, and had nothing to show for it. The daily meetings had become almost pointless; a repetition of what they already knew, which was zilch. In most murder investigations there were leads. In many instances, the victim knew the killer. Or blood, hair, fibre or semen samples were left at the scene. Fingerprints, shoe prints, tyre prints, a weapon or a witness proved the eventual undoing of most criminals. The processing of almost every scene gave up forensic evidence. But this killer was both clever and lucky. He left them up shit creek without a paddle. There was no reason to believe he knew his victims, and as far as they knew to date he had never been seen by a third party. The bodies had been thoroughly cleaned, and the sites offered up no clues whatsoever. The locations had been dumping grounds; just secondary crime scenes.

Laura reached into the drawer for a cigarette, but pulled her hand back. She felt nauseous, sick to her stomach as a result of eating too little, drinking too much coffee, and virtually chain-smoking. The continual, gut-wrenching knowledge that a girl was at that precise moment being held by a sadistic madman was almost too much to bear. The image of Shelley Stroud's ear pinned to a velvet cushion in a box was burned into her mind, searing deep into her brain tissue to cause an unrelenting headache that could have been generated by a red-hot branding iron. This psycho was reaching out, taunting and sneering at them as they careered about with all the vision of blind mice, impotent against him. They had checked the address in

Strensall, only to find that it was a vacant, weed-filled lot where a butcher's shop had once stood. And the name that he had signed the letter with and given to Shelley's father over the phone – Mark Chapman – was the name of the American nutter who'd gunned down John Lennon, way back in nineteen-eighty.

Laura had eventually lit a cigarette and nearly finished it before realising that she was smoking. Stubbing it out in the hidden ashtray, – that everyone from her team to the cleaning lady knew about – she rose and headed for the door. It was almost twelve-thirty. She needed time out: preferably a year on a Greek island. Christ, she needed a brandy, and would break her own rule of not drinking on duty to preserve her weak grip on the reality of what was happening. It was depressing to think that most people were apparently unaffected by anything less than terrorist attacks or the death of a high-profile celebrity like Cilla Black. It was a strange but undeniable fact that even as at that moment a young girl was suffering almost unimaginable torture, that no one should have to endure, birds still sang, the sun shone in a clear blue sky, and life was enjoyed as though all was well with the world. The ability of the human mind to disregard the plight of others and shut out all that did not affect it personally was an invisible suit of armour, worn as a shield against the unwholesome reality of misfortune that was too scary to confront. It was a quality that enabled optimism to flourish, and so promoted the continuance of the species. That all around her, fellow human beings could be more concerned and addicted to fictional characters in TV soaps than be touched by real suffering and cruelty, was an enigma that she found disheartening. It said little for mankind. Didn't they realise that they would never see another century in? That there was more to life than TV, football, material wealth and all the trivialities that preoccupied their sad little lives. How could they assimilate and filter out ninety-nine percent of all that was disagreeable to them, as though it was not relevant?

The phone rang as she gripped the door handle. She hesitated, wanting to ignore it, but turned back into the bleak utilitarian room, marched across to the desk and snatched up the handset.

"DI Scott," Laura said, her voice a flat monotone.

"Outside call for you. It's a Mr Elliott. He says it's important," Sue Jones – who they called 'Jones the Switchboard' – said, her lilting Welsh accent as strong as the day she had left Blaenau Ffestiniog thirty years ago.

"Thanks, Sue. Put him through."

55

"Laura?"

"Yes, Jim."

"I gave that stuff you sent me a look at. It may not be much, but I've put together a few notes that might give you some insight."

"I appreciate that more than you know, Jim. Could you send them to me as a PDF file?"

"No can do."

"Eh!"

"I can show them to you. I'm in York, sat in the Olde Starre Inne on Stonegate."

A moment's stunned silence. "You're in York?"

"Yeah. I cleared my diary for a few days. Is that okay with you?"

"That's great, Jim. I'll be there in ten minutes."

"Is it still brandy and ginger ale?"

"Yes. A large one."

Although he was watching for her, it was lunchtime and the pub was heaving with office workers and tourists. He could hear conversations in Japanese, German, and a New York twang, as well as various English accents. Laura materialised at his side as if spirited there, to bob her head and lightly brush his cheek with her lips before sitting opposite him to smile at his expression of surprise.

The smile was pinched, and the stress was manifest in her tired, concerned, yet still beautiful face. He felt a gangly, self-conscious teenager again. The touch of her soft mouth and the scent of her perfume sent ripples of near bliss through him, turning his limbs to jelly.

"Still wearing Opium," he said as an observation, not a question.

"Yes, a creature of habit. It's good to see you, Jim," she replied before sipping the brandy that had been waiting for her.

"So how's life treating you out here in the boonies?"

"It's been good for me. What I needed...until this serial started up."

"Apart from the job. You sure that you're okay?"

"It doesn't go away, Jim. You know that. It's an accommodation. The space is still there where Kara should be, but I've got a handle on it, now. I live with it and function. I can even look back on the good times and watch the videos, listen to her voice and enjoy her smile and the way she moved. She just went on ahead, too early. But she's safe, will never be hurt, disappointed or embittered by life. Overall I don't think she's missed too much. It's the survivors that get to do all the missing."

Jim vividly remembered the phone call, the pell-mell dash to be with Laura at the hospital, and the crashing wall of grief that met him when he'd arrived.

Kara had been the living image of her mother, just a younger version. Photographs of Laura at eleven could have been either of them at that age.

That sudden, black, heinous day had been the first time he'd seen Laura vulnerable, with her air of self-confidence shredded; torn asunder as her world fell apart around her as instantly as an earthquake victim. She had become a dazed, disoriented and forlorn figure, unable to believe that the most important person in her life had been swallowed up and was gone, never to return. What made sense of chaos had been obliterated.

Kara had kissed her mother goodbye just hours before, telling Laura that she would have spaghetti bolognese ready for the evening meal.

Laura remembered the last words her daughter had said to her: "So don't be late, Mum, or you'll have to eat it all dried up and stuck together like cold dog barf."

"Get out of here. Go and get educated. I'll be home on time…ish," Laura had replied, grimacing, sure that she would not be able to eat the meal that evening without imagining tucking into a pile of puke.

Kara went swimming. It was an organised weekly school trip to the local pool in Finsbury Park. She loved the water and rated herself almost as at home in it as Aerial, the Disney mermaid.

It had been a freak accident; a bolt from the blue...or into it. Kara had mistimed a dive from the three metre board and landed flat – a belly flop – hitting the water with a loud smack, dazing herself and swallowing the chlorine-tainted cocktail as she sank to the bottom, winded and in pain. The echoing slap of her body was as profound as a gunshot in a cathedral. Her classmates swam out to where she had gone under, to dive down, lift her to the surface and quickly heave-pull-push her up onto the non-slip edge of the pool. The teacher and an attendant made every effort to resuscitate her until the paramedics arrived. But she had gone, just blinked out with the untimely finality of a spent light bulb.

Laura had taken leave and begun her passage through the long and dark tunnel of grief. Her loss was an almost solid entity; a creature within her brain that ate at her reason, to compromise all former beliefs and erase healthy expectation. She had confronted death in many guises as a copper, and knew that it was as much a part of life as night following day. Death was as commonplace as birth, but was not the beginning of the journey, but the finality of all that has been: an end to all hopes and dreams and aspirations. Death is a door that slams closed and locks, never to be reopened.

It had been Jim Elliott who'd helped her overcome the pills and brandy-dependant state that she had escaped into. He'd somehow led her gently into the light, having personally been where madness dwelt. His firsthand experience of love lost to the grave helped him to guide her through the labyrinth of emotions that he recognised and had somehow found his way out of. Both metaphorically and physically he had held her hand and tiptoed through the minefield of her despondency, finally delivering her to safer, firmer ground.

"It'll never go away, Laura," Jim said. "And it shouldn't. If it did, you'd lose more than you could gain. You've found the resolve to live with the legacy of love that you and Kara shared, and move on. We're the casualties, like amputees who have had our legs shot out from under us. We had to heal a lot, then strap prostheses on to tender stumps and get up off our asses and learn to walk again. It's one faltering step at a time, and a lot of falling back down until you get the hang of it. Eventually you can walk unaided, but it's never the same. You move forward, but the feeling has gone; the sense of warmth or cold, and blood flowing through arteries and veins and aching muscles is missing. It's called adapting, and it sucks."

Laura smiled at Jim, more openly this time. She remembered feeding off his strength, using him as a support system until she had found the fortitude to pull free from the clinging embrace of melancholia. Her chief superintendent at the time, Alex Carter, had pulled strings, and her application for a sideways move had been expedited. The post up to Yorkshire, and the distance from all that she had known, including Jim, had aided her recuperation. It had been a rebirth that helped to subdue much of the pain. Her new job had kept her distracted; the work a pivot around which all other aspects of her life revolved.

Now, seated at the table of a crowded pub, Laura realised that she still loved Jim...had never stopped. She hoped that they could somehow find a way to bridge the ford that had risen and flowed between them since Kara's death, to perhaps give them a second chance to pursue what had been a far too short-lived affair.

"Another?" Jim said as Laura drained her glass.

"I'll get them," she replied, taking his glass, standing up and heading for the bar.

He couldn't take his eyes off her. They were locked on target; guided missiles that followed her every move. He appraised her slim figure, and his throat suddenly hurt as though filling with gravel. He remembered the happy moments that they had shared, along with the sad. He was a little ashamed to find himself mentally undressing her, imagining the firm body, pert breasts, and the small mole that graced the right cheek of her tight butt. He felt a healthy straining at the front of his jeans and was glad that he was sitting down with the table hiding his growing state of arousal.

Their relationship had been mainly snatched moments and rare evenings, with only two full weekends together in all the time that they had been lovers. It had not been easy, with Laura's career and Kara leaving little time for him or anything else in her life. And with the loss of her daughter, he had known that it was over between them. It had not been an abrupt ending, just a slow but sure separation, as sand through an hourglass; a gentle, insistent shifting.

Since Laura's move up north, Jim had enjoyed only one fleeting relationship that lasted less than a month, and several one night stands that he'd found to be shallow asides in the shadow of his deep feelings for Laura, that persisted, simmering on a back burner, contained but always threatening to boil up and bubble over. Sat now, studying her, he knew that he would always love her. That was why he was in York.

Laura could feel his eyes on her, his gaze an almost physical smouldering on her back, causing her cheeks to ignite in a hot flush. She paid for the drinks and then paused to steady her trembling hands and regain a measure of composure before turning and heading back to the table. His eyes met hers, and she read volumes in them. He still cared. She should have known that, just by the fact that he was here, and that he had studied the paperwork. It was a statement; an admission of his continued devotion. He would not have allowed himself to be drawn back into the world of pattern murderers by anyone else. As she placed the glass down in front of him, she made an instant decision. She wanted him to stay at the cottage; needed to be with him in every sense of the word.

"We need privacy to run through this stuff," Jim said, patting his briefcase.

Laura pulled a face. "The station is out. You can't officially be in the picture."

"I know. I'll book into a hotel, and we can meet up and—"

She cut him off. "Stay at my place," she said too quickly, her cheeks even more rubicund with embarrassment at her girlish outburst, and at what the invitation implied.

"You got it," Jim said, beaming with undisguised delight. "I'm not going to argue or say it's a bad idea. I want to be with you."

She fumbled in her handbag for her mobile and tapped in the stored memory number to connect her with Hugh.

"Hugh?...Laura. If you need me this afternoon, give me a bell. I'm checking something out," she said, grinning at Jim and looking him up and down.

CHAPTER NINE

HE followed her out of the walled city. York was a place he was unfamiliar with. It appeared to be steeped in history, and he was aware of its Viking and Roman heritage. He hoped that he would find the time to explore its narrow streets, preferably with Laura as his guide.

Pulling in behind her on the gravel turnaround outside the cottage, Jim switched off the ignition and stepped out of the Cherokee, closing the door with a sweep of the hip, due to carrying a holdall in one hand and briefcase in the other.

"I somehow pictured you in a flat in the city," he said as she swung her legs out of the car and, standing, smoothed her skirt down before heading for the front door.

"You like it?" she said.

"It's quaint. It just seems a bit rural for a born and bred Londoner."

"It keeps me sane, Jim. I love it out here. It's my sanctuary from all the brouhaha."

"Brouhaha?"

"This week's word: commotion, hullabaloo. I pick a word out of the dictionary every Sunday and flog it to death for seven days."

"Why?"

"To expand my vocabulary. Some people do crosswords or play scrabble. I find a word I like and bore everyone with it."

"Gorgeous, sexy *and* erudite. What a combination," Jim said, staring into her eyes. "Do you really think that it's a good idea...my staying here?"

"Yes. It's one of the better ideas I've had in recent months. We have a lot of lost time to make up for. I ran away from everything, and not seeing you is the only regret I've had. You're the only person I've missed. I just had to start afresh with a clean slate. And now I realise that you can't run away from yourself, and that it's today that really counts. Getting stuck in the past is just a waste of what little time we have."

Jim dropped his bag and briefcase in the narrow hallway, and they were in each other's arms, not speaking, just holding on, both with their eyes closed, time standing still as they kissed tenderly.

"Coffee?" Laura said, pulling away, gently, feeling weak, as though she were convalescing after a long, debilitating illness; in better health now, but still very fragile, and needing to take things slow and easy.

They sat at the table in the kitchen, and Laura told him of the latest developments. Of the grisly contents of the package, and of the note and Polaroid that had accompanied it. She also admitted that she couldn't sleep for the guilt she felt for provoking the killer during the TV interview, and by so doing causing his latest victim such suffering.

"He would still have taken her, Laura. That's what he does. But what the hell were you thinking about badmouthing him?"

"I wanted to draw the creep out, Jim. I thought that I could unsettle him, maybe make him careless."

"Oh, you've in all likelihood drawn him out of the sewer he lives in. You've made this personal, and probably added a new dimension to his game. Believe me; you don't want one of these monsters on your case. He's probably fixated on you now for calling him what he is.

"He'll see you as a player. Don't lose track of the fact that human life is almost an abstract to these freaks. He has no empathy or normal emotions that you can relate to. He's driven, needs to kill, and can't be dissuaded from whatever turns his wheels. You're not ever going to be able to reach him on any worthwhile level. He kills for the same reason that you smoke, because he's addicted to it."

"What's done is done, Jim. What else have you got on this guy?"

Jim opened his briefcase and pulled out two document wallets; one containing the sheaf of faxes that Laura had sent him, the other a wedge of his own printed A4 hard copy. "Here," he said, pushing both across the table.

"No, I'll read it all later, Jim. Tell me what you think. Give me a thumb-nail picture of him."

"Okay," Jim said, face now rock, eyes narrowed in concentration. "Firstly, the obvious. You definitely have a repeat killer out there. This is a guy with a serious personality disorder. I believe that we can attribute his present state of mind and behaviour to childhood imprinting, which has created an emotio-physical identity that has been influenced and is now an uncontrollable mechanism, patterned subconsciously by events that have their roots in his formative years.

"As a child he was almost certainly abused in some way, and became withdrawn and detached; a loner. His choice of victims and his subsequent treatment of them lead me to believe that his mother was the main instigator, the person responsible – to his way of thinking – for his present actions. He was...*is* fixated on her. She is most likely dead now, and his torn emotions of love and hate for her have affected his reasoning and compelled him to find an outlet to physically and emotionally continue to punish her for some action that he can't get past. He needs to continually recreate her, make her suffer, and kill her again and again. He may have actually murdered her. It would be worth checking up on all cases of matricide in the Yorkshire area over the last decade, to eliminate the sons from the picture. It's a long shot, but you may just get lucky."

"Why his mother?" Laura said. "Why not a wife or girlfriend who cheated on him?"

Jim shrugged. "There's an outside chance it could be, as I've intimated in the profile," he replied, standing, picking up their empty mugs and going to the counter to refill them from the softly gurgling coffeemaker that filled the cottage with the rich aroma released from ground Arabica beans. "Call it a hunch," he said, returning and setting the mugs down on wicker coasters. "But I know that this stems from his childhood, so his mother is a more likely stressor. Remember, a lot of this is conjecture. That's what I used to be able to do, come up with more right than wrong answers. But it isn't a perfect science. There's a chance that I'm way off base."

"But you don't think so?"

"No."

"What else, Jim? It's chilling but fascinating."

"I estimate him to be in his mid-twenties, thirty max. He's white, fit, and has to be physically strong. He manhandles his victims, strings them up to bleed out, and then moves them to outlying locations to be found. He transports them in the boot of his car, or in the back of a van, and carries them a distance from the vehicle, to be sure there are no tread marks to be found. I think he will be of above average intelligence, and that he is probably well liked by the people who he works with. He will have fostered a pleasant, affable personality, and is leading a double life, blending in without raising suspicion.

"He's also an arrogant bastard, who feels far superior to everyone else, but that won't show. I would be surprised if he hasn't killed a lot more young women and efficiently disposed of the bodies. All files of girls with blonde hair and blue eyes who have gone missing over recent years need to be re-examined. If we know where they were last seen, it could throw up a density in an area that is close to where he lives."

Jim paused and sat back. His shoulders slumped. He was pale, and sweat was beading at his hairline.

"That's enough for now, Jim," Laura said, needing to hear more, but hurting at what she could see it was doing to him. She knew that he'd opened a can of rotten worms, which must have been as hard an act for him to do as it would be for an agoraphobic to go shopping along Oxford Street on a Saturday afternoon.

"It's okay," he took a deep breath. "It just takes me back. They say if you're thrown off a horse, get straight back up in the saddle. I guess I've left it a tad too long. I'm finding it a little spooky remounting. I'd rather finish up now and be done with it."

"Okay, if you're sure. Why is he now giving up the bodies if he's killed more than the ones he's dumped to be recovered? Does that mean he subconsciously wants to be caught?" Laura said, lighting up and taking a deep drag of her first cigarette for over two hours, which was very nearly a record.

Jim shook his head. "Christ, no. He's just decided to show off his handiwork to an audience for some extra mileage and to get more of a thrill from what he's doing. This way he gets feedback and sees everyone panicking and running around like headless chickens. He'll be watching the news, reading the papers, and revelling in his notoriety. He's anonymous but infamous. If he isn't stopped, then all blue-eyed blondes better dye their hair and start wearing green or brown contact lenses."

"Is that the good news or the bad?" Laura almost whispered.

"There is no good news. Now, where's your john? I need to off-load about half a gallon of coffee."

"The loo is upstairs, first on the left," Laura said, smiling at his Americanism.

"I'll be back," he said in perfect Schwarzenese as he headed through the lounge towards the spiral staircase and vanished from view.

Laura made notes. Jim had already given her leads to follow that they had not even considered. His way of thinking, or feeling, was from out of left field and not hindered by just hard evidence, or lack of it. He had an insight that put him on the outside, looking in at an almost blank canvas, but able to conjure up the picture from just seeing the first few brushstrokes.

"That's better," Jim said, returning and mulling over the sheets of paper in front of him.

"What do you suggest?" Laura said. "How would you proceed?"

"Apart from checking out likely past victims and the matricide angle, there's not a lot you can do. To sum up, I think you're looking for a young Caucasian male, who may be fair-haired and blue-eyed. He's fit, probably works out, and will be around six feet or even taller. I'd bet the farm on him being local to the area, living alone in an isolated setting. He is left-handed, and most likely holds a position of authority in a field of work that he enjoys. As for the victims, he doesn't know them. He picks them out purely because of their physical appearance, and will then stalk them for a while to get to know their habits and assess how easily they can be abducted. He'll take no chances.

"He may be out of control and running amok from your point of view, but he's calling the shots, manipulating the proceedings, and would abort an attack if anything unforeseen came up. If he stops killing, then you may never know his identity. Like it or not, you need for him to carry on, and even then he could fill a graveyard before you get him."

"I'm impressed," Laura said. "But run through some points for me. How can you know so much about him from what I sent you?"

"The autopsy protocols say a lot. The downward angle of blows to the right side of the heads, correlated with the height of the victims, pins his approximate height. And that he cut the throats right to left confirms that he's a lefty. He has no need to pretend to be left-handed. Your handwriting experts will confirm that from the note. And the fact that only twelve to fifteen percent of the male population are left-handed cuts out a high percentage of men who might otherwise fit the bill. As for his colouring, I'm sticking with my theory that the girls represent an idealised version of how his mother looked. I choose to believe that he takes after her, which makes him a blonde, or fair with blue eyes. It's a stretch, but good odds. She hurt him, sexually abused him, or just pissed him off big time. Whatever she did, scrambled him. The rapes are violent and aggressive, and the stapling of the mouth is to shut his imagined mother up and prevent further lies, scolding, or any verbal communication."

"And what makes you so sure that this is his patch? Couldn't he be killing a long way from where he lives?"

"Not if he stalks them, and I know he does. This dude lives and works in the York area. He takes them back to his...lair, which is why I think he's single. He also keeps them for varying periods of time, sometimes days, so he has privacy. He's out in the country, lives in a semi-remote cottage, or on a farm. He has to have a place where his comings and goings don't attract attention. Based on what information you've given me, combined with calculated guesswork and gut feeling, that's the best I can come up with. At the moment he's holding all the aces. He needs to dominate, and thrives on it. He's a control freak. We...*you* need some luck, or for him to slip up and make a mistake. He isn't going to stop. He's driven; has a thirst he can't quench."

"Thanks, Jim. I know how hard it must be for you to get back into this again. But will you look at anything else that comes up?"

Jim shrugged. "I've got my feet wet now, so what the hell. I'll need to visit the sites where the bodies were found."

"I'll take you to them, tomorrow. I feel better about this case already, but sick to my stomach over the Stroud girl. I want to save her, but I don't know how to."

"I'm sorry, Laura, I think she's a lost cause, probably already dead. Let's call it a day. I need a shower and a change of clothes. And if you can face it, we can go out for a meal, my treat."

"Later, maybe," she said, reaching across the table and taking hold of his hand. "First I'd like to make up for all that lost time. If you want to."

"That's the best offer I've had all day," Jim said. "Come on, I need my back washing."

Laura gave him a seductive smile, stood up, led him to the staircase, and said, "Just your back?"

They began undressing each other, tentatively at first, then with an urgency soon to be matched by their fierce, abandoned coupling under the jets of hot water that steamed up the small bathroom. The sexual tension had been there since the first second they had met in the pub, as taut as a bowstring quivering with the strain of wanting to release the arrow. Time had not dulled their physical desire for each other.

Later, their ardour tempered, though not extinguished, they took time to towel each other dry, and then went to Laura's bed. It was as though they were revisiting a favourite destination that they had returned to and found even more exciting and beautiful than the first time; a location that they could now enjoy the fine detail of, not just the overall view. Laura sat astride Jim, and they moved slowly in synchronised harmony, until they overflowed and were as near to becoming one being as is possible.

Panting, perspiring, smiling, they said nothing, not wanting to break the spell that had pervaded and suffused them. They lay, still joined, embracing as lengthening shadows drew the light from the day and enfolded them in the warm embers of dusk.

All thoughts of death and past tragedy leached away. The love they felt for one another encapsulated and insulated them from everything negative or evil. They slowly drifted off into the mists of peaceful, contented slumber, spared the knowledge of the awesome personal danger that lay ahead, waiting to rend all their hopes and dreams asunder.

CHAPTER TEN

"SEE you in the morning," Brendan Wallace, the gatekeeper, said as he thumbed the button and the internal security door slid across behind Ron Cullen, who waved a hand in acknowledgement, while hefting the heavy bag further up on to his shoulder by its strap with the other.

Ron walked over to the main admin block and punched in the four digit security code to gain admission. The bag felt red hot, as though the ECR (Emergency Control Room) cameras that followed all movement, were X-raying it. He had almost turned back at the gate, to return to his car and off-load the modified shotgun and the cartridges into his boot. But what he had planned could only be accomplished on night duty. During the day everything *was* X-rayed at the gate, be it staff or visitors' property. Night-time was the only window of opportunity. The machine was unmanned, not thought a necessary measure at a time when scores of officers were crowding the gate to go off duty at the end of the day, to be replaced by just a handful of night patrols.

As he entered the corridors of the main residential wings, Ron relaxed a little, feeling safe now that he was inside. His first plan had been to wait for Heather's killer to be apprehended and then take him out in court, during the trial. Just gut shoot him in the dock with both barrels. That had been his intention as he had stood over his daughter's cold body in the small room of the mortuary to formally identify her, somehow stopping from screaming at the sight of her mutilated body. His stomach had churned, his vision had greyed, and the smell of air fresheners had almost made him physically sick. He remembered the look that the young DS had given him. The copper had seen his anger and purpose, as though it had been written in bright neon tubing on a sign above his head. Ron knew that he would have no success in killing the culprit in court, even if the animal was ever found and brought to trial. All crown courts had tight security these days.

It was later in the chapel of rest that he decided on this avenue of retribution, as he had been holding the gelid hand of the shell that had so recently been his beautiful, intelligent, life-loving daughter. The makeup on her face did not fully hide the puncture holes in her lips.   And although the high-necked shroud covered her stitched throat, he imagined, graphically, the tissue damage under the oyster gown.   She was gone, and a large part of him had died with her.   He now knew the frustration and anger that so many other bereaved parents of raped, mutilated and murdered children felt.   He worked among the sick and evil creatures that carried out these crimes, and listened to them complaining over the quality of food, and demanding to have more and more privileges.   He saw them laughing, wheeling and dealing in drugs, telephone cards and tobacco with others of their kind.   They were cared for and cocooned, living better than millions of pensioners, who struggled to make ends meet, many still having to ration heating and food to claw through each winter; an undisclosed number dying of hypothermia as successive governments gave them less support and human rights than they afforded enemies of society, who had surely forfeited any rights to anything, including life itself.

Reaching A wing, Ron dumped his bag at the side of the desk and plodded around the two storey quadrangle of cells, opening and closing the hundred observation flaps in the doors to do a body count, or roll check as it was officially called.   Back in the wing office, he rang his numbers through to the orderly officer, then waited for the prison roll to be reported correct, at which point the main gates were opened and the evening duty staff spilled out, a black-uniformed tide of laughing, whinging, shouting screws: an adult version of home-time from school.

Ron made a test call on his radio to the ECR, then poured himself a coffee and opened his book to the page where a photo of Heather marked his place and smiled up at him.   Until midnight he proposed to function normally, visit the pegging points every thirty minutes to turn his key in the slots and record – for an untrusting system – that he had not just gone to sleep or stayed in the office.   He would subsequently do what he considered to be a service to himself and society.   He would, in the name of natural justice, snuff out a few shitheads, whom he deemed to have enjoyed far too much borrowed time.

Just a few miles from the prison, Shelley Stroud was writhing, drumming her feet on the hard earth.   She was now more like a demented wild animal than a teenage girl.

He looked down at her.   She was lathered in sweat, soil, straw and blood, her blonde hair now matted and red.   The pad that he had taped to the raw hole where her ear had been had come loose, and her thrashing head had opened the scabbing wound. Her mouth resembled a zip fastener. He had gone a little overboard with the stapler.

Shelley was no longer sane. She had suffered the abuse, but the stapler clip...clip...clip...clipping her lips together had altered her state of mind. Adrenaline had pumped uselessly through her muscles, inciting her to take flight or fight, of which she could do neither. She reached a point where she knew death was imminent, and that there was nothing she could do to save herself. A crippling, absolute fear gripped her mind in a band of tightening steel as her brain fought to shut down and not be in this place of untenable horror. She prayed for quick release, to escape further torture, and her mind eventually came to her aid and began to fragment and crash like a computer invaded by a virus. She screamed, and the scream, like Shelley, had nowhere to go. The pressure of her attempts to vent the pain against the unyielding iron staples caused her cheeks to balloon out and her face to turn almost purple, distending hitherto unseen veins at her temples, and for blood vessels to rupture in her bulging eyes, sending crimson rivulets down her already bloody face. On the very brink of insanity, she felt a profound sadness for her parents, before her thoughts became an irrational, random and incoherent knot of mental static, and she retreated into a state of blissful unawareness.

He lay next to her, naked, and snuggled up against the now limp and mindless mannequin, his arm around her waist. "I love you, Mummy," he whispered, before drifting into a deep and dreamless sleep.

The night orderly officer left the wing, locking the gate behind him at 00.05 hours. Ron dutifully recorded his visit on the docket. He poured himself another cup of coffee and settled to finish up the last few pages of his novel. Fifteen minutes later, he closed the book and returned it to his bag. There had been big game hunting in Wilbur's fictional African adventure, but none to compare with the culling that he was about to perform. Taking out the shotgun, he broke it, loaded it, and filled his uniform jacket pockets with cartridges. He then wrote a final memo, addressing it to the prison governor as he chewed a thick wad of gum into a soft, malleable lump, and hummed an old lullaby that he had sung to Heather in her cot, back when the world had seemed young and full of promise.

All done. Time to go a huntin'! A nonsense rhyme popped into his mind. It was one that his uncle Arthur had recited whenever they had gone rabbiting together, when he (Ron) had been a tousle-headed youngster, back in the seventies. He said it aloud: "There was a little man, and he had a little gun, and over the fields he did but run, with a belly full of fat, an old tin hat, and a pancake stuck to his bum, bum, bum!" It still didn't make sense, but brought back good, solid memories. He rose and went to the barred entrance gate to the wing, where he took the elastic, pink gobbet of gum from his mouth, worked half of it into the lock, closed the inner wood door and kicked a wedge firmly under it. He then took the back stairs to the ground floor entrance to the wing and repeated the procedure, before returning to the office to collect his weapon and the list of cell numbers that he had carefully selected for special attention. He unclipped the leather, sealed packet from his key chain and ripped it open; an act reserved for life-and-death emergencies; the enclosed cell key only to be withdrawn after first alerting the orderly officer and control room staff. Ron alerted no one. He had a lot to do, and not a lot of time to do it in. Removing his boots, he set off along the landing, moving silently, not wanting the cons to hear his approach. Taking a deep breath, he opened the door of A2-7 with practised ease, turning on the cell light by way of the switch outside as he entered, to find the occupant beginning to sit up in bed.

Toby Martin was a paedophile. He was a pencil-thin, weasel-faced man with a curvature of the spine that both forced his head down and made him walk off centre, continually fighting to keep a straight line, as a car will try to wander when the wheel alignment is out of true. Toby had molested children for twenty-three of his thirty-nine years. He had done eight stretches for his compulsive sex crimes, and had finally been given a life sentence after getting carried away and strangling a young boy to death.

Eyes blinking, adjusting to the sudden and unexpected light, Toby wondered what the screw wanted at this time of night. He was clean. There were no drugs in his cell, and so a spot search was going to be a waste of their time. And then he became aware of the shotgun pointing at him.

"What the fuck are you doin'?" Toby said a second before the barrels crashed into his mouth, shattering his small, decaying front teeth.

"I'm reducing the prison population. And you have the honour of being the first no good little turd to start the ball rolling," Ron said, lowering the twin muzzles, pushing the cold steel up hard against Toby's groin and pulling the trigger.

Toby was still screaming and bleeding to death as Ron ejected the spent cartridge cases, reloaded, and opened the door of A2-16.

Titus Jackson was out of bed as the light came on, and even tried to reach Ron, but was blown backwards off his feet as the double blasts tore into his chest. The ebony-black rapist and murderer, his thick mass of dreadlocks flying above his head like a startled, many-legged spider, was dead before he hit the back wall and slid down it, to leave a sanguineness slick on the periwinkle-blue painted plaster.

Cell call bells sounded, and inmates shouted and screamed as the echoing blasts punctuated the night. Ron became intoxicated with the smell of cordite, deafened by the noise, and robotic in his movements, now distanced from his actions. He walked stiffly as if in a trance from cell to cell; the killing becoming an almost mechanical act. "There was a little man, and he had a little gun...There was a little man, and he had a little gun..." He kept repeating the mantra, though was unaware of doing so. He was perhaps a little insane now, in that his disordered mind was in some way functioning on automatic, as if his actions were part of a computer programme that was running its course.

Principal Officer Ray Manning, the orderly officer, ran to the wing accompanied by three other officers. It took them almost ten minutes to gain entry through the gummed-up gate lock and wedged door. And as they laboured to enter the wing, the unmistakable roar of a shotgun being discharged echoed through the internal corridors; the sound trapped, reverberating as it travelled around the enclosed landings; a deafening wall of noise that heralded the ministering of death.

He woke at the cusp of dawn as the first birdsong heralded a new day, and the greyness of morning filtered through the skylight. She was still out of it, conscious, eyes open, but staring with the vacant, glassy-eyed idiocy of a stuffed animal. This had been the first time that one of them had actually become catatonic. It was interesting. He felt as though he were in the presence of a warm-blooded vegetable. He fashioned a noose in one end of a rope and secured it around her ankles, then took the other end, threw it over the beam above them and hoisted her up like a flag, tying the rope off to the rail of a stall, to leave her hanging with the tips of her limp fingers only an inch off the ground, and her mane of pale hair brushing the compacted dirt. Firmly gripping her wide, childbearing hips, – that would never play their part in that function, – he ran across the floor of the barn, pushing her, and then letting go to watch her swing in a wide arc, backwards and forwards, rope and wood squeaking and groaning as she became a human pendulum. He watched amused as the living body passed in front of him, the displaced air wafting him with a cool breeze. He pushed her again, harder, and then lifted his knife, and as she sped by he lashed out to slit open her throat with the keen blade.

Shelley felt nothing – protected in a chrysalis of imbecility – as her jugular vein discharged the blood from her brain and a severed carotid artery pumped out much more, to paint him and the dirt floor in abstract patterns of bright red lines. He moved in, pushed her again, this time at a tangent; the angle of deflection causing her to circle him.

"Hey, Wendy, help me catch my shadow," he shouted as she flew by. But Shelley was past participating in any further endeavour, already turning right at the second star and going straight on to the wonderful world of Never Land. Her heart had taken flight, and she would truly never grow old, though would sadly be in no position to appreciate that in others' memories, she would remain forever young.

The sight, touch, smell and even the taste of the blood turned him on. He basked in its sticky, silky, coppery-scented warmth and waited until the pulses waned to become a dribble and finally just droplets, before taking a couple of photographs. He then went over to the wall-mounted hose reel, unwound several feet of it and turned the tap on, playing the powerful jet of the spray gun over the corpse and then himself. The rich lifeblood, if left for even a short period of time soon lost its charm, to become a sour-smelling, congealing material that proved stubborn to remove. This initial hosing down would make thorough cleaning and disinfecting a much easier procedure, when he had showered, eaten and returned to finish up later. He had no wish to cut them up, eat them, or keep any part of them as trophies. He wasn't a fucking idiot like Jeffrey Dahmer, the Yank who had got caught through a lack of discipline. Dahmer's killing had got away from him. He had corpses mounting up in his apartment; even heads in the fridge, and body parts in pans on the stove. The guy had been a raving lunatic, surrounding himself with the incriminating evidence. Christ knows what his apartment had smelled like. No, he wasn't about to lose control like that. He had buried many of his victims deep under the barn's floor, sealed in lime-filled, plastic fertiliser bags. And now, to save digging, and to add a new dimension to his exploits, he had started to leave them posed for the plods to find. The risk of transporting them to his chosen sites was calculated, and he reckoned, minimal. He enjoyed sharing his work, creating humorous little tableaux that he thought a nice touch. He was even leaving them with identification, to ensure that their families could give them a proper Christian burial. He wasn't all bad.

Ron knew that he was running out of time. He would soon have company, and then it would be over. It had been a success, but although he had moved quickly, the cons were now organised, and many of them had wedged and barricaded their doors against him. The hydraulic jacks that prised cell doors open in a matter of seconds, once in place, were not kept on the wings, but in the security office, separate from the residential areas, to be deployed when needed. They were effective, but too cumbersome and heavy for one officer alone to operate. Ron did have a set of Allen keys, and could have unscrewed the locking plates and reversed the hinge mechanisms, which would have allowed him to open the doors outwards, away from the barricades, but that also took time, which was a luxury he didn't have too much of left. Twenty from his list of twenty-five wasn't bad. He had wiped out a score of tossers who'd been a waste of space and a blight on society. They would never walk free, or have the chance to harm anyone else ever again. If his actions were deemed to be an outrage by policy makers who had wimped out, then tough shit. He wasn't looking for brownie points, but knew that most ordinary coppers, screws, and the majority of the general public would applaud his actions, even if they didn't voice their approval openly.

"Give it up," Ray Manning shouted as he rounded the corner of the spur and saw Ron covered in blood, breaking open the smoking weapon he held. "Put it down, Ron," he said, stopping ten feet from the officer, suddenly very scared as he saw the manic look in the other man's eyes.

"There was a little man, and he had a little gun..." Ron mumbled, thumbing two fresh cartridges into the sawn-off and bringing it up to point down the landing.

"Ron, no...Please!" Ray said, positive that he was about to die.

Ron blinked the sweat from his eyes and focused on the trembling orderly officer who stood before him with hands outstretched as if to ward off the lethal load he expected to be loosed. "I did it for Heather and Brenda, and for all the families out there who are still suffering because of what these lowlife's did to their loved ones," Ron said before turning the shotgun, pushing the hot ends of the sawn down barrels between his teeth, deep into his open mouth, and smoothly pulling the trigger, to blow his brains out.

Ray Manning and the other officers stood frozen to the spot in disbelief as Ron jerked backwards and fell to the floor.

"Fuck me!" Ray murmured, reaching for the radio that was clipped to his belt, already trying to imagine the shitload of paperwork that this unprecedented mess would generate, as in the first instance he told control to contact the duty governor, the Medical Officer, emergency services and the Home Office press office. As he spoke, a serpentine red stream flowed across the floor towards him from Ron's blasted head. He stepped back away from it as though it were acid, not wanting it to touch his shoes.

CHAPTER ELEVEN

THE iron steps were cold on Laura's feet as she hurried down the corkscrew staircase with a small, contented smile on her face. She felt truly alive for the first time since Kara's death, and was tingling under her oversize Winnie the Pooh T-shirt and brief cotton panties. The sensation of Jim still inside her and holding her persisted, arousing her again as she walked through to the kitchen and poured a steaming brew from the coffeemaker, that as usual had fired up as the timer triggered its operation, half an hour before her alarm clock buzzed like a fly and lured her from bed to turn it off. She switched on the portable TV – that was positioned in the corner, atop the marble effect counter between the bread bin and an empty spaghetti jar – before sitting at the pine table to watch the early morning news.

"…And now we go live to Long Hutton prison," the newsreader said, "where shortly after midnight a lone warder is alleged to have gone on a killing spree inside the jail. Early reports suggest that at least twenty inmates were gunned down in their cells." The newsreader turned to a large screen behind her, on which a correspondent was outside the well-lit walls of the maximum security prison. "John. Can you tell us what is happening at this time?" he said.

"Yes, Fiona," the suitably concerned looking young man, with sparse hair waving like corn in the light breeze, said. "A prison spokesman has confirmed that an officer on night duty smuggled a shotgun onto one of the wings, where he is believed to have coldly and methodically opened cell doors and executed inmates. Unofficial reports suggest that up to twenty category A and B prisoners, all serving life sentences, died before the officer turned the weapon on himself. As you can see," – the camera panned back to give a wide angle view – "there is a heavy police presence, and coaches full of prison officers have arrived from several other establishments, including Manchester, Hull, Leeds and Wakefield, due to the unrest inside. It is not yet known what the motive was for this unparalleled action, and the names of the dead inmates and officer have been withheld."

The picture snapped back to Fiona Clarkson in the studio. "That was John Kelly, live from outside Long Hutton prison," she said.

"We will keep you up to date with the situation, as and when we receive further details. I *can* tell you that the officer responsible for this tragic incident is believed to be the father of one of the so-called Tacker's victims. This may prove to be an act of indirect retribution carried out by a disturbed man. The Tacker is still at large and continues to prey on young women in the York area."

As the weather girl appeared, to theatrically wave her hands over a map of the British Isles and guarantee a humid day and high pollen count, Laura was already back upstairs getting dressed.

"What's the matter?" Jim asked, propping himself up on one elbow as Laura darted about the bedroom.

"A screw at Long Hutton went berserk with a 12 gauge and declared open season on inmates, then blew his own brains out. They didn't name him, but I know it was Ron Cullen, the father of one of the Tacker's victims."

"You sure?"

"Do bears shit in the woods?" Laura said, leaning over to kiss him on the cheek before running for the door.

"Meet me for lunch," Jim shouted as she clattered down the staircase.

"Same pub, one o' clock. Okay?" Laura called back.

"I'll be there," Jim said a split second before he heard the front door slam. Sitting up, he planted his feet on the cool, varnished floorboards at the side of the bed. Took a deep breath and exhaled slowly. God, being back in the sack with Laura had graphically brought it home to him just what he'd been missing. Sex with someone you want to be with and share your life with was more than just a physical act. It transcended just getting your rocks off. Making love with Laura was about more than fleeting gratification. It was a bonding; an expression of pent-up emotional needs that could not be replicated with another partner.

"It *was* Cullen," Hugh said, appearing at Laura's door within seconds of her sitting at her desk. "I knew he was a cold fish. He topped twenty sex offenders and murderers, all serving life, and then ate his shotgun."

"Who's mopping up at the scene?"

"DCI Thornton. He's out there now with the SOCO and the pathologist."

"It's tragic, Hugh. Cullen was in a position to take his revenge on the same sort of degenerates as the one who killed his daughter, and just flipped and did it. But it has no bearing on our case, other than being a direct result of what our boy did to Heather."

Hugh sighed. "A lot of screws and coppers are like loaded guns. I've heard more than one say that if he ever got diagnosed with anything terminal, he would do something similar to what Cullen's done."

"Yeah, but it's usually just talking the talk, isn't it? This is the first time that one has actually gone over the edge and done anything like this."

"Well, none of those wankers will ever be a threat to anyone again. He just reintroduced the death penalty for a limited run."

"You sound as if you approve of what he did, Hugh."

"Professionally, I see it as a crime committed outside the law. Personally, I think he provided a service that has been redundant for far too long. I'm one of those hard-liners who would not only bring back topping, but backdate it. The prison system is getting clogged up with lifers who should have been put down decades ago. What do you think, boss?"

"I think that my view on capital punishment is irrelevant. It's our job to catch them. I try to keep that as the only priority, and leave the courts to weigh them off."

"Was that a for or against the death penalty?" Hugh pushed, his eyes twinkling.

"Let's just say that if there was a system that could guarantee that no innocent man or woman was sentenced to death, then I would consider it in a different light for certain offenders."

"That was a yes, boss, whichever way you wrap it up."

"Shut up and pour the coffee, Hugh. You're giving me a headache."

Jim spent the morning going through the reports again, searching for the slightest detail that he may have missed. There was nothing. He showered, drank too much coffee and watched news updates on the unfolding prison drama. He had nothing but admiration for the killer screw. The dark side of him was always pleased to see bad guys get their asses vaporised. He had lived with violent, sudden death, and both seen and suffered the results of what sick and twisted psycho's could do. If milk is bad, you flush it away. And if meat has turned rancid, you bin it. He saw rotten humanity in the same light. If it was no good, feed it to the nearest waste disposal unit available. The lenient treatment of life's worst scum did not make the world a safer place for honest folk; ergo, the law was an ass, far removed and at odds with the society it was supposed to protect and serve. All decent Americans had been happy to hear that Bin Laden had met a violent end. Call it revenge, justice, closure, whatever. It had undoubtedly resulted in millions of folk punching the air and shouting *Yesss* at their TV screens.

Jim watched the hands of the carriage clock on the mantel in the lounge creep round with protracted, tortoise-like stealth. And finally at a little past noon he left the cottage and headed for York, eager to be with Laura again, missing her with a passion that he could not have imagined just twenty-four hours previously.

He was early, bought the drinks and settled at a small corner table in an alcove, from where he could see the door. It was exactly one p.m. when Laura breezed in, and his heart raced as she walked toward to him; the love light in her eyes shining, making him feel like saying the words to some 'Always and Forever' type of late night song that he had heard on countless smooch FM radio stations.

"I've got something you might find interesting," Laura said, producing a printout and handing it to him as she sat down.

"You've got a lot of things I find interesting," he replied, taking the piece of paper, but keeping his eyes firmly on Laura's, holding her gaze and speaking volumes without words, as she was held mesmerised by his magnetic stare.

"Stop it," Laura said, turning her head away. "I feel like a rabbit in a car's headlights when you do that."

"Do what? I didn't do anything. I was just looking at you."

"You know exactly what you were doing, Jim Elliott. It wasn't just looking, it was almost hypnosis. There should be a law against you Yanks coming over here and looking at womenfolk that way. You'll be offering me nylons and chocolate next like they did way back in World War Two."

"You should be so lucky. I don't offer bribes to the law."

"Shame. I'm open to a good bribe from time to time."

"Let's pursue this line of thought tonight, back at the cottage. I'm sure I can find you something as hard and sweet to suck on as a block of dairy milk."

"You'd better look at that list, before I run you in for...for making lewd remarks that are likely to make me blush."

Jim looked at the list of names and descriptions of a dozen missing teenage girls, and at the times and dates of their last known whereabouts. They were all fair-haired or blonde, with blue eyes, and they shared another common denominator; none had ever been seen again. The last on the list had gone missing just six months ago and the earliest over three years back.

"This looks good," Jim said. "I need to see a map to pinpoint exactly where they were last seen. It should give us his home territory."

"If it is him, all those locations are southeast of the city," Laura said, wanting to light just her third cigarette of the day, unable to in the pub, but pleased at the success she was having in cutting down. "I've got a map of the York area in the car. You can study it while I drive you to the crime scenes you wanted to see."

"Forget those, Laura. I wouldn't find anything. This is more important. Let's go back to your place and work on it."

As they rose to leave, Hugh Parfitt walked into the pub, saw Laura and pushed his way through the lunch-time crowd, making a beeline for them.

"Boss?" Hugh said, looking from Laura to Jim and back again.

"Jim Elliott...DS Hugh Parfitt," Laura said by way of briefly introducing the two men.

Jim shook the young cop's hand. It was a dry, cold, vicelike grip, intended to be challenging and slightly intimidating. Jim matched it, then increased the pressure as he smiled and returned the guy's fixed stare. For a fleeting hundredth of a second, he saw a soulless and uncompromising dark quality under the surface of affability, which seemed as wild as a storm-lashed and cruel sea. The youthful good looks and the too-quick pleasant smile were a mask that failed to hide a calculating, intelligent, and in some way dangerous mind from Jim's honed skills of character analysis.

"Good to meet you, Jim," Hugh said. "Can I get you both a drink?"

"Thanks, but no. We were just leaving."

"American, huh?...Jim Elliott. The name rings a bell," Hugh said. "Are you in law enforcement?"

"I used to be," Jim replied. "A long time ago."

"Got it!" Hugh said, grinning. "I've read about you. You were an FBI profiler. Didn't you catch a guy in Baltimore or Philadelphia? Called himself Lucifer and used to burn his victims when he was done with them, to supposedly deliver their souls to hell or something."

"It was Baltimore, and he called himself Lucien."

"So are you here to help us nail our killer, Jim? Or is your being in York at this time just pure coincidence?"

"Jim's an old friend, Hugh. He's not on the case. He's in PR now," Laura said, trying to end the conversation, walking towards the door as she spoke.

"Once a cop, always a cop," Hugh observed, turning up the voltage of his Burt Lancaster smile, before abruptly turning away and heading for the bar.

"Hugh is a good copper," Laura said as they drove out of the city in Jim's Cherokee. "He's just a bit overprotective of me. Looks after my interests."

"I never said a word," Jim replied.

"You didn't have to. I could tell you didn't like him."

"I don't like or dislike him, Laura. I don't know the guy. I just got a feeling about him. He isn't all he seems to be."

"Who is?"

"Point taken. I'm just on edge. His mother probably loves him."

That evening, he settled in what had been his father's armchair. It was worn and shiny-backed with frayed arms. Decades' worth of dust and sweat and grease had formed a patina of grime, overlaying the paisley pattern from all but the outer sides and rear of it. He had once dug his hands down the gap between the arms and seat and found a few pre-decimal coins; old pennies and even a dull, lacklustre florin that would be a ten pence piece nowadays. There had also been a black plastic comb, still holding some of his dad's Brylcreem-coated hair in its teeth. He had returned the items to the dark chasms of the chair, which was, as the farm around it, a time capsule; his link to a past that still played such a major role in his life. He had made few changes. The house was almost as it had been when he was a child. His parents' clothes still languished in drawers and hung limp and moth-eaten on wooden hangers in the utility wardrobe in the front bedroom. Old framed prints and monochrome photographs adorned the walls, preserving the colour of the wallpaper beneath, which had faded around them, and in places curled away from the encroaching damp. Outside, the land had been neglected. A large patch of weed-filled ground marked the spot where he had burned down the chicken shed. His memory of running around it whooping and shouting as the stinking hens clucked frenziedly as they were roasted alive still made him smile.

He sat forward, with a plate of ham sandwiches on his bare knees and a glass of milk in his left hand, grinning at the scenes being shown on the six o'clock news. It was giving updates on the previous night's fun and games at Long Hutton prison. It transpired that the screw who'd gone off his rocker had been the father of one of his mother's incarnations. It gladdened his heart that so many of the worst cons in the system had been offed in a twisted form of revenge, at his instigation. It was one of those days that seldom come along; almost equalling that long gone morning when he had been standing in the rain, watching his father die under the tractor, his body crushed and his last minutes full of pain and a fear that was so profound that he had almost been able to taste it.

The regional news came on, and Trish Pearson's head and shoulders filled the screen. "Last night," she said dramatically – as if she gave a fuck – with her eyes not making contact with his, but reading from an autocue next to the camera lens, "a tragedy took place inside one of Britain's top security jails. A warder, his mind crippled by the recent rape, mutilation and murder of his only daughter, lost control, and in a state of unimaginable mental anguish proceeded to shoot twenty inmates to death in their cells, before killing himself. There are two issues here. Firstly, how could a warder be able to walk into a prison with a shotgun and boxes of cartridges? And secondly, I think it safe to say that the real blame for what happened can be squarely placed at the feet of the mad-dog killer who continues to prey on young women in the York area. The sick and twisted coward who has been nicknamed the Tacker must be caught and caged for the rest of his natural life. And now we go to our outside..."

"You're next, you bad-mouthed bitch," he screamed at the set, shooting to his feet, causing the plate of sandwiches to fly off his knees to the matted carpet, as did the glass of milk, which slipped forgotten from his hand. "You've gone too far. It's time we met face to face... again."

CHAPTER TWELVE

HE waited for his strongest ally, which was nightfall, and then loaded the blue plastic fertiliser sack and its contents into the boot and drove west, into the city and out of it towards Knaresborough.

Crossing the bridge over the River Nidd and passing the entrance that led to Mother Shipton's cave, he left the road on to a forestry path, cutting the lights and driving at little more than walking pace, aided by pale moon glow. He parked in thick bracken among trees that hid the Mondeo completely from sight of the road.

He had reconnoitred the area, planned this novel disposal days ago, and was now excited at the prospect of his work being found. Detective Inspector Laura Scott and her posse of nose-blocked bloodhounds would get even more bad press as his reign of terror struck even deeper into the hearts of the population of North Yorkshire.

By the time he reached the edge of the rock cliff that overhung the cave below it, his shoulders were aching and his calves and thighs burned. The body was a dead weight, literally. And as he shrugged it off, for it to thud on rock that was only sparsely covered with a paper-thin layer of lichen and weed, he stretched and rolled his shoulders, twisting his neck from side to side, grunting at the complaining of his tight muscles. Hefting the sack over the spiked, six-foot-high iron poles of the security fence had tested him to the limit.

Fifteen minutes later, he was finished. He had taken the corpse from the sack and lowered it over the edge by a rope that was tied to one of its ankles at one end, and secured to one of the sturdy railings at the other. The cadaver hung, a grisly, ashen, spectral form against the wet limestone, to drip with water that was so rich in minerals that if the body were to be left, it would form a rock coating; a cast that would be as fine as any sculpture. It was a shame that the tourists – who would flock here in the light of the following day – would miss this new addition to the famous petrifying wall. But he was sure that it would be found, and that the attraction would be closed as the plods searched in vain for clues.

Thirty minutes later he pulled back out on to the A59 and headed for home with Tina Turner belting out that he was *Simply the Best* through all four speakers, and at a volume that inflamed his spirit and assaulted his eardrums with a decibel level that, given time, would have damaged his hearing permanently.

At the house, he stripped off his clothes to sit cross-legged on the bedroom floor, shuffling a thick pack of Polaroids as though they were playing cards, to turn them over one by one and place each face up on the pair of panties that had belonged to the pictured prey. Each was unique, generating sublime memories of his past exploits. His breathing became quick and laboured; pulse racing. Sensory overload made him dizzy. Selecting a pair of stained, black satin panties, he draped them over his erection and gently barrelled his fist around the silky material.

"The ones on the list were all taken within a ten mile radius," Jim said, drawing a circle on the map that encompassed an area with the village of Wheldrake at its centre. "He's in there somewhere. Now that he's giving the bodies up, he's started taking them from farther afield. He won't expect us to put it together."

"That's still a hell of a big area to check out," Laura said as she studied the map.

Jim was unfazed. "Think positive. We have the technology. The electoral roll will throw up all single men living at outlying addresses. And then it's just a matter of elimination."

Laura frowned. "You really think it will be that simple?"

"Yeah. Once you've got a list, a house-to-house will find him. There'll only be a few six-footers that fit the description. And with just a handful of suspects it will be easy to do background checks. I think he'll stick out like a sore thumb."

Laura reached for the phone and called Hugh.

"I'll see to it," Hugh said after Laura had run through the plan that she and Jim had formulated.

"I really think we're getting close, Hugh. He was careless with the ones he took earlier. He didn't bother going too far from his home for them, because he was sure that they were never going to be found. I imagine that when we locate him, we'll find the remains of more victims nearby, probably buried on his property."

"It sounds too neat to be that easy, boss. But I'll get right on it."

It was daylight when Vince Hopkins ambled along the concrete path that curved down towards the streaming face of the cave. He had been asleep in the small hut since before midnight, failing to carry out the required hourly patrols of the tourist attraction, complacent over his role as security guard, having only twice in ten years experienced minor problems with trespassing teenagers. And they had not caused him any grief. Just ran off when he shouted at them.

Vince was a fifty-nine-year-old tub of lard, who fuelled his obese body with a diet of junk food and vast quantities of Tetley's bitter. His tar-caked lungs wheezed as he stopped in front of the limestone cave and leant back against the waist-high railings that kept the punters at bay. Looking out over the river, he lit a cigarette and watched as five swans flew low over the glassy surface of the Nidd, their ghostly white forms appearing out of morning mist that would soon be burned off by the rising sun. They looked like a squadron of planes wing tip to wing tip, purposeful, on a bomb run of the bridge farther up the river. As they vanished around a bend in tight formation, he turned to look up at the array of articles hanging in various states of stone-clad petrifaction.

Vince's brain took long seconds to accept and recognise what his eyes beheld, and he dropped the cigarette and clenched his hands in white-knuckled horror as the realisation of what the new addition was rocked him on his feet.

She was naked, and her vacuous, blue eyes stared down at him, unconcerned of her condition or plight. His mind took in everything, as in stupefied fascination he studied the corpse that was suspended over the escarpment. He saw that her throat had been cut; the gaping maw a gleaming blue, purple and raw-meat red. Her mouth was a sealed line of glinting metal, and her nipples were missing from breasts that pointed towards him, weighed down by gravity. A noose of blue nylon rope encircled her right ankle and snaked upwards to vanish over the ridge above. Her other leg hung loose, down behind her, and his gaze lingered on the protuberant pubic mound and the wispy, sodden curls that matched the blonde colour of her hair.

The shock was too much for Vince. It was as if a gin trap had snapped its steel jaws around his chest, crushing his lungs and tearing at his heart, causing him to cry out in agony as he staggered a couple of steps before falling to crack his skull on the concrete walkway. A plume of gossamer-thin cigarette smoke drifted out from his mouth, to be carried away by the gentle breeze as a massive cardiac infarction robbed him of life.

Lying beneath the hanging corpse, Vince appeared to be engaging Shelley Stroud in a staring contest, their sightless eyes unblinking, and expressions impassive as they faced one another in mutual disinterest.

Neil Frampton, a newly appointed assistant manager at Mother Shipton's Cave Ltd, found the bodies as he searched for the errant security guard, who had not signed off duty. Neil was young, fit, a non-smoker, and although badly shaken by the scene in front of him, was not struck down by a heart attack, only the worry of how much revenue would be lost.

Standing back, Laura and Hugh waited for the duty pathologist to finish up his 'on scene' inspection of the corpses. Above them, where the rope had been tied to the security fence, a fingertip search was being conducted by officers. Shelley's body had been lowered to the ground after the forensic photographer had taken shots of her from what seemed a thousand angles. Both of the deceased now lay side by side under cover of an Arctic-white Incitent.

"You want to take a closer look?" the young pathologist asked, appearing at the front of the tent, holding back the flap as he addressed Laura and Hugh.

Laura walked over to a concrete litter bin, pushed her cigarette end into the sand-filled receptacle mounted in its top, and returned to enter the bright canvas shelter.

"What can you tell me?" Laura asked Ken Matthews, who she knew fancied her almost as much as his boss, Brian Morris, did.

"The security guard appears to have suffered a heart attack," Ken said. "The shock of seeing the corpse hanging there could have brought it on. Looking at him, I would say he was in pretty bad physical shape; a prime candidate. As for the girl, the cause of death will no doubt prove to be the cut throat. The blade has severed her jugular and right carotid artery, cutting completely through her larynx and vocal cords. She's drained of blood, and you can see the other injuries. Your boy has been busy again.

"The only other thing is this," he continued, hunkering down to wield a pair of what looked to be long eyebrow tweezers as he eased the thighs apart with a gloved hand. Protruding from the vagina was a piece of paper, wrapped in cellophane. "It looks as though it might be a note. Do you want it removed now or back under more controlled conditions?"

"Now," Laura said.

The pathologist drew the folded packet from the orifice with his tweezers and opened it out so that they could read the message that was written in bold, black capital letters, clearly visible through the slick, transparent protective covering. It read:

PLEASE FIND ONE (1) WELL NOURISHED BODY –

SLIGHTLY DAMAGED.

LATE TENANT WAS SHELLEY STROUD. MISSING

RIGHT EAR ALREADY IN YOUR POSSESSION.

REMEMBER, THIS ONE DIED FOR YOU, LAURA.

JOHN WAYNE GACY XXX

Laura knew what Ken or Brian Morris would find when they got Shelley on to the autopsy table and commenced cutting, probing, measuring and weighing; turning what had been a human being into marbled meat and assorted excised bloody organs. It had the unmistakable signature of the Tacker, without need of the note. The stapled mouth, missing nipples and cut throat were his trademarks.

"Thanks, Ken," she said. And to Hugh. "Come on, let's go. There's nothing here that will help us. The sad bastard is just playing games, getting his jollies again by putting his work on display and trying to provoke us."

"He's succeeding, isn't he?" Hugh said.

Laura shook her head. "Not really. He's baiting us, but every dog has its day. Between you and me, Jim Elliott is advising on this, unofficially. He's already worked up a profile, and has played this game for a lot longer than the dickhead that we're after has. Jim never gave up. He was like a Mountie; always got his man. It's not a case of if we catch this piece of shit, Hugh. Just a matter of when."

"I hope you're right, boss. So far we've got nothing. He leaves a clean kill. We've never found one single worthwhile clue."

"Are you forgetting the bite marks? Odontology can match his teeth to the last victim. And now he's done it again on the Stroud girl."

"We still need a suspect. The teeth marks don't help if we have nothing to compare them with. And I don't see how Elliott can be of any help. I heard that he'd cracked up and quit the FBI. He couldn't cut it any more."

"It wasn't that he couldn't cut it, Hugh. He walked because he'd had enough. He was sick of being in their minds, tainted by the evil and sickness that makes these monsters tick. He may never get involved again, but he'll see this through, now that he's committed himself to it. And that means our sicko is on borrowed time."

The following morning, Hugh came up with eight possible suspects in the area that Jim had homed in on, and arranged for uniforms to check them out.

Laura phoned Brian Morris, who had performed the autopsy on the Stroud girl, and could hear the undisguised disappointment in his voice. She just hadn't had the time or the inclination to visit the mortuary that day. She knew that the pathologist enjoyed seeing her, and that he probably visualised her being as naked as one of his cadavers every time she stopped by. But on this occasion, he would just have to make do with her voice. The unbidden thought of the lecherous, middle-aged little man sitting in his white-tiled office with his glasses steaming up as he jacked off whilst talking to her, almost cracked her up. It was hard to keep from chuckling as she spoke.

"Anything new, Brian? Or is it the same as the last one?"

"It may not be of any help, Laura. But he exsanguinated this one more thoroughly. Hung her by the ankle to bleed out, instead of by her neck. Also, the laceration to the throat was significantly deeper. From the angle of the cut, I believe he strung her up before inflicting the wound. I also think it fair to assume that the teeth marks will match those left on the Cullen girl, as will the staples. For some reason, he used twice as many this time. Oh, and the ear that you received did belong to this victim. I also found a residue of white powder on various parts of her body, where the water from the cave hadn't washed it off. It's gone for analysis. She may have been moved to the site in a container or sack that the powder had originally been stored or supplied in. If it turns out to be a specialist material, then you might just have a worthwhile lead."

"What do *you* think it is, Brian? Any ideas?"

"I think it might be some kind of fertiliser or ground up mineral, probably lime. But that needs confirming. The only thing that I'm one hundred percent sure of, is that the same lunatic is responsible for all these murders."

"Thanks. Next time I call by I'll bring cakes from Betty's, and we can pig out. How does that sound?"

"You sure know how to make an old man happy. I'll even stop working to eat them."

Laura winced. "Last of the romantics, eh, Brian?"

Only three of the men that were checked-out fitted Jim's profile. One had claimed to have been in Canada for the last six weeks, visiting his sister and brother-in-law. The second had no such checkable alibi for the pertinent dates, and had seemed very nervous and tight-lipped. The fact that he was confined to a wheelchair – paralysed from the waist down – and had been in that condition since a motorcycle accident back in oh-seven, was his saving grace. It was the third guy who interested them the most. He was too cool, slightly arrogant, and proved to be very vague when asked his whereabouts at specific times on relevant dates.

"The Canada story was on the level," Hugh said as Laura studied the reports on the three suspects, who all resided within the area Jim had indicated. "He was in Winnipeg, Manitoba for six weeks. He's clean. And the second guy will never walk again, and doesn't drive. So without an accomplice, he's in the clear. It's the last one, Derek Cox, who rings all the right bells. He lives alone on a smallholding. He's six-two, built like a brick shithouse, has hair the colour of corn, and eyes as blue as Paul Newman's were. The uniform that spoke to him says that he came across as evasive and unhelpful. He wasn't fazed at all and appeared to find the situation quite humorous."

"Tell me about him, Hugh."

"He sells organically grown produce and plays around with stocks and shares via the Internet. He has no real friends, no social life to speak of, and even the people in the village only see him when he drives through. He never uses the local pub or shops. The guy's a shadow. Oh, and both of his parents are dead. They bought it in a house fire that he walked away from with just mild smoke inhalation. That was twenty years ago."

"Bring him in," Laura said. "Let's talk to him, and if we don't get alibis that check out I'll get a warrant and we can take his place apart. Maybe we just got lucky."

CHAPTER THIRTEEN

TRISH sat alone and sipped at her glass of medium dry dealcoholised white wine. The Mousseux was as near as she permitted herself to get to alcohol. She had seen what booze could do to people and their careers, and was not going to allow herself to be ruled by the bottle, as her mother had been. Trish had watched her mum, Hilda, turn into a lush and age prematurely as she slurred and staggered through the last fifteen years of her life. Liver failure had taken her on her forty-eighth birthday, and Trish had been relieved when the source of her continual embarrassment had finally been reduced to ash, to be spread somewhere in the rose gardens of the crematorium in Hull, where all the late and never lamented Pearsons' wound up. Blood may or may not be thicker than water, but the effects of gin proved stronger than both and had quickly driven Trish from home, hating a mother who, to her way of thinking, was a weak-willed and pathetic specimen of human detritus.

As a child, Trish had been heartbroken and bewildered when her father walked out. Later, she understood why he had left. It had not been another woman who'd enticed him away, but his inability to live with a chronic alcoholic.

The Studio Bar was a cubby-hole compared to the likes of those at any of the major television companies. And as Trish sat nursing her drink in the shabby and dimly lit lounge, she decided that it would be advantageous to her career to let Jason Godwin screw her. Godwin had been drooling around her for months, copping the odd feel and making it clear that he was in lust with her. He was an executive producer at the station, and had been offered a lucrative deal by Channel 4. If he was prepared to take her along with him, and look after her interests, then spreading her legs was a small price to pay. She could fake orgasms as easily as she feigned emotions for the camera. Jason might just prove to be her best chance of getting the hell out of this one horse town and attaining the fame that she deserved, on national TV. It pissed her off to see some of the wooden, over-the-hill newsmongers making fat salaries. Her only fear was of letting the little shit dip his wick, to then tire of her before moving on.

Timing was everything. She needed to keep him interested and thinking with his cock, not his head. Touch wood, so far it was working.

"Trish, sweetheart, why not come down south with me? You know I adore you," Jason said, appearing as if conjured up by her thoughts of him. She was not to know that he was determined to get into her panties before leaving Yorkshire, without her.

Trish fluttered her eyelashes. "Jason, darling. You know how much I love my job. I want to be with you, but I couldn't function down there without work. I'd have to be sure that there was a contract for me. I already front a show, so I wouldn't want to have to start again from square one."

"I'll have a word with Gerald Archer," Jason purred, dropping into a seat opposite her. "He pulls the strings at C4. If he says jump, the only question is, how high? I'll show him some of your best material, including VT of this serial killer stuff that you're currently involved with."

Under the table, Trish stroked his leg with the side of her foot, and watched his eyes roll back a little as beads of sweat escaped from the front of a toupee that seemed to squat precariously on his head like the pelt of a dead animal. What remained of his hair at the sides was ash-grey, in stark contrast to the ginger tom-coloured rug that was taped or glued to his bald pate.

"I think we should spend the weekend at your place in the Dales and chill out," Trish said, her shoe now off, and her toes caressing the bulge at his crotch as she wondered whether he removed the wig and put it on a poly-head on his dressing table before humping. The thought of him standing naked and then ripping the piece off before leaping into the sack almost made her choke on the wine.

Jason had a large Scotch before heading back to the production office to tie up some loose ends for the following morning's six a.m. breakfast news. Trish had almost made him come in his boxers, then upped and gone, leaving him on the edge of more than just his seat. He knew the bitch was trying to play him like a fish on a line, but she was a challenge. What she didn't know was, that he would be gone the following Tuesday, and that the weekend at his rented cottage in the Dales would be the last time she would ever set eyes on him. She was a good regional presenter, but that was as far as she was going. She just didn't have the indefinable zing that it takes to command a national desk; that X factor that you either had or hadn't. Being attractive and competent was a requisite, but not enough.

True, the camera liked Trish, but didn't love her. He was surprised that she was still naïve enough to believe that sleeping with a boss would open up anything more than her own shapely legs. It was apparent that ambition and the lure of fame and greed lent credence to at least some blondes being dumb.

Trish left the building and followed the paved path to the small car park that lay beyond a landscaped belt of mainly conifers that were set among strategically placed rocks in a bed of weed-smothering shredded bark. She was reasonably confidant that Jason would keep his word. He was besotted. And after a weekend of her energetically catering to his every need, however deviant, he would undoubtedly want more. She would own him, emotionally, and dump him as soon as she was set up. She knew that Gerald Archer was in his late-sixties, and married, which to her made him a prime target for the flattery and not so subtle charms of a good looking woman who was young enough to be his daughter. Older men were susceptible, needing to prove that they were still desirable, still in the game, and still had the power to pull.

The first spots of rain dappled the concrete as she stepped off the path and angled across to her Scorpio, that was now, at eleven p.m., one of only a dozen cars still standing under the yellow glare of the perimeter lights.

Jogging as the dark sky began to hurl spears of summer lightning at the earth; Trish triggered the remote on her key fob and heard the metallic clunk as the door lock buttons popped up.

"Ms Pearson," he shouted as she pulled open the door and slid into the driver's seat.

She hesitated, squinted into the rain, then recognised him and relaxed a little.

"Yes?" she said when he reached the car, his jacket collar up against what was now a heavy downpour.

"I've got a lead on the Tacker that I think the media should know about. Are you interested?"

"Get in," she said, surprised, but eager to hear anything that would be a scoop and give her a high profile. Something like this could help her career as much if not more than fucking the brains out of Jason, who was currently the station's resident trouser snake. Everyone needed a stroke of luck as well as talent, and this could be her big break. The Tacker was beginning to make Sutcliffe – The Yorkshire Ripper – look like a saint. Sutcliffe had battered mainly prostitutes to death, but hadn't put the fear of God up the general public like this one. The Tacker was a nightmare, who made even the worst fictional serial murderers appear lightweight. This was reality, not a Hannibal Lecter, who was just a figment of the author Thomas Harris's dark and fertile mind, and ultimately a good vehicle for the acting talents of Anthony Hopkins. Fate had put her in the middle of one of the biggest ongoing crime stories for years, and being out in the sticks at this moment in time might just give her the chance to strike the mother lode. She could stay on top of it for as long as the killer remained free and continued to mutilate and murder teenage girls. So far, she had only suffered one setback; the ballsy female cop. The bitch had fucked-up what was going to be a scathing attack on the police's shortcomings, by somehow turning the interview around. She had said her well rehearsed drivel on air and then walked, leaving Trish looking like a dumb rookie.

"So what have you got for me?" Trish asked, turning to face him, her dismay at the rain dripping off him onto her soft, leather upholstery subdued at the prospect of being given a titbit that she might turn into tomorrow's lead story.

"Not here," he said. "I can't afford to be seen with you. And I can't be quoted. What I have to tell you is going to blow this case wide open. Drive me to my car. It's parked out on the Fulford road."

As she drove, he told her that the police knew the identity of the killer, and even gave her details of the depraved acts of mutilation that the victims had suffered, which had not been disclosed to the media. "He bites their nipples off, cuts their throats, and hangs them up to bleed out. I can also tell you that he's left-handed, and that he has killed at least a dozen more girls than you or the press know about."

"So who is he?" Trish said, following his directions and making a left into a lane adjacent to Fulford Golf Club, before parking behind his car.

He smiled. "You're talking to him, you stupid cow," he said, smashing his fist into her temple with enough force to bounce her head off the side window, causing her to groan and sink forward, conscious but with no control over her body; as a boxer, whose limbs turn to mush after a punch rattles brain against skull and robs him of all cohesive functions.

He hit her again and dispelled all thought. Bright colours fizzed behind her eyes, then dimmed to blackness.

Reaching over her and turning off the lights and ignition, he pushed the release on the safety belt's buckle and pulled her down across his lap, taking a reel of duct tape from his jacket pocket and quickly winding a length tightly around her head, once...twice...three times, covering her mouth, before biting through the tape and drawing her wrists behind her back to pinion them. He then pushed her sideways, unmindful of her head thudding into the door as he lifted her ankles up and bound them together.

After opening the front side window, he climbed out of the car, walked the couple of yards to his Mondeo and opened the boot. Looking about him, he checked that the tree-lined lane was deserted before going back to lift his latest acquisition out of the Scorpio and transfer it. He then emptied the contents of a two gallon can of petrol into the Scorpio, soaking the seats and carpet in both front and rear. The entire operation had taken less than a minute.

Reversing into a driveway, he headed back to the main road, but not before first pausing alongside Trish's car to strike a bunch of matches on the sandpaper strip of the Swan Vestas box and throw them into the open window.

Accelerating away, he was back on the Fulford road, heading for the A64 and well away from the scene when the Scorpio's petrol tank exploded and briefly lit the night sky in his rearview mirror.

As usual, Pam Garner had gone to bed early, to read a few pages of a paperback before becoming drowsy and putting the book on top of the small chest of drawers, to then switch off the lamp and go to sleep.

The thunderous detonation jarred her awake as her bedroom window imploded, and Pam was only saved from being peppered by a thousand shards of flying glass by the heavyweight cotton canvas curtains that billowed in under the shockwave, now as punctured as the heavens were by twinkling points of light. She leapt out of bed befuddled and ran out onto the landing, not knowing what had happened. Stopping at the top of the stairs to assess the situation as her head cleared, she realised that there was no smell of smoke, or the roar and crackle of hungry flames in the house. She reasoned that whatever had happened was outside, and that she was in no immediate, life-threatening danger. Walking back into the bedroom, she smoothed her nightdress down, put her slippers on and slowly approached the window with her feet crunching on the fragments of glass that had ripped through the material to fall down onto the carpet. Pulling back one of the curtains, just an inch, she looked out and was met by the flickering orange glow that emanated from a burning car in the lane, just twenty yards away from her house. Relieved, yet concerned, Pam rushed down the stairs, to telephone the emergency services for only the second time in her life; the first being when her late husband, Graham, had collapsed and died six years ago from a ruptured aorta. She recalled punching in the wrong digits three times with a wayward and shaking finger before managing to hit 999, as Graham made whooping noises and vomited blood onto the fitted lounge carpet that had only been laid the week before.

At first it was assumed that the burnt-out car had been stolen, and that joy riders had torched it. It was registered as being owned by one Trish Pearson of Hadley Court; a chic riverside apartment complex that overlooked the river and the city centre. A uniform called at the address, but there was no one home. It would be a further twenty-four hours before Trish was reported missing by her employers. And neither friends – of whom there were very few – nor colleagues had any idea of her whereabouts. She had just vanished into thin air.

She drifted slowly up from cold, black depths into shallower, greyer layers of awareness. Her lungs burned, aching in her chest, and in a panic-filled dream, as if she were a diver running short of life-sustaining oxygen, she kicked her feet and stretched her fingers for the surface, reaching for the effulgence and sweet air that was above her, almost within her grasp.

Pain drilled into her head, and a bright shaft of light found her face, making her close her eyelids tightly against the dazzling glare. She was now conscious, and terror began to worm into her brain.

"You're not my mother," a voice stated from the gloom beyond the cold sun of the torch's beam. "You're just the smug talking-head off the TV who thinks that I'm a sick piece of trash, a mad-dog killer and a cowardly, twisted little man."

The cone of light moved, circled her and blinked out to leave an afterimage blazing on her retinas; twin red planets hanging in a Delphic vacuum.

Trish couldn't talk, beg, scream or move. Her mouth was covered, and her hands and feet were bound.

"You're going to die, news lady," he whispered in the darkness next to her face. And as she grunted in fear and pulled away from the words and the hot breath on her cheek, she caught the unmistakable scent of Aramis. She was encompassed in silence and lay rigid with her muscles tensed in readiness for a piercing pain or heavy blow; her ears straining for sound, unable to follow his movements. She expected to be knifed or bludgeoned at any second. A squeaking, metallic shriek made her cringe for a moment, before ice-cold water hit her, drumming against her; a powerful jet that pummelled her body and face, hurting where it hit, rolling her over on to her side.

He hosed her down and then turned off the tap and lit a hurricane lamp. She was shivering, shaking uncontrollably as he cut through the tape at her wrists and replaced it with stock wire, using pliers to twist it tight, this time with her hands in front of her, and with one end of the thick wire wound and secured through a steel ring that was set into a large concrete block. On a whim he had decided to keep the bitch alive, for now. She would be there to use, to satisfy him; sex on tap. She was separate to his need, an added dimension to the game. It would be fun to have her watch when he worked on another with the knife and stapler. As a journalist, she would surely be only too pleased to gain such an insight to the Tacker; one that no one else had been privy to. He left her, suddenly ravenous, and locked the barn doors and headed for the house to relax and plan his next move. Having a minor celebrity of his own under lock and key gave him a rush. And he would be wanting much more from her than an autograph.

It was a consideration that the Tacker may have abducted Trish Pearson, but as an outside possibility, not a likely probability.

"She's a blue-eyed blonde, boss," Hugh said, stirring semi-skimmed milk into the brew he had made with Laura's gear, before walking back across the room to place the mugs on the only patch of desk that was not piled high with papers and files. "And she slagged him off something rotten on TV a couple of nights back."

"I bad-mouthed him too, and so have other broadcasters and the press in general. I don't see him trying to take out everyone that has called him what he is. We don't know that he took her, and she seems a little old for him."

"Meow."

"I'm not being catty, Hugh. He likes younger girls. Apart from one they were all teenagers. I think it's a coincidence, unrelated. Have we checked out anyone that she might have been having an affair with?"

"Her only affair seems to have been with her career. There was a rumour that she was screwing a producer at the station, but he seems to be in the clear. He says he tried it on but got nowhere; thinks she must be a dyke."

Laura glared. "It's amazing how many men accuse women of being bloody gay when they can't get their ends away. The chauvinist pigs need castrating with bricks."

"Ouch!" Hugh exclaimed, crossing his legs and grimacing. "I still believe that he took her. She was last seen leaving the studio at about eleven p.m., heading for the car park. I think she was snatched and driven, or forced to drive to where her car was found. It was a dark lane. He could have easily got her into another vehicle and then torched her car to destroy any evidence."

"You might be right, Hugh. But I think it's a long shot."

"If this is a mother thing, like you and the Yank believe, then she fits the bill. Her verbal attack and having the right hair and eye colour would pull his chain."

"Maybe, and for the record, remember that Jim isn't officially involved in this. We just go back awhile. We're old friends. He's helping us out on his own time with a few pointers."

"Hey, boss, it's me, not the super'. The guy was reputedly one of the best profilers in the FBI, but that was years ago. Excuse me for thinking that he might be a little rusty and out of date in his methods. I still think that he could put us way off track and confuse the issue."

"I doubt that. What Jim does isn't learned and forgotten, it's a gift. His input will be valid, and I'll feed anything that he gives me to you and the team. He happens to agree with you that Trish Pearson is in all probably the guy's latest victim. He doesn't believe in coincidences until all other alternatives have been ruled out. And then he still doesn't believe in them. I don't understand why you have a problem with him."

Hugh arched his eyebrows. "Call me a sceptic, boss, but I don't rate instinct, hunches or sixth sense when it comes to solving a case. I think formal investigative procedure and forensic science are the only way to go. You always hear about the successes that these behavioural science blokes have, but not so much about the ones they get wrong. I'm not impressed with profilers or the FBI in general. They're a legend in their own minds; overrated and full of bullshit."

"You shouldn't judge Jim's methods by what you've read in thrillers or seen on TV," Laura said, realising that she was jumping to Jim's defence, and that Hugh's ridicule of him and his talent had got under her skin. She was a little rattled. "He believes in formalistic investigation. Any hunches, as you call them, are just a part of the whole package. He proved countless times that he could process raw information and interpret it better than most other profilers. He takes what evidence there is and builds a mental picture of the offender from it. He doesn't pretend that he's infallible, but only a fool would underestimate his capabilities."

Hugh put his hands up submissively. "Point taken. It can't harm to consider every option. The only important thing is that we don't ignore the possibility that he *could* be completely wrong on this."

"When you're drowning, you grab hold of anything that floats by...right?"

Hugh lightened up and smiled. "Right, boss. I'll try to look at it that way."

CHAPTER FOURTEEN

THE fluorescent tube hummed continuously within a grimy plastic housing laden with the hot and brittle corpses of flies and moths. The diffused light shone down thinly on to the top of the ancient table below it, which was scarred by scratches and brown, lozenge-shaped cigarette burns; a captive, its legs bolted by brackets to the cold concrete floor.

Derek Cox was seated at one side of the table, slouched as nonchalantly as he was able to in the PVC bucket chair. He was wearing a black Adidas sweat suit, top of the range Reeboks, and was sipping bitter coffee from a polystyrene cup, wincing at the taste of the hot, acerbic brew that the station's vending machine deemed suitable for human consumption.

"Your coffee's crap," Derek said, grimacing and thumping the cup down on the tabletop and pushing it away with his fingertips as though it was a toxic concoction.

When asked to accompany them to the station, 'to help with their inquiries', Derek had been only too happy to comply. From the outset of the taped interview, he stated that he had nothing to hide, and saw no reason or need to ask for legal representation.

Laura and Hugh were sitting opposite him, trying to find a chink in his armour of affability and self-assurance. They couldn't rock him, and he remained unfazed by the insinuation that he might be involved in the spate of recent killings. Laura had not encountered a guilty person this unconcerned or relaxed. The young man before her could have been a Zen Buddhist; he was so 'together' and serene...outwardly. Christ, the average person was more uptight queuing at a supermarket checkout. In fact most of Joe public acted guiltier than Cox appeared to be if they spotted a police car in their rearview mirrors.

"You haven't really been able to help us at all, have you, Derek?" Laura said after formally reopening the interview with fresh tapes that had been unwrapped in front of their suspect, after they'd taken a fifteen minute break and left him to hopefully sweat.

"I'd love to be able to help you with this, DI Scott," he replied, a slight twist to the smirk on his face giving him the look of a young Harrison Ford. "But without having the foresight to know that I might need alibis, I haven't got any. I've told you, I don't get out as much as I should. If I were your man, I would have made sure that I had plausible, bullet-proof answers for all your moronic questions. As it is, I really can't remember the last time I murdered anyone."

"It's not funny, Cox," Laura said, feeling her cheeks prick with the heat of anger at the man's attempt at childish, school yard humour.

"I think it is," he said, looking from Laura to Hugh, then back to her, his eyes now fixed and penetrating; a small, cruel smile replacing his previously mild expression. "Humour is subjective. I've told you, I don't mind answering all your inane questions. That you don't like the answers I'm giving is your problem, and tough shit. I don't even know why I'm a suspect. Do I fit some description of your serial killer?"

"Listen, Mr Cox," Hugh said. "We want to eliminate you from our inquiries, and we'll be able to do that a lot quicker if you start being more cooperative."

Derek thrust his chin out in defiance. "No. You listen, *officer*. I could be awkward. But up until now I've been happy to waste a lot of time that I could have spent more productively elsewhere. Your procedures are interesting, better than watching Sherlock on Telly, but you just happen to have the wrong man. Why not just take my prints and some blood, hair and semen samples? You won't find anything to match them to, but it'll save a lot of fucking about. You've searched my property, and there's obviously nothing there, or you'd have charged me by now."

"I want an impression of your teeth, Derek," Laura said. "Is there any problem with that?"

"You can have an impression of my cock if you want," he said with a broad grin on his face.

"Maybe some other time," Laura came back. "For now, one of your much bigger mouth will suffice."

Laura arrived home to the empty cottage and prowled through it as a stranger in a strange land. The warmth had deserted it, gone as surely as Jim had left that morning. She was down in a bad place, where memories and needs pulled in every direction; ephemeral fingernails raking the scabs off old wounds in her brain, opening them to release fresh torrents of pain that threatened to drown her in a deep, dark well of melancholia. She was spinning ever inward and ever faster into a black hole that she had pulled free of once, only to now find herself back in its terrible gravitational clutch.

Jim had stayed until they got the lead on Cox, and had then gone – as though his presence had been no more than a flight of fancy – back to his life and work down south. The days that she had spent with him had felt so right. It was as though they were meant to be together. As if fate had ordained it. Now, the cottage that she had loved was teasing her with his smell, and the strong image of his presence; where he had sat, and what he had touched. She had let her past and present come together, and the collision of the two worlds had rocked the foundations of her universe.

Sitting in the kitchen, cradling a brandy-filled tumbler, Laura was unable to check the tears that ran freely from her now puffy eyes. It hit her like a freight train; a realisation that the cottage was no more than a retreat she had hidden herself away in. She was nothing but a runaway, using her career as a foil against the emotions that she kept smothered, cloistered in a mental convent that was detached from her true feelings. She loved Jim, wanted to be with him, but was scared to make the commitment. She had failed at marriage once, and was still, after all this time, low on self esteem.

Only Kara had made sense of everything. Her daughter's pointless accidental death had graphically illustrated that the journey between cradle and grave was just a haphazard and chaotic series of events. There was no such thing as security, and the future was of limited duration. Being a copper was no big deal. She had just made it one, to have some sense of continuity in a life that frightened her more with every passing day. Underneath the sham of being a hard-bitten DI, Laura now acknowledged the lonely, scared little girl that hid within, under the multi-layered persona that she had wrapped around her complex identity.

"You sad cow!" She said it out loud, almost a shout, before jerking backwards in the chair, standing up and walking to the sink to empty the brandy down the plug hole. Christ, she was pushing forty and looked on life as a half empty glass, not half full. Some imbecile had dreamed up the saying: 'life begins at forty', which was a crock of shit. Life was well ripe by then, and most people were on the down curve, like her, wondering what the hell they'd done with the most precious commodity of all, which was time, and angry with themselves at dreams not realised or even pursued, and surprised at how fast it had all gotten away from them.

Laura went upstairs and dressed in T-shirt, sweater, Levi's and Nikes, then returned downstairs and left the cottage by the back door to enter the woods that crowded up to the boundary of its small rear garden.

The sun was low in a dull, red sky as she walked along what she imagined to be a deer trail, tramping noisily over a carpet of dry twigs and pine needles, with the scent of conifers heavy in the evening air. A grey squirrel ran up the deeply fissured bark of a cone-laden fir as she stopped to light a cigarette. She watched, and the rodent headed up into the green canopy, bushy tail flicking with irritation at her presence, its movements jerky and comical. She had entered the woods to clear her mind, and found herself reassessing priorities and looking for answers to the enigma of existence, however pointless the exercise.

On a personal level, it all came down to the job. She was painfully aware that if she wanted Jim, she would have to jack it in and go to him. He had turned his back on the bureau and started over, finding a life outside the world of crime that she had steeped herself in. Walking on, she lost track of time, hardly aware as dusk sapped the heavens of light. She stopped by the side of a small brook to sit on the grassy bank, hugging her knees and staring at the still water and the black clouds of midges swirling senselessly above its surface. With a sudden clarity, the weight lifted from her, calmness pervaded her mind and lightened her spirit. She would see this case through, and then resign from a police force that was already looking to hang her out to dry over the Tacker. She had the deeds to the cottage, plus a couple of decent insurance policies and a healthy building society account. If Jim wanted a crack at being with her, then she would go to him, begin afresh, open a bloody florists or gift shop in Windsor and start to savour each day; take time out to smell the flowers. Christ! She had been little more than a fucking hamster, frantically running on the spot in a caged wheel and getting nowhere fast. It was time to jump off and get a life.

A crime scene team was searching Cox's smallholding while he was being questioned. He had raised no objections, and not even insisted on being present; just asked them to respect his property.

The forensic team arrived in two transit vans, stepping out of them wearing hooded coveralls, overshoes and latex gloves. Two of them carried bright aluminium cases, and the sunlight bounced off the reflective metal surfaces. Curious villagers were kept back by uniformed PCs, their apprehension combining with anger as whispers of contaminated waste or some deadly virus spurred them into confrontational mood.

"We're not bloody stupid," Stanley Price, the landlord of the Plough Inn, said to the constable nearest to him. "Those buggers are wearin' protective clothin'. An' last month there were crop circles in the field behind us. Somethin's up. We're not daft, lad."

"Do you think we'd be standing here if there was any danger?" PC Alan Fraser said, smiling cheerfully at the surly little man, who he thought capable of inciting the group of mainly pensionable-aged wrinklies and droolies into civil unrest. Jesus! That could result in embarrassing arrests of senior citizens, or at least bring about the odd heart attack, stroke, or both, judging by the look of some of them, who were all well past their sell by dates.

"You're paid to do what you're told, son, dangerous or not," Stanley retorted. "It's a copper's lot. So don't try to fob us off. Those buggers are dressed up to deal with some sort of catastrophe, and we have a right to know what it is."

Alan bit his lip. It was a hot day, and his shirt and underpants were sticking to him under the black uniform that soaked up the heat. The leather band inside his helmet was also sodden, and his hair and scalp were itching with sweat. The shifty-eyed little shit and his geriatric band of cronies were getting on his tits. Too many daft twats were watching repeats of the sodding X-Files and assorted Star Trek spin-offs nowadays. He would love to tell these yokels that a UFO had crash-landed, and that the forensic guys were really a team from Area 51 in the States, flown in to recover the craft and the little green aliens that occupied it. Having not won the lottery, and still needing his salary to pay the bills, Alan took a deep breath and pinned the pain-in-the-arse publican with a withering stare. "If you look closely, sir," he replied tersely. "You'll see that the buggers in question are not wearing fishbowl helmets, and haven't got oxygen tanks strapped to their bloody backs. This may or may not be a crime scene, and they are dressed in protective clothing because they do not want to contaminate any evidence that might be here."

Stanley glared, then coughed up some phlegm from his clotted lungs and spat it out through a convenient gap in his discoloured teeth, where a front tooth had been dislodged by the fist of a local farmer fifteen years previously: Stanley's attitude was not always suffered gladly. And had the viscous substance settled on Alan's highly polished boot instead of on the grass next to it, then the dour landlord might have been grabbed by his scrawny neck and nicked for assault. As it was, Alan counted to ten and refused to be drawn any further.

The house and outbuildings were clean. The only trace of human occupation, apart from that of Derek Cox, was an assortment of head and pubic hairs, mainly found in the bed and the bathroom. A few of them were blonde and would be analysed, but were short and most likely his. A vast collection of gay magazines and videos were discovered, and the bedside cabinet drawer held a healthy stock of condoms and tubes of KY jelly. Cox was obviously gay, and the only blue-eyed blondes that he was likely to be interested in would be of the male gender. The one item of dubious significance was a short coil of blue nylon rope found hanging from a bracket in the garage. It was bagged and taken, to be sent for comparison with the length that had been used to suspend Shelley Stroud. It was a routine procedure, not thought too significant, when taken into account that the product was generic and as commonplace in garages, garden sheds and car boots as knives and forks are in a kitchen drawer. The guy was a fruit, and it appeared that he would soon be eliminated as a suspect from their list of one.

CHAPTER FIFTEEN

IT was forty-eight hours later that Laura got a call from the Forensic Science Services in Leeds.

"The two pieces of nylon rope are a match, Laura," Dr Miles Atherton said. "Both are from the same length."

"Christ, Miles! Is that categorically and without doubt a hundred percent certain?" she asked, reaching for her cigarettes with her free hand, adrenaline pumping with the anticipation of what this bolt from the blue meant.

"Under the evil eye of the electron-microscope, no fibres can conceal their individual characteristics, my dear. In a world of uncertainty, this is unambiguous; beyond conjecture. This baby was cut with a serrated blade at a fifteen degree angle. The fibres are a perfect match. Also, the density and dye signatures are identical. And there are traces of blood on both pieces that are AB positive, which is the same as that of the Stroud girl. DNA matching will no doubt confirm that it is her blood."

"I think you've just wrapped up the Tacker murders for us, Miles. A mere thank you seems a little inadequate," Laura said, her hand clenching the receiver in a finger-aching grip, and her heart beating like a big bass drum.

"So buy me a malt whisky the next time you're in the neighbourhood, a large one. I'll have this paperwork hand delivered to you before lunch."

"If we get a conviction, I'll buy you a bottle of Scotland's finest, Miles."

Laura ground her cigarette butt out in the ashtray, slid the drawer closed and headed out of the office, down the corridor to a much larger office that they were using as an incident room for this case. Hugh and DCs Neil Abbott, Jack Mercer and Clem Nash were sifting through the case files again, searching for new leads, now that their suspect was looking whiter than white.

"We've got him! It *is* Cox," Laura said as she entered the room like a stormtrooper out of a Star Wars movie. "Arrange to have him lifted by an armed response team. If he thinks we're on to him he may go for broke. Forensic checked the rope, and guess what? It matches. It's even almost certainly got Shelley's blood on it. He doesn't appear to be stupid, but he has a licensed shotgun, so let's assume that he'd use it if push came to shove."

It took the Chief Superintendant's clout to pull strings and sanction an Armed Response Unit to be unleashed. What was commonplace in London seemed to be a big deal and take an interminable length of time to organise in the Vale of York. It reminded Laura that the overall pace of life in the sticks was several gears below the frenzy of the big city. Usually, that was no bad thing. But at times such as this she felt as though she was trying to operate in some foreign land with a 'mañana' mentality, where easy-going procrastination was the rule of thumb.

Derek was twenty-five yards from the house, knelt, planting seed potatoes, his bronzed body bathed in a sheen of perspiration. He wore only frayed-cuffed denim shorts, wrangler work boots and garden gloves. He thought he would make a prime candidate for a raunchy gardeners' calendar, though the picture that came to mind of a semi-nude Alan Titchmarsh or Monty Don reclining on a potting shed table amid spring bulbs and plant pots was, to say the least, off-putting. He froze as a distorted, magnified voice sounding like a Dalek, said: "Derek Cox. We are armed police officers. Put your hands behind your head, fingers interlaced...NOW."

He looked up, around him, and saw what appeared to be several SAS men, all in black, and all pointing what looked like submachine guns in his direction. He let go of the potato he was gripping and placed his hands behind his neck. It was a broiling August day, but he was suddenly very cold. The skin over his entire body tightened, and gooseflesh spread over him like a rash.

"Lay flat, face down. Keep your hands where they are," the disembodied voice crackled through an unseen bullhorn.

"The cheques in the post, whoever you are," Derek shouted, even as he obeyed the command, a second before being circled by a ring of armed police.

A gruff voice. "Shut the fuck up," followed by a knee digging in his back as his hands were roughly jerked down behind him and his wrists were cuffed. "You are being taken in for questioning. Anything that you say can and will—"

"Okay, enough. I've heard it all on TV shows. Cut the crap and help me up, this soil tastes nearly as bad as you heroes smell."

The knee ground down again, hard into his right kidney this time, making him cry out as he was yanked up by the ratchet cuffs with such force that he thought his arms would be popped from their sockets.

As Laura and Hugh interviewed Cox again, the Chief Superintendent stood behind a one way mirror, silent, content to watch and listen. As chief, he wanted to keep up to speed on what appeared to be the solving of the serial killings. He needed to be au fait with what he would step in at the right time and take the lion's share of credit for.

Derek could feel the pressure. It was the same as pre-storm static that quieted birdsong and weighted the air. A growing sense of impending doom flash-froze his spine. They had decided that he *was* the killer. Even the vibes from his solicitor – who had told him to answer nothing without his consent – did not inspire confidence. The dapper little geek might be representing him, but had already made up his mind that he was defending a murderer.

"The rope, Derek," Laura said. "It was in your garage. How do you explain that?"

He shook his head slowly. "I can't. It doesn't belong to me. I've never seen it before."

"Among the thousands of items that fill your garage, you expect us to believe that you can identify a piece of nylon rope as definitely *not* being your property. Is that what you're saying?"

Derek swallowed hard. "I've never owned any blue nylon rope. Somebody must have put it there."

Laura paused to exploit silence as a weapon, slowly taking a cigarette from the pack in front of her and hesitating for long seconds before lighting up. She inhaled deeply, tilted her head back and blew the smoke out and up into the air, to watch it rise and spread across the ceiling; a diaphanous cloud.

"Let's get this straight, Derek," she continued, eventually. "The killer picks you out at random, breaks into your garage and hangs a length of rope over a bracket, trusting to luck that for some reason we will suspect you and search your property. Does that sound plausible?"

"Don't answer that," the sallow-faced solicitor said. And to Laura. "My client isn't in a position to know what the killer did, and doesn't expect you to believe anything other than his innocence. He has never seen the rope that you allegedly found in his garage, and if all you intend to do is harass him over the same point, then I suggest that this interview be terminated. You are going to have to charge

Derek with what you have, or release him. And we both know that you haven't got a case that'll stand up."

Over the following two days, the smallholding of Derek Cox was turned into a building site. The lab boys used the latest sonic tomography equipment, which enabled them to scan beneath the ground and search for human remains.

"What exactly are you doing with this hi-tech gizmo?" Laura asked Dr Ed Wells, who looked remarkably like a younger version of Bruce Willis, though was not follically challenged and wore his long red hair in a ponytail that hung down between broad shoulders to the middle of his back.

"Sure can, er, sir...ma'am."

"Make it Laura. You don't work for me, so there's no need to be formal."

"Okay, Laura. This is a sophisticated radiography scanner. We bounce shock waves at a predetermined depth in the ground, and bingo, we have an image on a monitor in the van of any details within the selected plane. This will show us everything from a buried pitchfork or unexploded bomb, to a skeleton. It saves guessing, and more importantly, saves digging."

The scanner found the remains of a dog that had presumably been buried by a previous owner of the property, but nothing more sinister. And the house and Cox's car were clean. A lot of man hours and expenditure left them with the piece of rope as the only incriminating evidence against him. Then it all went down the pan. Odontology contacted Laura with results that put them back to square one. Their suspect, who was still being held in custody, much to his and his brief's annoyance, got a break.

"It wasn't Cox," Laura advised the team. "He may be an accomplice, but he didn't do it alone. His teeth don't match the bites. If he sticks to his guns, he's home free. We don't have enough to merit holding him for another second."

"He did it, I know he did," Hugh said, cracking his knuckles as he paced the office. "He could have worn special dentures over his own teeth to bite off the nipples. He's a clever bastard, but he fits the profile that your FBI buddy came up with. And finding the rope, well that ties it up for me...no pun intended."

"We needed a body, or bodies. At least some hard forensic evidence. We've got nothing but the bloody rope, that he denies owning," Laura said. "Put that together with his known sexual preference, and there's not enough to work with."

"More good news, if your name happens to be Derek Cox," Neil Abbott said, racking the phone that he had been talking on. "They checked his online times. When the first two girls were lifted, he was playing the market on the Internet."

"You mean, someone was online using his computer," Hugh snapped.

Laura shook her head. "Give it up, Hugh. We need more."

Derek had an irritating smirk on his face. "Any time," he said when they completed the paperwork, told him not to leave the area without informing them of his plans, and cut him loose. "Only don't send the bloody SAS lookalikes in again. Just give me a bell and I'll drive down."

Hugh wanted to drive his fist into the man's face. "If we lift you again, Cox, it'll be because we've got enough to put you away for the rest of your natural," he said. "You're guilty in my book, and I aim to prove it. So be aware that you're on a short leash."

"Are you threatening me?" Derek said, smiling contemptuously, and even stepping up close to Hugh, so that their faces were only inches apart.

Hugh fought to keep his cool. He leaned forward until their noses were almost touching. "Yeah, you murdering little queer," he whispered. "I'm on your case, big time."

Derek sighed. "It's a shame you feel that way. I like macho types, and you've got a lovely arse. If you ever want to have a really good time and try a little bit of something that I know you'd like, give me a call."

As Hugh's face flared red and his fists balled, Derek withdrew, blowing him a kiss as he hastily stepped out onto the street and vanished.

"You'll get yours," Hugh muttered. "All bad things come to those who wait."

CHAPTER SIXTEEN

TRISH shuffled across the dirt floor on swollen, bruised knees, and bobbed her head to sip water from one of the stainless steel dog bowls. She was now shackled with one ankle attached to the concrete block by a long rusted chain comprised of links as thick as her fingers. Her pale body was anorexic-thin, all sharp angles and protruding bones that pushed against taut skin mottled with sores.

He visited her once a day, removed the tape from her mouth and filled one bowl with fresh water and the other with what looked and smelled like cat food. The rules were simple: if she spoke without being asked to, he removed a fingernail. She had only lost one. He had withdrawn it with pliers, standing on her wrist as he wrenched it from its bed. She had never experienced pain like it before, and had wailed in agony as the nerve endings acknowledged the damage and her brain converted the signals to mind-crushing torment. And he used her as though she were brain dead; just warm flesh to pleasure him with. She had become an object; a non person with no rights, increasingly devoid of any hope or expectation.

The days and nights became a blur as darkness, light, heat and cold merged in her feverish mind. The skylight high above her was her window on the world; a square that presented an ever-changing vista of colours that formed a rich palette ranging from dawn-grey and robin egg-blue to sunset-red and lampblack. The grimed pane of glass became Trish's focal point; the centre of her now small universe. It was a gallery of heavenly art. She became aware of the beauty of clouds in all their changing forms and hues, and was excited by the fleeting glimpse of an unrecognised bird, and dazzled and burned by the sun at its zenith. At night a myriad stars appeared as twinkling diamonds, glittering against a black velvet drape. And at times the moon slowly passed across her field of vision like a ghost ship adrift on the high seas. It was as if she were in H.G. Wells' time machine, looking out from it as the days, weeks, months and years sped by. Time was without meaning as she grew weaker; centuries and millennia could have passed as she lost all focus and was driven by a semiconscious meandering current out into a vast ocean, with no reference points on the horizon to give perspective to her existence.

The fear of pain and the supposition that she would ultimately be murdered had been unbearable at first. Every time he entered, a hot wire burned in her stomach, and her heart skipped beats, almost stopping, then raced madly, pounding against the cage of her now well-defined ribs. She cringed from him at the end of her chain, hoping that it was only sex that he had come for. She was now anaesthetised to his member pounding into her; could disassociate herself from the act as though it was someone else's body being violated. She had become desensitised to his cruel acts; just so much numb and bruised flesh.

On occasion, he would lay out dozens of Polaroids in the dirt and order her to look at them, before showing her the tacker that he had used to staple the pictured girls' lips together. He would then press the cold metal of the tool to her mouth, trigger it, empty, and snigger at the distress it caused her. At other times he ran the blade of his knife across her throat so lightly that the honed steel could have been the kiss of a feather's tip.

"First I use them," he had said on his last visit, smiling at her, proud to share his secrets. "And then I staple their mouths. While they're alive I know that my mother inhabits them. I can see her hiding behind their eyes. The bitch comes back again and again, and I make her suffer. Then I cut their throats, hang them up and bleed them out. Once they die, I know that she's gone for a while. Did I tell you that this barn is full of them? They're under you, dissolving in lime. You'll probably join them soon and be under the earth and with them."

His threats became hollow. She finally reached a saturation point and her spirit broke. She was no longer the person she had been. The thin veneer of sophistication had been scoured away, and with it all the posturing and affectation she had created to shield her true self. She had cast off her cloak to reveal a naked, tortured soul who had acquiesced to the unremitting horror of her plight, as victims of the Holocaust must have done in Hitler's concentration camps; the torture, starvation and the palls of greasy, black smoke from the crematoria chimneys reducing them to silent, unmoving beings with staring, vacant eyes, awaiting the inevitable, with their former lives and loved ones gone and with no future to contemplate; all their hopes and dreams behind them. That was how Trish felt. There were odd moments when she was saddened at her predicament, but in the main she now just wanted it to be over with, to have release and eternal peace from the torment. Even the knife had lost its ability to frighten her, as apathy replaced continual fear. She imagined the blade piercing her throat, laying it open, and the sting of the cut and the warm spurts of blood that would rob her first of awareness, and then of life.

In the darkness, a sharp, stabbing pain pulled her from the edge of troubled sleep. She winced and drew her legs up as another bolt of liquid fire ate into her calf. Lashing out at the hunched form that clung to her, she felt razor-sharp incisors puncture the soft flesh between her thumb and index finger, ripping and tearing, shaking her hand as a dog would savage a slipper. She screamed into the tape and swung her arm against the concrete block, once...twice…three times before the huge, bristling rodent let go and scurried into the corner of the barn, vanishing among the dark pools of shadow.

Now, jerked back to vivid cognizance by this fresh danger, Trish moaned with renewed terror. She inched her weak body up on to the two-foot-square cube of concrete and huddled on its cold surface, like Gollum from *The Lord of the Rings,* to search the gloom for the new enemy that had found her and judged her to be no more than food. A deep-seated and petrifying fear of being eaten alive revived her flagging spirit, returning her to the harsh reality that she had not wanted to face.

The sound of the bolt sliding back was almost a relief. He would bring light, and the vermin would be kept at bay...but for how long?

He lit the hurricane lamp and frowned down at the pallid and gaunt woman who squatted on the concrete, reminding him of a chicken on a perch.

"What the fuck are you doing up there?" he said, putting down the lamp and ripping the tape from her mouth.

"R...rats...b...bit me...Want to die...Enough," she whimpered, her eyes downcast, not able to look him in the face.

He examined her and saw the thin streams of blood running from the bites on her leg, and the gaping rent in her hand that glistening muscle bulged from.

"Fucking vermin," he seethed. "They won't leave you alone now that they've smelt you out and tasted blood. I doubt that there'll be much left of you by morning; just gnawed bones with most of the marrow eaten out."

"So get it over with, you bastard. Fucking kill me and put me out of my misery," Trish shouted, her voice breaking, but loaded with anger that temporarily outweighed her fear.

He lashed out and backhanded her across the face, splitting her top lip, whipping her head back and knocking her to the ground. Unbelievably, she began to giggle as though her plight were some dark satire; a fictional two-hander play; the barn a stage in the round with an audience sat beyond the footlights in a hushed and unlit auditorium.

"Why are you laughing?" he asked her, wondering if she had slid over the edge into madness to escape him.

She spat blood, which coated her breasts and stomach in a fine spray. "Because if the rats don't eat me, you'll butcher me," she said. "I can't win, and it's so fucking sad that it's making me laugh. If that doesn't make sense to you, then tough shit. Now, why don't you just finish it? I think you've had your money's worth for what I called you on TV. Nobody likes a greedy bastard."

For a second he fully intended to kill her, there and then. But she had balls. He had stripped her of everything, snatched her from all that had made sense in her glossy, fickle, side-show world. But she had more grit than all the others put together. Her spirit was strong. She had even spoken without permission, *and* called him a greedy bastard. Even the fear of losing more fingernails could not override her need to talk back to him.

It was a little strange. He had actually got used to her being around. It had become pleasant to know that when he arrived home, she would be here, waiting for him, reliant on him for food and water...for life itself. Whether she hated him or not, he was now the centre of her small, restricted world. He wanted to keep her. She was the perfect woman, never refusing his advances, however debased and distasteful she must find them. Now that she was at the end of her tether both physically and mentally, he could take the game a stage further, develop it, and by so doing maintain the excitement of having total control over another human being. He would meet the challenge and try to gain her trust; brainwash her into appreciating him. During the lull in his activities this would be a fine distraction. He had decided to wait until autumn before resuming his acts of retribution against his mother. He was satisfied for the moment, and would start afresh with new methods; change his pattern to throw those who hunted him into turmoil.

Unshackling her from the cement island that stood in the sea of straw-covered soil, he then doused the lamp and lifted her up, noting how little she now weighed; how infirm and weak her body was. It was as though she was a cancer patient, her body hardly more than a shell ravaged by a malignancy that was eating her from within. He tingled with pleasure as her head fell onto his shoulder. She was safe, for the time being. He would care for her as though she was a wounded animal in need of treatment and warmth and nourishment.

Pushing the barn door closed with his knee, he turned and carried her across the yard into the house and up the stairs to the bathroom, where he sat her on the lowered seat of the toilet. He drew a hot bath, then lifted her again and gently placed her in the steaming water.

Trish thought that he was going to drown her; push her beneath the surface until her lungs filled like balloons, to burst as she suffocated on the hot liquid. Or maybe he would cut her throat or wrists, to watch as the water turned crimson and she bled to death. Instead, he reached out, picked up a bottle from the low windowsill above the taps and poured fragrant lavender Radox into the bath, stirring it with his hand. He knelt, rested his forearms on the edge of the bath and let her soak for a few minutes, saying nothing, just studying her. After a while he sponged the grime from her body, washed and rinsed her hair under the shower head, and finally sat on the toilet seat, smiling at her as though they were lovers, or husband and wife.

Trish felt the soothing heat melt the knots in her tight muscles, loosening them and relaxing her. As he gently sponged her, she began to cry softly, hardly able to face the comfort after so much suffering. Her eyelids felt weighted, her body jelly. And as he lathered her hair and massaged her scalp, she had to fight against sleep. She was sapped of strength, still scared, but now somehow sure that this would *not* be the time or place that he would kill her.

Helping her to stand, he held her arm as she stepped out of the bath, and then draped a thick, warm, fleecy bath towel around her shoulders. "Dry yourself," he said, turning to open the mirrored, wall-mounted cabinet and withdraw a new, boxed toothbrush. "Then brush your teeth." The smell of pet food on her breath offended him. "I'll find something for you to wear."

He left the bathroom, but almost immediately bobbed his head back around the door, locked eyes with hers and just stared, as though looking into her very soul, searching, probing. "Trish," he said. "Be sensible. Don't try anything stupid, or you'll be back in the barn, for good. You're on trust, do not abuse it."

She dried herself, towelled her hair and brushed her teeth; the spearmint-flavoured paste taking away the sour taste from her mouth. She brushed until her gums bled, before rinsing the foam of

Colgate and blood from her mouth and chin. The mirror above the sink was fogged. She wiped it clear of condensation with the towel and stared at the emaciated stranger that looked back at her; studied the dull, sunken, lifeless eyes that were highlighted by dark purple crescents beneath them. The chalk-white skin was stretched tightly over the underlying skull. She was still standing, mesmerised by her reflection, when he came back and led her by the hand, out of the bathroom and along a short landing to a bedroom. He sat her on an ottoman at the foot of the bed and handed her a baggy Bart Simpson T-shirt; the character's stupid yellow face beaming wide-eyed from the black cotton. He then passed her a pair of Union Jack emblazoned boxer shorts.

"Put these on," he said. "You'll feel better."

Trish slowly pulled the T-shirt over her head, grunting as her weakened, unused arm muscles shook with the effort. The shorts were ridiculously big on her, but the elasticised waistband kept them up under the T-shirt that hung almost to her knees like a short dress.

Once more he took her hand, led her out onto the dimly lit landing and down steep stairs, along a hall to a large country kitchen. He pulled a chair out from under the timber built table and motioned for her to sit, then went to a wall unit, returning with a bottle of antiseptic and a wad of cotton wool.

"This'll sting a bit," he said, soaking the cotton, before kneeling, lifting her leg and dabbing at the angry red rat bites.

The iodine stung as it soaked into the raw, deep rents left by the rodent's teeth. And when he pressed the wad against her more seriously bitten hand, she sucked in her breath at the deep throbbing pain that set her whole arm aflame.

He made sweet, hot tea and pastrami sandwiches for them both, and then settled facing her across the table and ordered her to eat. She nibbled at the fresh bread, tasted the filling of thinly sliced, salted beef and began to salivate, ravenous, her stomach growling. It took all of her willpower to take small bites and chew the food properly. She knew that if she bolted it down too quickly she would almost certainly be sick. Savouring each mouthful, she enjoyed the sandwich much more than she could ever remember relishing the finest fillet steak, lobster, or pâté de foie gras.

"You can speak, as long as you don't insult me," he said. "If you badmouth me, the rats will think it's Christmas come early. Do you understand?"

Trish looked him directly in the face for the first time in days. His eyes were deceiving; not as she would imagine the eyes of a killer to be. They shone a bright sapphire blue and appeared, erroneously, to be kind, harbouring no evil or the capacity to carry out the horrific acts that she knew he had committed. He was reasonably good-looking and even-featured, with a firm mouth and strong, dimpled chin. His hair was fair, thick, but cut quite short with a side parting. A lock of it fell across his forehead, giving him a boyish look. She judged him to be anywhere between twenty-five and thirty-one or two. Although she had known who he was, she had never taken much notice of him in the past.

"I asked you if you understood." he said, breaking her line of thought.

"Yes, I understand," she replied, nodding as she spoke, her voice now smoother, more recognisable from the gravel croak it had been; although too high, nearly soprano with anxiety.

"Thing is, Trish, I think you *have* paid for the slagging that you gave me on TV. The only problem is, I can't let you go, because you know who I am."

"I wouldn't tell any—"

"The fuck you wouldn't tell anybody," he said, his voice suddenly knife sharp. "Once free, you'd want me behind bars for the rest of my life. So don't talk shit or I'll staple your fucking mouth shut."

"No…please, don't. I'm sorry,"

"That's better," he said, reaching forward, taking her uninjured hand and squeezing it gently. "This could be fun. I've got no script for keeping someone alive. I'm just playing it by ear, because I really don't want to kill you."

Later, they sat in the living room and he showed her videos of the news reports that had been broadcast following her disappearance. Looking at footage of herself dressed in a power suit, lightly made-up, and with her hair carefully styled, she viewed the faintly smug and in-control anchor woman as though she was a stranger. For the first time in her life she looked at herself with a certain dislike. The on-screen Trish Pearson was not a person she would want to know. The insincerity that shone through was almost as irksome as the aura of superciliousness.

"You're no longer that stupid cow with an attitude, are you?" he said.

"No," she whispered. "I don't feel as though I know her. And I don't like her."

"So this has been a valuable learning curve, eh?"

She didn't know how to answer that, so didn't. It had in no way been worthwhile, but it *had* changed her, radically. She was different, in some basic way unlike the old Trish who she now saw as having as little depth as the two-dimensional taped image on the screen in front of her. How could she have been such a shallow, insensitive person for so long, without even realising it?

"Time for bed," he said, yawning as he stood up. "Follow me."

CHAPTER SEVENTEEN

A door in the kitchen opened on to stone steps that led down to a large and freshly whitewashed cellar. It held only two items of furniture: a single bed and a coffee table, its top littered with magazines and dog-eared paperback novels. In one corner stood a plastic chemical loo next to a large, stained and crazed porcelain sink, its single rusty tap dripping; the patter a heartbeat, echoing around a room that had no carpet to dampen the sound. A single low wattage pearl light bulb hung from the ceiling. It could be turned on or off from a switch in the cellar, or from one above them in the kitchen. The subterranean room was Spartan, but was as appealing to Trish as any suite in a five star hotel, compared to the barn.

"I work shifts, Trish, so you're going to be spending a lot of time down here," he said, sitting on the bed and patting the cover next to him, intimating that she should join him. "I don't want to have to tape your mouth or shackle you again, so I'm going to leave a voice-activated recorder on in the kitchen. If you start screaming for help, I'll know, and you'll be punished.

"Think on this...you're on a farm, well away from the road and out in the country. There are no neighbours, so no one could hear you. And the floor, walls and ceiling are two-foot-thick reinforced concrete. My dad, God piss on his soul, got the heebies back when Kennedy and Kruschev faced-off over the Cuban Bay of Pigs thing in the early sixties. He decided that World War Three was imminent, so turned what had been an old dirt cellar into this bunker. There used to be a generator and a complicated air filter system. The stupid bastard thought that after the bombs fell, he would be able to sit it out for a few months, live off canned food and bottles of water and then go back to farming after the fallout had somehow cleared. Oh, and the door at the top of the stairs is constructed of lead and sheet-metal, and I've modified it, there's no handle on the inside. You're on probation, Trish. No chain, no gag, but fuck up just once and it's game over."

He actually kissed her on the forehead and smiled warmly before rising and going to the stairs, pausing as he began to climb them, to turn back and call, "Goodnight, Blondie. I'll see you in the morning."

"G...goodnight," she replied. And seconds later fear and confusion, relief and tiredness vied with a sense of hopelessness as the steel door closed with the heavy sigh of how she imagined a vault or airlock door might sound. The metallic scrape of two bolts shooting home caused a sinking sensation in the pit of her stomach, and a sudden rise of panic took hold. Her cold skin crawled, claustrophobia hit her, and the cellar was transformed in her mind into a sealed sepulchre. She actually missed the skylight that had been a portal through which she had been able to view and somehow still feel connected in some small way to the outside world.

Leaving the light on, Trish lay back on the bed and closed her eyes against the sight of the low concrete ceiling that she imagined was moving down, soon to reach and flatten her with crushing force. The mattress felt soft and inviting after existing for so long on hard-packed earth. And the pillow and linen were dry. She almost floated, overwhelmed by a tiredness that obliterated all horrific thought in her numb brain, wanting to be asleep and find some respite from her suffering.

No Please, no. Jesus help me! Her surroundings began to transform. But how could they? The tap that had been dripping was now pouring with a steady flow, sounding like someone urinating. She was freezing to the bone, and her breath escaped her mouth in a mist of frigid vapour. Sitting up, she swung her feet onto the damp concrete, placing her hands on the patchwork quilt that she had been lying on top of. It too felt clammy. Looking down, she saw small coins of green mould or mildew clinging to its surface; the furry growths appearing to proliferate and mushroom out as she watched them. Standing shakily, she walked across to the sink and saw that the stream of liquid was thick, almost black, stank of raw sewage, and was nearly up to the rim, about to overflow and cascade down to the floor. Using both hands, she turned the resisting, squeaking tap off, before plunging her fingers into the opaque depths, sure that the plug must be in place, only to find a slimy mass blocking the hole. She tried to pull it free, clawed at it, and then leapt back, her hands whipping from the sink as though she had touched a live wire, as whatever filled the outlet pipe contracted and squirmed like a writhing eel.

Looking about the subterranean vault, the setting was not as she had first thought it to be. The whitewashed walls were powdery, flaking, and discoloured by brown patches that brought images of liver spots or blemishes of skin cancer on the back of ancient and anaemic hands to mind. In the shadows, where the walls met the ceiling, limp, black cobwebs hung with fat-bodied spiders clinging to them: sailors in the rigging of tall ships.

Stepping back the three paces to the bed, Trish saw a trail of fresh blood puddled on the concrete. Her gaze moved to her legs, and she cried out at the sight of the bloody rivulets that striped them and ran down over her feet. There were more than a dozen fresh bites on each leg; small open wounds on her shins, calves, thighs and feet. The end of the little toe on her right foot was missing, and the spur of disclosed bone jutted from the raw meat, a glistening white like a pointed stick of chalk.

She climbed up on to the bed and sat hunched, trembling uncontrollably as she searched the floor for movement. There appeared to be no holes at the foot of the walls; no way that they could enter, and yet they had reached her, somehow bitten her and even chewed off her toe without causing her to wake up screaming in agony. She knew that vampire bats anaesthetised with their saliva as they bit the legs of cattle at night to lap the warm blood from the unsuspecting animals. The disgusting creatures even introduced a fluid that stopped the blood from coagulating; could rats also have those abilities? She didn't know.

The quilt rippled with life. She froze, breath held as the moving lumps burrowed towards her under the bedclothes. One pointed head appeared from beneath the pillow, its large, oil-bead eyes fixed on her face, unafraid; snout and whiskers twitching as if smelling her. The light bulb dimmed, and the semidarkness galvanised the rodents into action. She lashed out as her body was weighed down by the stinking, bristling vermin. Sharp claws raked her, and sharper teeth bit into her flesh, tearing at her back, buttocks, stomach, breasts, neck, arm, legs and face. Muscle spasms caused her to buck and writhe and arch her back. She tumbled off the bed, rolled over on at least two of the plump bodies – that screamed like newborn babies – and forced herself up onto her knees, found her feet and scrambled for the stairwell. Reaching the top, she pounded on the door, simultaneously turning as she heard skittering claws from the tide of undulating fur rising toward her. The front-runners leapt, slapped into her breasts, stomach and thighs to knock her back against the cold steel. The pack covered her, latched on to her and dragged her down. What felt like a thousand knifes sliced at her. And as she tried to scream, a head darted into her open mouth for razor-edged incisors to cut through her tongue, ripping away a large chunk. They took her eyes, plucking them from the sockets, and the pain became a cloak of sheer agony. She lost all ability to think or resist the onslaught, and felt no further individual bites, just an overall flensing of her entire body, as from within her skull she suffered the unbelievable pain and waited for blood loss to bring her the mercy of unconsciousness.

Sitting bolt upright, hands clawing at herself, she grasped at the diseased bodies that were dissolving with the nightmare. The light bulb still shone brightly in the underground room, which she could see was as clean and freshly painted as when her captor had brought her down to it. Still tingling from the lingering, phantom pain of nonexistent bites, and without solace, she realised that this was her death cell, and that there would be no reprieve from the *real* horror that lurked above her. He would tire of her soon, take her back to the barn and perform his ritual act of murder. She could wait, subservient to his every command and perverted desires, or she could find a way to escape.

Trish lay awake, thinking of ways she might fashion a weapon with which at some stage she would employ to try to kill the maniac who held her fate in his hands. She wanted to survive; to somehow better her captor and get her life back.

CHAPTER EIGHTEEN

"**COME**," Chief Superintendent Raymond Cottrell called out as Laura rapped twice on the door of his fourth floor office.

She entered and was immediately uneasy in the large room that was intimidating by design, not accident. Walking self-consciously over the deep pile of slate-grey carpet, she counted the number of steps that it took her to reach the solitary chair that stood before the chief's behemoth, mahogany desk. Fifteen steps. Over thirty feet: a long, lonely walk that was intended to unnerve all visitors.

"Sit," Cottrell said, his voice a snake's hiss: the python Kaa of Kipling's Jungle Book.

Laura eased herself into the low, hard chair; eyes narrowed against the harsh daylight that almost but not quite silhouetted her inquisitor in front of the window that his high chair and buttress of a desk were strategically positioned. She studied the man. He was thin, sickly looking, with grey skin of almost the same hue as the carpet, and a loose wattle of flesh that hung – displaying white stubble missed by the razor – from his scrawny neck onto the front of his shirt collar, almost obscuring the small, tightly-fashioned knot of his maroon tie. His yellow-grey hair was sparse, slicked down to his scalp. It was only his eyes that burned with life, as if sapping energy from the rest of his apparently enfeebled frame. They were avian, with large and almost black irises that absorbed the light into unplumbed depths.

"To say that you had erred, Detective Inspector Scott would be a gross understatement," Cottrell said, drumming his almost pencil-thin fingers on a green blotter; which, apart from a telephone was the only other article on the highly polished surface of the desktop. "You jumped the gun and instigated the use of an armed unit to arrest an innocent man."

Laura waited until she was sure he had finished. He had a habit of leaving his discourse open-ended; a further ploy to disconcert. It worked.

"We had every reason to believe that Cox was the killer, sir. We found—"

"I know exactly what you found, Detective Inspector. I did not summon you here to discuss the matter. I want you to know that you are not performing your duties to an acceptable level. You should have kept the suspect under surveillance and waited for the results from the odontology department. You were too hasty by far.

"I am also informed that you have involved a civilian who was once employed by the Federal Bureau of Investigation," he said, almost spitting the organisation's name out with undisguised disdain.

"The man was a topflight profiler with the Behavioural Science Unit at Quantico. I was using any means available to me to try and close the case," Laura said in defence of her actions.

"I am not suggesting that initiative is without merit, Detective Inspector," Cottrell said, his refusal to ever use acronyms an annoyance to Laura. "But only results can go some way to excuse less than professional methodology. I shall take it under advisement as to whether you should be removed from this investigation. And I will not tolerate any further association with the American. That is all."

Laura had been summarily dismissed. The reprimand was over, for the time being. She wanted to tell the anal retentive megalomaniac just what he could do with the case, the job, and even the oversized desk that he preached from behind, as though it was a raised pulpit. It was with a great deal of difficulty that she somehow managed to maintain an outwardly calm, unruffled demeanour. Most people had some sense of humour, but the police chief was seemingly the exception to the rule, bereft of any sign of even suppressed levity. It occurred to her that Jim would have been able to produce a written vignette of Cottrell, setting out the premise that he had been denied breast feeding and was raised in a loveless environment that accounted for his morose personality and piss-poor attitude. Or maybe he suffered from a stomach ulcer, haemorrhoids or a nagging, frigid wife. Whatever the reason, Laura found the man to be as personable as a cockroach. Cottrell spoke *at* people, not to them. His only interest was results.

Laura stood up, her lips pursed, then nodded curtly and made the long trek back to the door, sensing the police chief's eyes boring into her back; her mind conjuring him raising an unseen smile that she was pleased not to be able to see, knowing that it would make her flesh creep.

Resisting a powerful urge to slam the door behind her, Laura left what she thought to be an unwholesome place. The little man's mild body odour seemed to have adhered to her, making her feel unclean and in need of a hot shower to remove the invisible layer of contamination from her skin.

"You look angry, boss," Hugh said when she strode past him into her office and made a beeline for the desk drawer and her hidden cache of cigarettes.

"Cottrell just carpeted me, Hugh," she said, lighting up and sucking the calming smoke deep into her lungs. "He is without doubt the most contemptible little bastard that I've ever had the misfortune to meet. And he stinks."

"What did he say?"

"In short, that I wasn't hacking it. He wants results. It was basically a smack on the wrist for moving too fast on Cox. He thinks I overreacted, and he's right, damn him. What really pissed me off is that he knew about Jim. Somebody dropped me in it from a great height."

"Not me, boss," Hugh said. "I might not rate Elliott, but I wouldn't be disloyal to you. I hope that you know that."

"I didn't accuse you, Hugh. But someone on the team ran off at the mouth."

Jim was sitting out on the balcony sipping black coffee and pondering on whether to water the potted japonica, which was wilting with the heat; the mixture of compost and peat that it grew in, dry, its surface cracked like the earth of some drought-ridden African plain.

He drained his mug and got up, pausing for a few seconds to watch a jet angle up from Heathrow, to be encompassed by cotton-candy clouds. As it vanished, he went inside for more caffeine.

Rummaging through two units in the kitchen, he found a plastic jug, filled it with cold water, returned to the balcony and set the coffee down before pouring the life-giving water over the baked crust that was losing its ability to sustain the plant's life. At first, the water pooled, and then slowly began to drain. It took several minutes to absorb the two pints that he patiently fed to it, and he could almost imagine hearing a sigh of relief as the ornamental quince sucked up the sustenance through its dry and withering root system. He left the empty jug next to it and sat down again, staring off to the castle's round tower, that stood resolute and might have been a permanent, natural feature of the landscape; oblivious to man and his transient passing before its aged edifice.

Since driving back from Yorkshire, Jim had been unable to settle back in the groove. He saw to business in a perfunctory, offhand manner, with no appetite for the sham of reinventing personalities and mollycoddling celebrities of dubious, usually fey character and questionable ability. He now saw his life as a dreary canvas, faded, the bright pigments obscured by a patina of grime that clung to its surface, thickening with inchmeal accumulation that vexed his spirit and obscured any worthwhile aspirations.

Laura cared deeply for him, he knew that. And he loved her and wanted to be with her with a need that was consuming him. Her personality was a convoluted maze, strewn with dead ends and detours. Her career was a crutch, and had helped her to cope with loss and grief and the crippling weight of emptiness. The job was her security blanket; a constant that could not just be ripped away and confiscated, but had to be cast aside willingly, when the confidence to function without it came about naturally, by choice. And that might be something that would never happen.

She had phoned twice since he'd returned home. They had planned to see each other again, as soon as the Tacker case was solved, for a weekend on neutral ground; maybe stay at a quiet hotel in the country and avoid newspapers and television. That in itself would be a giant step forward, if it ever materialised. In the meantime she was keeping him abreast of developments. The suspect, who lived within the area that Jim had designated, seemed involved, although the only evidence was a length of rope that he insisted he had never seen and therefore, to his mind, must have been planted by the police. With no other leads, the guy had walked. Jim now waited for her e-mails and phone calls, hungry for more details that might help him fill in some of the blanks and add to the jigsaw that was taking shape in his mind. He had found all the edges, and was working towards the centre, now feeling as though one elusive key piece would fully disclose to him the identity of a figure that was almost revealed.

Going back inside to his computer, Jim began to compile a simple list of what he considered to be the pertinent facts. Laura's latest mail, received the previous day, had given up another clue, hardening his conviction that the killer lived on a farm. The traces of white powder found on the last victim's body had been calcium oxide. Lime; a substance usually spread on the land as a fertiliser by the farming community. The molecular structure of the lime had been degraded and was believed to be at least twenty years old. The assumption was that the corpse had been transported in a bag – plastic, as confirmed by forensic – to where the body had been found hanging.

Jim made a list:

1. PAST RECORDS OF MISSING BLONDES...ALL FROM SOUTHEAST AREA OF YORK.

2. UNKNOWN SUBJECT'S LOCALE WITHIN THAT DISTRICT.

3. ISOLATED FARM/SMALLHOLDING/DOMICILE.

4. LIME...WHICH WOULD MAKE A FARM MOST LIKELY.

5. MATCHING SECTION OF BLUE NYLON ROPE/DEREK COX.

6. KILLER/BLUE EYES/FAIR HAIR/LEFT-HANDED/TALL?

7. TEETH IMPRESSION...NOT COX'S.

8. MOTHER/MATRICIDE/COMPULSION.

9. SADISTIC PERSONALITY DISORDER. VIOLENCE AND CRUELTY USED TO CONTROL AND DOMINATE. NEEDS TO INFLICT PHYSICAL AND PSYCHOLOGICAL PAIN. OBSESSED WITH TORTURE/DEATH.

10. INTELLIGENT/COMPETITIVE/GAME PLAYER.

11. COX + ACCOMPLICE...OR ROPE PLANTED BY KILLER. WHO KNEW THAT COX WAS A SUSPECT? THE POLICE?

Jim stared at the screen and let his mind spin like the reels of a Vegas slot machine. The facts clicked into place...Jackpot! The Tacker was a cop. He reached for the phone.

"Jesus, Jim, are you positive?" Laura said, holding the receiver close to her ear, even though she was at home alone and could not be overheard.

"Hell, no, I'm not positive, but sure enough. I'm working on the assumption that if Cox was involved, then you would have found more than just one glaring, incriminating clue. You found nothing. His house and land were as clean as a whistle. And he's gay. He doesn't fit the bill. Whoever put the rope in his garage was pointing you at a suspect who fitted the rough description of the killer, and who lived in the right surroundings in the area that we were locked on to. Cox conformed to the profile, superficially. You need to make a list of everyone who had access to the information. Then just home in by process of elimination. You've got a killer cop, Laura, I'm sure of it. He's going to loosely fit the picture that we've built up of him. And once you've narrowed it down, you'll find that he lives out in the sticks, and all the clues will be there to nail him. I'm convinced that he took Trish Pearson as well. She may even still be alive. And Laura, for God's sake be ultra careful. If he thinks that you're getting close to him, he'll take you out."

"Thanks, Jim. I'll get on it. Unfortunately it's not just confined to the team. Quite a few others have been involved in the investigation and know a lot of the case details. It could take a while."

"It shouldn't. His address will point him out."

"I'll keep you informed of—"

"I'm coming back up," Jim interrupted. "I don't intend to sit down here like a spare prick at a wedding, wondering if he's cottoned on to what you're doing. Remember, if it is a cop we're looking for, he thinks like you and is without doubt monitoring every move that you make. Don't lose sight of the fact that this guy is a killing machine. Trust no one who has any knowledge of the profile, or could feasibly be who you're after."

"Go straight to the cottage, Jim. I'll leave a key in the woodshed out back, above the door on a nail."

"I'll be there by noon tomorrow...I love you."

There was a pause. "Good. We need to talk."

"Take care."

"And you. Bye."

He felt like the proverbial cat on a hot tin roof. He'd declared himself by saying 'I love you' and disclosing the depth of his feelings. He hadn't planned on saying it. The words had just tumbled out unbidden. With the exception of Pamela, Laura was the only other person he had ever truly loved, apart from his parents. Images and memories of his mum, dad and Pamela assailed him. All three were now gone. His parents had died together in the twisted remains of his father's Ford pickup. A local drunk had passed-out at the wheel of his old Mercury and perished with them in the resulting head-on collision. They had been driving back from church along a quiet country road on a bright spring day in ninety-nine when it happened. God, how the years flew by. It seemed like only yesterday he had got the call. You never get over life experiences like that, just accommodate them somehow and let time do the rest. And Pamela, dear sweet Pamela, who had been gunned down during the attempt on his life. That had been the hardest cut of all. Guilt was cruelly endurable. He had come to accept it would always be on his shoulder berating him interminably like a fucking parrot with a bad attitude. But there was absolutely nothing he could do to change one second of what had gone down. Life isn't like the movies; you only get one take. And that one rainy night in D.C. had left him thinking of how things might have been. Pamela should still be alive, and wasn't because of what he had been. And now he was going back to it. He was obviously one of those people they talk about that never seem to learn from their mistakes.

Shaking off his relentless demons, Jim made a phone call and cleared the decks yet again, relaying his intentions to Diane, his long-suffering secretary, who he thought he should make a junior partner for the way she ran the office and kept everything together, gliding as smoothly as ball bearings in a tray of engine oil.

"Di, I'll be away for a few days, York again. Call me if anything comes up that you can't deal with. And give some thought as to whether you'd like to be a partner in this circus we run. We'll discuss a new inflated salary and details when I get back. Okay?"

"Shit, boss, are you in love or something?"

"Or something. Now hang up, Di."

"Be good. And if you can't—"

"I'll be bad and careful. Now get back to earning us some money, while I spend it."

It was past one a.m. when he hit the sack. He'd showered, packed, and set the alarm for six, already impatient to be with Laura again. Jesus! Had he *really* lost control and told her that he loved her. It had just come out, as the actress said to the bishop. But he was glad that it was now in the open. Just the intonation and pitch of her voice when she had said: 'Good. We need to talk', had implied that she was contemplating a future with him in it, unless he was being presumptuous in reading more into it than there was.

Laying in the darkness and allowing a modicum of optimism to rear its head, he had no sense of impending doom; could not foresee the disaster that would strike within hours and threaten to erase all that he now cared for in life.

CHAPTER NINETEEN

APART from Jim, there was only Hugh that she could fully trust without reservation. He was her sidekick; Lewis to her Morse, a loyal colleague and friend who was above suspicion. It flashed through her mind that he was tall, with fair hair and bluish eyes. Thank Christ he lived in the city. He had a swank, top-floor bachelor pad that looked out on The Lord Mayor's Walk and across to the east side of York Minster, which rose like a Gothic leviathan, defiant against the centuries that ebbed and flowed around it. Laura had stood at the flat's lounge window and looked up at the cathedral's twin towers, fancying that she could hear the bells ring, their clappers striking discordantly as the hunchback, Quasimodo – on loan from Notre Dame – swung from rim to rim of the hollow, cast metal cups to impress a horrified Esmeralda.

Laura had been to Hugh's gaff several times, seen framed photographs of an elderly couple; his parents, now both retired and living in Bournemouth. There had also been a shot of a pretty young woman in mortar-board and gown, proudly clutching a rolled, ribbon-wrapped scroll: his sister Deborah, he had said with pride, who now worked for NASA and was based across the pond in Houston, Texas.

"Car park, Hugh," Laura said, motioning with her head for him to follow as she rushed out of her office and made off down the corridor to the stairs at the rear of the station, clutching her cigarettes and lighter.

"So what's with all the cloak and dagger stuff, boss?" Hugh said after Laura lit up and casually looked about her, to assure herself that no eavesdropper was sitting in a car nearby with a window wound down. *Welcome to the wonderful world of paranoia.*

"It looks as though it could be one of us," Laura said, staring off towards a stand of tall poplars that towered high above the wall of the car park, wavering, their leaves rustling in a gentle breeze.

Hugh's brow knitted in a frown. "What might be one of us?"

"The Tacker. He could be a copper. Jim is almost positive that he is."

"Bollocks! I don't want to go there, boss. Or even think that it could be a possibility. I'm beginning to *really* dislike Elliott. I know he's your uh...friend, but his theories suck. He sounds as though he's fishing without a net. He'll have us chasing our own tails while the Tacker carries on killing with impunity."

"Hugh, there was nothing at Cox's place but that piece of rope hung where we couldn't help but find it. If the man is guilty, how come he was so meticulous in not leaving any other shred of evidence, but stupid enough to overlook the bloody rope?

"And his teeth impression doesn't match the wounds. So without grasping at straws in the wind and inventing an accomplice, he was just a patsy."

Hugh shook his head. "So humour me. Why does that point to one of us, for Christ's sake?"

"Because Jim targeted the area that Cox lives in. The killer couldn't have known where to plant the rope without inside information of that fact. There's no credible possibility of it being coincidence."

"I still prefer to think that Cox is involved. It makes a lot more sense than a bloody maniac copper on the loose."

"But you can see that if Cox isn't involved, then it has to be someone who has access to the investigation. Can't you?"

"Yeah," Hugh said, reluctantly accepting the premise. "I don't like it, although I can grasp the logic. But for the record, I think that this line of inquiry is going to prove a complete waste of valuable time."

"Hugh, I—"

"You don't have to say anything else, boss. I'll pull the team's files. Shit, I'll pull all male personnel's files," Hugh said, hiking his shoulders and holding his palms up in resignation. "We should be able to narrow it down through duty rosters and addresses. Anyone living in the target area that was off duty when the girls were lifted will be red-flagged."

"Don't forget the SOCO's, and every other department that has been involved with the case."

"I'll even screen the civvies, right down to the messengers and the car park attendant."

"Thanks, Hugh. And try to have a little more faith in Jim. He didn't want to be involved with this in the first place. I asked him to come on board. That he has contributed is a bonus. We deal with crime in general, and most murders we get are domestic, drink/drug related, or carried out during a robbery. Jim was a specialist. He dealt almost exclusively with pattern murderers like this one. He knows how to hunt them down. The Met has a behavioural science unit of sorts. But they don't have the practical experience; it's mostly theory. Fortunately, we don't have the same problem with these psychos as the States do. Out there it's rife."

"You really think that he can nail this guy, don't you, boss?"

"No, Hugh. I *know* that he can, and will."

It was midday when Hugh walked into Laura's office with a printout of thirty-two names. "What do you say we look at this lot over a beer, boss?" he said.

"I didn't drink on duty till this case was dumped on me, Hugh. I still don't approve of it, so I'll let you buy me a Coke. And you can make do with a shandy," Laura said, slipping on her jacket, glad of the excuse to stretch her aching back, and making a mental note to indent for a new and more comfortable office chair. "Have you got anything promising there?"

"I can't believe that any of these might be our man. But any one of them could be. They all live in outlying locations, and some even fit the description that Elliott dreamed up. You'll have to decide how to proceed from here. What do you propose? How the hell are you going to check out over thirty serving officers, ranging in rank from a DCI down to PCs, without causing a shitstorm of hitherto unseen proportions?"

"Jim will be back on the patch tomorrow. He can look at the list and go though the descriptions and addresses, before I decide on anything."

"You do realise that if Cottrell gets wind of him still being around, then your next job will be mopping out the holding cells and changing bog rolls?"

"So don't mention him again in front of the team or anybody else, Hugh. You fucked up the other day in the incident room. That's the only way Cottrell could have got to learn Jim was involved in the first place."

"That means one of the squad is in the old goat's pocket, reporting back to him. I won't slip up again. Scouts honour."

They walked down the road to the Royal Oak. It was only a two minute stroll away from the station, but brought them both out in a sweat as the heat bounced off the pavement; the soaring temperature unabated by what was now only the whisper of a breeze.

Laura sat in a quiet corner of the lounge bar, away from the shaft of sunlight that shone through a large window to cut a hot path across the faded, paisley-patterned carpet. And while Hugh went to the bar for the drinks, she ran through the list he had given her, to provisionally mentally delete some names as belonging to officers who she deemed too old, too short, or who she knew to be married with families, and therefore outsiders in the field that should throw up a likely candidate. Only one of the team directly involved with the case was on the list: Clem Nash. Clem was twenty-seven, single, and a solid five-eleven, with mousy hair and blue/grey eyes. He had only been a DC for six months, but had been an outstanding uniformed constable with a high arrest rate and above average intelligence. He was taciturn by nature, and didn't get close to anyone. She had mentioned this to him at an interim interview, pointing out that although a good copper, he was not getting into the spirit of being a team player, and that she was monitoring him, hoping that he would come out of his shell a little before she had to do his ASR. If there was one aspect of the job she hated, it was doing annual staff reports on the junior officers under her command. It was human nature to be antagonised or dispirited by criticism (however constructive the comments) so she went to great lengths to forewarn anyone of what she would be writing, making them aware of any shortcomings or areas that she considered needed working on. She recalled that Clem had said that he wasn't concerned with developing relationships, just doing the job to the best of his ability.

'Just write it up as you see it, boss. I'm not political, and I don't want to play mind games to score points,' Clem had said to her, giving one of his rare half smiles as the interview reached its conclusion. Laura noted that Clem lived on a converted barge on the river, out near Bishopthorpe. Surely there were far too many other boats and nearby caravan sites in the vicinity to give a killer the privacy he needed. The longer she looked at the list, the more she began to have doubts about everyone on it. But the most unlikely men could be closet killers. She recalled a spate of rapes that had been committed during the summer of oh-six, all carried out on Hampstead Heath. The rapist – when caught in the act – proved to be a fifty-year-old bank manager who lived out in the burbs. He'd been supposedly happily married for twenty-eight years, had two daughters, both at uni, and was on the surface a model citizen who had just reached whatever the male menopause is and gone berserk, raping a total of seven young women in as many weeks. As a copper, she knew not to take *anyone* at face value.

"One Coke with crushed ice, ma'am," Hugh said, placing a large schooner in front of her.

"And what's that?" Laura said, pointing at his pint.

"That's a shandy. Or to be perfectly honest, a pint of best bitter with a lemonade top, which is as near to being a shandy as I can bring myself to ruin a good pint."

Laura grinned as Hugh attempted to con her with his boyish charm, but then was suddenly disturbed as he took a sip from the glass, holding it left-handed. She had not previously noticed that he was a lefty. If it hadn't been Hugh, she would have been convinced that she was sat opposite a leading contender for the title of 'most wanted serial killer in recent British history'. Thank God that he had family and lived in the city.

"Are you all right, boss? You look as though you just got hit by a lorry," Hugh said, a concerned edge to his voice.

"I...I'm fine, Hugh. I just feel a little light-headed. I think I might need some food on my stomach. I've been skipping meals."

"They only do snacks and sandwiches and stuff like that in here. Would you rather go somewhere else and get a proper lunch?"

"No, a sandwich will be fine; roast beef if they have it," Laura said, surprised at how steady her voice sounded.

"Back in a sec," Hugh said, standing up and heading to the bar.

If I were Jim, I would be looking at Hugh as a suspect, she admitted to herself. Her DS at least merited being on the list that he had furnished her with. After all, it had been Hugh who'd come up with Derek Cox as a suspect. It was feasible that he had set the man up by planting the rope.

"There you go. One roast beef sarny and a packet of crisps for you, and a pork pie with mustard for me. Next time the meal's on you," Hugh said as Laura made room for him to put the plates down.

His cheeky grin and kind, laughing eyes smothered her suspicion. Christ, she had worked with Hugh for long enough to know that he was a straight copper; one that loved his job and had no time for criminals. He had made no secret of the fact that he would top rapists, paedophiles and murderers to protect society and make the world a safer place to live in. He had once beaten the shit out of a guy that had hospitalised his wife for the third time, and then arrested the wanker for assault. That, to her, wasn't the actions of a monster that preyed on women and did what had been done to the victims. Jim had planted the seed in her mind that it was a copper, and now she was letting it propagate and grow out of control.

Hugh left half of the pie, pushed the plate away and took a large mouthful of his beer, which had not been tainted by even a single drop of lemonade.

"At least ninety percent fat and gristle," he said, scowling at the pie as if it was road kill, and considering whether or not it was worth taking back to the bar to complain about.

"The beef's fine," Laura said, averting her gaze away from the teeth marks he had left in both the crust and the unhealthy looking greyish meat.

Less than twenty minutes later they left the pub and began walking back through the growing crowds of office workers that had been let loose for lunch.

"Damn," Laura said, stopping, turning. "I'll catch up, Hugh. I took my cigarettes and lighter out of my bag and left them on the table."

With her back to the bar, she wrapped the half-eaten pie in a paper napkin and secreted it in her shoulder bag with a dexterity that would have brought praise from a stage magician. Her furtive action was lost on the disinterested girl behind the counter, who was pulling a pint and suffering small talk from a punter who was leering at her ample and barely covered breasts, while plying an unoriginal chat up line to deaf ears.

Rejoining Hugh, the cigarettes and lighter in her hand, Laura felt as guilty as most of the criminals she interviewed looked when they'd been caught bang to rights. She felt as though Hugh could see through the black leather shoulder bag. As if with X-ray vision he had located the remains of his lunch and knew that she suspected him.

They both went off duty together that evening at six p.m. and walked across the car park to their vehicles, which were next to each other.

"See you bright and early in the morning," Hugh said, climbing into his car.

"Early, yes but bright, doubtful," Laura replied, opening the door and throwing her bag onto the front passenger seat.

"Not planning a night on the town, are you?"

"No, Hugh. Ten hours' sleep seems more appealing at the moment. I'm knackered. I must be getting old."

"It's a state of mind."

"So maybe I've got an old state of mind."

Hugh keyed the engine into life and drove off, waving to her as he made a left past a line of cars and headed for the barrier.

CHAPTER TWENTY

LARRY Hannigan took the napkin and folder from Laura and listened to what she had to say as he placed the small parcel on the Formica top of a work bench, unwrapping it carefully to examine the contents, before opening the document wallet, removing the photos from it and studying them.

"This has to be off the record for the moment, Larry," Laura said, giving the bearded odontologist a conspiratorial wink.

Larry looked over the top of his tinted 'John Lennon' spectacles, which were part of his image; a hippy growing old disgracefully, complete with a faded T-shirt featuring a picture of Bob Dylan on the front, and patched, flared jeans under his open lab coat. "You want me to do an unauthorised comparison with the boob bites, then report back to you personally. No pen to paper, uh?" he said.

"That's right, Larry. I know it won't match. But I need to eliminate it for my own peace of mind. Can you do that for me?"

"Cool," he said. "I'll get to it as soon as I finish up the job I'm on now. It'll be later tonight, maybe ten or so before I'll have anything."

"I'll give you a bell in the morning," Laura said, turning to leave. "And thanks, Larry, I really appreciate this."

"Make it after nine. But what if it is a match?"

She stopped, pulled out her note book, scribbled her home and mobile numbers down, ripped out the page and handed it to him. "If it is, then call me, no matter what time you get finished up. Then it *will* be official."

"Rock on," Larry said, giving her the peace sign; still in Woodstock time-warp mode, from his long, greying hair, down to his open sandals.

"Yeah, groovy, man," Laura grinned, returning the sign and making for the door, her short heels clipping like horseshoes on the tiled floor as she left.

Larry poured himself a coffee, put an ancient LP vinyl record on the turntable in his office, cranked up the volume and, leaving the door wide open, went back to working on a reconstruction of a jaw that came from a corpse found by hikers on the North York Moors. The body had been face down, head and shoulders in a stream, just half a mile west of Rievaulx Abbey. There had been nothing to identify it, and decomposition had reduced it to a near skeleton. It was estimated that it had lain unfound for between three and six months. The damage to the skull had indicated foul play, with fractures resulting from blunt force trauma to the temporal plate and the mandible, which had split in half and was missing several teeth. Larry was basically putting the jaws back together and resetting the teeth that had been recovered. He had painstakingly realigned the lower facial bones, cementing them together, with the result that an individual occlusion – whereby the maxilla was positioned behind the mandible – would assist identification, once a cast had been taken and a reconstruction expert had fleshed out the copy skull with clay or Plasticine to build up facial musculature prior to overlaying it with features. It wasn't an exact science, but could in many instances produce a likeness to the deceased that could help with recognition.

The music from the flower-power days he was fixated on seemed to make time fluid and speed by unheeded as he performed his art, pausing only to change discs, to hum along to Dylan, Joplin, the Byrds and their ilk.

It was almost nine-thirty when Larry cemented the last tooth in its socket and stood back, putting his hands up to massage and knead his aching neck. Going back to his office, he removed his lab coat, opened the window, took a joint out of a cache at the back of his desk drawer and lit up. *Time to chill out, then hit the road, man*, he thought, sitting back with his feet up and eyes closed, enjoying the mellow hit of the weed.

Ten minutes later, approaching the door with his finger reaching for the light switch, he was all set to lock up for the night when his eye caught sight of the napkin on the counter. *Shit! The fucking pie that Laura had left for comparison*. He had said he would check it out, tonight. She would be phoning him in the morning for the result. He couldn't let her down. Laura Scott was a cool babe, knew where he was coming from, and reminded him a little of how Joan Baez had looked in the seventies, apart from the short hair.

It ended up being eleven-fifteen when Larry returned to the lab. He had met his partner of six years, Zandra, at The Bombay Garden, a first-floor Indian restaurant on Coney Street, and had consumed a feast fit for a Maharaja, washed down with a couple of lagers to cool the fiery vindaloo. He'd then phoned for a cab, for Zandra, promising to be home by two a.m., latest.

The last partial bite into the firm meat of the pie had left a near perfect impression. The 10x8 close-up shots of the teeth marks that had removed the nipples of two of the Tacker's victims, plus the casts made from the wounds were enough for a visual confirmation that the same person who had been eating the pie was responsible. He had tests to run, but the spacing and slightly exaggerated overbite looked identical.

Larry's balls tightened, and the hair on his forearms tingled. He realised that Laura must have been with the killer that day.

It was a little after one a.m. when he was certain beyond all doubt that he had a positive match. He reached for the phone, retrieved the piece of paper from his lab coat pocket and punched in Laura's home number. On the fifth ring she picked up.

Laura scrabbled for the phone and lifted the receiver, pulling herself up into a sitting position in the dark. "Uh, yeah," she croaked, still more asleep than awake.

"Laura? It's Larry."

"Yeah, Larry. What can you tell me?" she said, a stab of apprehension sharpening her senses.

"I got a near as damn it positive result. I'd need more for a courtroom, but I'd bet my house on it that the bites are from the same teeth. Whoever was eating that pie is your killer."

"It can't be!"

"Believe me. There's no doubt. I double-checked, then double-checked again."

"Okay, Larry, now it *is* evidence. Stick it in the freezer, or whatever you do with something perishable. And do the bookwork. I'll get back to you. And thanks, Larry, I owe you. Goodnight."

The click and subsequent unbroken tone sounded loud in her ear, like the steady purr of a big cat. She kept hold of the receiver, reached for the bedside light switch with her other hand, fumbling, nearly pulling the lamp over as her trembling fingers searched for the button. The sudden sensation of not being alone made her pause, and then stiffen and gasp as a cold, solid object was pressed against her throat.

CHAPTER TWENTY-ONE

AFTER leaving the station, Hugh drove across town to his flat, pulling into the small, walled car park through a porte-cochere that bore a large overhead sign stating: Sherburn Tower Apartments. Residents Only; and below in large red letters the warning: 24 hour security. Unauthorised vehicles WILL be clamped. The sign dissuaded all but the most stupid or dyslexic of space seekers from using the prime city centre parking area.

Standing at the window in the shadow of the Minster, Hugh casually separated the junk from his mail, tearing up Readers Digest crap, which for what seemed like the thousandth time informed him that he was a winner, and urged him to read the contents carefully and return the Yes or No envelope within Christ knows how many days.

The flat was his official residence; the only address that the force, bank and every other relevant party had on file for him. He passed through at irregular intervals and unpredictable times, made a point of being on speaking terms with his neighbours, and even stayed overnight once in a while. The interior of the apartment was little more than a carefully staged set, furnished to appear to be what he thought would be a typical bachelor pad. It was reasonably tidy, with just enough clutter and appliances to convey the desired effect. He kept beer in the fridge, CD's and clothes on view, and the bed carefully unmade, with an open Ian Rankin paperback face down on top of the bedside cabinet. All the little touches were there to allay any possible suspicion. He even had photographs of a make-believe family on display; the bounty from a raid on a photographer's in Hull, when he had been on detached duty there as a young PC. They had found several hundred prints of children performing every lewd sexual act imaginable, with both other children and adults. The guy ran a respectable trade as a front, doing weddings and portrait stuff, but had a more lucrative tax free sideline in child pornography. Hugh had lifted a couple of envelopes of uncollected regular shots, and used the odd one to strengthen the false image that he had invented, by framing them for the rare visitor to see.

The mortgage on the farm had already been paid in full when his father had been crushed by the tractor. His mother had been left everything; the property, over forty thousand pounds – that she had not known existed – and a fat insurance payout, due to the old man's accidental death. Later, after the car crash that had killed the slut and the councillor who she'd been screwing, Hugh had inherited the lot. The farm was now his secret lair. There was no phone, and he had nothing delivered there, and no work done by outside contractors. No one had reason to visit the place. The utility bills were paid by standing order under an assumed name, and a sign at the entrance gate, that stood a quarter of a mile from the house, warned of guard dogs. Over the years, the hedges and trees around the perimeter of the property had grown unchecked, until the house was hidden by a profusion of trees, bushes and tall undergrowth. The weathered, mainly wooden outbuildings had faded with neglect, to blend with their surroundings. For years he had led a well-planned double life; the flat and his career being the perfect cover for his separate alter ego of serial murderer.

It had been a split second expression on Laura's face that had revealed to him that he was in danger. He had seen the workings of her mind in that single fleeting moment. The cop in her had subconsciously put it together. She had momentarily looked past his being her easygoing and likeable DS, to view him as a potential suspect who fitted the Yank's description. It was as if a dark thunderhead had passed in front of her eyes as he had lifted his glass...left-handed. Eureka, he was suddenly on the list that he had compiled and obviously left himself off.

It had been a shock when Elliott targeted the area that the farm was in. The ex-FBI shithead really *was* good. He'd done his homework and put it together that the common denominator was the locality that so many girls had been abducted from. Hugh had not thought it significant at the time, but now the skeletons in his cupboard – or to be more precise, under the barn floor – were back to haunt him. He knew that at some stage Laura would check him out, to convince herself that he was not the blonde, blue-eyed six-footer they were after. He couldn't take the risk of her digging too deep. His cover might hold, but he wasn't going to put it to the test. Her next revelation might be that he had personally come up with Cox as a suspect. Even Stevie Wonder would be able to clearly see the possibility that he had planted the rope in the guy's garage. It was a bitch. He didn't want to kill his boss. He had a lot of time for her; had grown to respect as well as like her. They had hit it off from day one, and he valued her friendship and considerate nature. That she had insulted and taunted him on the TV was okay, he would have done the same; although he had chastised her with the letter and the ear, laying some guilt off on her for the girl's suffering. Now, in the short term, he would have to take her out of the picture, while he put the final touches to a plan he had hoped he would never have to use. If all went well, Hugh Benton Parfitt would vanish from the face of the earth, to resurface down south in a week's time, his appearance changed and safely embarking on a new life. He had laid the foundations down over three years ago; his prospective alias risen from a Leeds graveyard; a dead child who would have now been his age was firmly reborn with driving licence, bank account, passport and a history that would stand up to any amount of close inspection in this computer dependant society. He would soon be John Anthony Lyndhurst, with dark hair which he would grow shoulder length, and wearing green contact lenses. His new home would be somewhere in London, blending in with the seething masses; a shadow and nonentity. Once established, he would seek out his mother again in all her guises, being more careful in future, learning from his past mistakes. That he would have to lose the farm and flat was annoying, but he had funds and had always known that this day might come. Nothing lasts forever.

Leaving the flat, he made small talk with an elderly neighbour who was standing at her open door, taking the air. He even stooped to stroke her stinking tomcat, which wound around his legs, jabbing its face against them. It always seemed to smell of piss, and he would have loved to snatch it up by the scruff of the neck and hurl it over the balcony. It would be interesting to see if cats really did always land on their feet.

"Oh, by the way, you won't see me around for a couple of weeks, Mrs Harriman. I'm off to Florida for a holiday, so don't be concerned," he said to the blue-rinsed old fart, knowing that she missed very little of what went on in Sherburn Towers.

"Well, say hello to Mickey for me, and have a good time," she replied, her ill-fitting dentures clacking loosely in her pursed mouth.

"I'll even send you a postcard," he lied, making his way down the first flight of stairs.

His plan was simple. He would get rid of Trish, permanently, then abduct Laura and install her in the cellar. With her safely stashed, he would have the breathing space necessary to carry on as normal for twenty-four hours, or even longer. He would go to work as usual in the morning, find time to make large cash withdrawals from his two bank accounts, and also collect the several thousand pounds that sat idly in a safe deposit box. Going off duty as scheduled, he would dump his car in a city car park and steal another to drive down to the capital. The only possible threat was the Yank. He was a loose cannon and unpredictable. But an idea was already taking shape in his mind to wrong foot the clever bastard. He would have him racing around like a clockwork mouse, searching for the lovely Laura in all the wrong places.

Laura had driven home feeling stupid and more than a little ashamed. She recalled all the good times that she had experienced while working with Hugh. He had always been protective, never above showing that he cared for her, and more often than not able to cheer her up when she felt down. It was inconceivable that he could be a cold-blooded killer, let alone one who would have sent her the photo, note and ear. He had been as shocked and mortified as her when the package had arrived; as angry and upset as she had ever seen him. Up until today she had been convinced that if they found the murderer, then Hugh might have to be restrained from attacking him. But now, because Jim suspected that it was a copper, she had even doubted the closest colleague she had. There had been a time, shortly after her transfer, when she and Hugh had been only a whisper away from being lovers. They had gone to a colleagues retirement 'do', and she had overindulged. Hugh had driven her home and stayed over, sleeping on the settee downstairs. Had he not been her DS, and so much younger, then who knows? He was attractive and personable. She'd still had needs that she had suppressed, but like thirst and hunger, the urge to satisfy her sexual appetite was gnawing at her. Abstaining from sex hadn't been a conscious life choice, and her libido was still strong. If Hugh had come on to her, she may have had something to regret or be happy about the following morning. Maybe he just hadn't fancied her. But screwing a junior officer on her team was a no-no. Like birds, cops shouldn't shit in their own nests. Being emotionally involved with a work colleague could only cause problems. It clouded the issue and interfered with decision making.

Now that Jim was back in her life, she was glad that nothing had happened. Bottom line was, she had trusted Hugh and hated the fact that she felt the need to eliminate him from any shadow of guilt. When Larry confirmed that Hugh's bite marks did not match those on the corpses, she would feel even more foolish and a little ashamed...but very relieved.

She opened the windows front and back to create a through-draught and let some of the day's built-up heat escape the cottage, before taking a ladder-backed chair outside the kitchen door to sit down on it, smoke a cigarette and drink a cup of tea as she enjoyed the quietude of her surroundings and the scent of blossoms and pine that drifted invisibly across to her from the garden and the dense woodland beyond. Tomorrow, Jim would be here, and the thought of his imminent nearness excited her. If he had been with her that second, then she would have led him into the woods, stripped both him and herself and lain naked in a cool glade amongst waist-high ferns that would hide them from view. She closed her eyes and imagined the breeze to be his breath, and of what they would do together.

Stop it, woman! Standing, she walked back into the kitchen. The fantasy had made her feel as horny as hell.

She ate late: Weight Watchers sweet and sour chicken with rice, which took all of fourteen minutes to cook from frozen in the microwave. With a calorie-laden brandy and ginger ale, she ate half of the bland meal, and then settled with her feet up on the couch and watched the last forty minutes of a prehistoric movie – *The Philadelphia Story* starring Cary Grant and Katharine Hepburn – before going to bed feeling mellow, relieved that Larry hadn't phoned, and that the saga of the partly eaten pie was over with and Hugh was in the clear.

He drove back to the farm and changed into shorts and T-shirt and a pair of old trainers, before going out to the barn with a spade and digging a hole in the earth. It was a three-foot-deep rectangle, just long enough to accommodate a body when the time came. At the moment it was no more than an excavation with a pile of dirt behind it, but would soon be a grave, with the earth shovelled back over a fresh corpse, and a deep covering of straw strewn across the barn floor to at least buy some time before it and the other remains were discovered.

In the garage, he started up the Jeep he'd stolen over a year ago. He had acquired it for just such an emergency. Forward planning was his forte. The vehicle was regularly serviced, by him, and he drove it around the farm every week or so, to ensure that it didn't seize up. He would now use it for a single one way trip that night, before dumping it. The engine purred, and after a couple of minutes he turned the ignition off, satisfied that it would not let him down.

After showering, he wrapped sandwiches in sheets of paper kitchen towel, poured milk into a splinter proof Perspex beaker, and headed for the cellar with them on a tray. The stone beneath his now bare feet was cool. He felt totally relaxed and in control. Now that he had formulated a plan, the idea of starting a new life was exhilarating. He had been in a rut and needed to spread his wings and start over.

She was where he knew she would be, on the bed, sitting with her legs drawn up, arms hugging her knees. He placed the food and milk on the coffee table, and then sat down on the edge of the bed next to her.

"Take your shorts off and kneel, Trish," he said. "I haven't got long, so this will have to be a quickie."

Trish obediently removed the shorts and presented her rear to him, gripping the iron rail of the headboard and clenching her teeth in readiness.

It was over with in seconds. He didn't hurt her, and seemed preoccupied. He left without saying another word.

It was much later when she drank the milk. She could not face the food; too nauseous and petrified by the look that he had given her before leaving the cellar. Instinct told her that her time was nearly up. He had become more detached, distant and thoughtful. To her way of thinking, his overall demeanour was a portent of doom. She had the impression that she was suddenly of no more interest to him; had become a liability or inconvenience. Intuition – that she was not about to ignore – told her that the next time he entered the cellar might well be to kill her. If she was going to make a move, then it would have to be then.

A few minutes later she heard the distant sound of a car start up, and waited until the engine noise had completely faded before setting to work assembling a makeshift weapon. She determined not to just acquiesce to whatever fate he had planned for her. She had suffered too much at his hands to just meekly allow him to slaughter her like an animal. Somewhere deep within her was an as yet unfound reserve of strength that was rising up, to aid her in what would be a last ditch effort to survive.

CHAPTER TWENTY-TWO

HE pulled the Jeep off the road, through a gap in the decaying split-wood stake fencing, cutting the lights as he manoeuvred the vehicle uphill and swung it into high bracken between the trunks of mature firs. After turning off the ignition, he lit a cheroot, happy to smoke in the stolen vehicle; a practise that was taboo in his sweet-smelling Mondeo. Only Laura had got away with lighting up inside it. Now, sitting in the darkness and listening to the tink of hot metal as the engine began to cool, he visualised his impending actions, mentally rehearsing what he regarded to be a delicate mission, that he would rather not have been forced into executing.

It was twelve-fifty a.m., and he was maybe five minutes on foot away from Laura's place. Moonlight filtered through thin cloud cover, giving him enough ambient light to pick his way through the forest to the solitary cottage. He was dressed in black from the Balaclava that he wore pulled down over his face, to the trainers on his feet.

Stopping at the edge of the tree line behind a fallen and rotted pine, he looked through the screen of evergreen foliage that separated him from the dark silhouette of Laura's retreat. He listened to the night, but heard nothing, save for the soft sigh of the breeze that whispered through the needled branches, and to the fast thud of his heart beating in his ears as the adrenaline level rose in anticipation of the deed he was about to carry out.

Sitting on the decaying tree trunk, he swung his legs over it and stopped again as his foot snapped a dry branch, resulting in a loud pistol-shot crack that echoed through the darkness. Shit! He waited awhile, and then moved on, a shadow among shadows, seeming to glide over the small lawn at the rear of the cottage to the kitchen door.

The window next to the door was open an inch, and the blade of his knife quickly slipped the antiquated arm loose from the metal post that was screwed to the wood frame securing it. Was Laura stupid? Being a cop, she should know better than to go to bed without locking everything. No one was safe in this day and age. Burglars were like vermin, skulking in the night, ever ready to take advantage of easy pickings. One had even broken into the

144

farmhouse eighteen months ago. The creak of a stair had roused him, and he had waited, standing behind the bedroom door, to let the intruder enter the room and shine a torch around it, before grasping the guy by the back of his overlong, greasy hair and jerking him backwards off his feet. Two hard blows from his fist had knocked the trespasser unconscious.

Ronnie Smithers had come to in the barn, naked and chained to the concrete block.

Hugh wasn't even angry. All's well that ends well. He spent over two hours with Ronnie; talked to the young man, to partly get to know the individual that he had decided to punish, after first confirming that he was working alone, and being told where he had parked his vehicle. He pointed out the error of Ronnie's ways, and explained that he was to be made an example of.

Before having his lips stapled together, Ronnie had cried a lot and begged to be released. But as Hugh had told him, you had to be prepared to face the consequences for your actions in life.

Ronnie's threshold to pain had proved to be very low. And the fear that he exuded in invisible waves was as tangible as the smell of his sour sweat and strong-smelling waste. He had passed out several times under the ministrations of the knife, before blood loss eventually sapped the life from him. Hugh had buried the partly flayed corpse in the barn, then driven the late Ronnie's beat-up old Cortina to a flooded sand pit and committed it to the murky depths, on the bottom of which all manner of discarded junk was rotting and rusting away. Hugh reasoned that crime would be dramatically reduced, if not wholly eradicated, if all wrongdoers were subjected to his harsh but effective form of justice. The law needed to get real and stop mollycoddling the shit of the Earth.

Enough reminiscing. He donned latex gloves and pulled the Balaclava back up to his forehead before easing himself up and through the open window, moving a vase of cut flowers farther along the sill before slipping over and dropping lightly to the vinyl-covered floor. It was an entry without any fear of the unexpected. He knew that Laura had no pets, and that she lived by herself. No Doberman was waiting, muscles bunched, its body quivering as it tensed to leap at him from the black wedges of shadow that filled the room. And no cat would trip him, or howl with pain as he inadvertently stood on its tail or a paw.

The cottage was silent, save for the hum of a fridge, and an old wood-cased clock, its resonant tick-tock calming, soothing; a measured cadence that lowered his heart rate.

He moved to the spiral staircase, the soles of his trainers noiseless on the iron treads as he ascended with all due care. He knew the layout well, having been inside on several occasions; the last time less than a month ago, to pick Laura up for duty when her car was off the road. He had once even stayed the night, and not even tried to get his leg over. She had been well-oiled, but he had too much respect for her to try it on. It would also have complicated their working relationship; a negative move, so he had kept the status quo. It had not been that he did not find her alluring. He did. She was a very attractive and intelligent woman. But sometimes it was prudent to keep business and pleasure completely separate from one another. He had known that there could be no future in getting involved romantically with Laura. Although it crossed his mind that being with someone like her may annul the need he felt to kill and kill again. To fall in love may dispel the systematic, deadly compulsion he had to punish his mother. But should he ever find someone with the qualities to effect a modification in his personality, it would not be Laura. He had seen how she looked at the Yank. There was history between them. He recognised that she still felt something for the man.

Pausing on the landing, he drew his knife and then moved unhurriedly to the open door of her bedroom.

The sudden loud trill of a telephone pierced the syrup-thick silence. He flattened himself to the wall, not breathing, heart racing again like a jackhammer. As she stirred, he slipped into the room. He had his night vision and could make out her shape. She was propped up on one elbow, holding the receiver and talking with the slur of sleep. He waited, and as she reached for the bedside lamp, her call finished, he moved to her and pressed the flat, cold side of the blade against her throat.

Laura couldn't breathe. Sudden shock and fear coursed through her entire body. She was paralysed, unable to move, her lungs and muscles cramping. She felt the sensation of her chest expanding to the point of bursting like an over inflated balloon.

She had become almost paralysed, and had to consciously force herself to take air in small snatches, her mouth opening and closing like that of a fish out of water. She wanted to jerk back from whatever was touching her skin, to kick out against the presence that she could now feel as a solid form in what should have been an empty space. Messages from her brain demanded that she act, but her body was less responsive than a frozen carcass hung in the frosty air of a butcher's walk-in cold room.

"Go on, boss, turn on the light, I won't bite," Hugh's disembodied voice said from the murk, so close that she could feel his warm breath on the rim of her ear.

It was funny how the mind reacted to unexpected intimidation. She was at once twelve again, sitting by herself in the local flea pit; the Gaumont. She had often gone to the cinema unaccompanied during school holidays, to enjoy the solitude and the awe-inspiring magic of the movie stars on the giant silver screen. As a youngster, going to the pictures and reading books were her chosen avenues of escape from the less than exciting reality of day-to-day life. She didn't just watch the films or read the books, but was absorbed by them; to almost become one of the fictional lead characters.

Sucked back through the years, Laura gazed at the giant, patched screen, engrossed and entranced by the much larger-than-life images and the booming soundtrack. She was unaware of the middle-aged man who had walked the full length of a row of seats that only she occupied, to sit next to her in the ill-lit stalls.

She had felt a slight tickle on her right leg, just below the hem of her pleated skirt, and had scratched absently, squirming a little on the maroon, velveteen seat covering. A few seconds passed, and the tickle was back, higher up, under the material on the inside of her thigh. Sudden comprehension of what was happening had frozen her solid. She could not move as trembling fingers stroked the front of her panties, and the heavy breathing of the man who was molesting her, quickened. A hot digit slid under the elastic and searched out her centre, and she had remained rigid, incapable of any action. While one clammy hand invaded her, the other took her hand and gently guided it to his lap, to place it on something warm, firm, smooth and...and sticky, like the paper glue she used to paste pictures of pop stars she had cut from magazines into her scrapbook. The shock-sensation of touching something unseen yet throbbing with life, gave her the jolt needed to break the spell. Pulling away, she half fell into the aisle, stumbled to the exit at the rear of the cinema, and broke free into the brightly lit foyer. Without once looking behind her, she had fled the theatre and run all the way home.

That singular experience at the Gaumont stole a part of her childhood, and left her with a dislike for cinemas that still persisted. She had not mentioned what had happened to anyone, feeling ashamed, as though she had in some way been partly to blame for the assault; not just the innocent victim of a paedophile. And now, all these years later, she was transfixed again, back in the dark stalls of the cinema, unable to speak and numb with fearful expectation. This was now only the second time in her life that she had found herself unable to react against someone who was intimidating her.

CHAPTER TWENTY-THREE

JIM'S eyes snapped open. He stared into the gloom with the face from his dream still vivid in his mind. He leapt from the bed, glancing at the glaring, green display on his alarm clock: 1:50 A.M. He ran through to the lounge, picked up the phone, tapped in Laura's number and listened impatiently to the ringing tone as he gathered his thoughts.

It had not just been a dream that had drawn him from the rim of troubled sleep. His mind had been sifting through and filing information, collating all the facts of the Tacker case and piecing them together as he dozed. The conclusion that his subconscious mind had woken him with was a numbing revelation: Hugh Parfitt, Laura's DS, was the killer.

Jim replayed his brief meeting with the young cop and remembered the stony, fleeting gaze that had quickly been masked by a bland expression; a mask coating the cop's face and softening the look in his piercing blue eyes.

It all fitted. Parfitt was the right height, right colouring, and had been in a prime inside position to have selected suspects in the area that Jim had targeted. He had no doubt that the detective had planted the rope in Cox's garage. Not only was he positive that it was a cop now, he *knew* which cop. Closing his eyes, he reran the encounter, flicking through every word that he had exchanged with Hugh in the York pub, pausing, freeze-framing each moment with near photographic memory. 'Once a cop, always a cop', Parfitt had said, before turning and walking off towards the bar. He had done something else; he had reached into his trouser pocket, presumably for cash. It had been his left-hand pocket, ergo, he was left-handed.

With no capacity to consider coincidence, Jim put it all together, and was certain that Detective Sergeant Hugh Parfitt was the serial killer whom they sought.

'Hi. I can't get to the phone at this moment, but please leave your name, number or a message after the tone and I'll call you back'. Laura's sultry, taped voice answered.

"Pick up, Laura, it's Jim," he said, then waited, to be answered by a beep and mind-numbing static, and so he left a message, "Phone me on my mobile number. It's urgent." He then rang her mobile.

No answer. He phoned the police station in York, to be advised that she was off duty.

He quickly dressed: Blue chambray shirt, beige chinos and crème loafers. Snatched up his car keys and holdall and left the flat on the run, to rocket down the six flights of stairs to the ground floor – too impatient to summon and wait for the lift – and out of the rear of the building to the car park. Less than fifteen minutes after waking he was on the road, ignoring speed limits, but keeping a watchful eye out for police patrol cars. His only concern was to reach Laura, knowing that if she managed to look beyond her close working relationship with Hugh and put it together, then she would be in mortal danger if she handled it wrong and put him on his guard.

By the time he reached the M1 he was wound too tight, almost on the edge of panic, his hands aching from the vicelike grip he had on the steering wheel. He fought to relax, turned on the radio for distraction and tuned into a night-caller style of programme, its fodder; the bitching of phone-ins from insomniacs, bored shift workers and borderline crazies, mixed with middle-of-the-road music to sustain them through till dawn. It was instantly forgettable fare of the kind which was vomited over the airways world-wide. People were people with the same hang-ups and problems, whatever the country or language. After thirty minutes of listening to the puerile remarks of the callers, he could understand from their comments why they were without love, hope or friendship. In his opinion, only sad bastards rang radio stations to bare their souls to total strangers. Unable to stomach any more, he changed station, running through the preset buttons and finally settling for Radio 4 and the World Service.

All being well, he expected to be at Laura's by five-thirty a.m., and was already anticipating hammering on her door and seeing her look out through the bedroom window, before rushing down to let him in, bleary-eyed, but hopefully pleasantly surprised. He was sure that once he could get her to think outside the box and view her sergeant with professional detachment, then she would have to agree that Hugh at least merited checking out. They would have to scrutinise his past, and turn over every stone. Should he be found to be whiter than white, then nothing would have been lost, though Jim expected a trail of pointers from his childhood that would expose his personality disorder and prove him to be the killer. He had glimpsed the alter ego behind the facade of normality; should have recognised the psycho who dwelt within the mind of Hugh Parfitt.

It should be easy to wrap up. Hugh would be unsuspecting and in the lion's den; apprehended in the police station as he pretended to investigate the crimes that he was guilty of committing. But nothing in life ever seemed to pan out as expected. Bitter experience told Jim that very few things went down as planned. The art was to try and be prepared for all possible connotations and complications; to appreciate that if it could go wrong, then as sure as night followed day, it would. The bonus in this case was that Parfitt was on the inside, feeling secure in the belief that he was in control, leading the team away from himself.

Jim slowed as the Cherokee's headlights bounced back at him from a hovering white wall of luminescence, and drove – eyes straining – for the next half hour at less than twenty miles an hour through low banks of fog that were sitting at irregular intervals across the six lanes of the motorway. It was as if it had been sent, a nefarious obstacle, to keep him at bay; a manifestation to show him from the outset that he was in danger of being thwarted in his mission.

Ceding to fatigue and conditions that could result in a multi-vehicle pileup Jim stopped at Woodall service area near Sheffield. His bladder was throbbing to be relieved, and he needed caffeine in the form of black coffee to give him a jolt and wake him up. The concentration of driving through the early morning summer fog had given him a headache, and threatened to lull him to sleep.

As he sat in the almost empty cafeteria, drinking expensive but low quality coffee, he tried Laura's number yet again, having already attempted to contact her four times as he had driven north. He slammed his Nokia onto the tabletop in frustration as her recorded message once more talked at him impersonally. A waitress and the few customers turned to stare at him. He glowered at each in turn until they looked away.

The coffee scalded his mouth and brought tears to his eyes as he drank it too fast, eager to set off on the last leg of his journey, now running late. It was still only four-forty-five, but fully light.

The fog had magically dispersed as he pulled back out onto the M1 and accelerated smoothly up to ninety. He was trembling with an unshakeable presentiment of doom, which manifested itself in what felt like cold fingers wrapped around and squeezing his intestines. It was the same gut-churning fear that overcame him every time he arrived at an airport terminal to catch a flight; a sickening, sinking, leg-weakening sensation that sapped his strength and reduced him to a quaking mound of Jell-O. He knew that the unexpected may be waiting for him; a sudden catastrophe that could not be reckoned on, and which he was powerless to deal with appropriately. A lot of what life threw at you was from out of left field, catching you completely by surprise and bowling you over like a ninepin.

Daydreaming as he drove, Jim journeyed back in time to relive an early experience of how a planned and professional operation could turn into a major-league fuck-up.

The incident now seemed a lifetime ago, but he could recall every heart-stopping second as if it had only taken place yesterday...

...As a rookie field agent back in Arizona, with brush cut hairstyle, brand new charcoal-grey suit, and full to bursting with pride and the need to prove himself, Jim had been on his first case; the junior member of a team that were approaching a remote timber-frame bungalow in the shadow of the Sauceda Mountains, halfway between Gila Bend and Ajo. They had parked the off-roaders well back, behind tumbles of time and wind-shaped sandstone over a hundred yards from the property, then donned Kevlar vests under the black jackets that were stencilled FBI in large white letters on the front and back. He had been armed with a pump-action Mossberg shotgun and a holstered Smith & Wesson 38 Special. They had moved carefully through the saguaro and rock-strewn landscape, to take up positions around the bleached, sagging building, that looked as though it would collapse under the next strong gust of hot, desert wind.

Jim was bathed in sweat by the time the snipers were in position and the stage was set to commence the operation. He was on a high, ready to follow orders and prove himself worthy of the shiny new bureau badge that was now his most treasured possession and seemed to burn against his ribs through the leather wallet it was seated in. He felt invulnerable; justice and might on his side. He was an agent of the Federal Bureau of Investigation, and the fidelity, bravery and integrity that the letters also stood for filled him with pride, and a false sense of security.

An attempted bank robbery at a First National location in Tucson had turned into a blood bath. Three raiders had disarmed the security guard and subsequently ordered him, the tellers and the sixteen customers present to lie face down on the floor. The bank guard was an ex-cop and carried a backup piece in an ankle holster. He had, stupidly, drawn it and managed to shoot one of the trio in the throat, and another in the leg, before the third opened fire with an AK-47, killing both him and a teenage boy who had unwittingly made the fatal mistake of lying next to him.

The two surviving would-be robbers aborted the raid and fled, taking a middle-aged female customer as hostage and quitting the scene in a stolen Chevy Tahoe.

The State Police had given chase, calling the bureau as a matter of course, due to the kidnap of the woman being a federal offence.

There must have been eighty cops gathered, waiting for the action as Agent In Charge, Curtis Baur stood and faced the bungalow, a bullhorn to his mouth, about to start the negotiation procedure.

It had been then that reality in all its sudden inequitable, unforgiving and indiscriminate purposelessness hit Jim with the force of an eighteen-wheeler.

A bullet ploughed through the AIC's forehead, causing a strangled, amplified grunt to be emitted from the hand-held speaker. A baseball-sized hole opened up in the back of the agent's head, and Jim – who had been knelt behind Curtis – fell back on his ass as a spout of blood and steaming brains covered him, followed by the full weight of the twitching but already dead body of the late negotiator. All professionalism died with Curtis Baur. A deafening staccato of return fire split the arid air, peppering the house, shattering the windows and reducing the one-storey building to match wood. With no concern for the plight of the hostage, just a bloodlust and determination to exact swift retribution, the gathering of law enforcement officers expended enough ammunition to decimate the population of a small town.

After what seemed an eternity, the firing ceased. No one moved, and for long seconds the only sound came from the groaning of splintered timbers, which were losing their battle to hold up the cedar-shingled roof.

As they stood transfixed, the remains of the door swung open. One of the kidnappers appeared, hands held high, waving to show that he was unarmed. He walked forward hesitantly, out into the bright sun with his eyes narrowed to slits, squinting against the dazzling light.

Jim pushed the corpse of the team commander off him and rose to his knees, just in time to see the execution of the now defenceless felon. A hail of bullets caused the less than able robber to dance like a marionette in the control of a demented puppeteer. Bright red florets blossomed from his shirt and pants as hot lead crashed into his body, turning him into a bloody rag doll; spinning him, driving him back into the doorway that he had just exited from.

They moved in, fingers on triggers, ready to open fire again at the least sign of movement. In the bungalow's living room, among the bullet-riddled furniture and fittings, the two fugitives lay side by side, staring blankly at the ceiling, no longer a threat to anyone. The hostage was in the bedroom, curled up on a mattress as though asleep, with a single bullet hole in her temple, which would later – thank Christ! – be found to be from one of the killer's guns. The paperwork that was subsequently cooked up between the state and bureau somehow made the foul-up look more like the taking of Iwo Jima, and Jim had quickly come to terms with the reality that however well-trained and prepared, anything could and did happen. The best laid plans of mice and men, and especially men, when adversity and guns were involved, often turned to shit when human nature in all its unpredictability was involved.

The reverie, though depressing, had helped eat up the miles. Jim cut the engine and stepped out, his butt numb and neck aching. The first thing he noticed was that Laura's car was missing from its usual spot at the front of the cottage.

He rushed to the front door. It was locked, and his knocking, shouting, and even the throwing of gravel up at her bedroom window brought no response. He ran around to the back and found the kitchen door also locked, but the window next to it open. A damp chill pervaded him, as though embalming fluid had been injected into a vein, to be circulated through every part of his being by a labouring heart that was now full of icy liquid dispelling his blood.

Not bothering to go and retrieve the spare door key from the garage, Jim climbed through the window, noticing that the sill was clear, and suspecting that the large vase of flowers farther along it had been moved to allow prior unrestricted access. Lowering himself to the floor, he slipped off his loafers and quickly made his way through to the living room, his awareness to the surroundings heightened as he tried to ready himself for any eventuality. Silently, he wound his way up the metal steps. The house felt empty, but he was on guard, tensed for a sudden attack, his muscles as tightly coiled as the spiral staircase. In the bedroom, he found no clues. Laura just wasn't there, though the bed had been slept in. The pillow was dimpled from where her head had lain on it, and the ruffled sheet had been thrown back. There seemed nothing untoward. Perhaps she was at work now. He checked the other small bedroom and the bathroom, before going back downstairs and finding a note on the coffee table, its corner pinned down by a heavy onyx ashtray. He read it twice, studied each word, and came to the sickening conclusion that Laura was in the hands of the killer.

A further meticulous search of the cottage confirmed his worst fears. On the jamb of her bedroom door was a small smear of blood, almost dry, not yet set hard to the gloss paint; still bright and easy to rub off on to the ball of his thumb. He went back to the bed and found a single red blot that appeared almost black against the background of the plum-coloured pillowcase. If not specifically searching for it, he would have – as he had on first inspection – missed it. Back downstairs he read the note again: Jim, I've had enough. I'm sorry, but I need time out from the job and everything else. I thought getting away from London would be the answer. But you can't run away from yourself. I still haven't come to terms with Karah's death. And this case with teenage victims has got to me. Please don't try to find me. I need to work things out. I'll give you a call when I get it back together.

It was definitely Laura's handwriting, but Jim knew that she had been taken from the cottage against her will. However messed up her mind was she wouldn't – even under dire stress – have misspelled Kara's name. The addition of an H was her message to him, telling him that the note was bogus. Also, though maybe not intentional, the extra letter was significant; H, for Hugh. He pocketed the piece of paper and went back through to the kitchen for his shoes, and then made for the front door, opening it as the phone began to ring. He rushed back to answer it before the machine kicked in.

"Hello," he said.

"Hi. Is Laura there?"

"Who's calling?"

"Larry."

"Larry who?"

"Larry Hannigan. Odontology. Who am I speaking to?"

"Jim Elliott. I'm a close friend of Laura's."

"Well, er, Jim Elliott. I need to know that she's okay."

"I don't think she is okay, Larry. I just got here and she's missing. Why are you so concerned at this time in the morning?"

"I rang her with some results, just a few hours ago, and the more I thought about the implications, the more worried I got. My karma's fucked up, and I think she's in danger."

"I need to know all you know, Larry. What results are you talking about?"

"Sorry, pal, no can do. I don't know you from Adam. I'm going to ring her department."

"Larry, whatever you do, do *not* ring the police. It's a cop that's involved in this. You could get her killed if you talk to the wrong person."

"Give me one half decent reason why I should believe you."

"Because I've got no reason to lie to you. I needn't have answered the phone, or told you that she was missing. I need help, Larry, or Laura might not make it."

There was a long pause. "I'll buy that for now. Call in at the lab within an hour and convince me that I should trust you," Larry said before giving him the address and disconnecting.

Jim left the cottage and headed for the city, the bunching muscles in his cheeks being the only outward sign of his agitation.

The small office he was ushered into was a world apart from the white, sterile looking laboratory he had passed through. The room was a scruffy den, pure sixties. The Dell pc on the paper-laden desktop clashed with garret-like surroundings that reflected Larry's appearance and demeanour.

"I met Dylan in D.C., back in '93 at Clinton's inauguration 'do' at the Lincoln Memorial," Jim said as he stared at the giant poster of Larry's folk hero, which held pride of place, tacked to the wall above the desk. "He seemed a cool dude. I remember he sang 'Chimes of Freedom'."

Larry was impressed. His raised eyebrows and rapid blinking said so. "So, er, Jim, just who the hell exactly are you? And what's happened to Laura?" he asked, pouring them both black coffee from a machine that could have been – and in fact was – a model manufactured in the 'Swinging Sixties'.

"I'm an ex-FBI profiler, Larry. I knew Laura in London when she was with the Met. After her daughter died, I helped her get past it, and we got tight. She needed to move away, and I didn't want to live with her and the force. Anyway, she contacted me over this Tacker case and asked if I would give a few pointers. The bottom line is, that I've got it narrowed down to a list of one; a cop on her team. I arranged to be at her place today, and arrived early. When I got there she was gone. I found traces of blood and this phoney note," he said, withdrawing the folded sheet of paper from his shirt pocket and handing it to the technician.

"This is bullshit, Jim," Larry said, reading it and passing it back. "She was up, on top of this. Christ, man, I was talking to her on the phone at one a.m. She wouldn't have just taken off."

"I know that. Help me on this, Larry. It could save her life."

"She came to see me yesterday, late afternoon, with a fresh, partly eaten pork pie, and asked me to do an 'off the record' bite comparison with the two victims who'd had their nipples bitten off. I got a positive match and phoned her. She told me to treat it as evidence and do the necessary paperwork. I rang back because I couldn't get it out of my head that she must have been with the killer yesterday, probably eating with him at lunchtime. I had bad vibes."

"I know who he is, Larry" Jim said. "He must have realised that Laura was on to him, and abducted her. I don't want him panicked. He may have already killed her, but if he hasn't, I need for him to feel safe until I can locate her."

Jim fell silent, looking down into the dregs of coffee in the old Greenpeace mug. He had voiced his fear that Laura might already be dead, and in saying it, had made it seem more of a probability than a possibility. And he didn't know if he could deal with that, if it turned out to be true.

"Larry," he said after gathering his thoughts. "I don't want you to do anything till I get Laura back. Can you trust me and believe that I'm her only chance?"

"You really love her," Larry stated.

"You'd better believe it."

"Keep me posted, will you? She's a special lady."

"You got it, Larry. Thanks."

CHAPTER TWENTY-FOUR

LAURA reached out slowly, found and pressed the light switch and half-closed her eyes against the sudden glare. Hugh was withdrawing a long-bladed knife from the side of her neck, smiling cheerfully as he sat down on the bed next to her.

"What the fuck are you doing, Hugh? Why are you here?" Laura said, trying to feign ignorance, and simultaneously cope with the genuine shock and astonishment of what had transpired during the last few seconds.

Hugh's smile vanished. "Nice try, boss. But it's too late to act dumb. Thanks to your colonial friend coming up with a pretty good description, and putting it into your head that the Tacker was a copper, I've had to think up a whole new game plan. You suddenly put two and two together at lunchtime in the pub. Why?"

"It just fell into place," Laura said, dropping all pretence. "Jim thought it had to be someone on the case. I hoped it wasn't you, even when I saw that you were left-handed. Funny, I'd never really noticed that before. The phone call I just got sealed it."

"Who were you talking to?"

"The lab. They did a comparison for me, and your teeth marks were identical to the killer's, which means that you're the maniac who gets off on killing young defenceless girls."

"Careful, Laura. Push me and it can end right here and now. Where did you get my teeth marks from?"

"The pie you only ate half of in the pub."

"So that's what you went back for?"

"That's right, Hugh. It's over."

"It isn't over till it's over, Laura. I'm betting that you were waiting to see if it *was* a match before you told anyone else. That means I'm still in the clear."

"So what are you going to do, Hugh, kill me?"

"I hope not. I may not have to if you don't try to do anything stupid. I need you out of the way though, under wraps until I get organised. But if you fuck with me...well, you know what I'm capable of. You've seen enough of my work."

It didn't make any sense to her. "Why, Hugh? You're a good copper. Why did you murder all those girls?"

"You don't need to ask. Elliott had all the answers. He's too smart for his own good. I think I'll kill him for fucking up my life and forcing me to have to start over. What I do to them is personal. I'm a liberated man, and what I do has nothing to do with anybody but me and my whore of a mother. She has to pay."

"I thought that your parents lived down south, Hugh?"

"You were meant to. I watched my father die under a tractor, and spat on his dead face. Later, I fixed my mother and her fancy man. The flat and the photos are just a front. Edgar fucking Hoover Elliott was right again. I own a farm in the area that he pointed us at."

"But if—"

"That's it, Laura. No more talking. I've got a lot to do. Let's go."

With the point of the knife's blade pricking the skin of her neck, drawing blood, Laura got up from the bed and allowed herself to be guided to the door, where Hugh stopped her with a hand on the shoulder.

"Remember, Laura, if you try to run or make any heroic moves, I'll cut your pretty head off and leave it on a plate in the fridge for lover boy to find."

She put a hand up to her neck, felt a bead of blood, and then lowered her arm back down to her side. "I'm not going to give you any reason to hurt me, Hugh," she said, furtively wiping her finger on the door jamb as he urged her forward and down the stairs to the living room.

He dictated the note, and she wrote it word for word. He had known that her daughter had died in tragic circumstances; even knew her name. But he did not how it was spelt.

Laura had no warning of the blow. As she finished writing, her head lit up with a starburst of light and she was instantly dead to the world. His fist, clenched around the worn, wooden handle of the knife, had flicked out with the speed of a cobra's tongue, catching her skull behind the ear, hard, jarring her brain into unconsciousness.

As her head snapped sideways and she began to topple from the chair, he gathered her in his arms and lowered her onto the carpeted floor, face down. Pulled a reel of duct tape from a pocket and quickly secured her wrists behind her back and her ankles together, and finally covered her mouth. He was gentle, even pulling her Disney night-shirt down over her thighs, aroused by the sight of her bare buttocks, but covering them out of long-standing high regard for the woman who was now his defenceless captive. Taking the car keys from her shoulder bag, he scooped her up and draped her over his shoulder like a rolled-up rug, then carried her outside and carefully placed her in the boot of the small Fiat, ensuring that she was on her side, even taking the time to retrieve a throw from the rear seat to fold and place under her head.

Back inside the cottage, Hugh set the scene, filling a holdall with a selection of clothes from the bedroom drawers, and taking essential toiletries from the bathroom. He then returned downstairs and left the note on the coffee table, its corner pinned by a large ashtray, and left.

Driving Laura's Fiat back past where he had dumped the expendable Jeep, he lit a cheroot and thumbed the cassette that jutted from the stereo into the slot. It was Sinatra; Laura had taste. He played it loud enough so that she would be able to hear it in the boot, should she have regained consciousness. He even sang along with 'Old Blue Eyes'; a splendidly out of tune rendition of *My Way*, sung his way.

Trish sat on the bed and concentrated, examining every item available to her as she deliberated and eventually formulated a plan that might save her life. The sick copper would get more than he bargained for when he next ventured down into the cellar. She had no intention of making it easy for him; was not the cowed, pathetic prisoner that he supposed her to be. Her readily submitting to his every demand had been out of fear, and now that same fear was motivating her to fight for life and freedom. He did not seem to realise that if she had nothing to lose then, like a cornered, frightened animal, she would expend her last ounce of energy on defending herself.

Removing the books and magazines from the coffee table and turning it onto its side, Trish brought the sole of her foot down onto one of the two legs that were now eighteen inches from the floor, stuck out horizontally like the stiffened legs of a dead sheep. The effort caused her to cry out in pain as the unyielding timber bruised her bare foot. After massaging her sole, she placed open magazines over the leg as padding, stood on the bed and jumped down with her feet together and knees flexed. The leg sheared off with a sharp crack as the dovetailed and glued joint snapped, causing her to fall awkwardly over the table, her left side connecting with the raised edge as she put her outstretched arms out in front of her to save her head from hitting the concrete. Screaming against the pain, she slid down into a sitting position and held her side, moaning as every shallow breath caused sharp, stabbing pains, convincing her that she had cracked or fractured one or two ribs.

After waiting for the agony to subside to a dull ache, she examined the now detached table leg. It was a heavy length of hardwood that tapered to a diameter that she could hold comfortably in her hand. She now had a weapon; a club, but doubted that she would be able to use it against him effectively in her weakened state.

Necessity truly being the mother of invention, she turned her attention to the small portable loo. It was constructed from a hard plastic material, and gave her an idea.

Using both hands, she lifted up the foul-smelling container, her stomach heaving at the stench of her own waste, that mixed with the disinfectant liquid was a potent brew that almost made her vomit. She breathed through her mouth, hefted the loo up to the edge of the sink and emptied the concoction, gagging as the liquid slowly seeped away to leave a clotted layer of faeces, that even the running water from the tap would not clear. She rinsed out the receptacle and then swung it with all her might against the corner of the wall, where it rebated into the stairwell, to turn her head to the side as it shattered and left her holding the handle. The loo disintegrated and was reduced to an array of blue shards that flew off in every direction, to land on the cellar floor and the top of the bed.

"Yes...Yesss!" Trish cried out in triumph, hugging herself and grimacing as her ribs complained at the physical exertion.

Crawling around the floor and gathering the pieces into a pile, she inspected the various sized fragments of plastic. Finally, she selected and picked up a twelve-inch long spearhead-shaped shard and pressed it against her palm, laughing as it pierced her skin with the sharpness of broken glass.

An hour later, Trish was as ready as she ever would be. The coffee table was again upright, standing like a three-legged dog, with the books and magazines back on its top. She had put the end with the missing leg farthest from the stairwell, and then gone over to the bottom step to look back and survey her work, content that without close inspection, nothing seemed untoward. She then gathered up all the other pieces of the loo and placed them in a heap in the corner to the left of the steps, out of direct line of sight from anyone entering the underground room. Sitting on the bed, she examined her work. The table leg she had broken off was now no longer a cudgel, but a shaft. The pointed plastic shard was a blade, bound tightly to the wood with strips of bed sheet.

Timing would be critical. She rehearsed the scene over and over in her mind, 'seeing' Parfitt walking down the stairs with a tray or plate in one hand, and a drink in the other. He was arrogant, too sure of himself, and that was in her favour. He could not now imagine her as a threat. In his eyes she was just a weak and compliant plaything with no will left; reduced to a cringing and pitiful creature that relied on him and feared him. Making a move against him would be the last thing he would expect her to do, with the threat of pain, or worse, to be returned to the rat-infested barn and shackled to the cement block. As he leant forward to place whatever he was carrying on to the tabletop, she would lunge forward with the spear that she had fashioned. In one smooth movement she would bring it from concealment at her side and drive it into his face, throat or chest, then leap over the end of the bed, race up the steps and throw the door shut behind her and bolt it, to trap him wounded, dying or dead in his own stinking cellar.

She shook in a state of mingled fear and excitement at the thought of being free, daring to contemplate success, and already picturing herself phoning the police as the Tacker beat his fists against the door and screamed obscenities at her. If this didn't prove to be a career-enhancing opportunity, then nothing ever would be. Christ, she could write a book of her nightmare ordeal as his prisoner: the true story of how after suffering at the maniac's hands, she had finally not only escaped his clutches, but ensnared or killed him. It would be serialised by a tabloid, without doubt be at the top of the best seller list, and would in all likelihood be made into a movie. There would be a very lucrative upside to recompense her for the near-death experience, and rightly so.

The element of surprise would be on her side. She played the scene over and over again, even practising the move that would save her life, repeatedly bringing up the spear from her side and thrusting it – like a quick draw gunslinger – to where she expected him to be. Her hatred for the demented copper who had tricked her, abducted her, and used her so repeatedly and violently, gave her the strength and the resolve to do whatever was necessary to live to tell the tale.

He parked the car in the barn, remained seated and listened to Sinatra finish up singing *The Lady is a Tramp*, before ejecting the cassette and pocketing it. He then left Laura in the boot and walked across to the house. There was still a lot that had to be done before the night was through. No rest for the wicked. Ha!

Once ready, with a claw-hammer secreted under a tea towel on the unit top behind the kitchen table, he went upstairs and changed back into the shorts and T-shirt. He planned to bring Trish up from the cellar, allow her to sit at the table in the belief that he was going to make her a hot drink and allow her to shower, and then kill her with one devastating blow to the skull with the hammer. He would immediately put a bin liner over her head and tape it around her neck. What little blood escaped would quickly mop up. It should all be over in a few seconds, and he would then bury her in the shallow grave and transfer Laura to the cellar. He did not intend for Trish to suffer unduly, or even for her to be aware that it was time for her to check out. He bore her no ill-will. She had just outlived her usefulness; had become excess to requirements.

The sound of the bolts being drawn back caused Trish to whimper with fear at the overwhelming significance of what the next few seconds held. She was under no illusion and firmly believed that this was truly a life or death situation. She sat at the head of the bed, legs stretched out in front of her, and the weapon – that seemed so puny now – at the side of her leg, with the blanket bunched up to help conceal it.

His feet, bare legs, shorts, upper body, and finally his head and shoulders came into view as he descended the steps and smiled at her.

Her heart tripped, skipped, and felt as though it was being crushed in the grip of an iron fist. He had stopped three feet from the foot of the bed, and had nothing in his hands. Trish stared at him, horrified, her plan evaporating. The rehearsals had been a waste of time. For ome reason he was not going to come within striking distance. Panic seemed to drain her mind of all ability to think, and her limbs were rigid, muscles locked. The smile on his face had transmuted to become a look of disgust as his eyes narrowed and his lips drew back and twisted in a scowl.

"Jesus, it stinks down here. Have you just been?" he asked, taking another step forward before turning his head towards the sink and seeing the blue-brown swamp in the sink, and immediately knowing that the malodorous stench emanated from the pungent, heady mix of excreta and disinfectant. He then saw the broken remains of the loo: the pieces of plastic gathered together in a small heap, as if it were kindling ready to be lit. For just a second he was dumbfounded and could not understand why she had done it. What the fuck was the stupid bitch hoping to gain by smashing her toilet to bits?

A blur of movement in his peripheral vision jerked his attention back to the bed.

Trish knew it was now or never. She hurled herself forward towards him like a coiled spring, thrusting the short spear out straight-armed in front of her; a guttural scream of combined terror and rage escaping her lips as she leapt catlike into mid-air.

He twisted and pulled back to avoid her, but felt a searing flash of pain in his side. Falling to his knees, he realised that she had a weapon, had stabbed him, and that if he had been a fraction of a second slower he would have been skewered through the stomach. He gasped as she withdrew the hand-held spear, and threw himself sideways as she struck out again, to roll across the cellar floor, cursing as another stinging slash opened his cheek to the bone.

Trish hesitated. She had stabbed him once, felt the plastic point enter him, and watched as he folded to his knees. She pulled it free, and saw the resulting outpouring of blood seeping through his cotton T-shirt, resembling a spreading wine stain on a tablecloth. She tried to take advantage, lunged again, jabbing at his face. And as he rolled away from her she took her chance, dropped the weapon that had served her so well and dashed up the stairs to the open door and freedom.

Bad timing. Had she kept up the onslaught and continued to stab him as he lay on the floor, momentarily helpless, then she could have killed him and been done with the whole sorry business. But her second of hesitation and subsequent decision to flee proved to be a monumental mistake.

He was fast. Knew that if she had the composure to pause and close and lock the cellar door on him, then he was finished. As he raced up the stairs, she was already swinging the door to. It shut with a heavy thud.

Trish fumbled the top bolt, hand shaking as her brain screamed directions to it, willing it to grasp the head of the bolt and slide it smoothly into place. At last her trembling fingers found it and...

...He hit the inside of the door with his shoulder as he heard the bolt scrape across the metal surface. The iron finger slid into thin air, and he careered out into the kitchen.

Trish stepped to the side, turned and made to run, but he grabbed a handful of her hair and dragged her backwards. She twisted, wild-eyed, with her mouth darting at his face, jaws snapping, attempting to bite him.

Hugh reacted. Swung her against the kitchen wall, once...twice...three times, before letting go and walking over to where he had secreted the hammer, as she slid down to the floor, leaving a swathe of blood from her split forehead in her wake on the faded wallpaper.

Trish was conscious, but could not find the strength to move. She was knelt, head hung between her shoulders as if in prayer, knowing that she had lost the battle for life and was about to die. She felt nothing, was dazed, consumed by a weariness that overcame her, robbing her of all resolution, to infuse her with a strange acceptance while awaiting her fate: a condemned prisoner acceding to the inevitable, climbing the steps to the gallows almost willingly, having come to terms with what was unavoidable.

The gleaming hammer arced down on to the crown of her head, and the round barrel of steel split her scalp open to punch a hole through her skull and plug into the underlying brain tissue.

Trish felt a stabbing, piercing pain, and was at once paralysed and struck blind, although still aware. She could hear a loud whining, stammering sound, but had no idea that it was an emission from her own mouth. She was jerked back as the tool was wrenched free from her skull, and having been rendered sightless, was spared seeing the glistening hammerhead as it scythed into her forehead and terminated all perception of being.

Standing back, Hugh dropped the hammer and placed his hands on his knees, gasping for breath as he watched the blood pool out onto the cracked and worn linoleum.

What a fucking mess! He would need more than a bin bag now. She was still convulsing, thrashing about like an epileptic, and the sight was riveting; one he thought would have been enhanced by a suitable backing track of upbeat dance music.

It took him over an hour to clean up. He wrapped the body in a plastic dust sheet, took it out to the barn and buried it as planned, then returned to the house and using a mop, cloths and a bucket of hot water he went to work in first the kitchen and then the cellar, removing every trace of body fluids, and even clearing the blocked sink, breathing through his mouth as he poured a full bottle of pine-scented disinfectant down the plug hole. Back upstairs he examined the ingenious weapon that the sneaky bitch had fashioned. He couldn't help but admire her effort. Had he been a fraction of a second slower, she would have probably killed him with it. He threw it outside the back door, along with the other pieces of what had been the Chemiloo, to join his blood-sodden T-shirt and shorts. He determined to bag the lot up and dump it when time allowed.

In the bathroom he showered and inspected his injuries. The sharp plastic had gone through his side. It was painful, but only a flesh wound. No big deal. He stepped out of the shower, dried off and then poured TCP antiseptic into the jagged gash and used a full roll of bandage to wrap tightly around his waist. The cut to his face merited a few stitches, but a large Band-Aid would have to suffice. He dressed in fresh T-shirt, jeans and trainers, and went to get Laura; his last task of this long, eventful night.

Laying Laura on the bed in the cellar, he removed the tape from her mouth and held the knife in front of her face.

"Listen very carefully, boss, I've had a long day," he said. "And believe it or not I'm going to work later, so I need some shuteye. There's a jug of water and some biscuits and fruit on the table next to you. Plan on making it last for about twelve hours. I'm afraid there's no toilet down here, just a bucket in the corner. If you behave, you'll be free by this time tomorrow. Once I'm well away from the area, I'll phone the station and tell them where you are."

"Why should I believe you?" Laura said, wincing as her swollen jaw complained.

"Because if I'd wanted to kill you, you'd already be dead."

"You must know that you'll never get away with this, Hugh."

"Save the lecture, boss. Remember, I'm a cop, like you. And if you've any sense, you'll pack the job in. You don't really make a difference. Shit has always happened, and always will. You're just an aspirin trying to treat a cancer."

He cut the tape from her wrists and ankles, and then walked towards the steps.

"Hugh," Laura called after him.

"Yeah, boss?" he answered, pausing and half turning.

"Why the staples, and...and all the other mutilation?"

"Because she deserves it," he said. "She's a whore...a fucking slut. She has to pay."

"Who is, Hugh? Who deserves it? Who has to pay?"

His eyes clouded and became unfocused with a thousand yard stare. His face went slack, and his mouth dropped open. A muscle began to twitch in his right cheek, drawing his top lip up in an unwitting impersonation of Elvis Presley. For just a moment, Hugh had left the building.

"Mummy," he murmured absently. "Mummy has to pay. She has to keep being punished for what she did to me."

A Hugh Parfitt that Laura did *not* know once more showed her his back, and trudged heavy-footed up the stone steps. As the door thudded into place above her, and the bolts snapped across, she could hear sobs. He was actually crying.

CHAPTER TWENTY-FIVE

JIM knocked at the door, took a step back and waited. It was six-forty-five a.m. He had been given Parfitt's address by Clem Nash, who'd been on duty when Jim called in at police headquarters. Clem had been introduced to him by Laura on his previous visit, and the young DC gave up his colleague's address with little reluctance, although he wondered why the American couldn't wait, pointing out that Hugh would be in at eight o' clock.

"He's away on holiday," a harsh voice called out as Jim once more rapped on the door with his knuckles. He turned and was faced by an elderly woman. She was standing at the partly open door of the next flat, her blue-rinsed hair in rollers, and a large ginger cat gripped to her matronly breasts, claws tearing at the quilted housecoat she wore as it tried to escape her grasp.

"I said, Mr Parfitt is away, young man. He won't be back for a fortnight."

"When did you last see him?" Jim asked, not moving towards the old woman, sure that she would shut the door in his face if he approached her.

"Teatime, yesterday. And who might be asking?"

"I'm a friend, Jim Elliott. I'm up from London on business and just called on the off chance that Hugh might be in."

"American, are you?" she said with a derisive edge to her voice, before coughing wetly to clear lungs that were as smoked as kippers, due to sixty years of being addicted to unfiltered cigarettes.

"That's right," Jim said, forcing a smile to cover his mild revulsion at the liquid sound of phlegm being brought up and then swallowed. "Do you know Hugh well?"

"No. He keeps pretty much to himself. In fact he's hardly here at all. Just drops by to collect his mail. He very rarely stays over."

"Do you happen to know where he's gone?"

"As a matter of fact, yes, I do. Florida. Is that where you hail from?"

"Er, no, I was born and raised in Arizona, Mrs..."

"Harriman...Nancy Harriman."

"Well, thanks for your help, Mrs Harriman. I'll give him a call when he gets back."

"You'd have more chance writing. Do you want me to give him a message?"

"No need, it's nothing urgent," Jim said, walking past her towards the stairs, stifling a chuckle as the displeased cat finally wrenched free from her liver-spotted hands, scrambled over her shoulder and went down her back, growling as it leapt to the floor at a dead run and vanished along the hallway.

"Now look what you've done! You've frightened poor Marmalade," Nancy shouted after him, before slamming her door shut.

Jim found a small back street café adjacent to the River Ouse, ordered black coffee and asked to borrow the establishment's copy of the Yellow Pages. The sallow-faced Italian waiter seemed disturbed at being asked for something that was not on the menu, and could not therefore be charged for, but returned with the bulky directory and placed it before Jim as though it were a tagliatelle or spaghetti dish, before retreating to the rear of the cafe. Thumbing through the grimy, out of date tome, Jim found the section he needed, but was faced with little choice. There were very few private investigators in the York area. He plumped for one situated nearby which was advertised as being a specialist in missing persons, or traces as Jim called them.

It was a one man outfit with a seedy office located over an antiquarian book shop on Micklegate. Threadbare carpet led up a narrow stairwell onto an equally narrow landing. The black lettering on the cracked, frosted glass panel of the solitary door read, Talbot Investigations. Jim could imagine the interior of the office to be a 'Mike Hammer' scene of worn furnishings; a picture of hand to mouth existence bordering on insolvency.

"Yeah, come on in, it's open," a stony voice called out after Jim had tapped lightly on the glass.

The office was almost exactly as Jim had envisaged it would be; dowdy and functional, but not what he would deem inspiring to any prospective client. The PI – who in the book was advertised as being an ex-police Detective Inspector with over thirty years experience – was pouring boiling water into a mug.

"You're an early bird," Leo Talbot said, giving Jim what appeared to be a cursory glance, but which Jim recognised as being a professional once over that took in more than the average person would see in a month. "Coffee?"

Jim nodded. "Black, no sugar."

"Take a seat and tell me what you need doing that you can't handle yourself," Leo said, dropping a sweetener into his own stained mug and stirring the brew vigorously.

Jim immediately felt that he had made a good choice. The guy had an aura of hard-assed capability. He was mid-fifties, with short, steel-grey hair and a checkerboard-lined face that was testament to a wealth of experience and a lifetime of incident. He was bulky, maybe five-ten, but looked strong and able. His eyes were sharp and clear, studying Jim as he placed the steaming mugs on the cluttered desktop. Jim had the unsettling feeling that his life had been read like an open book by the down-at-heel-looking ex-cop. As the PI sat and stared across at him with raised eyebrows, waiting to be given details, Jim couldn't help but notice his striking resemblance to the late American actor, Richard Boone, who had, among many parts, starred as Paladin in the old TV western series *Have Gun Will Travel*. His laconic, laid-back attitude and even the husky voice reinforced the illusion. It was only the Yorkshire accent that broke the spell.

"I need background on a serving cop. Everything you can dig up, and then some. And I need it yesterday. Can you do that for me?" Jim said.

"Yank, eh?" Leo said, turning away from a dusty, dented and squeaking desk fan – blades sluggishly cutting through the warm air – and sheltering the flame of his lighter from it as he fired up a cigarette, prior to reaching for a pencil and notepad.

"Yeah, but I'll be paying up front in sterling, not bucks."

"As an ex-copper myself, I'd need a good reason to start digging around in a serving officer's life? Is he in trouble?"

"This cop *is* trouble. I haven't time to feed you crap. His name is Hugh Parfitt, a local DS. And there's every possibility that he's a serial killer who has at least one woman stashed away in the York area. We're talking about life or death here, with no bullshit exaggeration."

"What's your involvement?" Leo said, talking through a haze of cigarette smoke that the crippled fan was having trouble dispersing.

Jim gave the PI a thumbnail sketch of the case, of his connection, and of his fear for Laura's life.

"Fuck me!" Leo said. "This would make a good movie; retired FBI profiler helping to nail a serial killer in the UK."

"So you'll join the cast, uh?"

"Yeah. Give me a bell in about an hour, and I should have some basic details on Parfitt."

Jim took five twenty pound notes from his wallet and handed them across the desk. "Will that hold you till I can get to an ATM?"

"No sweat. We'll worry about fees when the lady... or ladies are safe."

Jim shook the gumshoe's hand and left, already feeling better for having Leo Talbot on the case.

Parking the Cherokee in an official slot outside the police station, Jim went in and asked the cop at the counter if he could speak to Clem Nash.

Clem came through to the foyer, a worried man with a frown on his flushed face. "Over there," he said, pointing towards a green vinyl-covered bench seat that ran the length of the rear wall. "You'd better tell me what the hell is going on, Mr Elliott?"

They sat out of earshot of the uniformed sergeant and WPC who were manning the front desk. "Hugh is upstairs," Clem said. And he seemed less than happy when I told him that you were looking for him."

"Clem, listen to me for sixty seconds with an open mind," Jim said. "The Tacker is a cop, and the cop is Parfitt. He's abducted Laura. I have no solid proof, yet, but it's him for sure. Will you work with me on this?"

Clem was speechless. He replayed what the Yank had said, running it through his mind and evaluating the implications of what he had just been told. He had little time for Parfitt; thought that he was a smug bastard, but found it impossible to imagine Hugh as a psycho serial killer.

"Convince me," he said to Jim after a long pause. "Give me something to stop me thinking that you're dealing with a short deck."

"Okay," Jim began; knowing that how he sold this to the young cop could prove critical in saving Laura's life – if she was still alive – and nailing Parfitt. "Only a cop could have known to plant that rope on a likely suspect in the area that was targeted. And it was Hugh that came up with Cox...so he did it. Also, Laura got Larry Hannigan over in odontology to do a comparison between teeth impressions in a partly eaten pork pie that she had got somewhere yesterday when she went to lunch, and the bite marks on two of the dead girls. They were a match, so—"

"Holy shit!" Clem said. "The boss went for a pub lunch with Hugh yesterday."

Jim looked on as an expression of stunned amazement settled into one of growing acceptance on the DC's face. He said nothing more, just waited for Clem to assimilate what he had been told.

After a long pause. "What do you want me to do?" Clem said.

"Nothing yet, I don't want him spooked. If he thinks that we're on to him, then we might never see Laura again. I want him to feel snug as a bug in a rug. I need to see him, and convince him that he's not under suspicion."

Clem waved to the desk sergeant, who hit the button that unlocked the door to allow them through into the station proper. Upstairs in the squad room, Hugh was busily wading through computer printouts. Jim noted the dark smudges under his eyes, which contrasted sharply with his paler than usual complexion. He also wondered what had caused the need for the large plaster taped to his cheek.

"Jim," Hugh said, rising, pushing the papers to one side and offering his hand. "Good to see you, again. Where's the boss?"

Jim shook his hand with false enthusiasm, reached into his pocket and withdrew the note from the cottage and handed it to the DS. "I was hoping you might know, Hugh. Read this. She's done a runner, and I haven't got a clue where to start looking for her."

"Why would she do this?" Hugh said, shaking his head in measured, mock surprise as he read the note that he had dictated just a few hours' earlier.

"God knows. She's still fragile. She hides it well, but hasn't been able to come to terms with her daughter's death. She's been on the edge since it happened, holding herself together with little more than spit. I think that this case; the murder of these girls, has put her back to square one. There's a chance that she'll do something stupid if I don't find her."

Hugh's shoulders slumped and he manufactured a suitably concerned expression. "She seemed fine yesterday, Jim. Where do you intend to start looking? I want to help."

"Thanks, Hugh, I appreciate that. But I think she'll have headed back down south. London is her home ground. I'll make some phone calls, but I doubt it will do any good. Knowing Laura, she'll have found somewhere to be alone, to feed on her low self esteem and wallow in the guilt that she'll be feeling for running away from responsibility. Her depression will have probably put her back on the bottle. I'll stay at her place tonight, and then head back down south in the morning."

Hugh placed his hand firmly on Jim's shoulder. "Jim, if there's anything that I can do...anything at all. I don't just work with Laura, we're a team. And I care for her a lot."

"I realise that, Hugh," Jim said. "If I get lucky, then you'll be the first to know. That's a promise."

CHAPTER TWENTY-SIX

CLEM accompanied Jim back down to the main entrance of the station. They took the stairs instead of the lift and stopped on the first floor landing to talk. Jim gave Clem his mobile phone number.

"Hugh seemed genuinely concerned," Clem said. "And he thinks the world of the boss. Are you sure that—?"

"Forget that he's a cop, Clem," Jim said. "People from all walks of life can be killers. Look at that Manchester doctor, Shipman. They still don't know how many patients he murdered. The tally was up in the hundreds. But until he was caught he was just a nonentity; a low-profile, middle-aged GP. No one knew that he was playing God and taking life as and when he saw fit. Don't look for rationality or sound reasons for these sickos' actions. Just try to accept that they are totally unpredictable, and that the Hugh who you think you know is just a veneer that covers a damaged, malformed personality. He's driven by sexual and homicidal lust that in the right conditions will make you nothing more than prey. Don't underestimate him. Killing you would be as easy for him to do as standing on a bug."

Before going back upstairs to keep a close eye on Hugh, and still finding it hard to imagine him as the Tacker, even with evidence that seemed irrefutable, Clem went into the gents, took a leak and rinsed his face with cold water. He let what Jim Elliott had told him rattle around his brain, and tried to make sense of it. The American had said that Hugh was basically two people, and that the side of him that was a savage ritual murderer would not hesitate to kill anyone that threatened his freedom.

A shiver ran up the length of Clem's spine as he re-entered the incident room and saw Hugh sitting at his desk, drinking coffee and ostensibly looking through printouts that might lead to the killer.

"You and Elliott buddies?" Hugh asked Clem.

"I don't have buddies," Clem said with a straight face. "And if I had, a full of shit Yank profiler wouldn't make it to my Christmas card list."

Jim left the Cherokee in the NCP car park next to the Railway Museum. Rented a Sierra from Herz; a precaution in case he had to tail Hugh, who would recognise the 4x4 on sight. He then gave Leo Talbot a call on the off chance that the PI had made some headway, not expecting to be given information that slotted neatly into place and confirmed his worst fears with chilling clarity.

When Jim had gone, Leo settled in front of the one piece of equipment in his office that was state-of-the-art, and that he was an expert user of. His PC saved much time and shoe leather, reaching out for him to garner information in minutes, that without the technology would have taken many hours or even days to procure; though Leo preferred fieldwork, which on some cases was still the only way to operate. Matrimonial and surveillance for insurance fraud and the like – with the additional requirement of photographic or video evidence – essentially involved long hours' of staking people out, sometimes for days, and occasionally even weeks or months. But nearly all background assignments could be done with his arse firmly seated in front of his desktop. He could hack into agencies and extract information, be it within or outside the public domain.

The registrar's and council offices databases gave up everything that he initially needed on Hugh Parfitt; a potted history.

Hugh had been born to Samuel Parfitt, a farmer, and Jennifer Parfitt née Bowman. Their address had been Westwood Manor Farm, Escrick. Samuel had died in '93, and Jennifer just five years later, when Hugh was nineteen. A little more digging showed that neither of Hugh's parents had died from natural causes. Samuel had been crushed under a tractor, and Jennifer had been killed in a car crash that made the front pages of the local rags, due to her being in a car with a married man, who also happened to be a local councillor and high profile businessman in the area. An interesting find was that Hugh paid council tax on two addresses: a city centre flat, and also the family farm that he still owned.

The phone rang and Leo picked up, not surprised that it was the American on the line.

"Leo?"

"Yeah."

"Anything?"

"A little. Well, more than a little. Are you close by?"

"Yeah."

"Call in. I'll have some fresh coffee brewed."

"I'll be with you in ten minutes," Jim said, ending the call and starting up the Sierra.

Clem found it impossible to engage Hugh in conversation, and was glad of his own reputation for being uncommunicative and never using two words when one would suffice. His laconism was coming to his aid.

Hugh got up, unrolled his shirt sleeves, buttoned the cuffs and slipped his jacket on. "I've got to go to the bank, Clem," he said. "Then I might just call in at the hospital and have my face looked at," he added, fingering the Elastoplast. "I turned around too quick and smacked it on the edge of a kitchen cupboard I'd left open. I think I could have fractured my cheekbone."

"Will you be coming back?" Clem asked him in as casual and not give a damn tone as he could muster.

"I'll give you a bell if I'm not going to. I feel crap, so I might just call it a day."

As Hugh left the station, Clem followed at what he hoped was a safe distance, knowing that he could not afford to be seen and arouse suspicion.

Across town, Jim had parked the car. He was jogging down Micklegate to Leo's office, hardly able to contain himself from breaking into a dead run. He had felt urgency many times in his former career, but only once that bordered on the near panic he felt now. He vividly remembered the capture of the Blue Ridge Killer, and the race to save his last victim, who they knew had been buried alive in the mountains of western Virginia.

Lloyd Purvis had been waylaying and raping females at various points along the Blue Ridge Parkway for over four years. He was a strange individual, who had an aversion to blood and death that was almost as strong as his dark compulsion to obtain sex from unwilling strangers.

Married with two teenage boys, Lloyd was a garage owner and lay preacher; a popular guy in Laurelburg, which was a small township six miles west of Culpeper; a town that would later be widely known as being the location where the late actor Christopher Reeve suffered the catastrophic riding accident in '95, that was to paralyse and confine him to a wheelchair for the rest of his life.

Lloyd was forty-five, rugged and dependable looking, with honest open features and a winning smile. Had his wife, Melinda, seen fit to make out with him more than once a month, or had shown more response to his lovemaking than he would have expected from screwing a knothole in a plank of ponderosa pine, then he most likely would not have resorted to the actions that ultimately led to his being a serial killer, high on the FBI's most wanted list.

Once or twice a month, Lloyd would patrol the Parkway in his recovery truck. And several times a year he would get lucky, coming across a lone female driver who had broken down at the side of the road. On rare occasions he had picked up a hitchhiker. And twice he had taken foolhardy, solitary female backpackers who'd thought that the mountains were a safe haven, only to pay the ultimate price at Lloyd's hands.

His method was simple. He would hit his victims over the head with a wheel brace, dazing them and giving him time to tie-up, gag, and secrete them in a packing crate in the bed of his truck. He would then drive to an isolated off-road spot, remove them from the crate and rape them repeatedly. To cover his actions, he would then replace them in the crate and bury them alive. Almost all of his victims were conscious when interred, to endure a lingering death by suffocation in stygian darkness. Three of the crates had been found; the last exposed by burrowing animals attracted by the smell of corruption. Fibres from the recovery truck's seat covers, and a partial thumbprint on one of the corpse's remains had been retrieved, which was enough to prove guilt, if or when they found a suspect. Semen traces had been present, but were too degraded to be of any use. Hair samples, other than the victims, that had been recovered from all the sites were similar, and came from a Caucasian male with predominantly mid-brown hair.

Jim had compiled a profile, and his conviction that the killer was local to the area, hunted regularly and would strike again, led to a massive undercover operation being mounted, with female agents posing as hitchhikers, backpackers and stranded motorists. Only three weeks later, it proved successful, leading to Lloyd being arrested as he attempted to abduct Special Agent Susan Alvarado, who was parked at a scenic overview at the southern end of the William & Mary tunnel. Lloyd had been about to attack her with the wheel brace, only to find himself staring into the muzzle of a gun and being ordered to drop the weapon or be shot dead. His rampage was over. Tormented and seemingly genuinely relieved to have been stopped, Lloyd immediately admitted to being the Blue Ridge Killer, stating that he had raped and buried at least sixteen women in the region; the last just several hours before his arrest.

Shania Farnsworth was eight months pregnant, sitting in her Dodge Neon with the hood up, listening to Alan Jackson singing *Here in the Real World* on the car radio while she waited for assistance. Lloyd had snuck up, pulled her door open and struck her across the head. He was carrying her limp body back to the truck before he noticed her condition and immediately lost interest (and his erection), turned off by her swollen belly. But she had seen his face, stared at him momentarily as he swung the brace, and would no doubt be able to identify him to the police. Even though unused, he had no choice but to bury the pregnant woman. Later that day, still frustrated, his need for release inflamed by the previous failure, he was hunting again. The mental lure of having sex with a bound, struggling stranger was as compelling as the chum of rotting meat, fish and buckets of blood that drew sharks into the wake of a boat. Attacking an armed undercover agent was his first and last mistake.

Lloyd led the agents through the thick undergrowth. They had parked as near to the burial site as was possible, and were now running pell-mell, feet crunching, crackling over the forest floor. Lloyd, cuffed to an agent, was crying, his remorse overwhelming him, now that it was over and he was in custody; his reign of terror at an end.

"There," he had said, stopping in the dappled sunlight that danced through the breeze-blown canopy above the small clearing, to point at its centre with a shaking hand.

They had dug frantically at the loose earth, using tyre irons, broken lengths of tree branches and even their hands, hoping against hope that the young woman and her unborn child would still be alive; praying that the crate was large enough to hold enough air.

Reaching the top of the box, scraping it clear, an agent removed a bent nail that had been employed as a fastener through the hasp and, prising back the lid, pulled it up to reveal Shania laying on her back, eyes huge, staring, bulging orbs. Her hands were raised up, clawed, the finger ends bloodied and raw, with the nails broken, some ripped back away from the beds, due to scratching at the rough wood of what had been her coffin. She had a fixed look of pure terror on her sweating, tear-streaked face, and more than that, emptiness, as though she had lost all reason. Jim's stomach did a back-flip at the sight of the heavily pregnant woman. They were too late. No...they were not. Her hands began to move as she started to scratch at thin air, where the lid had been. She was alive. Had somehow survived the ordeal and would live to have nightmares for the rest of her life.

Lloyd Purvis had sunk to his knees and thrown up at being faced with the aftermath of his deed. He had lost an element of his sanity at that moment and had withdrawn into a world of his own, unable to contend with the abhorrence he felt at the sight of what his other victims must have suffered as a result of his sick actions.

Never to utter another word or communicate again with the world outside his broken mind, Lloyd was now a permanent patient and inmate of the Parkerville Maximum Security Facility for the Criminally Insane in West Virginia.

The sweet taste of success, and more meaningful, the saving of life was what had made the dark profession of Jim's choosing worthwhile. He had seen Shania much later; when she sought him out to thank him for his part in saving her and the baby. Jim had wept with her as they embraced and celebrated life.

CHAPTER TWENTY-SEVEN

SWEAT was beading his hairline and popping on his back as Jim took the stairs two at a time. He knocked once and entered the office, to find Leo standing at the window, from where he had watched Jim's hurried approach.

"Easy, Jim, you'll have a bloody heart attack. Less haste, more speed," Leo said, turning and lifting the electric kettle to pour boiling water over granules and brew the instant coffee.

"I work out, even do half marathons, so I'll survive," Jim said, trying unsuccessfully not to sound out of breath.

"Read that," Leo said, nodding to a sheet of paper on the desktop.

Jim lifted the sheet of computer paper and hungrily scanned the tightly packed text.

"It all fits," he said. "I wouldn't be surprised if he had something to do with his parents' deaths. The farm is where he operates from. It's where he takes his victims to; his private killing ground, that nobody has any knowledge of. If Laura is still alive, that's where she'll be."

Leaving the coffee untouched, Jim was up on his feet again, folding and stuffing the piece of paper into a pocket as he made to leave.

"You need backup on this, Jim, I'll come with you," Leo said, knowing that the American would not waste valuable time attempting to convince the police of how grave the situation was, or take the risk that even if they believed him and went in mob-handed, that Laura would have much chance of walking away from the scene in one piece.

"Thanks, Leo, but no. Unless you've got a .45 in your drawer to blow the son of a bitch away with, I'll handle this on my ownsome."

"Sorry, old son, this is York not New York. Best I can do is this," Leo said, rummaging on a shelf full of everything from civil law books to Dick Francis paperbacks, and finding a local map. He opened it and quickly found the farm, highlighting it with a red circle.

"Thanks," Jim said, taking it and heading for the door. "I'll catch you later."

Clem was standing in a menswear shop, idly sorting through a rack of ties, his hands fingering them as his gaze remained fixed through the store window onto the entrance of the Barclays branch on the opposite side of the street, where Hugh had entered several minutes before. He had followed Hugh from the station, parked in the open air car park next to Clifford's tower and tailed his DS, first to a building society, then a Lloyd's branch, and now to Barclays. It was obvious that the hospital-then-home story was a crock of shit.

Ten minutes later, Clem was back in his car, watching Hugh pull out. He followed the black Mondeo as it headed south out of the city to pick up the A19. As he drove, Clem phoned the number that Jim had given him, but got no reply.

Back in town, Jim started the Sierra, pulled away from the kerb, and noticed his mobile phone on the passenger seat where he had left it. "Stupid bastard!" he said aloud, pissed at himself for leaving the phone in plain sight for any would-be thief to be tempted by, and more importantly, annoyed for cutting off his only line of communication for over fifteen minutes. He would have to employ a more professional attitude if he was going to successfully deal with this mess. He needed to calm down, but that was easier said than done when so much was at stake.

Clem kept a minimum of four vehicles between himself and Hugh, braking and easing back even further when his quarry turned off onto a country road that was bereft of traffic, save for a distant oncoming tractor. He risked losing sight of the other car spasmodically, as bends in the road – which were lined with trees in full leaf of summer – separated them by a distance of more than a third of a mile. Rounding a wooded curve, he was faced with a long, straight stretch of clear road. The Mondeo had vanished. Slowing, Clem continued for maybe five hundred yards before seeing the entrance to the only property that Hugh could have pulled into.

The flaking letters on a blistered wooden sign that hung askew from a large stone gatepost were hardly legible, but could still be deciphered, and read: Westwood Manor Farm. He could not see a farmhouse or outbuildings through the trees, brambles and thick foliage that screened any dwelling from sight of the road, so drove on, parking in a wide break behind high hedging a hundred yards farther along the little used highway. Taking his mobile, Clem made his way back towards the farm entrance, and once inside the gateway he slipped under cover of bushes that hid him from both the drive and the road and tried Jim's number again.

"Yeah," Jim said, answering as he drove south through Fulford.

"It's Clem. Hugh is out at a place called Westwood Manor Farm, near Escrick."

"I know where it is," Jim said. "I'm heading there, now."

"I'm on the property, watching the driveway."

"Good. I should be there in a few minutes. Don't do anything, Clem. Just wait for me. We'll go in together."

"Okay, Jim. I'll get back to you if he leaves."

Jim pressed END, dropped the phone back onto the passenger seat and put his foot down to accelerate, overtaking other traffic with an almost reckless disregard for his or their safety. He was so stressed that he thought he may have developed an instant ulcer. His stomach was on fire and felt how he imagined it would if digestive acids were burning through its lining. Every second might count if he was to save Laura. Parfitt was now in the house with her, and the knowledge of what he had done to other women filled Jim's thoughts, creating uninvited, loathsome images of Laura suffering the same fate. He drove on, faster still, frustrated and hardly able to contain the overwhelming tension that was tearing at his emotions.

Laura was sitting on the bed hugging her knees against the cold. She was wide awake and trying to ignore the throbbing pain in her jaw, which was a reminder of the punch that had rendered her unconscious. As Trish had before her, Laura was planning how to disable or even kill Hugh, to save her from whatever he intended to do. She could not allow herself to believe for a second that he would keep his word and let her live. The cellar was no more than a holding pen; a death cell from which he would at some time take her from, to execute. She could not expect a last minute phone call to reprieve her, or to be found and rescued. That was for the movies. If she was to survive, then it would be as a direct result of her own actions. Her first thought was to simply wedge the cellar door and prevent his entry. *Shit! Outwards! The fucking door opens outwards, you dumb bitch. Get with the programme.* She looked around her, searched for anything that she could use or adapt as a weapon, but there seemed to be nothing. Diversion, not attack, was the only action she could think of that might give her a chance to escape. She needed to get away from him, not confront him physically. Hugh was strong and fit, and obviously deranged. She could not overpower him, and so the only feasible way to turn the tables was to employ a diversionary tactic; something that would stop him dead in his tracks for a second or two, and give her a half chance to make a getaway. With her bladder pounding, she went across to the bucket he had left in the corner and squatted over it. The acrid fumes from the three inches of blue chemical disinfectant he had poured into it was sharp in her nose and stung her eyes, as it was agitated by the stream of her urine.

It was then, still hunkered over the strong-smelling mixture, that she formulated a plan. She took the water ewer from the coffee table, drank half the contents, then emptied the rest into the sink and refilled the jug with the concoction in the bucket, placing the cocktail on the floor between the table and the bed. When Hugh next came down the steps, she intended to throw the liquid into his face, to momentarily blind him, giving herself the precious instant needed to duck past him, to not only escape the cellar, but also to lock him in it. She had no doubt that when she made her move, Hugh's natural reaction would be to put his hands up to his face and simultaneously draw backwards. She would have one roll of the dice, and fate would decide how they fell.

CHAPTER TWENTY-EIGHT

LEO went over to the window and pushed down the dust-covered slats of the Venetian blind so that he could watch the tall American run along the pavement, threading and jostling his way through pedestrians, almost knocking a woman to the ground in his eagerness to get back to the car and head off into what was without doubt going to be a deadly situation.

Leo couldn't settle. It was too much to expect him to sit back while a client – who had paid a retainer up front in readies – tried to deal with a suspected serial killer, alone. He did his utmost to resist the urge to get involved, but couldn't. However good the Yank was, he may need all the help he could get. Turning away from the window, Leo paced the office like a caged bear, on edge, scratching at his scalp, unaware of the dandruff that was dislodged to rain down on to his shoulders. Coming to a decision, he went to his desk, unlocked the bottom drawer and withdrew a weapon from under a stack of old files, checked it and pushed it into the side pocket of his jacket. He had only ever used it for target practise, but knew that it had the power to inflict serious injury or even death if ever employed as a last ditch defence at reasonably close quarters. He now wished that he'd offered it to Jim. The Crosman CB40 pistol was a comforting two and a quarter pound of zinc chromate; a gas pistol, almost as reassuring as a real firearm, but without the need of a certificate. It held an eight shot magazine of pointed pellets that would penetrate flesh and muscle with destructive force.

Leaving the office, Leo walked briskly to the NCP car park across the river, keeping his hand on the gun in his pocket, visualising emptying its load into the killer's thighs or kneecaps, to take him down and negate any threat that he might pose. Leo had no intention of rolling around on the ground and fighting with a much younger, fitter man. Not at his time of life. He had enough aches and pains without adding to them.

Jim drove out of the city and turned on to the back road that led to the farm two miles away. As he anticipated being at his intended destination in under two minutes, a muffled explosion startled him. It sounded like a blanket-covered balloon being burst. The steering wheel pulled sharply to the left, almost spraining his wrists as he wrestled to keep the car on the tarmac surface. He slowed, straightened the Sierra and brought it to a stop, half up on the grass verge.

I don't fucking believe it! That's all I need. He stepped out of the car and kicked the bodywork savagely. The front offside tyre was flat to the rim.

Fifteen minutes crawled by, and with still no sign of Jim and a growing fear that every second could be Laura's last; Clem decided to approach the farmhouse and play it by ear. After all, he was the cop, Elliott was a civilian.

Dark clouds had been drifting in from the west and stacking up, and the first coin-sized drops of rain began to patter through the leaves of trees, forerunners of the imminent storm. Keeping to the side of the driveway, Clem moved quickly, as stealthily as possible, ready to dive into the undergrowth at the slightest untoward sound. A barn and farmhouse came into view. And Hugh's jet-black Mondeo was parked outside the house's front door. Clem shivered, as though the car was a hearse. The skin on his arms and belly puckered, and a fleeting sense of intense apprehension ran through his whole being. He bent low, crossed the drive fast, edged along the weather-bleached side of the barn and stopped at the corner to make sure all was clear. Pausing to decide what to do next, he wished that Jim would arrive and save him from having to go it alone.

The summer storm became torrential. The thunderheads shed their load; the deluge announced by chains of lightning racing across a pumice sky, and sonorous cracks of thunder that split the air in deafening accompaniment. The tapping of raindrops on the corrugated-iron roof of the barn became a solid drumming, the beats inseparable; a single continuous unyielding detonation.

Clem took a risk and ran, feet squelching on ground that was now pooling mud; clothes immediately soaked and clinging to him, cold and uncomfortable. Reaching the front of the house, he made his way around the building, staying close to the rough, whitewashed walls, dropping down on all fours to pass ground-floor windows unseen. At the rear of the house he took a furtive peek through a window, into what was a large farmhouse kitchen. No one was visible. He grasped the brass knob on the back door, slowly turned it and found it to be unlocked. He then froze and his mind suddenly went blank. He was at a loss as to what to do next. Should he enter the house and carry out an unprovoked attack on a superior officer, because he believed him to be a serial killer? Now that he was at the point of taking some action, the situation seemed ludicrous. He had let the Yank's fervour ignite him. But now, standing there dripping wet, he found that his conviction had been cooled by both the lashing rain and the absurdity of the premise that his DS was holding Laura Scott hostage, or that Hugh spent his spare time mutilating and murdering teenage girls. He could imagine the scene: entering the house like a drowned rat, confronting Hugh and asking him if he was the Tacker, and inquiring as to whether or not he had the boss trussed up, or perhaps butchered and reposing in a freezer, ready for dumping off at a picnic area, or maybe outside WH Smith, sat with her throat cut and a stack of the Big Issue on her lap.

Clem reviewed what Jim had told him, re-examining the facts that pointed to Hugh being the killer, then steeled himself and eased open the door, holding his breath as he waited for a loud squeak from swollen wood or rusted hinges. There was no giveaway noise. He entered the kitchen and closed the door behind him, then removed his shoes and tiptoed across the room, to pass by a bolted, steel-faced door which he instinctively knew would lead to a cellar, and on a subconscious level wondered why it would be bolted as a police or prison cell is…to denote occupancy?

The interior hallway was gloomy, musty-smelling due to dampness, bathed with only the dull light from the open kitchen door and a window at the top of the stairs. Clem jumped back as a photoflash of lightning produced jagged shadows that seemed to leap towards him. His nerves were stretched to breaking point, his heart pounding in his ears, and his stomach queasy, threatening to rebel and eject its contents from his mouth, his bowels, or both. Looking about him, he saw a golf bag standing next to the front door. It ran through his mind that Hugh played off a handicap of ten; a bandit who, in competition could play to six.

Clem eased an iron club from the bag, grasped it two-handed and immediately felt a surge of confidence run through him from the weighty cudgel, that if necessary he would use against the other man without the slightest hesitation. He was now decided that Hugh *was* a vicious and cold-blooded killer, who would not give up without a fight to preserve his freedom.

Taking one slow step at a time, Clem climbed the stairs; the soles of his damp socks tacky on the dust and grime-laden carpet.

Halfway up, a board creaked under his weight, and so he stopped, breath held as his mind conjured-up an inhuman figure rushing from an upstairs room, wielding a gleaming butcher's knife; a keening wail escaping its mouth as it attacked, slicing and hacking at him. He waited an interminably long thirty seconds, then continued on up, reaching the landing before pausing again, straining to hear any movement that would indicate where Hugh was. The sound of rain still filled his ears. It was too loud— It wasn't rain. The thrumming, running water was inside the house, emanating from what must be the bathroom. The door ahead on the right was slightly ajar, and a cloud of steam issued from the lit gap, dissolving as it met the colder air on the landing. His courage blossomed. The thought of Hugh unaware of his presence, standing under the shower and deafened to his approach, gave Clem a false sense of inflated superiority, dulling his guard against danger.

Hands aching from the firm grip he held the shaft of the golf club with, Clem walked up to the door, took a deep breath and kicked it open.

Leo pulled in and stopped behind the Sierra, just as Jim was stowing the flat in the well of the boot. Stepping out of his car, Leo turned up the collar of his jacket against the whipping rain and approached the bedraggled American, who looked up in surprise, then slammed the lid of the boot down and wiped his wet and dirty hands on his soaking trousers.

"I decided to come along at no extra charge," Leo said.

Jim nodded. "Thanks. I may need the help. Although one cop is already there, keeping an eye on the place. He tailed Parfitt to the farm."

"I'll follow you," Leo said, before running back to the shelter of his car.

Jim climbed back into the Sierra, started it up and stabbed at the accelerator, to speed away from the verge with tyres spinning for a second on the slick grass, before they found purchase on the road. His heart felt heavy in his chest; a dead weight of growing panic. The contemplation of being too late was almost too much to bear.

Passing the gateway, almost missing seeing it through the semi-opaque veil of rain, Jim braked, skidding on to the long grass at the side of the road and fishtailing to a stop. Leo drew in smoothly behind him. They both climbed out, hesitating for a few seconds, expecting Clem to appear from hiding.

"Let's go in," Jim said, raising his voice and leaning close to Leo to be heard over the hissing rain and background crackling of thunder that echoed through the low ceiling of cloud above them.

"Take this," Leo said, pulling the gas gun from his pocket and thrusting it out towards Jim. "It's not a .45, but it's an attention-getter."

Jim took it, looked it over and pushed it into the waistband of his trousers. "An air gun?"

"CO2, eight shot. It'll stop him at close range."

They jogged along the undulating track, feet splashing through muddy puddles, approaching the house warily, but with little hesitation. Jim had now decided on a full frontal assault, hoping that the element of surprise and the gas gun would give him all the advantage he would need. Skirting Hugh's car – that squatted, dark and still, as if it were a hell-hound standing guard for its evil master – he depressed the handle on the front door of the house and finding it locked, ran around to the rear with Leo following in his slipstream, wheezing, lungs aching from a lifetime of smoking that had reduced his ability to absorb oxygen into his bloodstream by up to forty percent.

The kitchen door was unlocked, and the wet, mud-caked shoes on the floor inside it led Jim, correctly, to assume that Clem had become impatient and was already in the house, somewhere.

Clem narrowed his eyes in the steam-filled bathroom, squinting to try and make out a shape behind the dolphin-illustrated plastic shower curtain that hung inside the bath. As he summoned up the nerve to pull it aside, a devastating blow to his back sent him hurtling forward to crash into it. He let go of the golf club and put his hands out, scrabbling at the smooth, wet material, dropping heavily as his knees collided against the bath's rim, pitching him into it. His weight ripped the curtain down from the plastic hooks, for it to fall and drape him. And he cried out as intense pain travelled the length of his spine with flaring, bright agony that reached up through his neck into his skull, and down into his buttocks and legs. He lay still, unable to move, attempting to breath, sucking open-mouthed against the plastic that was encompassing his head and held in place by the powerful jets of hot water that pummelled and compressed the clinging fabric to his skin.

"Fucking amateur," Hugh said, jerking the curtain up to reveal himself standing naked, shotgun held one-handed as he uncovered

Clem. "Thought you'd just sneak up and brain me with a seven iron, eh?"

Lying on his back, one leg hooked over the edge of the bath, defenceless and at the armed man's mercy, Clem now knew beyond any doubt that Jim Elliott had been correct in pegging Hugh as the Tacker. He wished that the ex-FBI man had been off-base, because knowing that Hugh was the killer could only allow for one outcome to his brash trespass. He was going to die, there and then, and had no means to stop it happening.

Hugh backed up, not taking his eyes off Clem, to sit on the toilet seat, the double-barrelled 12 gauge that he had driven into Clem's spine now across his knees with the twin black maws of the muzzles pointing at the DC's head.

"Let's make this easy, Clem," Hugh said. "I want to know why you followed me here, and who else knows about this place?"

"Fuck you!" Clem said, knowing that talking wouldn't buy him any favours.

The blast was deafening, ricocheting off the tiled walls of the small bathroom; an eardrum-pounding roar that masked the high-pitched animal scream that Clem emitted as three toes were blown off his right foot.

Blood mixed with the running water and swirled down the plug hole. More had covered the white tiles and ceiling; a splatter of crimson that was slowly diluted by the condensation to form rivulets and run down to the cast-iron bath, which now sported a pitted and holed area, bereft of enamel.

Hugh inhaled the warm, damp, cordite-laden air and watched as Clem writhed and wailed in abject agony. "Let's try again," he said, his attention focused on part of a toe, complete with nail, that was slipping down the wall and leaving a snail-trail of gore behind it.

"El...Elliott," Clem stammered through gritted teeth, not looking at Hugh; mesmerised by the bloody, misshapen end of his foot, and wetting himself as terror of a magnitude he had not previously known could be experienced, consumed him. "He knows that you're...that you're the Tacker. And he...he knows that you took the boss."

"So, Mr FBI is coming to the rescue. Am I right?"

"Yeah. And he'll f...fucking nail you...you mad bastard."

"Well, whatever happens, Clem, you won't be here to see it. It's time to die, old son."

"No! Hugh, please, don't do it. I swear to God I won't say anything," Clem whined. "I don't want to die."

"You pathetic, grovelling little shit," Hugh said, smoothly pulling the trigger.

The dense clump of lead-shot missed Clem's head by inches, shattering the tiles and leaving a crater in the wall.

Clem screamed as hot, jagged fragments of tile and lead pellets rebounded and pierced the back of his neck and scalp. And then he passed out.

Hugh laughed aloud as he dragged the unconscious DC out of the bath, before going to his bedroom, to return with handcuffs and tape. He looped the cuffs around the thick outflow pipe at the back of the toilet and ratcheted them tightly to Clem's wrists, then taped his former colleague's mouth.

He wasn't some homicidal maniac who killed wantonly. He was a good cop. Trish had been an unavoidable, regrettable casualty. He had no intention of harming Clem – anymore than he'd already had to – or Laura, or even the Yank. He just wanted to give himself time to vanish and regroup.

Back in the bedroom, Hugh ejected the spent cartridges, reloaded the shotgun and placed it on the bed and went over to the chest of drawers and took his knife and a key from under the pile of panties in the top drawer. Going back out on to the landing, he stopped outside the second bedroom, unlocked the door and entered. Closing it behind him, he turned to the bed and was met by sparkling blue eyes, and a smiling face framed by vibrant blonde tresses that flowed over the pillow.

CHAPTER TWENTY-NINE

LAURA heard the two muffled reports, and recognised them as being too short and precise to confuse with the claps of thunder. The explosions could have been a car backfiring, with a stretch of the imagination. But her situation compelled her to believe that the source was of a more iniquitous nature. Sitting bolt upright at the sound of the first blast, she swung her feet onto the floor between the bed and the coffee table, to hide the jug from view, gripping it by the handle, tensed, waiting expectantly, sure that it would not be long before he came. She hoped that the blasts had been shots, and that Hugh had done the world, and her in particular, a big favour by blowing his own brains out. But that was wishful thinking. In her estimation suicide wasn't something Hugh would even contemplate.

Looking down, Hugh saw that her night-dress was rucked up over her hips, so averted his eyes and adjusted it, before sitting on the bed cross-legged, next to the shrunken, brown-skinned and almost skeletal remains that he had eviscerated before curing in tannic acid so many years ago. Rusted staples pinned the leathery lips together, but the glass eyes and cheap nylon wig gave the late Jennifer Parfitt a horrific semblance of life.

Hugh had returned to the quiet country graveyard as darkness fell, just a few hours' after his mother had been laid to rest. Now, all these years later, he held her shrivelled hand gently and let the events replay...

...There were no high, wrought-iron fences or locked gates to negotiate. This was not a landscaped cemetery with neat, regimental flower beds, crisp gravel walkways, or carefully manicured lawns and hedging. The majority of the gravestones leant like the dark stumps of crooked teeth, spotted with lichen and losing the slow battle against gravity. And the coarse grass was shin-high, ready for the local farmer to put his sheep in to nip it short, right up to the granite and marble bases. Should he be discovered waist deep in his mother's grave by an insomniac vicar, what would he do? Maybe put his spade across the man of the cloth's head and send him prematurely to his maker, depositing his earthly remains in the coffin beneath his feet, which would soon be vacant. Waste not, want not.

He could not afford to be caught; to probably be charged with grave-robbing, or at very least, vandalism. And the papers would have a field day. He could almost see the headlines: 'Mentally disturbed local teenager discovered digging up the body of his recently interred mother'. They would treat him like a raving lunatic. Probably lock him up in an asylum. That was not going to happen. She…Was…Not…Dead. It had been a terrible, terrible mistake. She could be resurrected, returned to him, and they would be together again, just like before. Everything was going to be just fine. He could make things right.

Under the light of a full moon, he dug down to her coffin, reclaimed her, and set her down gently next to a nearby oak, from where she could watch him return the grave site to the condition he had found it in. Once finished, he carried her to the van, placed her on a blanket in the rear, covering her with half of it, and arrived back at the house as the grey half-light of dawn broke.

He envisaged a perfect relationship, with a reborn, obedient and forever faithful mother. It was at that moment in time that his way of thinking became a little unhinged.

At first he would just talk at her, but then, with time, a growing delusional state overcame him, enabling him to imagine her animated and – in his mind – able to converse freely with him and move independently. He was able to suppress his illness to the outside world, possessing an internal switch that he could switch on and off at will. Having bestowed 'life' into the corpse, he found there was a downside. She had taken to berate him sporadically with verbal condemnation of his deeds, which had resulted in his stapling her mouth; an act that proved futile, due to her power of speech being projected wholly from within his own troubled psyche.

Hugh snapped back to the present. "I don't know what to do, Mummy," he said, snuggling up close to her on the damp bed. "They know what I've done."

"Stop worrying, baby," he said aloud in a falsetto reply to himself, his eyes glazing over as he saw his mother as she had been in life; smooth peach-blossom skin, full lips, teeth so white and even. "They know nothing," 'she' continued, reaching out, with his assistance, to cup his face with her hand. "Only the bitch in the cellar, the cop in the bathroom, and that American know what you've been doing to all those girls. Kill them all and we'll be safe. You'll just have to stop butchering those sluts…for a while."

"But the police won't stop until they find me. We should go away from here, just vanish. I have a plan."

"This is my house!" she screamed. "And it's where I plan to stay. Fit-up that bastard, Cox. But do it properly this time. Put Laura's body at his place, with the knife. And then make the cocksucker write a suicide note, admitting to being the Tacker. And be sure his fingerprints, hair and semen are all over the whore."

"But the teeth impressions on the bodies aren't his."

"So what? He had an accomplice. It'll be in the note. He can plead that he did it with some other maniac. Christ, Hugh, make him write anything you like. First, wait for the Yank, and kill him. Then finish Clem off and take your split-arse boss to Cox's and do her there."

"Okay, Mummy," Hugh said, climbing off the bed and leaving the room, to return to his own and retrieve the shotgun.

Jim paused at the door that led down to the cellar, and turned to face Leo. "See if Laura and Trish Pearson are down there," he whispered to the PI. "And if they are, get them away from here and call the police."

"But—"

"No buts, Leo. I'm counting on you to save Laura's ass. Just do it."

As Jim edged out of the kitchen into the hall, Leo gingerly slid the bolts back, careful not to make a sound, pulling the door open with all the caution of a bomb disposal expert opening a package suspected of containing a pipe-bomb wired to the lid.

Laura tensed as she heard the whisper of the door being opened. Oh, Christ! This is it, she thought. Her whole body stiffened, muscles locked. Inwardly she felt utterly weak and boneless, scared that she would be powerless to act, as she heard the first light footfall on the steps: leather on stone.

She couldn't look up; felt sure that Hugh would read the intention in her eyes if she faced him. She stared at the top of the coffee table, her gaze riveted to the cover of a National Geographic magazine, the photo of an aborigine staring back at her, his dark, sun-creased face daubed with beaded whorls of white spots; wide nostrils flared, and deep-set eyes fixed on the camera lens with more than a little condescension. The red sandstone monolith of what her generation would always call Ayers Rock grew out of the heat haze behind him to form a dramatic backdrop.

He was so close, now. Almost down there with her. *Please, sweet Jesus, help me!*

With perfect timing, Laura swung the jug up from the floor as the figure appeared in her peripheral vision. The blue liquid found its mark, splashing into the face of a man she thought looked vaguely familiar, but who was *not* Hugh Parfitt.

Leo reached the bottom of the steps and saw the woman sitting on a single bed, head bowed, unmoving. As he opened his mouth to speak, she moved in a blur of speed. He recoiled, instinctively put his hands up, but was a split second too late to stop the tide of liquid that hit him from filling his mouth, stinging his eyes, and burning his sinuses as he inhaled it through his nose. He reeled backwards, shocked, coughing, blinking and wiping at his smarting eyes.

Laura ran straight at him, hit him in the groin with all the force she could muster, fist clenched in an underarm swing, then elbowed past him and bounded up the steps, her legs rubbery, shaking, threatening to give out. She threw the door shut behind her, slammed the bolts into place and headed for the kitchen door.

Leo felt a sudden, sickening agony spread through his compacted testicles and flare up into the pit of his stomach, before he fell sideways grasping at the main source of tribulation, to strike his head on the concrete as he gagged on the chemical mix he had inadvertently imbibed. He heard the door above him close, and the bolts shoot home: Knew that he'd blown it, but could not have foreseen the woman's attack against him. Christ, he'd come to rescue her, and been half-blinded and kicked or punched in the balls as reward. He got to his knees, reached up to grip the edge of the sink and pulled himself upright, immediately vomiting and collapsing back down to the floor on all fours, where he stayed until the pain dulled and the retching subsided. Standing again, he turned on the tap, cupped water to his eyes, rinsed out his mouth, and tried to assess how deep the shit he had got himself into might be.

Laura stumbled out through the kitchen door and jogged around to the front of the house, looking about her through the steady downpour of chilling rain, before heading for the barn, from where she had been carried after being abducted. There was a thick chain through the handles of the doors, but the padlock that held it in place was not locked. She pulled it free and entered the murky interior, to be faced by the sight of her Fiat parked up, standing on a thick carpet of straw that covered the earthen floor. Rushing to the driver's side, she pulled the handle and the door opened. Relief surged through her. Within seconds she would be driving away from the farm, to raise the alarm and seal Hugh's fate. She sat, dripping wet, and fumbled under the steering wheel, only to find the ignition empty. The key was missing. Anger and fear welled up inside her, and tears of frustration pricked her eyes. She had no idea where she was, and to run blindly through the rain, in his territory, seemed a more frightening prospect than staying in the barn. The last thing that he would expect her to do was remain in the vicinity. Surely he would think that she had made good her escape and was going for help. With any luck he would panic and leave. Whatever happened, she would stay put until dark, then find the road and ultimately another house, where she could call the cavalry from. She left the car, ran to the back of the barn and parted a thick drift of straw, crawling in and pulling armfuls of it over her, to hunch up, hidden and already warmer; to begin what she thought would be a long wait.

Jim was halfway up the stairs when he heard the door to the cellar slam, and seconds later the kitchen door shut. He sighed with relief. Laura must be safe. A voice at the back of his mind told him to retreat, go after Leo and Laura, and maybe Trish, and leave it to the police to mop up. It was foolish to try and finish it himself. And yet he continued on up to the landing; a dog with a bone, unable to let it go and back off. And where was Clem?

Jim reached a partly open door and eased it back with his foot, searching for a target with the gas-operated gun held in a two-handed grip, his right shooting hand cupped in his left, elbows bent, and the left side of his body slightly forward of the right, balanced and ready to squeeze the trigger at the slightest provocation. The coppery smell of blood mixed with acrid spent gunpowder hit his nose at the same time as Clem Nash came into view. The young cop was sprawled on the floor. Jim immediately spun round, expecting Hugh to be behind him, to then feel a surge of relief to see that the landing was empty. Pushing the bathroom door to, he knelt and felt the blood-smeared neck for a pulse, surprised at the strong beat that met his fingertips. He ripped the tape from Clem's mouth, and the cop moaned and opened his eyes.

"He...he's got a shotgun, Jim," Clem whispered, his voice ragged with pain.

"Stay calm and keep quiet, you're going to be fine. I'll be back soon," Jim said, turning and easing the door open. He saw two further doors along the landing, both closed, and presumed that Parfitt must be hiding behind one of them. He reached the nearest, turned the handle and kicked it back. As he made to enter, the other door, twelve feet away, flew open to reveal the pale, naked and blood-streaked figure of the rogue DS, who rushed from the shadows, raising a shotgun as he screamed hysterically at Jim.

"Keep out of there," Hugh screamed. "Leave my Mummy alone."

Jim fired once, and then threw himself into the room as the shotgun roared.

As Hugh tightened his finger on the trigger, a sudden sharp pain burned into his shoulder. The 12 bore bucked in his hands, and a gilt-framed photograph of his mother – which hung on the wall at the top of the stairs – disintegrated. He dropped the heavy shotgun and went back to his room, reappearing with a knife in his left hand.

"Hugh, help me...help me!" His mother screamed in his mind, and with no thought of caution he rushed to her aid.

Jim rolled as he hit the floor, to come up in a crouching position against a wardrobe at the far end of the bedroom. White-hot pain bit into his back, and he knew that at least some of the lethal load had caught him as he had dived into the room. He took deep breaths, suppressed the urge to groan in acknowledgement of his wound, and went to the other side of the bed, to crouch in the gloom with the gun trained on the open doorway, fully expecting Parfitt to appear any second and start blasting. It was only then that he saw the withered corpse on the bed and reeled away from it, unable to stifle a cry of agony as his raw and bleeding back slammed into the wall.

Hugh entered the room at speed, his crazed eyes spotting Jim instantly. He came round the bed, slashing in front of him with the razor-sharp knife; a continuous high-pitched whine escaping his lips as he attacked.

Jim had moved forward, about to regain his feet, but stopped to track the advancing figure with the barrel of the pistol and squeeze the trigger three times. The gas-driven pellets found their target. The first hit Hugh in the neck and the second and third both entered his chest, within an inch of each other, just below his collarbone. But they did not have the stopping power of bullets, and Hugh kept coming, (seemingly too enraged to feel or react to the pain), lashing out with the knife, its blade cutting through the air no more than a playing card's thickness from Jim's face as he snapped his head back to avoid it. Hugh struck again and sliced into the back of Jim's hand, severing tendons and causing him to drop the pistol to the floor. Without hesitation, Jim drove his left fist into Hugh's face, knocking him backwards into a sitting position, and then gripped the other man's left wrist to prevent further use of the knife.

Hugh lunged forward and bit down on Jim's forearm, ripping the flesh from it with a sawing motion of his teeth.

Grimacing, but ignoring the fresh pain, Jim brought his head forward with as much force as he could muster, and heard the crack of his attacker's nose as it shattered under the impact of his forehead.

If pain has a colour, then Hugh saw it; a blinding flash of bright scarlet that almost matched the gout of blood that sprayed from his nostrils. He released his grip and screamed, dropping the knife and scrabbling away from Jim, finding his feet and running for the door.

Jim was up and after him half a second later, only a few feet behind, diving for the other man's legs, before being hit in the temple by the edge of the door as it was thrown back against him.

"Get the bitch!" Hugh's mother's voice screamed as he ran along the landing, flaying the soles of his bare feet as he crunched over the fragments of glass from the photo frame he had inadvertently shot from the wall minutes earlier. He tripped halfway down the stairs, fell sideways and crashed through the banister, ripping out several of the wooden uprights and breaking the handrail, which split apart with the crack of a tree branch being broken over a knee.

Landing hard, Hugh lay on his side, winded, his whole body pounding with pain from the pellet wounds, his broken nose, feet torn, and now a sharp stabbing pain, which he thought may be broken ribs from the fall. If the Yank had appeared at the top of the stairs at that moment, then he knew he would have been finished. But there was only the steady beat of water from the bathroom, and a rumble of thunder from the passing storm. A few seconds, he thought, and he would go for Laura. She would be his passport out of this fucking pigs breakfast of a balls-up.

CHAPTER THIRTY

AS she huddled under the straw, Laura wondered about the man whom she had locked in the cellar. He had looked familiar, and that bothered her. His strong features were striking; not good looking, but charismatic, with a quality of lived-in ruggedness that suggested he had earned the deep lines that etched his face like fissures in timeworn rock. Her thoughts drifted to Hugh and his grotesque double life. She felt unclean at the closeness she had felt to him, now that she knew he had carried out such horrific acts.

A PI...An ex-cop! Laura's mind had been subconsciously sifting, searching through a mental mugshot book, and had found a match for the middle-aged man in the cellar. She recalled being introduced to him, soon after taking up her post at York. He had just handed the police a murderer on a plate, and was being thanked with an official dinner and much backslapping and acclaim from old colleagues, ranging from DCs to Chief Superintendent Cottrell. She remembered thinking that the ensuing media coverage must have brought a lot of new business to his door.

Leo had been asked to investigate a possibly fraudulent insurance claim. A woman by the name of Amelia Grant was in line to pick up a million pound payout following the supposedly accidental death of her husband.

Quentin Grant had gone horse riding with his wife, and Amelia, suitably and convincingly distressed, had phoned for an ambulance soon after. Her story was that Quentin's horse had bolted after a low-flying jet had passed directly overhead. She had said that after careering through a wooded area, her husband had been knocked from his mount as a branch struck his face.

Maurice Iveson of M.I. Insurance was not certain, but hopeful that there had been foul play. The policy had only been taken out six months previously, and he needed to be convinced that the coroner's verdict of death by misadventure was the correct one.

Leo had quickly ascertained that the grieving widow was screwing a guy twelve years her junior, and that the stud in question was Ralph Jameson, an ex-con with previous for GBH, burglary, and an acquittal on an attempted murder charge. It transpired – after much foot-slogging – that on the day of Quentin's fatal 'accident',

Jameson had been in a village pub, not far from the Grants' house. The landlord recognised him from a photo that Leo was touting around, and also remembered that Jameson had stayed in the bar for over two hours that afternoon. He recalled that the man appeared agitated and ill at ease, continually looking nervously at his wristwatch and fidgeting with a mobile phone. After receiving a call that lasted all of ten seconds, he had rushed out to his car and driven off at high speed. The date could not be confused. The day that Grant had died was also the landlord's wedding anniversary. It put Jameson a two minute drive away from the road adjacent to the wood were Quentin and Amelia were riding. The line from Hamlet came to mind, when Marcellus had said to Horatio that something was rotten in the state of Denmark.

Leo had called to see Amelia. Told her that he knew that she – aided by her boyfriend – had conspired to murder her husband and make it look like an accident, to get hold of the insurance money. He also told her that Jameson had spilled his guts to a mutual friend, and that he had proof of their relationship and of lover boy's presence in the area on the fateful day. The clincher was when Leo said, erroneously, that as a freelance investigator, with gambling debts and the tax man on his back, he would forego reporting what he knew to the police, and even give her a letter implicating him in the cover-up, for a one-off payment of fifty thousand pounds. To his surprise, the cold-hearted bitch not only agreed to the deal, but offered to substantially increase the amount that he had asked for, if he would get rid of Ralph Jameson permanently for her. He said he would contact her the next day, when he would expect half the cash up front. Leo then went straight to the police with a tape he had made of the damning conversation. The police carried out their own investigation, and Amelia and Ralph were both arrested and charged, to be subsequently tried and convicted of Quentin Grant's murder.

It emerged that just prior to leaving the stables that day, Amelia had phoned Jameson at the pub, confirmed the route that they would be taking, and then led her husband to his death. Ralph had leapt out from the side of the bridle path, dragged Grant from his horse, and struck him a single blow across the forehead with a stout tree branch, killing him instantly.

In court, they had tried to lay the blame off on each other, but only dug themselves in deeper with a jury that unanimously returned a verdict of guilty as charged.

The thought of going back into the farmhouse made Laura physically shake with fear. But she couldn't leave...Taylor – no, not Taylor, Talbot, Leo Talbot was his name – at the mercy of Hugh. There was no way she could just sit it out, knowing that when Hugh went down and found him, he would undoubtedly kill him. There was no choice, she had to go back and set him free, or his death would forever be on her already guilt-ridden conscience.

Pushing her way out of the straw, Laura immediately began to shiver violently, her wet night-shirt clinging to her, and pieces of dull-yellow chaff sticking to her from head to toe. She lurched across the barn, past a concrete block with a large metal ring set into its top, then reaching the doors, looked out into the rain, expecting to see Hugh, but didn't and was both relieved and thankful that there was no sign of him. She trudged back across the muddy yard, retracing her steps to the rear of the house, feeling vulnerable, scared and weak, and knowing that if she paused for even a second, then she would lose her nerve and run blindly, as far as her legs would carry her in any direction that took her away from Hugh Parfitt. At that moment, collapsing in a ditch a mile away with her lungs almost bursting and her chilled body scratched and torn by thorns and branches, seemed far more appealing than the thought of going back into the waiting arms of a homicidal maniac.

Leo tried the door, but it was solid, unyielding, hurting his shoulder as he ineffectively threw his weight against it several times. He went back down the steps; eyes still burning, vision blurry. The female DI had been inventive and quick as a fox. He admired the adeptness with which she had escaped; could appreciate that she had not expected anyone but her captor to enter the cellar. He now wished he had called out before going down into what had proved to be the lioness's den. Absently reaching for his cigarettes, he lit one and took a deep drag, squinting around the small room to familiarise himself with his surroundings. It took him only a few seconds to realise that there was no other way out, nowhere to hide, and nothing that would serve as an effective weapon. He almost choked on lungs full of smoke as the sudden, deep, resonant blast of what could only be a shotgun, echoed above him. There was no way he could be optimistic. The probability was that Jim Elliott had just come across Parfitt, and not survived the encounter. Now, if he was to get out of the house alive, he would have to rely on his own wits and a whole lot of luck. He couldn't help but think that his future had all the hallmarks of proving to be a bleak and very short-lived one.

Impending danger was a catalyst for inspiration. If he could not escape or arm himself, then he would have to defend himself as ably as possible and ride it out on a wing and a prayer. Sweeping the books and magazines off the top of the coffee table, he lifted it, noticing that one of the legs was missing. Climbing the steps, this time holding the table in front of himself as a shield, he rested the bottom edge of it on the top step and waited, ready to slam the heavy piece of furniture into the door as the bolts were drawn back, to hopefully gain advantage over the killer cop.

Jim fought against the racing tide of blackness that swept over his consciousness, but succumbed. The effect of the blow to his skull drew him down into a dark pit, to briefly curtail all interest in the situation.

He came to confused, uncertain for a few seconds as to where he was or what had happened to him. And then the events prior to being struck by the door flooded back. He tried to climb to his feet too quickly, only to fall, with his head spinning, pounding. He could taste the blood that had run down the side of his face and into his mouth from a deep gash above his ear. With supreme effort, he got up, but could not stay upright and fell back. Reaching out, he grasped a handful of the bedspread, jerking it, inadvertently pulling the bewigged husk of Jennifer Parfitt over the edge, for it to fall on top of him, the withered legs astride his hips, gnarled, long-nailed fingers on his chest, and face up against his with its puckered, stapled mouth resting against his lips.

Jim cried out and pushed the grotesque, dried-up body away, horror-struck as both of the staring blue eyes popped from their dark, musty sockets, to bounce off his face and roll across the floorboards into the shadows. He struggled to his knees, made it to his feet, but had to sit on the edge of the bed as a grey mist swirled in his mind, almost overwhelming him and holding him in a state of languid torpor. Taking deep breaths, he steadied himself and waited until his head cleared. When able, he assessed the situation.

The pain from his head, back and hand, helped to concentrate his mind. He looked down at the twisted bundle of skin and bone that had been Hugh's mother, realising that his profile on the case had been as close as he had ever got to think his way into the mind of a serial killer. The mentally ill young man had obviously exhumed her, refusing to let death stand between them. Jim surmised that Hugh's widowed mother had provoked him beyond endurance. It wasn't a stretch to imagine that they had been involved in an incestuous relationship, and that when she had found a new lover, Hugh had engineered the car accident that had killed her and the man who she had been with. Being unable to kill her again, he had found look-alikes to punish in her place. Jim knew that there would be periods when Hugh would be oblivious to reality, living in a state of delusion. Given time, his ability to differentiate between the two worlds that he inhabited would degenerate, and he would collapse into a state of complete insanity.

Having seen the look in Hugh Parfitt's eyes, Jim fully perceived the depth of madness that lurked behind them in his warped and disassembling psyche.

CHAPTER THIRTY-ONE

LEO leaned back against the whitewashed wall at the top of the shadow-filled stairwell. He was as prepared as he could be, and although nervous, actually felt confident. There was no way that Parfitt would be expecting a sixteen-stone man to plough into him as he opened the door. And as Laura had proved earlier, the element of surprise was a powerful foe to contend with.

In a strange way, Leo felt more alive at that moment than he had done in years. The present danger had given rise to a chemical reaction within him that he thought had dried up, crystallised and blown away long ago; no longer within him to trigger the tightness he now felt cramping his stomach, or initiate the false sense of regained youth that seemed to permeate though his muscles with a warm, burning sensation of tense readiness, obviously due to an adrenaline rush.

It was almost five years since Leo's wife had died. Soon afterwards he had taken early retirement from the force. Sheila had been his rock; the foundation upon which he had built his life. She had brought order to chaos, and had always been there for him, supportive and yet independent; his true love and best friend.

It had been septicaemia that had so suddenly and unexpectedly taken Sheila from him. She had undergone relatively minor surgery; a knee replacement, and should have been out of hospital in forty-eight hours, but instead, had died, drugged to ease the pain, robbing him of even a chance to tell her how very much he loved her, and say good-bye.

He had entered the dark and desperate world of grief; a bitter place that left him languishing in accursed resentment of life and the cruel lottery that it had proved itself to be. Turning his back on the faith he had shared with Sheila, he disclaimed the concept of a higher, all-seeing power, choosing to perceive existence analogously with the wild order of nature, where only the fittest survive at the expense of the weak, infirm and aged, which they decimate with impunity, until in turn they become victim of the same age-old and endless process. The struggle for life over death seemed a hollow, meaningless and empty pursuance to Leo. Bad enough to be born only to die; but to be aware of the inevitability of such an ephemeral reality was, to him, an extortionate price to pay for the supposed higher intellect that a freak of evolution had bestowed upon his species. As the composer Hector Berlioz had said— 'Time is a great teacher, but unfortunately it kills all its pupils'.

For six weeks after Sheila's death, Leo had for the most part sat alone and disconsolate in the small bungalow that had been home for the duration of their marriage. He had felt himself fading away, as a growing emptiness replaced the spark of life that was bleeding unseen from his mind and body. He contemplated suicide, but chose to live, on his own terms; a solitary existence. He eventually regrouped, handed in his papers and left the force, to almost immediately open the agency, so that he would have a reason to climb out of bed each morning and face another day. With time, the involvement with hapless or troubled clients proved a distraction from his own despondency, allowing him to function on a level that became at least tolerable.

The bungalow had become a neglected, dust-layered mausoleum that he frequented less and less. Most nights, he slept on the sofa in the small room next to his office, visiting the house only once or twice a week, to try and feel closer to Sheila, causing himself renewed pain as he opened wardrobes and drawers, to touch and look at the clothes, jewellery and other personal effects that she had worn or used or enjoyed possessing. They gave him no solace, and yet he could not bring himself to bag up the material residue of her life in bin-liners and dispose of it piecemeal to Oxfam or the tip. That was a final undertaking that he had postponed and shirked away from, as he had with his beloved wife's ashes, which still reposed in a rosewood casket atop her piano in the lounge, where they had spent so much of their life together. Sheila had loved Whitby, and the sea, which she had viewed as an eternal living entity encompassing and reflecting all human moods, from composed tranquillity to mindless rage. Its tides and flow never ceased to fascinate her, and the lunar forces that affected it were a mystery which both enthralled and excited her. Leo had intended to scatter the cremated dust, that was her mortal remains, over the cliffs that they had walked along hand in hand so many times in the past; to release her into the bracing salt air that she had so enjoyed and been invigorated by. They had spoken of buying a stone-built, sea-facing cottage in the area when he retired, but that dream never came to pass.

Now, standing on the cellar steps, he determined to fulfil what was the duty of the living. If he survived this day, he would clean and clear the house, then – on what would have been Sheila's fifty-sixth birthday in two weeks time – make the trip to Whitby and metaphorically free her from all earthly constraint. He now felt ready to let go; believed that she was with him, watching over him, and waiting for him along the road a ways.

Laura re-entered the kitchen, paused to listen, but heard no sound. She took a towel from the rail behind the door to wipe the rain and straw from her face and hands, before walking out into the short hall and stopping in front of the metal door, dropping the towel to the floor as she reached it, to stand, her hand on the top bolt, fearful that Hugh would suddenly appear and once more incarcerate her below ground, or just stab or shoot her to death where she stood.

Easing the bolt back, Laura subsequently squatted to release the second, sucking breath through clenched teeth as it scraped noisily, metal on metal, worse than fingernails raking a slate blackboard.

Leo smashed the tabletop into the door as he heard the bottom bolt slip free from its bracket. He lunged forward, eager to take advantage and negate the threat of the man who he believed was about to enter the cellar.

Laura staggered back on her heels as the door knocked her off balance. She fell to the floor winded, then looked up to see the detective glaring wide-eyed over the top of the table he was holding.

"Laura?" Leo said, frowning, surprised.

"Y...yes," she replied, her voice a gruff whisper.

"The other woman?"

"I've not seen her."

"OK, Let's get the hell out of here," Leo said, throwing his makeshift shield aside to crash end over end down the cellar steps as he reached down with his hand outstretched to pull the bedraggled looking woman to her feet.

Standing, Laura turned and ran, back outside, heading for the barn with Leo following. Once inside it, her intention was to hide in the deep straw again, but Leo put his hand on her shoulder, stopping her in mid stride.

"Up there," he said, pointing to a wide wooden ladder that was fixed to the timber wall and led up to an open hatch that gave access to a loft that ran the entire length of one side of the building, twenty feet above their heads.

Laura went first, as Leo watched the doors, sure that a shotgun wielding maniac would appear, intent on blowing them both to kingdom come. He waited until Laura was two thirds of the way up, then climbed after her, his wet, leather-soled shoes slipping on the smooth rungs as he moved too quickly, feeling vulnerable with his back to the entrance. Looking up, he momentarily stopped, his sore eyes forgotten as they fixed on the sensual sight of Laura's buttocks and the wedge of hair and tantalising glimpse of pink flesh among dark curls, which redirected his attention away from possible danger. Blood rushed to his face with the embarrassment and shame that he felt for not averting his eyes from her lush nether regions, which were visible under the nightdress she wore.

They nestled into the stale, old straw, both trying to suppress sneezes initiated by the bone-dry particles that had been disturbed and were floating in the air around them, to be seen as a spiralling cloud of motes in the pale shaft of light that pierced the skylight in the roof and formed a grey column, illuminating the block of concrete below it.

"What are you doing here?" Laura asked Leo as they sat with their backs against the wall at the rear of the loft.

"I came with Jim Elliott," he said.

The skin on Laura's neck and scalp prickled. She again heard the gunshots blasting through her mind, now more significant, knowing that Jim must have been the target, and by his absence, convinced that he had been killed as he tried to rescue her.

"I'm so sorry," Leo said, reading her expression. "Parfitt must have got the drop on him. The bastard had a shotgun. I heard it go off."

"It was fired twice before you came," Laura said woodenly, her eyes brimming with tears as she sank into a well of grief that was bottomless and soul destroying.

Leo said, "There was another copper here. He followed Parfitt out to the farm, and he's missing as well."

"But what if Jim is still alive?" Laura whispered, not believing it could be true, but grasping at the remote strand of hope she needed to give her the will to function. "He may just be wounded and need help."

Leo shook his head. "That's wishful thinking, Laura. What do you want to do? Go back in there and get blown away?"

"I came back for you. I have to go back for Jim. I have to know that I tried. Can't you see that?"

"No. My phone is in the glove compartment of my car. Let's try and get to the main road and call for help."

Laura shook her head. "That's as risky as going into the house. We could be caught out in the open. He'll expect me to run, not to go back. He's probably outside now, searching for me."

Leo sighed. He could see that her mind was made up. Shit! He had no choice but to accompany her, even though he thought it would probably turn out to be the most stupid decision he had ever made. With no further discussion he went to the ladder and began to climb down.

CHAPTER THIRTY-TWO

AT the same time as Laura and Leo had run from the house, Hugh had got to his feet and limped past the open cellar door and into the kitchen.

Gone! The Yank must have let her out before going upstairs. But she was lost out there, probably hiding nearby. He had not heard a car drive away. He would have to find her, or he was finished. His eyes locked on to the selection of knives; their dark ebony handles protruding from slots in the large wooden block that stood on the counter next to the bread bin. He withdrew a long, thin-bladed boning-knife, immediately feeling stronger, as though a power radiated through the haft that he now gripped so tightly in his hand. It was as if Elliott had ceased to exist. His mind was blotting out all but a single line of thought at a time. He walked out into the slanting, driving deluge slowly, mechanically, no longer feeling pain from his wounds, and with the blood diluted with rain and being washed from his body he made his way to the front of the house, and then stopped to look about him, determining where he would seek refuge in Laura's position.

The barn doors were not closed to. There was a vertical black line of shadow; a gap between them. His mouth pulled up to the side in a crooked grin. The stupid bitch had thought to hide in his personal abattoir, unaware that it was his alter of sacrifice, or that the ground it encompassed was filled with so many of his past victims. She had brought him nothing but trouble. Her living even long enough to be butchered at Cox's place was no longer a consideration. He would find her, tie her to the block, staple her fucking mouth shut, and cut her throat. After that, her dead body would be bagged-up and transported to Cox's house, where he would stage a macabre scene of murder and suicide. Later, he would attend the scene again, when the corpses were discovered. He would be there in an official capacity, to act suitably shocked and mortified at the atrocities committed on his boss.

Opening the right-hand barn door just wide enough to allow him to slip through, Hugh immediately moved to the side of it, into the shadows, to stand for a few seconds and give his eyes time to adjust to the low light.

Now disentangled from what had been Hugh's mother, Jim scrambled over the top of the bed and reached down to pick up the knife that Parfitt had attacked him with. The gas gun was not in sight, and he denied himself a few extra seconds to search for it, shuffling back across the bed, to step down to the floor and hear a sharp snap as he inadvertently put his foot through a brittle ribcage. He jerked back, and then returned his attention to what his clearing mind appreciated might be the ace in the hole.

Looking along the gloomy length of the skirting board, he saw the two false eyes, three feet apart, staring out into the room. The thumb, index and ring fingers of his right hand were numb; the result of the deep laceration that gaped open and streamed with blood, forcing him to put the knife on the floor while he retrieved the glass orbs with his left hand and forced them back into the sunken sockets. Then, with the match stick corpse under his right arm, he retrieved the knife and set off in search of Hugh.

Who the fuck is that? Hugh thought, watching the burly figure step down to the ground from the hayloft's ladder, with Laura above him, carefully descending it a rung at a time.

Leo denied himself a repeat viewing of Laura's attractive bare bottom, turning away from the vista of firm flesh, just in time to see the naked figure of a man running across the barn towards him. And as he raised his arms in defence he knew that he was too late. The glowering face, maniacal staring eyes, and the blur of shining steel were too close to allow for any evasive action.

The blade arced upwards, to enter his abdomen, sliding smoothly to the hilt. Leo gasped as a sharp, paralysing pain made him double over. Had he not known better, he would have believed that the cramping, crippling agony in his torso was the result of a sudden, massive heart attack.

Hugh put his right hand around the man's neck, to pull him forward as if greeting an old friend, to then twist and wrench the weapon in all directions to cause as much internal damage as possible. He worked the blade, – as his victim jerked and tried to pull away – only withdrawing it as the other man sank to his knees and ceased to struggle.

Hugh looked up to where Laura clung to the ladder. The shuddering, moaning, dying figure at his feet was already dismissed from his mind. He stepped over it and advanced.

209

Leo tasted warm blood in his mouth, coughed once and sprayed the air with crimson droplets. He knew that he was dying; could feel a coldness creeping through him that he recognised as being a withdrawal of blood from his extremities; a last ditch attempt by his body to protect the major organs and preserve their functions. Lying on his back, he was surprised that instead of experiencing fear, a spiritual revelation, or the vision of a benign figure calling to him, hand outstretched to lead him into a tunnel of scintillating white light, or whatever the hereafter might be, he found himself once more looking at Laura's bottom as she hung high above him. It was a truly delectable sight under the clinging hem of her Mickey Mouse nightdress.

Laura climbed back up, too fast, losing her footing and almost falling into the arms of what was no less than waiting death. She somehow held on to the smooth rung, and with muscles stretched and burning, hauled herself back up into the loft, throwing the hatch down and searching in the straw for a catch or bolt to secure it. There was no fastening, or any object she could see to employ and weight it down to keep him out. With no alternative, she knelt on the trapdoor, hoping that her own soaking wet body on the hatch would be enough to keep him at bay. Unable to foresee any escape now, she felt trapped, vulnerable, and very alone.

As Hugh climbed the ladder with the blood-coated knife gripped between his teeth, a scene from his favourite childhood book popped into his mind: *Treasure Island*, and Israel Hands climbing the rigging of the Hispaniola, intent on murdering Jim Hawkins, who quaked above him in the crosstrees.

With neck and shoulder tight to the underside of the trap, he pushed upwards, straining every muscle, groaning with the effort, but driven by sheer determination and a flood of adrenaline that had surged through him as he ran across the barn to gut the man at the bottom of the ladder. The wood creaked and raised an inch, then two. Above, Laura felt herself being lifted and knew that her weight was not nearly enough to hold him back, as she began to slide down the rapidly increasing incline.

"You're going to die, boss," Hugh mumbled as the trap flipped back, dislodging Laura from it, to dump her in the straw on all fours.

She was between the devil and the deep blue sea, or more aptly, separated from the ground so far below her by a devil in human form. She snatched a glance over the edge of the loft. If she leapt down to escape Hugh, then in all likelihood she would break her ankles or sustain some other injury that would render her unable to move. Better to just throw herself at him now, before he could climb the last couple of rungs and step on to what was in essence a boarded balcony. If they fell to earth together, then with a lot of luck, he may break her fall, and hopefully his neck, or choke on the blade of the knife that was clenched between his teeth, dripping Leo's blood on to his chin, chest and stomach.

In the instant before she threw herself forward in a final attempt to survive, a voice split the near silence.

"Hey, shithead, look who I've got," Jim shouted, entering the barn, looking up and seeing how close Hugh was to reaching Laura.

Hugh stopped, turned his attention to Jim and let the trapdoor drop back into place as he lowered himself part way down the ladder.

"Don't hurt her," Hugh wailed, snatching the knife from between his teeth as he saw a vision of his mother squirming in the grip of the American, who held a blade to her tender, milk-white throat.

Jim's right arm encircled the corpse's shoulders, and with his uninjured hand he pressed the sharp tip of the knife against the creased and leathery-brown skin. "Drop the weapon and climb down, now, or I start cutting," he said.

"You so much as graze her, and I'll rip your fucking lungs out with my bare hands," Hugh said as he obeyed and released the knife to let it tumble down onto the straw-covered floor of the barn.

Once that Hugh was back on the ground, he walked purposely towards Jim, hands clenching and unclenching at his sides.

"That's far enough," Jim said, for a moment convinced that Hugh was too far gone to be able to hold back, even at what to him would be the certain death of his mother. "Stop right there and sit on the ground." And to Laura, "Get down here, Laura, quick as you can."

Laura almost collapsed with relief, at both Jim being alive and at what seemed a last minute reprieve from what she knew would have been the end of her. In the low light, it appeared as though Jim was holding a bewigged dummy in front of him, but the absurdity of the situation was outweighed by the still dangerous position they were in. She swung the trapdoor back all the way and scrambled down the ladder, giving Hugh a wide berth, even though he had now sat down and totally ignored her, his gaze and concentration firmly fixed on the mummified body that she could now see was what Jim held.

"In my pocket, left side," Jim said as she reached him. "Get my keys. The car's at the end of the drive, out on the road. Bring it back here."

Laura did not argue, just found the keys and ran from the barn, down the muddy track, hardly aware that the rain had stopped, and that a watery sun was lightening the slate-grey sky.

"Now what, Yank?" Hugh said, almost spitting the words out; hatred as cold as permafrost radiating from his bulging blue eyes.

"You get up slow and easy and back off, all the way to the far wall, and then sit down again. When Laura gets back with the car, I let your mother go, and leave."

"How do I know you won't kill her?"

"Because you're the sick bastard who gets off on killing helpless women."

"Do what he says, son," Jennifer Parfitt said, exclusively to Hugh. "He hasn't got the balls to hurt a defenceless woman, unless he has to. He'll keep his word."

"Okay, Mummy," Hugh said, slowly rising to his feet.

Jim felt a worm of revulsion and horror writhe in his brain. Knew that Parfitt believed he was communicating with the mummified corpse.

Hugh walked stiffly backwards, not stopping until his back came up against the bleached and warped boards of the wall, where he slid down, to sit forlorn-looking, but generating no pity from Jim, who knew him for the heartless scum that he was. Hugh Parfitt was the same as all the other countless serial killers that he'd profiled, back in the days when he had worked from a maze of offices sixty feet below the FBI Academy on the U.S. Marine Base at Quantico, Virginia. As so many times before, he had put himself into the mind of a repeater murderer; had journeyed into the dark world where evil dwells. Jim knew that they were all individuals; each and every one of them similarly twisted, but dancing to a different drum. What they *did* all have in common was the same insatiable need to inflict suffering, both mental and physical; to dominate their victims and punish them for some wrong that they most likely imagined had been meted out to them by parents or the world in general. This type lacked the capability to feel any compassion for humanity. They might as well be of another species. Jim had once again evaluated and analysed the specifics of the crimes, and had developed a near perfect profile on the killer who would forever be labelled the Tacker.

Jim heard the car approaching. He took three paces backwards to the partly open door, and as he did the bony feet of his inanimate hostage dragged along the ground, their long, curved, horny toenails parting straw and gouging furrows in the underlying soil.

Laura stopped outside the barn and opened the car window. "Jim, he stabbed Leo," she shouted, to be heard above the noise of the engine. "He might still be alive."

Jim looked across to where the PI lay almost hidden in the straw, unmoving, his body a rose madder hue from chest to thighs in the dim light. Moving forward, not taking his eyes from Hugh, or the knife from his 'salvation's' throat, he reached the body. One glance was enough. Leo's eyes were open and glazed with the pupils fixed. His mouth was gaping and slack, dripping blood. Across the front of his shirt, the bright red stain was still spreading like an animated Rorschach blot, which to Jim resembled an octopus, its tentacles unfurling over the slashed white cotton that covered the dead man's chest.

Jim had an almost irrepressible urge to hack the head off the corpse he held, knowing that Hugh would hear his mother scream and see a phantom gout of blood rise from the stump of her neck as the head fell to the ground. He wanted the maniac to suffer the torment that he so readily inflicted upon others. And when Hugh then attacked him in an almost blind rage, he would stab the man repeatedly, not stopping until he collapsed with exhaustion, unable to raise his arm any more to plunge the knife into the psycho killer's flesh. Instead, he backed away towards the door and the light, then threw the lifeless husk across the floor and darted outside. He fed the chain through the handles and secured the padlock, locking the one and only entrance and exit to the barn.

As Jim climbed into the passenger seat, Laura swung the wheel, reversed back across the farmyard past the black Mondeo and the front of the house, and then stopped a safe distance from the now imprisoned murderer. She picked up Jim's mobile and phoned the incident room direct, to give DC Neil Abbott brief details of the situation, her location, and telling him to get an Armed Response Unit and a paramedic team rolling as soon as she rang off.

Jim heard Laura talking, and knowing that they were now safe, and that only the clean-up remained, he passed out, relinquishing his grasp on the willpower that had kept him going while there was a threat of danger. He acquiesced, allowing his multiple injuries – including a mild concussion – to overpower him.

CHAPTER THIRTY-THREE

LEO was *not* dead. He was near to it, but still conscious, and had heard everything, but was unable to move as he had looked up into Jim Elliott's face. He could not even blink, and knew that he must have appeared to be beyond help, which in fact – although still hanging on to life by a very slender and fraying thread – he was.

With supreme effort Leo moved his head a fraction to the left and let gravity take over, to pull his cheek down to rest on the ground. He saw Parfitt knelt next to something that he thought should have been hidden from sight, swathed in bandages and securely locked away in a sarcophagus in the bowels of a pyramid, or deeply entombed below the sandy earth in the Valley of the Kings. The naked killer cradled the shrunken head of the leathery figure; a bizarre and chilling sight, as the man stroked the blonde wig – that sat askew on its skull – and stared into the gleaming artificial eyes, before bobbing his head to kiss pinched lips, that appeared to be stitched or wired together.

Leo shuddered inwardly as Parfitt raised his head, nodded, and began a one-sided conversation with the abomination.

"Yes, Mummy, I will," Hugh said. "They'll both pay for what they've done to us. We'll get away from here. And in a few weeks time when it's safe, we'll visit Laura and kill her. The Yank can live. Losing her will be his punishment."

Leo concentrated. He now had reason to not just let go and drift into oblivion, but to live long enough to make a difference. He withdrew into himself, cleared his mind of every thought except for a determined intent to move his right hand. At first there was nothing. He had no control over his body, which was without sensation, somehow separate from him, beyond his ability to communicate with and direct with instructions from his brain. It was as though he were trying to employ psychic powers or telekinesis to move some inert, remote object. He reached into hidden depths that he had never before plumbed, and willed his limp, unresponsive, perfidious limb to obey direction. And with a hitherto unimaginable focus of thought, he broke through, felt a twinge, then a rush of warmth and feeling as blood was pumped back into his arm to prickle and tingle painfully, coursing down the length of it to the tips of his fingers. He fisted the hand in triumph, before slowly easing it into the side pocket of his jacket and carefully gripping the old, gold-plated Calibre lighter that Sheila had given him as an anniversary present, what now seemed like a lifetime ago. Withdrawing it, he wished that he could have one last fag, safe now in the knowledge that he would not survive this day to fall prey to lung cancer, heart disease, or any other warning made by EEC Council Directive on every pack of cigarettes.

Letting his hand rest on the tinder-dry covering of the barn floor, Leo summoned up the strength of both body and spirit to accomplish what he knew would be his final act. Flicking the lighter's wheel with his thumb, he felt the heat from the flame, and offered it to the bed of straw, conscious of the fact that he was in essence putting a torch to his own funeral pyre. The initial crackle of igniting grain stalks became a greedy roar that was almost music to his ears. And then a wall of flame erupted next to him, taking hold of his wet clothes; steam coalescing with smoke as the searing heat swept over him and raced to all corners of the barn.

Leo had read many accounts of supposed out of body experiences that some people reported after being resurrected by medical intervention. And as the trial by fire became an almost exquisite sensation, he rose, drifted up to a far corner of the barn where the walls met the roof, and looked down at his own, charring body, that was twisting under the heat, fat dripping from it like tallow from a candle as it was consumed. He felt no pain now, only a feeling of well-being, and an overwhelming awe and sense of peace that he could not have previously imagined attainable. He saw the figure of the man who had released him from earthly bonds gather up the empty shell of what had once held the spirit of his mother, to retreat to the rear of the smoke and flame-filled inferno. And then, as if putting what were childish things behind him, and no longer a part of what had been mortal mayhem, Leo was absorbed by a light far brighter than the conflagration below him. He was imbued with the knowledge that he was about to embark on an enthralling journey of enlightenment, where Sheila would be his guide into a new phase of existence.

The smoke billowed out through a million cracks and gaps in the structure, finding every chink that offered it escape. And in what seemed a fiery rage, the barn exploded outwards, the blast exacerbated by the petrol tank of the Fiat as the highly flammable liquid detonated.

Laura watched spellbound, then started the car and reversed back farther from the blaze. With the engine idling, she waited, half expecting Hugh to emerge from the wall of smoke; a human torch, carrying his smouldering charge in his arms. But he did not appear, and as the seconds passed, she knew that it was over. Hugh had been cremated, burned alive, and was hopefully enduring an ordeal of the damned in the deepest abyss of hell for the acts that he had committed and the suffering he had caused others.

Putting the Sierra into gear and gunning the engine, Laura accelerated away; the car sliding sideways across the muddy ground as she over-steered. Spinning the wheel into the skid, she increased speed and shot down the bumpy quagmire of the drive, out onto the road, towards the sound of approaching sirens.

Elation and sadness welled up as a potent cocktail to overwhelm Laura in almost equal parts of intoxicating, dizzying relief and sorrow. She cried. The knowledge that Hugh was dead, and that she and Jim had somehow survived, was an intense and exhilarating feeling. But the cruel loss of the PI, and of a police detective who was probably one of her team, soured the tears that ran down her cheeks.

CHAPTER THIRTY-FOUR

JIM was floating on the edge of consciousness; dreams and reality fusing into a badly edited film. For a while he was back a dozen years, on a weekend yachting trip off Martha's Vineyard, lying below decks on a narrow bunk with the sea-swell rocking him gently back and forth. For some reason Pamela was sitting next to him, a half-smile on her lips. Not possible. Pam was dead, he knew that. So how could this be? And as he returned the smile, her face slowly morphed, melting and reforming, until he was looking up at Laura; was aware that he was in an ambulance, and that the yacht's bunk was in reality a gurney; the sensation of a heaving ocean being the vehicle's suspension responding to the undulations of a country road.

He drifted again, to find himself in the bedroom of the farmhouse, struggling with an animated, eyeless corpse that straddled him, its claw-like hands around his throat, hooked fingernails piercing the skin as it tried to strangle him. The apparition opened its toothless mouth, scattering rusted staples from puckered lips, to emit a demented, bowel-loosening wail. The fetid stench of decayed breath in his face made him gag and turn his head away.

"Jim...Jim! Can you hear me?" Laura said, squeezing his uninjured hand.

"He's concussed, love," the paramedic said after examining Jim's head wound and checking the pupils of his eyes. "He'll be in and out of it for a while."

"What's this week's word, huh?" Jim suddenly asked, his voice slightly slurred as though he'd been drinking.

"Uh, what?" Laura said.

"I said, what's the word? I thought you picked an obscure one out of the dictionary every Sunday, and used it as much as possible for a week."

She smiled. He was going to be okay. There was nothing wrong with his memory.

"Misanthrope," she replied.

He frowned. "Is that like lycanthrope? Some sort of werewolf?"

"I suppose there's a vague similarity. It's a hater of mankind; one who avoids human society."

"A fur-ball with attitude?"

"They're not necessarily hairy. They just have an attitude."

"Are you saying I'm one?"

"No. Although you aren't short in the hair department."

Jim smiled and passed out again, immediately dreaming of a figure that was a cross between Lon Chaney Jnr and the beast from the movie *An American Werewolf in London*. The setting of his vagary was Arizona, and the creature was loping from cactus to cactus, eyes glowing embers, reflecting the light of a blood-red moon.

Jim *had* suffered a mild concussion, and his back was a mess from the shotgun blast that had strafed him, but would heal, once all the lead shot was removed. It was his hand that was the main cause for concern.

A consultant strolled into Jim's room the following morning; a gaunt-faced man who peered over gold half-frame spectacles, his hands deep in the pockets of his Versace trousers. He looked dressed to play golf at some swank private country club, not deal with the sick or injured. He proved to be droll, an antithesis of his outwardly morose persona.

"Do you play the piano, Mr Elliott?" Dr Nigel McMillan asked in a refined lowland Scottish accent.

"Er...No. Why?" Jim said.

"That's good, because it's going to be a wee while before your hand starts to pull its weight again."

"What's the damage, Doctor?"

"Severed and partially severed tendons. Your index finger may never serve as an efficient nose-picker again."

"I don't pick my nose."

"Another plus. But seriously, I'll be operating on your hand as soon as your shaken but not stirred too much brain has settled down. With physio and the possibility of further surgery down the line, you should regain maybe eighty percent mobility in it."

As the consultant left, Laura arrived toting a carrier bag.

"Not fruit and flowers?" Jim said, hauling himself up into a sitting position.

"No, Coke, the 'real thing', not the nose-candy variety. I also brought you my MP3 player and headphones. There's a terrific selection of music on it; The Sound of Music, Des O'Connor's Greatest Hits, and a Disney sing-a-long."

"You've gotta be kidding."

"I am. There's Springsteen, Chris Rea, Old Blue Eyes and quite a lot of country and western, which should make you feel at home."

"Thanks, but I'll be out of here in forty-eight hours."

"Who says?"

"I do. I don't like hospitals, and I'm fine apart from the hand."

Laura leant over and kissed him on the mouth, easing her tongue between his lips and teeth as she ran her fingers lightly through his chest hair. He reached out to touch her breasts, but she pulled away, grinning, looking down between his legs at the now tented sheet. "Is that a gun, or—?"

"No. I'm just pleased to see you. Now, either strip off and climb in, or take a seat. No more prick-teasing, or I'll soil the linen, and the nurse will probably spank me."

"In your wet dreams, Elliott," Laura said, sitting back on the uncomfortable plastic chair, which she thought was a less than subtle ploy to discourage lengthy visits.

"Bring me up to speed, then," Jim said. "What happened after I passed out?"

Laura slipped off her jacket, thought about having a cigarette, and then remembered that she was in a no smoking area.

"The barn was gutted," she said. "I hung around until I was sure that Hugh couldn't have survived, and then drove out to the road. You were transferred to an ambulance, and I came to the hospital with you. The forensic team are picking through the remains. Clem is in surgery this morning. His foot is a mess, but thank God, he survived."

"He should have waited for me to arrive. But I think he was too anxious about you, Laura."

"He's a good copper. A bit of a loner, but I like him."

"I saw a newspaper earlier," Jim said. "You're almost a celebrity over this case. You should reassess your career. There's got to be a book deal in the offing. I can see it now; *The Tacker* by Laura Scott. Then it'll be a movie. Although they'd probably relocate it to Los Angeles instead of York, and cast someone like Mark Wahlberg in the role of Hugh. It would bear no resemblance to what you wrote, but it would pay big bucks."

Laura shook her head vehemently. "I don't want to profit from all the misery that a fellow officer caused. Christ knows what the final tally of victims will be. I doubt that we'll ever know."

"Business as usual, then?"

Laura felt the mood change. It was as if a sudden icy draught had entered the room to lower the temperature by a few degrees. The cold shadow of her job was there between them, festering; a wedge driven deep between her and all that she wanted from life. Unbeknown to Jim, she had made the decision to walk away from the sleaze, now sick of a life that was ruled by violence, drugs and the worst elements of human nature.

"I'm taking some leave, Jim. I think I'd like to see Arizona, as soon as all the debriefing and paperwork are out of the way. A guided tour might be best. Any idea who I should book with?"

Jim's disposition was instantly modified. "Elliott's Golden West Tours are incomparable," he said. "You get as much sex and scenery as you can take. It's a personally conducted, tailor-made romp through the Southwest. You'll see Monument Valley, the Grand Canyon, the Painted Desert, Vegas; the whole nine yards. But watch out for that guide, he's a randy piece of work, given half a chance."

"It sounds like just what I need. Can I book now?"

Laura left the hospital walking on air, so excited at the prospect of starting over with Jim that she forgot to have a cigarette until she had reached the car park. She was now ready to enter a new phase of life, to break free from the cocoon of her career and spread her wings. In the final analysis, it was only people and relationships that were worth a damn. Her job was just an endless war that could at best result in the winning of only small battles. The overall picture was grim. Crime in all its multifarious forms was a part of human nature, as natural as eating, making love, taking one breath after another. It wasn't something that could be cut out like a diseased appendix. Good and evil came in many varieties, and she was no avenging angel put on earth to fight the Devil in all his guises. Her close call with Hugh – which could have so easily resulted in her death – and the still gut-wrenching memory of the swiftness with which Kara had been taken from her, combined to give a fuller comprehension of the brevity of life. Nothing that happened, however bad, would knock the world off its axis, bar it being struck by a large enough asteroid. Had she died at the farmhouse, then it would have been newsworthy for a fleeting moment, for strangers to read about as life marched on unaffected by her passing. It was now time to look out for number one. As far as she was concerned, she'd paid her dues in service to an uncaring society; had been there, collected the emotional scars and got the ripped and bloody T-shirt.

Egotistical would be her chosen watchword for the coming week. She was ready for a large dose of systematic selfishness, and fuck anyone who didn't like it.

It was ten o'clock the next morning when Laura got a call from pathology.

"Laura? It's Brian Morris."

"Yes, Brian."

"Are you okay? I heard what happened. It's hard to believe that it was Hugh."

"I'm fine, Brian. If you walk away in one piece, you can't complain. And *I'm* still trying to come to terms with it being Hugh. It seems you never really know anyone. Only the side of themselves that they let you see."

"I thought you should know that you still have a big problem," Brian said, his voice lowered as though what he had to impart was a state secret of such magnitude that he was scared of being overheard telling it to the world at large.

"In what sense?"

"We found seventeen bodies in the barn. Sixteen were in shallow graves, and one of them was Trish Pearson. The others are too badly decomposed for a quick ID. They'd been buried in quicklime. Above ground, we only found one charred corpse. I think dental records will confirm that it's Leo Talbot. There were *no* other remains."

"But Hugh was trapped, locked in the barn for Christ's sake! He *must* have been there."

"No, Laura. He got out. Believe me, he was not inside it."

"Fuck! Who else knows about this?"

"Officially, you're the first. When I hang up, I'll have to make more calls and let the dogs of war loose, so to speak."

"Thanks, Brian. Was there anything else?"

"We found a glass eye in the barn. I say glass, but it was actually a high density resin compound. It had melted; looked like a fried egg with a blue yoke. I still can't figure Hugh as being so sick. He always seemed the type who I would have been proud to have as a son-in-law."

After Brian rang off, Laura lit a cigarette. Dragged on it nervously. Paced the office. The news that Hugh was still alive and on the loose had come as a complete shock. She could not fathom out how he could have escaped being burned up in the inferno. He would now be the subject of a massive manhunt, but being a copper he would know exactly what procedures would be employed, and what measures to take to lie low, vanish and avoid capture. She imagined that he was many miles away by now, almost certainly in London, or any large city that would provide an environment in which he could become anonymous among the masses.

In actual fact, Hugh was less than a thirty minute drive from where Laura was standing. He was planning what he thought to be a fitting revenge on both her and Jim Elliott. They had conspired to bring him down, and almost succeeded in their endeavours. But he could not, would not be stopped, and was not one to forgive or forget. As an enemy, he had no equal. Everyone got to pay the piper, eventually. And in their case it would be sooner rather than later. He and his mother had survived a terrible and potentially fatal experience. Now, his former life was irretrievable, but he had the strength to overcome adversity. Laura and the Yank had killed Hugh Parfitt in name only, forcing him to adopt another identity. He would move on, after first meeting the challenge and prevailing. They would come to know that he was a living nightmare; one that they could not wake from to flee and escape. The only feeling left for Laura now was a burning hatred. The saying, 'You're either with me or against me' came to mind. Well the lovely Laura and Mr FBI were certainly not with him. They were the opposition, and would soon know that they were on the losing team.

CHAPTER THIRTY-FIVE

DOMINIC Armstrong was one of three GP's operating out of a small surgery in Skelby; a village west of the A19, situated in the lush pastorage of the Neame Valley, alongside the banks of the River Ouse.

Dominic left his last house call, out at Dutton's Farm, at six-thirty p.m. and headed for home. Alfred Dutton, a sixty-year-old sheep farmer, had been suffering from chest pains, and having already recovered from one heart attack, which had struck at a time of enormous stress during the foot and mouth epidemic (which had resulted in his entire flock being slaughtered), Dominic quickly made the decision to call for an ambulance. His policy being an old and faithful one; 'better safe than sorry'.

Having waited for paramedics to arrive, Dominic drove down to the valley floor, relishing the thought of being off duty for the next two days, barring unforeseen emergencies.

Home was a detached Yorkstone house – on a little-used minor road, a mile outside the village – at which he lived with his wife, Paula. The location was idyllic, a far cry from the Chapeltown area of Leeds, where he had previously been in practise for over twenty years. Break-ins by junkies desperate for drugs had become commonplace, and the workload, although shared with five colleagues, had been mind-numbing and without letup. He had dreamed of being part of a country practise for a long time, and not a day passed without him consciously appreciating the opportunity which had arisen and led him to Skelby.

Dominic and Paula now enjoyed a quiet rural life; just the two of them, since their daughter, Caroline, had flown the nest after gaining a place at Durham University.

Pulling into the circle driveway, Dominic parked under the leafy mantle provided by mature chestnut trees; their leaf-laden branches reaching for the front of the house, painting it in dappled light and shade.

"I'm home, Paula," Dominic shouted, setting his battered medical bag on the hall table, and hanging his trilby, which was as dilapidated as the bag, on one of the pegs of the wall-mounted rack above it.

"In here," Paula called from the lounge.

Entering the room, he saw that they had company. Paula was sitting in an armchair, facing him. And from where he stood, he could see the back of another woman's head, her blonde hair apparently and bewilderingly flecked with pieces of straw.

Walking to the centre of the lounge, he froze, and his legs nearly gave way as he saw the mummified corpse that was sitting opposite his wife; the single eye in its hideous face canted to the side, as if staring into the fireplace.

"Unh!" That was the only sound he uttered, as his brain attempted to interpret the macabre scene before him.

The cold steel at his throat caused him to jerk sideways, resulting in a shallow cut from the sharp blade.

"Easy, easy," Hugh said, pressing the knife that he had taken from the kitchen drawer even harder against the doctor's wrinkled neck. "Mother, this is Dr Armstrong. He's going to fix me up. And if he behaves and does exactly as he's told, and keeps his shit together, then I won't have to disembowel the lovely Paula."

"I'm sorry, Dom," Paula said, unable to staunch the tears that ran down her pale cheeks. "He told me that if I tried to warn you, he'd kill both of us."

"That's right, Dom," Hugh said conversationally. "I *will* kill you if necessary. I know it's an antisocial trait, but everyone has their little foibles. Now sit down next to the lovely Paula and I'll explain what's going to happen."

Dom struggled to move, legs feeling set in concrete, only able to respond when a sharp blow to his lower back started him off, for him to totter forward and almost fall across Paula. It was only then he noticed that her wrists were bound with silver duct tape.

"I'm only going to say this once, Dom," Hugh said, sitting next to his mother and holding her hand in his. "We've had a very, very bad day, haven't we Mother?"

"Yes, son, dreadful," she replied, her words and wan smile lost on the captive couple.

"I've already had to kill once today," Hugh continued, his full attention now back on Dominic. "So please don't give me the slightest reason to add to that. I've been shot by some kind of air gun, and I think that a few of my ribs are cracked. Also, my nose is broken, and my feet are cut up. The deal is, you patch me up, and then after a couple of days, when I'm feeling chipper, I leave you locked in your cellar and vanish."

Hugh had been extremely lucky, and knew it. As the barn had been engulfed by fire, he had picked his mother up and charged at the rear wall, shouldering his way through weak, brittle boards that had offered barely any resistance to the sudden impact. He had run through the thick stand of trees, out to the road, to lay his mother down in the long grass, out of sight. He then waved down a Post Office van that – fortuitously for him – had been passing at the right time and place.

"My barn's on fire," he shouted, leaning into the driver's open window; the smell of singed hair, scorched skin and smoke convincing the uniformed postman of what was in fact the truth. "Do you have a phone to call for help?"

As Jason Harper reached for his mobile, Hugh hit him; a powerful, fisted blow that caught the young man just above his ear and knocked him sideways.

Hugh pulled the door open and struck the dazed man another four times, only stopping when sure that he was unconscious.

Placing his mother gently in the back of the vehicle under a jumble of parcels and mail pouches, he then bundled Jason into the front passenger seat, where the young man slipped down into the foot well.

After driving east on back roads for two miles, Hugh drove through an open gateway that led into a field of wheat that rippled wavelike in the breeze; a golden sea under the strengthening light of the sun. He dragged the stricken postman out on to the ground, stripped him of his uniform and lifted up a large football-sized piece of rock, with the full intention of pulverising the man's head to a pulp, but on a whim, cast it aside and bound him hand and foot with twine that he removed from a large parcel. Bunching one of the young man's socks into a ball and stuffing it into his mouth, he tied it securely in place with his necktie to gag him, and secreted him alongside his mother, before donning the uniform and driving northwest, skirting the city of York and picking up the A19.

Feeling uneasy and vulnerable, knowing that he would have to find somewhere to rest up and lie low for a while, Hugh made a left onto a minor road, slowing after several minutes as he passed a solitary house that was set back from the highway, almost obscured behind a screen of tall and leafy trees. The brass plate screwed to one of the large, brick gateposts informed him that this was Mayfield House, the residence of Dr D. Armstrong. Without hesitation he drove up the curving driveway and stopped outside the front of the house.

Stepping out of the van, keeping his head down to hide his bloody, swollen nose, and with a parcel in hand, he approached the door and pressed the old fashioned porcelain bell push.

As a middle-aged woman opened the door, he rammed the parcel into her chest, forcing her back into the hall with such force that she fell heavily, to end up on the floor in a sitting position, looking up at him in mute surprise.

"Listen, lady," Hugh said. "Answer my questions quickly, or I'll fucking kill you, it's that simple. Is there anyone else in the house?"

"N...no," Paula managed to reply, thinking that this was a burglary; having no idea that mere robbery would have been a Godsend.

"When does the good doctor get home?"

"In...in about an hour. But it could be longer."

"Who else lives here?"

"No one. There's just the two of us."

"Okay, get up. We're going to get in the van and hide it around the back of the house. Then you follow my instructions to the letter. Don't give me the slightest excuse to hurt you. Understand?"

"Yes," Paula said as she climbed shakily to her feet.

"What's your name, lady?"

"Paula."

"I'm Hugh, Paula. Take it easy and you'll be just fine."

Once the Post Office van was parked in a disused stable block and covered with a tarpaulin sheet, Hugh found thicker rope and tied the now semiconscious postman more securely, tethering him to a post at the back of a hay-strewn stall and taping his mouth. He had no intention of murdering anyone else, unless he had to. He was not a fucking thrill killer who wasted people for the sake of it. He determined to be disciplined and remain in control. These people were not a part of his problem, and he bore them no malice. To leave a trail of corpses was not in his game plan.

Following instructions, Paula carried the mummified corpse into the house and propped it up in a sitting position on the settee. It was then that she knew true fear and became wholly aware that the stranger was stark raving mad, as well as bad.

"Make me a coffee and something to eat," Hugh ordered as he looked about him, holding the shaking woman with one hand, his fingers and thumb gripping, digging into the nape of her neck. "Does your husband own a shotgun?" He then asked. "And if you say no, and then I find one, I'll use it on him when he gets home."

"Yes. There's a gun safe in the cellar," Paula replied. "The keys are in the cutlery drawer, under the plastic tray."

Before the doctor arrived home, Hugh ate a large chunk of mature cheddar cheese served with pickles and homemade crusty bread, and enjoyed two mugs of strong, sweet coffee. For very dissimilar reasons, neither Paula nor his mother had an appetite.

Now, with Dominic seated on the settee next to his mother, Hugh took off the blood-spotted blue shirt and retrieved the shotgun from where he had propped it behind Paula's chair. He then wound duct tape – furnished by Paula – around her neck several times, before tightly taping the ends of the 12 gauge's barrels to the back of her skull. Finally, with his hand taped to the stock, finger on the trigger, he was ready.

"Got the picture, Doc?" Hugh said. "You inject me with anything other than a safe dose of local anaesthetic and antibiotics, or try to be a hero, and I pull the trigger and blow Paula's head off. Now feel free to go and get what you need. And if you phone the police, remember that even if I was shot through the window, Paula would still die. So move your arse. You've got less than a minute to join us in the kitchen."

An hour later, Dominic had finished up. He had excised three of the four pellets; one from Hugh's neck, a second from his shoulder, and a third from his chest. The fourth was too deeply imbedded, lodged behind a major blood vessel. He explained that he didn't have the training to even attempt to remove it; that he was a GP, not a surgeon. He then bound Hugh's ribs, three of which were cracked, and finally removed slivers of glass from, and dressed his unsolicited patient's feet.

"How am I doing, Doc?" Hugh asked, free of pain for a while, due to the injections that had artificially induced an absence of sensation to all but his fractured nose.

"You'll live. But you need more surgery to remove the other pellet from your chest."

"I'll get round to it. Now let's go out to the stables and fetch the postman. I think that you and he can share each other's company for a while."

The cellar was perfect, with no windows or secondary exit.

"You're lucky," Hugh said to the postman, (who was conscious but concussed), before locking him and Dominic in the underground room. "This is Doctor Armstrong, who is now your personal physician."

227

Cutting the tape between her head and the shotgun, Hugh used a tea towel to blindfold Paula, and then bound her hands behind her.

"I won't be long, Mummy," he said, and led Paula up the stairs into the bedroom, pushed her onto the bed and used more tape to secure her by the neck to the brass bed head. He then sat next to her and stroked her pallid and creased cheek with the back of his hand. "I don't want to gag you, Paula," he said. "So please be quiet and patient. What happens over the next couple of days will largely depend on you and your behaviour. If you comply with everything I ask of you, you won't die."

After showering, then shaving with the doctor's electric razor, he returned to the bedroom and rifled through the wardrobes, finding a clean shirt, slacks, socks, and a pair of brogues that were only slightly oversize. Once dressed, he cut Paula free and removed all her bonds, allowing her to visit the bathroom, but staying outside the door to listen as she cried, threw-up, then resumed crying.

Paula could have climbed out of the window, dropped down on to the flat roof of the garage and escaped, but knew that Dominic and the young postman would pay for her actions. She also briefly considered concealing a pair of hairdressing scissors about her person, but knew that she lacked the resolve needed to attempt to kill him. If she tried and failed, then he would almost certainly murder them all. After composing herself, but still feeling more afraid than she had ever been in her life, she walked back out on to the landing, to see her captor turn from where he was sitting at the top of the stairs.

"Now listen up, Paula," Hugh said, managing a small smile, even though the act exacerbated the throbbing pain in his nose. "I need you to behave and act normally, and see to it that any callers to the house or on the phone don't think anything is wrong here. You'll want to run or give me away if you can, but that would be a very bad idea. If you want your hubby to make it through this in one piece, just do exactly as you're told."

"I'll do whatever you want. Just please don't hurt us."

Hugh stared at her with solemn-eyed sincerity. "I've got nothing against you folks. I just need to keep my head down for a day or two. That means it's in your best interest to make sure that nobody figures out where I am. I promise that you won't come to any harm, if you help me," he said, reaching out, taking her hand and leading her down the stairs.

For three days, Hugh watched news bulletins, taking little pleasure from the initial and premature reports of his death, and not in the least surprised when the forensic teams – after sifting through the ashes – determined that his remains were not among them. He allowed Paula to take food and drink down to the cellar at regular intervals, while he waited at the top of the stairs with the shotgun aimed at her back, in case one of the men went for broke and tried to escape. Each night he used Paula for relief, having no need to take her by force, as she passively endured his demands in the hope that her compliance would gain favour. After sex, Hugh made her take three strong sleeping pills, and taped her wrist to his, before dozing fitfully as he fine-tuned both his short and long term plans.

He had fled the farm with nothing. His false ID and money were lost to him, and he would now have to initially live dangerously until he could assume a new identity. Each evening, under cover of darkness, he had Paula drive her husband's Rover to cash points as far afield as Thirsk and Harrogate, where he would sit in the car while she made withdrawals from ATMs. Added to the money that had been in the house, he amassed a total of over two thousand pounds.

Paula rated an Oscar, he thought. She had phoned the surgery on the second morning and told Dr Jeremy Farnsworth – the senior partner of the practise – that Dominic had left for Cambridge, where his ageing father had been rushed into hospital and was in a critical condition following a massive stroke. She said that she would keep the surgery updated on the situation, but did not think Dom would be back on duty for several days. She had also conducted a lengthy telephone conversation with her daughter, Caroline, who rang at least twice a week, and came home once a month for a long weekend.

Paula thanked God that Caroline had only visited the previous week, and that she had not been at the house when the rapist and killer had made their home his temporary hideout. The thought of him subjecting Caroline to all that she had been through was too much of a nightmare to contemplate. She had chitchatted with Caroline, told her that her dad was on an emergency call-out, and managed not to sound anything other than her normal and cheerful self. She finally hung up, and then started shaking uncontrollably, more with a deep sense of relief than from any other emotion.

The television news had disclosed the identity of the maniac in their midst. He was, of all things, a policeman; Detective Sergeant

Hugh Parfitt, alias the Tacker, who was by all accounts a serial killer and had escaped from a burning barn earlier on the day that he had turned up at their door. The public was warned that he was highly dangerous, and that he should not be approached under any circumstances.

Commonsense told Paula that when he left, he would not leave them alive to bear witness against him. And yet she could think of no way to prevent what seemed inevitable.

It was on the fourth evening as dusk fell, that Hugh made ready to leave.

"I've got a few things to do, and then we'll be on our way," he said to Paula. "Have you got a road map or an A to Z of London?"

Paula found him a motoring atlas, and then waited in a state of terror, positive that he would live up to his reputation and slaughter everyone in the house.

"Make up a couple of flasks of coffee and some sandwiches if you want, Paula," Hugh said. "I'm going to lock you in the cellar with Dr Dom and Postman Pat. I expect you to try and escape, but be very sure that I've left before you do."

Paula hesitantly prepared the food and drink, and placed it in a plastic supermarket shopping bag, hoping beyond hope that this was not a sick ploy, and that the madman really was going to keep his word and let them live.

"My mother and I thank you for your hospitality," Hugh said as Paula walked stiffly down the cellar steps, expecting to be blasted by the shotgun with every shallow breath that she drew; her whole body tensed, ready for the imagined impact and pain.

Hugh locked the door, put the 12 gauge on the kitchen table, and then manoeuvred a weighty Welsh dresser up against their only way of escape.

In the bathroom, he applied a semi-permanent hair colour, of the shade that Paula had used for nearly a decade to dye her greying hair. He then cleaned up all traces of what he had done and pocketed the empty dye bottle. His former fair hair was now a deep chestnut brown, dramatically altering his appearance. He had left the farm naked and on the run, but had swiftly regrouped and now had temporary transport in the form of the doctor's Rover, and enough money for the time being. He would have to initially live on the edge, until he could assume a new identity. It was time for him and his mother to move on. The Armstrongs' would no doubt make good their escape, eventually, or be found. And it would hopefully be assumed – as he had asked her for a London A-Z – that he was on his way, if not already in the capital. The last thing they would expect was for him to stay under their noses, and to kill again before disappearing like a ghost.

CHAPTER THIRTY-SIX

TWENTY-four hours after undergoing surgery on his hand, Jim discharged himself from the hospital. He had been dressed and ready to leave when Laura arrived for what she had assumed was to be just another visit.

"I thought they were keeping you in until at least tomorrow," Laura said.

"So did they, but I declined the invitation to stay on. My head's okay and my hand has more bandaging than a boxer's. I'm just taking up valuable space, and I'm likely to die from boredom if I stay in here another minute."

Outside, after Jim had signed a release form to officially gain his freedom by relieving the hospital of all responsibility and liability, Laura lit a cigarette as they walked towards the Cherokee, which she had picked up for him after returning the rented Sierra to Hertz.

"Will you stay at the cottage for a while?" Laura asked, hearing the imploring edge to her voice and feeling embarrassed at what sounded a blatant, almost beseeching request, rather than the offhand enquiry she had meant it to be.

"I've no choice," Jim replied, smiling mischievously. "I need a full-time nurse, driver, cook and lover...and not necessarily in that order, until my hand heals up. And you know what they say. A volunteer is worth ten pressed men."

"You chauvinist pig, Elliott. It's a good job I love your worthless hide, or I'd leave you at the kerbside and cancel our trip to Arizona."

"There is one other reason why I'm going to stay at your place," Jim said, his smile fading, to be replaced by a worried frown. "Hugh will attempt to kill you."

Laura shook her head. "I don't think so. I doubt he's within two hundred miles of here. And anyway, the chief's put a round-the-clock watch on the cottage. Hugh's too clever to walk into a trap. He'll have enough on his plate trying to keep one step ahead of us. I doubt he'll give me another thought."

"You're wrong, Laura. Stop using logic. He's lost it. He'll want revenge. And in his unsound mind, it's you who's caused his life to nose-dive. He won't be able to let it lie. You should move out of the cottage until he's safely behind bars, or permanently if he doesn't get lifted."

"If you're right, then he'd find me wherever I moved to. He's a detective, remember?"

"Okay. So we wait for him, and when he makes his move we'd better be ready for it, or we're history. He's a crazy sonofabitch, but slick as snake-oil."

That first night back at the cottage, they talked of hardly anything but Hugh, his victims, the sad loss of Leo, and the events that appeared to have warped Hugh's mind, creating a monster within him that he had obviously been able to hide and control for many years; an undetectable part of his character, that he unleashed when the irresistible urges bubbled up and demanded to be nurtured and pacified.

"I have no doubt that he had an incestuous relationship with his mother," Jim said. "One that she most likely instigated and encouraged from when he was a young boy. He was in love with her on a multilevel basis. He would have been devastated when she started an affair with another man, and couldn't accept it or get his mind round it. We'll never know whether he tampered with the car and caused the crash that killed her, but I think it's a safe bet that he did. Digging her up and preserving her was a denial of his loss. He needed her so much that he just couldn't let go."

"But all the killings and mutilations, Jim. Why did he do it?" Laura said, pouring them both large brandies, as once again she reflected on the countless hours' that she had spent with a man who she had considered to be a caring friend, as well as an honest, decent colleague.

"I'd say he never forgave his mother. So to punish her, he transferred her personality to living girls who bore a superficial likeness to how she'd looked in life. He could then vent his anger and frustration on her: kill her over and over again at will, and make her suffer endlessly for what he chose to think of as her sins."

"Christ, it's so obscene and ghoulish. I can't believe that I never saw a glimpse of that side of him. How could he hide it?"

"A lot of sicko's are ingenious, Laura. They can blend with their surroundings, and can project whatever emotions or part of their overall personality is required to maintain the illusion of normality. The side of Hugh that he allowed you to see was real. He probably loved his job, and gave the caring side of his nature full rein. The ability to keep his dark side hidden is a mechanism that many serial killers are capable of controlling. A percentage of them are even married with a family. They can be good fathers and husbands; trusted and respected members of the community. I found that it's usually the people closest to them that are most shocked when they are eventually caught. They defended them all the way to the booby hatch, prison or lethal injection chamber in most instances."

"Enough," Laura said. "I want to put it out of my mind for a while. Let's go to bed, wedge the door, and see if your injuries have affected you in any other department."

"It's my hand that's damaged. All the important parts are in perfect working order."

"I'll be the judge of that," Laura said, picking up their empty glasses and taking them through to the kitchen, then checking the new window locks for the third time, and ensuring that the front and back doors were locked and dead bolted.

They lay naked, a single cotton sheet covering them to their waists. The summer night was humid, and they were both coated in a fine sheen of perspiration. They kissed slowly, lips parted, tongues teasing, probing.

"God, I needed that," Laura gasped a few minutes later. "You were right; the important bits are in perfect working order."

"Flattery will get you everywhere," Jim said, reaching behind her to caress her buttocks as she leant forward to kiss his lips.

Climbing off him, Laura headed for the bathroom, and he raised himself up on his elbows to admire her shapely form as she walked out on to the landing.

"Are you tired?" Jim shouted, after listening to the splashing in the toilet bowl, and acknowledging that every action, however commonplace, was in Laura a special and sensual event.

"Not really. Why, are you still feeling randy?"

"No, I'm famished. Let's have some cheese and biscuits, and open a bottle of cabernet."

They talked until almost dawn, but skirted around the subject of their future together, as though broaching it would somehow spoil what had been a perfect evening. Both of them were scared to be specific as to what they envisaged or hoped for from the relationship, though each wanted to be with the other, greedy to make up for the time that they had spent apart.

"Where do we go from here?" Jim said, heart in mouth as he turned the conversation to what felt like an almost taboo area that was fraught with emotional pitfalls; deep traps with sharpened stakes, waiting for him to fall on to and be speared. "Is this just another quick fling? Or do we stir in a little commitment for flavouring and make a meal of it?"

"I love you, Jim, and I want to be with you. I intend to quit the force, but it's daunting. I can't just sit back and wait for you to come home every evening. I wouldn't make a good stay-at-home-do-the-housework kind of wife."

"You could join the firm. PR isn't brain surgery or rocket science, but it's a step up from dealing with all that's rotten in society, and it pays better."

"It's not just about money, Jim. Don't you miss being with the FBI? Be honest."

"I miss certain aspects of it. But that's only natural. Overall, I miss it like a bad tooth. Life moves on, and change is part of the process. Even if you stay a cop, retirement will start tapping on your shoulder. All of a sudden you'll be in your fifties and the big six-O will be looming. Come the day, you'd still have to make a fresh start and find a point to it all, but with less time left to do it."

"Christ, Jim, that's a gloomy outlook."

"It's the truth, honey. If you're thinking of quitting, then you've already realised that you don't need another twenty years of swimming against the tide. You've got to start looking forward. Your career might have helped you to become the person you are today, but you don't owe it a damn thing. You need to believe that, and walk away from it."

"If what you say is true, how come so many ex-cops and even FBI profilers stay on the fringes? A lot go into crime consultancy, or write books about it, or end up in security or private investigation."

"They can't let go, so they stay connected from a distance. But for every former agent like John Douglas, who uses his experience to write best-sellers, there are scores like me, who go into non-related second careers. I admit that law enforcement gets into your blood. It's like a drug, and can be just as dangerous for your health as snorting coke, popping pills or mainlining. With me, it became a mission to get inside a monster's head and think my way into his mind; to understand what rang his bell, and then home in on him. But there are healthier and better ways to live each day. You just have to set new and more fulfilling goals, and find something to fill the gap...the part of your nature that thrived on a certain aspect of being involved in evil, till you're past the cold turkey stage and the sun comes up brighter and warmer than ever."

"I can't even stop smoking, Jim."

"That's because you don't want to enough. You can see the benefits, but your heart isn't in it. You may never stop. It takes more than willpower, or the toll on your health. It takes desire."

"You're right, and I know it. When we get across the pond and start Elliott's Golden West Tour, I'll get some distance and perspective, and work it out. What really did it for you, Jim? Was there a defining moment?"

"No, nothing like a sudden revelation. It was a build up, like tartar. People that I cared about were killed, and I nearly bought it myself. I started to wake up feeling bad every day, and knew that I was losing the plot. I remember sitting up all night and watching the sun come up over D.C. one morning. It was fall, and the gold and copper of the trees was also on the grass in drifts of leaves that were as bright and alluring as an open chest of pirate's treasure trove. There was a film of mist clinging to the surface of the Potomac, and a skein of geese flying above it in formation. It was a beautiful and peaceful moment, and I suddenly got to thinking that you only get to be part of this gift called life for a limited amount of time. Each day is a one off, never to be got back experience. I cottoned-on then, at that moment, to the fact that this isn't a rehearsal; it's a one act play. I was down in the grounds of an empty coffee cup; couldn't get any lower. I just knew as I sat and looked out of my apartment window at the beginning of a new day that I was at the end of a book, and had to close it and start another. I'd reached a point where I knew that if I'd kept on going as I was, I would've been overwhelmed and gone under and probably ended up in some rubber room, doped up on Thorazine for the duration. I don't mind admitting that I'd reached a wall I didn't want to climb over."

Laura poured them both another glass of the ruby-red cabernet. The bottle was now empty, but the crackers, brie, wedges of cheddar and the small wheel of Gouda that she had put out sat untouched and forgotten on the coffee table.

"Do you think you could put up with me full-time?" Laura said.

"I don't think I could, I *know* it," Jim said, reaching across the table to hold her hand. "We deal with Parfitt, and then get on with the rest of our lives, together, right?"

"You really believe that he's stupid enough to stay around and try something, don't you?"

"He'll come, Laura, and soon. He's driven with a hatred for you that must be stuck in his craw like broken glass. You put it together and identified him. But he won't imagine that we'll be ready for him. He knows that he's expected to run and hide, so he'll be too confident, and that gives us the advantage. Remember, he's basically insane, and wants what he feels is justice for what we've done to him and his mother. While you're at the station tomorrow, I'll buy some self protection items. We'll be ready to give him a proper welcome."

"Don't forget, the cottage is under police surveillance. There are two armed officers watching out for me."

"He could get past them, Laura. Better safe than dead."

"You really know how to make a girl feel secure."

"I don't want you to feel secure. I want you to feel very ill at ease, until it's settled."

Minster Firearms was situated inside the city walls, down a side street not far from the tourist-choked Shambles. Jim pushed open the sturdy security door, to be met by an Aladdin's cave of weaponry, and the rich familiar, evocative smell of gun-oil and leather. He walked across to the display-case counter and nodded at the bored-looking and bearded guy who sat behind it on a wooden chair; an imposing Orson Welles look-alike with the remains of an unlit cigar clamped between his teeth as he looked up impassively from the girlie magazine that lay limp, well-thumbed and dog-eared in front of him. Jim studied the impressive array of handguns behind the glass, which he could not procure without a firearms certificate. He then looked up at the walls, where among rifles and shotguns he saw a weapon that – although deadly – could be purchased over the counter, without any formalities or attendant paperwork.

He selected a Barnett 'A.P.' System Rhino crossbow, incorporating a loading mechanism that would allow him to arm it one-handed. With a dozen bolts, or quarrels as 'Orson' called the short heavy arrows, of which six could be clipped into the weapon's curved structure for speedy reloading, he felt almost equipped to face any adversary, although an Uzi or a .44 Magnum would have been his preferred choice of personal weapon for the confrontation that he was convinced was waiting to be played out in the not too distant future.

Back at the cottage that evening, Jim felt more at ease. He felt confident that he could deal with an attack that could not be a surprise, because he expected it. He had also decided that he had no intention of making any effort whatsoever to take Parfitt alive. He would use extreme prejudice on sight of the man. This was life or death, and he would not hesitate in negating any threat, to ensure that both he and Laura survived to make memories together.

CHAPTER THIRTY-SEVEN

"IT won't be for long, Mummy, I promise," Hugh said, lowering her gently onto the folded blanket in the boot of the doctor's rover, and placing a pillow under her head before closing the lid. "Sweet dreams."

With all the unaccustomed handling and movement, the corpse's left leg had become detached. The paper thin dried skin and rotted tendons had parted at the knee as he had carried her along the hall. But he did not notice the mouldering limb lying on the carpet as he went back for the supplies he had packed. A part of him would always see her complete and in pristine condition; alive and robust, with no disfigurement or impediment. His mind had imbued her with eternal youth, and would allow nothing to blemish his perfect image of her. The lower part of the leg had therefore become completely invisible to him as it fell away from the corpse.

After incarcerating the three nonentities in the cellar and making ready, he had sat for a while on the settee next to his mother, his face slack and without expression as the electrical charges in his brain almost short-circuited, holding him in a state similar to that which an epileptic experiences immediately after suffering a seizure. Only his eyes moved, jiggling rapidly from side to side. And as the mental spell broke, he was confused, taking over five minutes to regroup his thoughts and become aware of who and where he was. It was becoming increasingly difficult to keep his two incongruous personalities apart. Like matter and antimatter they were on a collision course that would prove untenable if and when they met. He was as unstable as a stick of sweating dynamite, on the verge of disassembling by way of a cerebral meltdown that would result from the pending internal explosion.

"Laura," he whispered. "Must deal with the bitch. She is a betrayer; a modern-day Delilah."

With the shotgun, a box of cartridges, a hammer, six-inch nails and a selection of the darkest clothing that Dominic had owned all secreted next to his mother in the boot, Hugh locked up the house and drove away. He now wore a pair of the doctor's horn-rimmed glasses, with the lenses removed. And with his now dark hair and swollen, broken nose, he bore little resemblance to the man that the police would be searching for.

Driving past Laura's cottage at first light, Hugh noted the unmarked Vauxhall Cosworth that was parked almost opposite, up on the berm and in the deep shadow of the low, thick limbs of a mature oak tree. Behind the partially misted windows of the car, he caught a glimpse of two figures, who he knew would be armed coppers, probably special branch.

The Yank's Jeep Cherokee was in Laura's drive, so it was obvious that they were taking no chances, and had prepared for the unexpected. He would make preparations and return after dark. He determined that the police presence would prove more help than hindrance.

Eric and Molly Champion had parked their car and caravan in a lay-by on the A166 adjacent to a large picnic area that was set well back from the road amid trees that shielded the tables, benches and vehicles from sight, and dampened the noise of passing traffic. They had driven up from Birmingham the day before, their plan being to stop off at several spots along the east coast, then cut back inland from Whitby to cross the North York Moors. They were seasoned caravaners, but liked privacy, and so tended to avoid overcrowded official sites, preferring to stay in quiet, usually deserted locations. They were both fifty-nine years old, and were looking forward to retirement the following year from the social security office jobs that had brought them together thirty years earlier.

Up at six a.m., Molly had put the kettle on to boil for tea, before stepping outside on to the dew-laden grass at the side of the caravan. She stretched and yawned, enjoying the fresh and invigorating morning air. A sudden movement caught her eye, directing her gaze to a man who emerged from the bushes and walked across to the vehicle that was parked up behind them. Molly grinned. It was obvious that the guy had been for a leak, or maybe to take a dump, due to there being no toilets in the lay-by, and the fact that he was zipping up his trousers. The man gave her a quick glance; looked a little embarrassed, as if knowing what she was thinking. Another few seconds and in his cab, and the lorry's engine roared into life. Molly watched as the large eighteen-wheeler passed by her, to rumble out on to the road, heading west.

There was only one other vehicle in sight, a green Rover parked about thirty yards in front of them. It crossed her mind that it was probably a sales rep that had stopped for a couple of hours' kip during the night, and no doubt slept for longer than planned.

The whistling summoned her back on board. She moved quickly for a big woman, stepping up into the caravan and turning the steaming kettle off before it woke Eric up. She put tea bags into the brightly coloured Garfield pot, and filled it with the boiling water, before turning the portable radio on for a fix of easy listening, courtesy of Radio Two.

Sitting at the small dinette table, Molly looked ahead to the day that she and Eric could leave Birmingham permanently, to perhaps set up home somewhere in North Yorkshire. They had lived in the same semi in Smethwick throughout their marriage, but both preferred the countryside; hence the forays into it at every opportunity. There was nowt so queer as folk, Molly thought. Their next door neighbours, Colin and Joan Miller, had accompanied them for a long weekend to the Welsh borders the previous summer, and had both been on the verge of having panic attacks. They viewed anything other than the comforting, overpopulated brick and concrete habitat that they had spent their entire lives in as unsettling and in some way threatening. The great outdoors was obviously not everyone's cup of tea. Funny how wide open spaces could in some way disconcert townies.

With her back to the door, Molly looked out through the opposite window. She smiled at the sight of two grey squirrels. The cute rodents scoured the tops of the picnic tables and investigated a waste bin, looking for scraps left by the previous day's visitors. This, as usual, was a world away from the stress of city life, with its frenetic pace and attendant noise and pollution. Molly was positive that without these tranquil breaks, the pressure of their jobs – dealing with men and women that demanded benefit in the form of money, and who became angry or distraught if they did not qualify for payment – would overwhelm them.

As Molly thought to take Eric a cup of tea, something clamped her mouth from behind and dragged her up onto the balls of her feet.

"Listen to me very, very carefully," Hugh whispered in her ear, showing her the knife that he held in his other hand, before pressing the edge of its cold, keen blade against her cheek, with the point almost piercing the fleshy pouch under her right eye. "If you follow my instructions precisely you will not be harmed. Do you understand?"

Molly could not move or respond. Her heart trip-hammered and a ringing sounded in her ears as her high blood pressure rose to signal a dangerous artery-bulging level. She felt as if a geyser of hot liquid had surged into her brain, compressing it, incapacitating her, suspending her on the brink of unconsciousness. She was at once sweating yet shivering, held in rigid mortification and a brittle spasm of fear.

"Do you understand?" Hugh said for the second time.

Molly somehow found the will to give a slight nod of her head.

"Good girl. I'm going to take my hand away from your mouth. And when I do, I want you to tell me your name, and who else is on board. Keep in mind that it's very important that you don't lie to me or call out. If you scream, it will be the last thing you ever do."

The pressure of the hand eased, allowing a gap through which she could smell her own warm, mint-scented breath, rebounding from the cool palm.

"My n...name is...is M...Molly. There's just Eric...my husband and me," she said in a library whisper. "He's still in bed," she added.

Eric's low, evenly modulated snoring stopped abruptly in a loud snort as Molly – under instruction – shook his sheet-covered foot. His eyes snapped open in surprise, and he grunted; a slow smile dying on his face even as it formed, on seeing the figure standing behind his wife, holding a knife against her throat.

"Good morning, Eric," Hugh said to the thin, balding man, who reared up into a sitting position and stared at him as though he was Freddy Kruger. "I'm afraid that I'm going to have to interrupt your vacation for a while. I don't intend to harm you or Molly, but I need you to understand that if you cause me any inconvenience whatsoever, then I *will* kill you both. Do I make myself clear?"

Eric's mouth dropped open, his lower jaw instantly weighted with stupefaction. He was speechless, unable to readily comprehend the scenario at the foot of the bed.

"I'll take that as a yes," Hugh said. "Here's what we're going to do..."

A little later, Hugh went for the Rover. Parked it almost bumper to bumper with Eric and Molly's Citroen and transferred his mother and other effects to the caravan, before properly inspecting his new temporary home. The twenty-two-foot long Gazelle Road King had a large dinette-come-living area, partitioned off rear bedroom, and a generous sized bathroom complete with shower. The furnishings and fittings were in immaculate condition, which indicated that the caravan was almost new. After carrying out a meticulous search of the vehicle, he found a further five hundred pounds in cash to add to his kitty, and a pair of Ray-Ban metal wrap, steel-grey framed shades that were a vast improvement on the doctor's glasses, which he binned.

Later, having feasted on bacon and eggs and enjoyed two cups of tea from the smiling Garfield pot, he set off for a day at the coast. The abandoned Rover would soon be just one of many vehicles parked at the picnic site, raising no suspicion until at least late evening. Even when found, it would give up no worthwhile clues as to his whereabouts, as by then he would be many miles from the area.

Horizontal stripes of light seeped through the louvered doors, allowing Eric and Molly to look into each other's eyes. They were sitting face to face in the dim, cramped confines of the stuffy, narrow, built-in wardrobe. Their wrists were taped behind their backs; legs overlapping, taped together, joining them. Their mouths were also taped, to stifle any ill-advised temptation to cry out for help.

Later that morning, sitting on a cliff top a couple of miles north of Scarborough and looking out to sea, where the smudge of an oil tanker ploughed a slow path across the horizon, Hugh grinned with boyish glee. When night fell he would cause mayhem, get even with Laura – who had fucked up his career and his life – and give the far too clever FBI dropout a display that would probably tear his mind apart. He would then head south, settle down with his mother (his one true love) and keep a low profile as he adopted a new way of life and a respectable front. He would refrain from killing for a while; suppress the urges that built up like the magma under a volcano. And when he did resume, there would be no further games or interaction with the plods. Bodies would not be found in future. He would take only strays and runaways with no fixed addresses or reasons to be missed; flotsam that society overlooked and turned its back on. The killing would be a public service; pest control, clearing the streets of scrounging, scumbag no-hopers, who were of no discernible use to themselves or anyone else. Everything was looking decidedly brighter. He felt invincible. It was as if the world revolved purely to serve his needs and desires; a table of plenty; hors-doeuvres to be sampled at his leisure.

CHAPTER THIRTY-EIGHT

MARTY Drury snapped the mag back into his Glock 17 and returned the weapon to the shoulder holster under his left armpit. The interior of the car was illuminated with a brief flare of light as he then proceeded to light a cigarette, before turning to Vic Buchanan, who was already dozing only ten minutes after they had relieved the two-till-ten shift.

The handover had been a gruff verbal report from Herbie Parnell, to the effect that the female copper and her boyfriend were inside the house and had no plans to leave the cottage again till morning.

"For fuck's sake, wake up, Vic," Marty said.

"I am awake. I was just resting my eyes."

"Yeah, yeah, and I'm the jolly green giant. If you think I'm going to check in every hour while you get your ugly sleep, then you're wrong."

"Christ, chill out, Marty. We're babysitting a split-arse DI and a bloody Yank, not guarding a fucking royal. Parfitt isn't going to show. He'll have done a runner and be keeping his head down. He knows that every bobby on the beat between Lands End and John O'Groats will be looking for him, hoping to get a bloody medal or promotion for being the one to collar him. The sooner they catch the bastard or blow him away the better, and we can get back to something less boring than sat out in the fucking sticks, freezing our balls off."

"It's pigging red hot, you dummy," Marty said, opening his window almost all the way, flicking the half-smoked cigarette out, to watch as the red end sparked briefly in the darkness.

"What time do we do an external check of the house and then get coffee off the tart?" Vic said.

"Eleven. After we've radioed in," Marty replied, tweaking up the volume on the car radio a notch, to pierce the silence of the night.

Marty was already bored out of his skull. It was hard to be expectant, keyed-up and ready for action when it was obvious that nothing untoward was going to happen. Most of his working life was spent waiting, watching and doing fuck all. Years ago, when still in uniform, he had envied the gung-ho, gun-toting cops in civvies that seemed to have an adventurous life, beset with intrigue and danger. The truth was, he had been far happier as an overworked PC. He had just spent the best part of a year as a small cog in an operation to smash a large drug cartel, only to see it all come apart and go down the drain. It could be soul-destroying work, and did little for the ego. He was tempted to jack it in and join the firm of an ex-flying squad officer he knew, who had offered him a job in the growing field of personal protection for celebrities, politicians and the like. He could see himself as a highly paid bodyguard. He might try to work a medical retirement and give it a go. At least that way he would then have a pension of sorts coming in, should it not pan out.

The car door opened, and even as Marty began to turn his head, the blade of the knife was driven into his ear, to imbed deeply in brain tissue.

The attack was so fast that Vic thought for a second that his partner had opened the door; was maybe going for a piss. But Marty let out a thin, strangled whine and slumped forward in his seat. It was only then that Vic saw the figure, dimly lit by the dome light over the rearview mirror.

Hugh had slipped silently from the trees, knelt next to the car and listened to the conversation. As he pulled the door open and skewered the nearest copper, he put his hand under the dying man's jacket and removed the handgun, chambering a round and aiming the pistol at the other bewildered looking man's face.

"Hands on the dash, now, or you get to join your buddy in the big police station in the sky," Hugh said, his voice calm, low and ice-cold with menace.

Vic did as he was told.

"Good man," Hugh said. "I want call signs and procedures. Then we do a test call, and if you've lied to me, I'll kill you. If you behave, I'll lock you in the boot and you live to fight another day. First, take your weapon out, thumb and finger only, and toss it in the back."

Vic slowly removed the pistol from its holster and dropped it over his shoulder onto the rear seat.

Hugh grinned. "So far, so good. Now, make the test call."

The call checked out and, at gunpoint, Vic pulled the boot release and got out of the car, walking slowly to the rear and climbing into it as ordered. As he struggled to find a measure of comfort in the cramped space, Hugh clubbed him over the head several times with the gun's butt, only stopping when he was sure that the copper was unconscious or dead. He then pulled the lid down and gently pressed it until the catch clicked into place.

Sitting in the driving seat next to the corpse, which looked like someone asleep, with its head lolling forward, Hugh withdrew the knife from its head, wiped the blade clean on the body's trousers and waited until eleven o'clock to make the hourly test call. He then left the car, armed with the Glock, the knife and the mobile phone-sized two-way radio, and walked across the country road, whistling nonchalantly as he opened the gate, to make his way up the path to the front door. He rapped on it four times, and then paused before tapping twice more, exactly as the copper had told him to.

There were developments on the evening news. Laura and Jim stared at the screen, hanging on to every word as an outside broadcast from the village of Skelby showed the exterior of a floodlit house among the trees. The report verified that Jim had been right in believing that Hugh was doubtless still somewhere in Yorkshire.

A doctor, his wife and a postman had been discovered alive in the cellar of the house. They had been found by another doctor, who had become suspicious when his colleague's wife had phoned to say that due to serious illness in the family, the GP would not be at work for several days. Paula Armstrong had said that her husband's father had suffered a stroke which, considering he had been dead for over two years, was highly unlikely to say the least. Dr Jeremy Farnsworth had, after a great deal of contemplation, been unable to let the matter rest. He could not entertain the possibility of Paula or Dom lying to him. And it was even more inconceivable that they could under any circumstances have mistakenly attributed the reason for Dom's absence to the poor health of a deceased parent.

Jeremy had knocked at both front and back doors. There was no answer, and only as he walked back to his car did he hear the muted shouting from inside the house. Without hesitation he had broken a window to gain access.

It was thought – due to Parfitt asking for an A-Z of London – that the wanted man may already be down south. Dr Armstrong's Rover had been found abandoned in a lay-by on a road in East Yorkshire, but it was not known what vehicle had been stolen as a replacement. No other details were being released by the police, and the Armstrongs and the postman were being kept incommunicado.

"Looks like he *has* gone down The Smoke," Laura said when the programme moved on to race riots in a West Yorkshire city, and forest fires much farther afield near Los Angeles, that were claiming houses of the rich and famous.

"He's gone nowhere, Laura," Jim said. "He won't move on till he's finished up here. You're his main concern at the moment. Everything else is secondary. He'll be totally fixated on venting his hate for you and me. He's driven by a need to punish us for exposing him for what he is."

"And all we can do is sit and wait," Laura stated. "He has the advantage."

"No, we have the advantage. We know his agenda. We just have to wait him out and be prepared to finish it without any hesitation."

"You mean kill him in cold blood?" Laura said, her expression showing the inner conflict that she felt.

"Sometimes our worst nightmares are outstripped by reality, Laura. Don't think of Parfitt as a person. He's more dangerous than a rogue elephant. If you think for a second that he deserves any compassion, then your life is on the line."

"But could you really—"

"Kill him? You'd better believe it. I'd have more qualms over destroying a mad dog.

His mind is diseased. It might not be his fault. He may not be able to control his actions, but that doesn't cut him any slack. I know that when it comes to push or shove, and it's him or us, I won't be looking to argue the toss with him."

Laura got up and headed for the kitchen. Jim rose and followed, as though he was scared to let her out of his sight for even a second. And that was the truth of it. He didn't underestimate Parfitt. He had learned not to underestimate anyone in life. You had to be aware that each individual possessed unknown potential. Complacency was an enemy, ever ready to pounce on the unwary.

"You hungry?" Laura asked.

"Not particularly. A little peckish, maybe. You?"

"No, but I need to be busy. I've got the urge to cook something."

"So let's cook. What have you got in mind?"

"Just something quick and tasty."

"I'll help. Tell me what to do."

With three boned, skinless chicken breasts defrosting in the microwave, Laura gathered together an array of ingredients. Following instructions, Jim peeled and chopped a clove of garlic, then grated the rind off and squeezed the juice from a lemon into a bowl. Laura heated oil in a wok; cut the chicken into roughly 5cm sized cubes and tossed them in a mixture of plain flour with the lemon rind and garlic that Jim had prepared. While she cooked the nuggets until golden, Jim peeled and grated ginger, mixed it with stock and sugar, and passed it to her to add to the chicken for another few minutes. He then blended the lemon juice with an egg yolk, to be stirred with the rest until it thickened into a rich sauce.

"Wash your hands and open a bottle of wine, while I finish up," Laura said, testing egg noodles that were simmering in another pan. "It'll be ready in a couple of minutes."

As Jim poured out two glasses of Merlot, Laura added parsley and seasoning to the meal and then drained the noodles and served it up.

Jim sniffed at the air like a Bisto Kid. "That looks and smells delicious," he said. "I've suddenly got an appetite."

"Me too," Laura said as they clinked their glasses together.

"What do you call it?" Jim asked, preparing to take a mouthful of the steaming dish.

Laura grinned. "Food. But if you need a name for it, let's call it lemon chicken surprise."

"That sounds like a dessert."

"Even more of a surprise that it isn't, then. Just eat."

Twenty minutes later, Jim sighed with contentment. "That was some supper dish," he said, carrying the plates to the sink.

"Glad you liked it," Laura said as she made up a flask of coffee and screwed the lid in place, just seconds before the prearranged knock came at the door. "There's our goodnight call."

Laura realised that she was no longer consumed by fear. Jim was strong and reliable, and his experience of dealing with the type of threat that was facing them was without equal. But the knowledge that Hugh might be nearby and intent on revenge was playing on her mind. He was smart, capable, and had so far managed to kill with impunity and stay ahead of the game. There was no guarantee that good would triumph over evil. That was the stuff of fairy tales.

CHAPTER THIRTY-NINE

WALKING from the kitchen and along the short hall to open the door, Laura had a smile on her face to greet one of the graveyard shift cops. Maybe it would be Marty Drury, who was the youngest and by far the more affable of the two. It wasn't. As she opened the door her smile froze a split-second before she was struck savagely on the shoulder. The blow spun her round, and the flask flew from her hand to crash to the floor and spin away with a sound that might have been loose pebbles being shaken in a seaside bucket.

With his forearm around her neck, exerting pressure on her throat and cutting off her air supply, Hugh rammed the muzzle of the Glock up against Laura's temple.

Jim kicked back the wooden, ladder-backed chair he'd been sitting on and rushed out into the hall, to stop abruptly at the sight of the man holding the gun to Laura's head, and the almost plum colour of her face, caused by slow asphyxiation.

"Hi, Jimbo," Hugh said, kicking the door closed behind him. "I was in the neighbourhood, so I thought I'd just call by and repay you and the boss for all the trouble you went to over the last few days to fuck me up."

Jim could hardly recognise Parfitt. His hair was dark; he wore shades, and his nose was badly swollen. "Hugh, listen—"

"No, Elliott, *you* listen. Do exactly as I say, or I end it here and now. Go into the lounge and lay face down on the floor, arms together behind your back. You know the drill."

Jim obeyed. He walked woodenly into the middle of the room, knelt down and slowly lowered himself to stretch out on the carpet. Within seconds he felt the bite of a plastic restraining strap as his wrists were pinioned together. He then grunted in pain and surprise as Hugh brought the gun's barrel down hard on his bandaged hand, which blossomed with blood as the stitches burst and the surgeon's work was undone.

Hugh had been holding Laura face down next to Jim, his knee in her back. He side-swiped her twice with the gun, hard enough to daze her, and then reached into a pocket for a reel of duct tape and proceeded to tape her hands behind her before, as almost an afterthought, he also used it to bind Jim's ankles together. Once satisfied that neither posed a threat, he hauled them to their feet, one at a time, and pushed them onto the settee.

Sitting on the chair opposite the two people he most hated in the world, Hugh placed the Glock he had purloined from the copper he had killed on the top of the coffee table. He smiled broadly, enjoying the fact that he was in complete control of the situation.

"This is cosy," Hugh said, removing the police radio and his knife, hypodermic, a phial of fluid, hammer, and two six-inch nails from his pockets, to set them down neatly before him on the tabletop. "Just the three of us, and plenty of time for me to demonstrate my skills. You're going to experience suffering that you can't properly imagine, Laura."

He remained unmoving for a few minutes, savouring the moment, and then sighed, got up and went into the kitchen, returning with a bottle of French brandy and one balloon glass. Settling down again, he opened the bottle and poured himself a large measure. God, he felt up for it. This was too good to rush. He swirled the brandy around the glass and inhaled the bouquet before sipping the golden liquid; the mellow spirit startling his taste buds before being swallowed to hit his stomach with spreading warmth. He was relaxed and totally at ease. Only now mattered. There was no past or future in his mind to dilute the moment. He was eager to start in on what would be his most memorable act. No enemy can be greater than one who has been a trusted friend. Laura had turned on him; a Judas. Her treachery would now be repaid in full. He had given her respect, loyalty and a certain amount of devotion, and she had been ready to throw him to the wolves; *had* been the leader of the pack.

"Now, are you sitting comfortably? No, of course not, but I'll begin anyway," Hugh said, grinning at his prisoners. "I've given it a lot of thought, and have decided to skin you alive, Laura. It isn't original, I know. It's an art that has been practised throughout history, and no doubt more expertly than I will be able do it justice. But I'm prepared to give it a go if you are.

"And you, loverboy," he sneered at Jim. "You get to watch the whole show from a front row seat. Worse, you get to live to remember that if you hadn't been so fucking clever, this wouldn't be happening. You'll probably crack up after this is over; maybe top yourself, because you've got no grit, Elliott. You can only handle being on the winning team. When things go wrong, you fold like a wimp."

"Where's that hideous prune you call Mummy, Hugh?" Jim said, his whole body tensed, ready to kick out if he could goad the other man into attacking him. "Doesn't mummy's little boy want her sitting here to watch him being naughty? Or has she finally fallen apart with all the exercise she's had of late?"

Hugh's left eye began to blink rapidly, and his mouth worked soundlessly, but he didn't make a move from his chair, just glowered at Jim.

"Well, motherfucker?" Jim pushed, wanting a response; needing to unsettle Parfitt and modify the situation, desperate to change the course of events that loomed horrifyingly in front of him. "Can you only go up against defenceless women? Not got the bottle to deal with someone your own size, head on, huh?"

Hugh took deep breaths, and found composure. "It isn't going to work, Elliott. Your FBI mind games aren't going to get you or Laura out of this," he said, lifting the syringe, drawing a small amount of morphine into it – which he had taken from the doctor's house – and quickly leaning forward, to plunge the needle into Laura's thigh.

Jim lurched forward off the settee, to do no more than fall across the coffee table and roll on to the floor beyond it, helpless.

Hugh jumped up and drove his foot into Jim's ribs, twice, then kicked him a third time in the side of the head, sending him sprawling on his back, to be enveloped by a dark veil that negated all interest in the proceedings.

Laura felt drunk, and not from the wine. She tried to speak, but her tongue felt too big for her mouth, and the words that she tried to form just sounded like a toddler's gibberish.

Hugh's cheeks dimpled in a smirk. He began to cut her clothes from her, and she could only watch, numb, her body unresponsive as the effects of the narcotic paralysed her. He cut the tape from her wrists, and she tried to lash out to defend herself and fight for her life, but her arms hung limp and unresponsive at her sides. She was powerless; completely at his mercy.

Hugh chose the wall opposite the spiral staircase, removing a framed photo of Laura and her late daughter from it, to hurl across the room, where it shattered against the kitchen door. He then examined the feature of the upright oak posts that protruded from the plaster and ran from floor to ceiling, four feet apart. Lifting Laura, he carried her to the wall, and pinning her between the rough plaster and his own body, facing him, he raised her right arm up above her head to the side as high as he could, with the back of her hand against the dark wood.

A white-hot stab of pain blazed through Laura's hand and raced along her arm to her shoulder. And as she cried out in agony, her other hand came alive with the same crippling forks of excruciating fire.

Hugh moved back away from her, and Laura's body sagged, causing more pain as her spiked hands took her full weight. She somehow managed to lift her head and look up to her left, to see the rivulet of blood running from her palm, and to stare in disbelief at the two inches of gleaming nail that protruded from her flesh. The bastard had crucified her to the wall beams. A vision of Christ on the cross materialised in her mind. Her spirit gave way, snapping under the burden of fear. She didn't want to die, but if this was her time to, then she wanted it to be over with quickly, but knew that Hugh had other plans; knew that the real suffering had not yet begun.

Jim came to his senses in a sitting position, his back up against the cold metal staircase. He tried to move, but his neck was taped to one of the cast-iron uprights. Before him, Laura was hanging, naked, with blood dripping down her arms from where nails affixed her hands to the vertical wall beams.

"I got things set up while you were having forty winks, Jimbo," Hugh said conversationally, appearing in front of Laura, his recharged glass of brandy in his right hand, and a wicked looking knife with a thin, six-inch-long blade in his left. "Now, what I intend to do is make a Y-cut, but not too deep, because this isn't an autopsy. I'll just be peeling her like a tomato. And every time she passes out, we'll take five and wait for her to come round. I don't want her to miss a thing. In fact I think I'll work from her neck to her thighs, and try to flense her torso like a jacket. Then I can slip it on and wear a part of her while she's still alive. I may have to give her another shot of morphine when I start in on the head. Removing her face and scalp might just smart a little. Can you imagine what will be left, writhing on the wall, Jim? It'll be like some butchered thing out of a horror movie, but *we'll* both know who it is, won't we?"

"You fucking sick bastard!" Jim cried out, tears filling his eyes to mist his vision as his stomach cramped with leaden fear, frustration, and anger at his helplessness to do anything but watch.

"There's no need to be insulting, Jimbo," Hugh said, a theatrical expression of hurt on his face. "You've dealt with enough serial killers over the years to know that we're driven, without the ability to show any empathy. We feed off suffering, thrive on domination, and really get off on having control over others. Christ, I'm only following a blueprint. It's a genetic thing. Look at nature; hunters and prey. What I do is as natural to me as fox hunting is to the well-heeled minority of dickheads that try to justify their actions as being necessary culling. Blood sport always has its critics. But I don't attempt to justify anything. I just need to do it. I'm like a furnace that needs stoking."

"You'll get caught, Parfitt. Sooner or later they'll hunt you down and—"

"And what, Yank? This isn't the good old U S of A. There's no death penalty here, so even in the unlikely event that I did get caught, I'd be put in some shit-hole for the criminally insane. Big deal. But I don't intend for that to happen. I'm going to vanish when I've finished up here and start a new life. And you'll know that I'm out there somewhere, laughing at you. But enough banter. Let's get down to it, shall we?"

"You've lost the plot, Hugh," Jim said. "I thought that you were repeatedly killing your mother for what she must have done to you. Why are you doing this? It isn't part of your demented, delusional crusade."

"If it hadn't been for you and Laura, I would still be at the farm with mother, and still be a copper. You've both ruined everything. You have to pay."

Hugh turned to Laura, raised the gleaming blade of the knife to her eye, and then let the point trace a line over her cheek, to follow her jaw line down to her neck, and further, to linger at the side of her right breast, then caress the nipple to involuntary erection with the cold steel. He smiled at the unbridled fear that manifested in her wide eyes and frantic expression. It was time. He was aroused, and began to moan in anticipation as he made the initial cut at her right shoulder and started in on the wet work.

CHAPTER FORTY

VIC Buchanan took deep breaths, fighting nausea, ignoring the pain in his head and clenching his teeth until his cheek muscles ached. Reaching up in the darkness he could feel the deep gashes in his scalp and the wetness of blood in his matted hair, which also trickled down his forehead into his right eye. He was surprised to have survived, though, having believed that Parfitt was going to kill him.

Easing round, knees bent, Vic put his feet together and started kicking against the back of the car's rear seat. It gave way on the fourth attempt, and he rested, pacing himself, hoping that he wouldn't pass out before he could nail the bastard who'd attacked them and may have already killed the copper and her boyfriend. He had no way of knowing how long he'd been out. Maybe it was already over.

With supreme effort, Vic found the willpower to pull himself through from the boot into the rear of the car. His gun was in the foot well, and he slipped it back into his shoulder holster as he leaned forward to look at the dashboard clock. The green numerals were fuzzy, his blurred vision almost doubling them. He concentrated, narrowed his eyes and fought to focus. It was 11:38 PM. He had been out cold for at least thirty minutes, maybe longer. Reaching over to where Marty was slumped, he put his fingers to his partner's neck, to feel only the stillness he had expected.

Opening the car door, Vic fell out onto the grass verge, his legs weak, trembling. Lying there for a minute, he battled against an insistent voice in the back of his mind that urged him to just close his eyes and go to sleep for a little while. It was with an iron will that he forced himself to stand up and stagger across the narrow road to the cottage. And it was mainly anger that fuelled his determination; an unbridled resolve to deal with the lunatic who'd murdered Marty. He lurched drunkenly as dizziness disoriented him, and slammed into the gate, folding over it, pitching forward onto gravel that bit into his cheek and temporarily revived him. With what took monumental effort, he climbed to his feet again and wove his way to the door like a Saturday night drunk; his free hand pressed against one of the head wounds that bled profusely. He could have been twelve again. Back then, the boy he had been had woken with terrible stomach pains. His mother and father were at work, and he was off school, it being half-term. For weeks he'd suffered with a dull pain in his side, but had ignored it, said nothing, and hoped that it would go away.

With his pyjamas saturated in sweat, the young Vic had set off on the longest journey of his life. The pain was so intense that he could not climb out of bed, but had to roll onto the floor and crawl. Every movement was a colossal challenge. He made it to the top of the stairs on his hands and knees, and then passed out. When the escalating agony brought him round, he edged down the stairs one at a time with a continuous moan escaping his lips, and tears mingling with the perspiration on his chubby cheeks.

The journey along the hall and into the living room at the rear of the house took him almost twenty minutes. And the effort to gain his feet next to the sideboard and snatch the phone from its cradle was an act that took strength of will he had not known he possessed. After dialling 999 and telling the operator that he needed help, Vic had passed out again, to be found unconscious by the ambulance crew that forced entry to the house. Within forty minutes of arriving at hospital, Vic was being prepped for emergency surgery. His appendix was on the cusp of perforating, and had he not found the fortitude to reach the telephone, then he would have most likely not survived.

A minute passed. For sixty long seconds Vic leaned heavily against the wall next to the door to rest and summon up enough strength to be able to function. He waited until tattered sails of fog drifted across the face of his mind to leave it clearer. Adrenaline swept through him as he readied himself and took deep breaths. He drew his gun and curled his finger purposely around the trigger. He reckoned he might have one slim chance. If he could kick the door open, he would have to use the split second of surprise to find his target and shoot. If the door held, blowing the lock out was his only other option, and would result in him losing any element of surprise.

The sudden scream from inside the cottage galvanised Vic into action. Disregarding his injuries, he stepped back apace, and with all the force he could muster, kicked the door at a point an inch to the side of the brass handle, relieved as with a splintering crack the aged wood gave and shot back, ripped away from the lock. Vic entered a hall, rolled forward and came up on to one knee at an open doorway, searching for the rogue copper, his gun now held two-handed, the barrel moving in coordination with his eyes. In an instant he saw the man who had attacked him and Marty. The killer was now turning to face him, holding a knife in his hand. Vic also noticed the naked woman, standing against a wall with her arms raised, and the Yank sitting at the foot of a spiral staircase, apparently tied to it.

"Flinch and I'll empty the mag in you," Vic said, his Browning Hi-Power sighted on the man's chest. "Drop the knife and take three steps towards me, and then lay face down."

Hugh was totally shocked by the sudden, dramatic entrance of the armed copper. It was hard to believe that the blood-drenched figure was still breathing, let alone conscious. Or that he could have escaped from the boot of the car and managed to break down the door. That the man was swaying, almost out on his feet, and that blood was still flowing from the deep lacerations to his head, was encouraging. Hugh knew he had a chance; play along and wait for the man to keel over. It was only willpower that was keeping the stupid plod standing upright.

"I said, move," Vic slurred. "You need to know that if I even think I'm going to pass out, then you're history."

"Okay, okay, take it easy, don't get your knickers in a twist," Hugh said, dropping the knife and stepping forward, to slowly lower himself to his knees and adopt a prone position on the carpet.

Vic pushed himself up, using the wall at his back for support. He walked towards the stairs with faltering steps, not taking his eyes off Hugh for a second and giving him a wide berth. Picking up the knife, he went to Jim and sliced through the tape that held his neck against the stairs, and then cut through the plastic tie that bound his wrists. It was all he had the strength left to do. Vic had given his all, lost consciousness, and fell across Jim's lap.

Taking his chance, Hugh crawled across the floor to the coffee table and grasped hold of the gun he had taken from the other copper. He leapt to his feet, turned and fired twice.

One slug hit the staircase next to Jim's head, to ricochet off it with a loud pinging sound and imbed in the wall scant inches from where Laura was hanging. The other bullet thudded into the shoulder of the insensible police officer, causing his limp body to jerk.

Jim snatched the Browning from the inert copper's hand and returned fire, loosing off three shots without having time to take proper aim.

Hugh felt a searing pain in his thigh. He fired again wildly as he limped-stumbled-careered into the kitchen, to unlock the door and stagger away from the house, across the back garden and into the woods that loomed; a black wall in the night at the end of the small lawn.

Jim eased the cop off him on to the floor, got up and went to Laura. "No, Jim, finish it. Kill the bastard," she said. "I'll live."

Hugh ran through the thick bracken for twenty yards, grunting with pain, half-hopping, to finally trip and fall into the waist-high ferns. He sat up and scrabbled backwards, pushing with his uninjured leg until he was up against the trunk of a tree. This, he decided, was where he would wait, knowing that the Yank would follow and search for him. His only chance of making it the half mile back to where he had stashed the car and caravan was if he killed Elliott. His first shot would have to count, or his pursuer would take cover and pin him down. He should have hesitated the extra second it would have taken to aim properly in the cottage. He had actually panicked. All he could do now was listen and watch and be ready to end this fiasco. He still had the advantage, and would not waste it. He took off his belt and buckled it around the top of his thigh, pulling it as tightly as he could bear, before securing it. He would need treatment, but at the moment that was the least of his problems.

Jim saw the trail of blood; shiny black on the paving stones of the patio under the silver glow of the moon. He followed the direction of the glistening teardrop-shaped spots, running, bent low, zigzagging to present as small a target as possible, out across the lawn and into the trees beyond. He had hit Parfitt, seen the entry hole appear in his leg, four or five inches above the knee. It was a wonder he had not gone down. With a little luck the bullet had ruptured his femoral artery, though that was wishful thinking; there would have been much more blood. One thing he *was* sure of, the bastard would not have got far, and was probably waiting for him nearby, concealed in the semi-jungle of ferns and saplings that blanketed the forest floor. He assessed the situation and moved on, now without stealth, purposely treading on dry twigs and cones to announce his presence. He then stopped, eased the magazine out of the gun butt and fired twice; the loud metallic clicks followed by an exclamation of "shit!" being the bait to draw his quarry out.

Hugh heard the snap of twigs and the crunch of pine needles underfoot. The sounds grew louder as the Yank drew near. He then saw his outline, black on dark grey amid the tree trunks, standing, working his gun. The two hollow, echoing sounds of the mechanism, and the low oath that followed, confirmed that the weapon had jammed, or the mag was empty.

Pushing himself up on his good leg, Hugh levelled the pistol at Jim, took careful aim and squeezed the trigger.

Jim heard the rustle and scrape of clothes on bark, off to his left. He dropped to his knees, discarding the gun and shrugging the crossbow – which he had taken the time to collect from the bedroom before leaving the cottage – from his shoulder in one smooth movement as he stood back up.

The whoosh of the nine-inch bolt hurtling through the air was masked by the roar of the Glock. Jim felt a slug tug at his side as he pulled another bolt from the retaining clips of the bow and reloaded. In the gloom, as his night vision returned following the blinding muzzle flash, he could see Hugh, standing against a tree. He fired again, wondering why the other man had not continued to shoot at him.

Hugh felt an impact in his throat as he fired. The back of his head was slammed into the rough, fissured bark of the eighty-foot-tall pine, and he could not move. A pulsating pain shot up into his brain, and down into his shoulders and upper arms, causing him to drop the gun and reach up to the source of his agony. His shaking fingers found the feathered fletching of the shaft that protruded from just a fraction to the left of his larynx, and by touch, he guessed that it must be an arrow. His mind was numb with astonishment, unable to comprehend the manner in which he had been wounded. And as he attempted to come to terms with his plight, a second piercing stab of pain; a lance of fire in his chest, resulted in him being pinned even more securely to the tree trunk. He clawed frantically at the fresh source of throbbing, cramping torment, but could only feel the very end of the bolt; the slotted plastic nock standing proud from his right breast like a third nipple. He pulled forward, trying to rip free of the two aluminium shafts, but the tearing pain was unbearable. Again, he tugged at the metal arrow in his throat, but was unable to grip it and find purchase as his blood-covered, fumbling fingers slipped off the viscid projection. Finally, he stopped, fixed to the trunk, a low, keening, almost inhuman howl issuing from lips that bubbled with a bloody froth.

Jim dropped the crossbow. He retrieved the Browning and rammed the mag home, working a shell into the chamber as he approached the moaning figure. Reaching Hugh, he stopped in front of him and realised that it was over, so pushed the pistol into the waistband of his trousers.

"Shit on a stick, eh?" Jim said, studying the now helpless killer.

Hugh tried to spit in Jim's face, but the blood pulsed out of his pursed lips with no power, to dribble down his chin and drip onto his bloodied shirt front.

"How does dying feel?" Jim asked, smiling at Hugh and acknowledging that he was satisfied with the payback he had meted out.

Hugh attempted to answer, but could only produce an unintelligible wheeze as he tried to ask Jim to finish it and put a bullet in his brain. He felt death invading him, slowly creeping through him; a sly, stealthy but unmistakable final adversary that could not be evaded, bargained with or fought off. He experienced clarity of thought that he had not known since something had snapped inside him, back when he had been a teenager standing next to his mother's grave. His rage was now subdued by a stronger emotion; uncontrollable dread. He shuddered as a flash of lucidity forced him to face the full weight of all the abhorrent acts he had committed. He knew that he had been deluded to have imagined that his mother was alive and wholesome; capable of movement, speech and all living functions. That he could have vented his anger at the corpse of the person it had once been by killing so many innocents was now beyond his newfound power of reasoning.

The piercing scream that Hugh somehow found the strength to emit sent ice-cold ripples down Jim's spine and raised gooseflesh on his arms, stomach and thighs. He could feel the hair stiffening on the back of his neck as he watched the dying man arch his back and pull his head forward, straining to uncouple himself from the bolts that skewered him to the tree. With the sucking sound of a boot pulling free from thick mud, Hugh's head shot forward, free of the impediment, to droop down onto his chest.

The brief struggle was over, and the insight that Hugh glimpsed through the many faceted, stained-glass window of his fragmented personality, consumed him. He shut down, unable to face the reality of what he was, or the enormity of what he had done. He retreated, back in time, erasing the years as though he were in a lift, plunging down past many floors at sickening speed, away from the present, to finally open the doors on a warped memory of a long gone episode that still haunted him.

He was almost thirteen again, outside the chicken shed at the farm, trying to summon up the courage to open the door and enter. He felt the cold wind whipping through his clothes, and looked up at the low, lead-bellied rain clouds that were about to discharge their load. His numb fingers ached with the force he exerted on the egg basket he held. Steeling himself, he pulled back the door and entered the shed. The fowl were at once crowding, milling about him; a solid circle of hot, stinking, feathered, fluttering avian horror that began to tear at him with snapping, fang-lined beaks. They flew up into his face, hung from his arms, covered him from head to foot in a suit of feathers, and then dragged him down into the slimy, shit-coated straw, their frenzied clucking filling his mind and drowning out all thought.

In his befuddled state, as the black tide of death surged through his brain, Hugh's last image was of the corpses of his parents entering the gloomy hut, their accusing eyes holding a promise of merciless, unrelenting purgatory for all that he had done.

Jim saw a look of pure terror materialise on Hugh's face, as the dying man raised his head and stared at some hideous vision that only he could see. He coughed, and a welter of blood spurted from his nostrils and cascaded from his gaping mouth, overflowing from his liquid-filled lungs. With one retching gurgle, he became still, and all expression faded from his now lifeless blue eyes.

Back inside the cottage, using the wounded police officer's radio, Jim summoned the emergency services, then wrapped a blanket around Laura and supported her weight as he held a glass to her lips and allowed her to sip a little brandy.

"You're sure that he's dead?" Laura said.

"He's pinned to a tree with a crossbow bolt, Laura," Jim replied. "I put one through his throat, and another in his chest. I watched him die. Believe me, it's over."

"What a way to spend Easter," Laura quipped, somehow finding black humour at her state of crucifixion, and the manner in which Hugh had met his fate.

"It isn't Easter," Jim said, managing a strained smile, admiring her strength of character; a flood of relief almost overwhelming him at what seemed a near miracle that had saved her from a fate he could not bring himself to properly imagine.

The officer – who Jim had dragged a few feet away from the bottom of the staircase – was now conscious, sitting up with his back against the wall and his shoulder wound padded with a towel. Jim had already thanked Vic profusely, acknowledging that he had undoubtedly and radically changed the course of events by performing his duties to a level far above and beyond all expectation of a man in his injured state. His heroism would not go unsung, though both Jim and Laura owed him a debt that could never be repaid.

"Well it feels like Easter, hanging here," Laura said. "Can't you use the claw end of that hammer and get these nails out?"

"No, Laura. The fire-fighters will do it. They have special equipment for removing women from oak beams."

"Sure. I bet they do it all the time."

"It's a dying art, like thatching," Jim said, now grinning broadly. "There's not been a lot of call for it for centuries."

They kept up the banter until the distant sound of sirens became a deafening two-tone wail outside. Within minutes the cottage was heaving with fire-fighters, paramedics and armed police. Under medical supervision, the beams were cut above and below Laura's hands, and she was released from the wall with a block of wood still firmly nailed to each, that would be removed surgically on arrival at York District Hospital.

Jim led the police out into the wood, to where Hugh's body was affixed to the lofty pine, before being taken to a second waiting ambulance, to once more face hospitalisation, surgery to his damaged hand, and treatment for the flesh wound from the bullet that had passed through his side.

CHAPTER FORTY-ONE

JIMMY Parker and his best pal Malcolm Briggs – who was known as 'Frog' by his peers, for the simple reason that he looked like one – had camped overnight in what was known locally as Bluebell Wood. The two teenagers had set off on a bike ride the day before from their homes in north Hull, and picked the secluded location to pitch their small tent as dusk fell, after riding along a bumpy, rutted access road that was only infrequently used by the employees of the company that owned the wood.

Frog was awake at dawn, and crawled shivering out of the tent. He stretched and moaned aloud. His whole body ached from the hard earth that both the ground sheet and his thin sleeping bag had failed to cushion him from, even though he and Jimmy had removed all the loose stones from the level patch of ground on which they had chosen to erect the tent in a small clearing.

Lighting a cigarette, Frog wandered into the bracken and unzipped his jeans, urgently needing to relieve his pounding bladder. Looking about him, as he let the strong stream play on a tree trunk, a small patch of pure white among the greenery caught his eye. Finishing up, he crept through the high ferns until he could make out what stood in the much larger clearing before him. It was a caravan, hitched to a Citroen car. He retraced his steps and crawled back inside the tent to shake Jimmy awake.

"Uh! What?" Jimmy grunted, lashing out to knock his pal's hand away.

"Come see what I've found. Hurry up," Frog said.

Jimmy sat up and groaned as his muscles complained, then yawned and combed his long mud-coloured hair back out of his bleary eyes with his fingers. "This'd better be good, Frog. I was dreamin' that Adele was about to sit on my face."

"Adele who?"

"The pop singer, dummy."

"Yucch! Why would you wanna dream that?"

"Never mind. What've you found?"

Frog retraced his steps, with Jimmy sauntering along behind him, lighting a cigarette and coughing as he inhaled the first drag.

"Look, there it is," Frog said, pointing at the caravan.

"What's so interestin' about a friggin' caravan?" Jimmy said, shrugging, still only half awake, and starving; his stomach rumbling.

"Let's check it out," whispered Frog. "It's probably been abandoned."

They crept up to the edge of the clearing, then hunkered down and listened for voices or music from a radio. But apart from their breathing, and Jimmy's belly gurgling, all was quiet.

"They might still be asleep," Jimmy said.

"We can see in the window. There's a gap in the curtains," Frog said, moving out into what he thought of as no mans land; becoming Rambo in a jungle setting as he approached the enemy stronghold in a crouching run. Jimmy strolled out after him, hands stuffed in his pockets, eyes screwed against the smoke that curled up from the half-smoked cigarette dangling from the side of his mouth. He was not caught up in what Frog thought of as an adventure.

Jimmy was a skinny five-nine, three inches taller than Frog, and could look inside the vehicle without having to jump up or stretch.

"So, what can you see?" Frog asked.

"Nuthin'. Looks empty," Jimmy replied, squinting into the dark interior, unable to see anyone.

"I told you. It's been dumped. C'mon, let's go in and see if they've left anythin' worth havin'."

"It hasn't been dumped, dummy. It looks new, and the car's in good nick."

Frog ignored him and tried the door. It opened. He stepped up and entered furtively, waiting for Jimmy to join him before venturing any further.

Jimmy eased the door closed behind them, and they both moved forward into the dimly lit dinette.

"Check the back," Frog said, noticing that the caravan was not unfurnished and stripped out as he had expected it to be. There was a portable TV on a work surface, and the clutter of occupation all around him. If the owners were just early risers and had taken a dog for a walk, then the shit would fly if they came back and found him and Jimmy on board. They may even still be in bed, though surely if they were, the door would have been locked.

Jimmy walked the few feet to the open door of the bedroom, then stopped, totally fazed at the sight before him, unable to move or speak, and unaware of the spreading warmth that stained the front of his jeans.

"What's up?" Frog said, turning to see Jimmy rooted to the spot. "What've you found?"

Frog walked up behind his friend, looked round him, and saw the blonde-haired figure in the shadows, sitting upright on top of the bed against the headboard, staring back at him with a single bulging blue eye and a gaping, dark cavity where the other should have been. He joined Jimmy in stupefied horror, his brain trying to make sense of the mummified corpse. The face was creased and leathery, its mouth partly sealed by metal staples. Part of its nose was missing, disclosing yellowed bone, and the forearms and hands that were skeletal and birdlike under tatters of flaking skin, as was the one leg that jutted from the garment it was clothed in.

What had been Jennifer Parfitt was as Hugh had left it, reposed in a peach-coloured housecoat that belonged to Molly Champion. Hugh had, in his mind, left his mother watching the small, portable TV.

The spell broke, and both boys reeled backwards towards the door, fighting and gibbering with fear as they scrabbled at the handle, to fall out face down on the ground in a tangled heap of flailing arms and legs. They found their feet, crashed through the undergrowth and mounted their bikes, to pedal away down the track, not stopping until they had reached the road and ridden flat out for over a mile; the tent and all else abandoned as they imagined the atrocity in hot pursuit, gaining on them. Lungs burning and leg muscles aching, they finally dropped the bikes on to the verge and sat down on the grass next to them.

"W...What do we do?" Jimmy said, examining the now cold, wet patch at his crotch, as if it had appeared there by magic, not generated by unbridled fear.

"We phone the police and report it," Frog replied. "But we don't give our names. Then we forget about it. We never saw it."

But they *had* seen it, and although they would never mention it again, even to each other, both boys would have nightmares and carry the picture of Hugh's mother's remains etched on their brains for the rest of their lives.

Half an hour after the anonymous phone call had been received, a police car pulled up near the clearing in Bluebell Wood, and a much relieved Molly and Eric Champion were found and released from the cramped wardrobe. Both were aching and dehydrated, but had survived their meeting with the man that they would soon learn had been the killer known as the Tacker. Their experience led to a change of lifestyle. Never again would the couple take to the open road on caravan holidays. They subsequently sold the Gazelle and joined the masses that took package holidays, believing, justifiably to their minds, that they would be far safer in the hotels of Florida or Spain, than parked up in a lay-by in the British countryside.

EPILOGUE

STANDING up against the guard-rail at Yavapai Point, they looked out across to the pink, gold and blue hues that were unveiled as the sun rose over the far rim of the Grand Canyon.

"This is...it's just, well, it's awesome," Laura said.

"I know. There are no words that can do it justice," Jim said, shivering slightly in the sharp, cold, dawn air and tightening his grip on Laura's shoulder, to pull her closer to him. "It never looks the same twice."

They had arrived the previous afternoon, late, just in time to see the sun sink from view over the western horizon in a blaze of deepening reds and purples, to be quickly devoured by the dark wedges of shadow that crept into the mile deep chasm and extinguished its beauty to human sight for another day.

Over two months had passed since the night at the cottage, from where Laura had escaped with her life, and Jim with his sanity. Most of the t's had been crossed and i's dotted on the Tacker case, and the world had moved on to new atrocities, acts of terrorism, mindless murder, natural disasters and violent loss of life in myriad other ways, that took place every day.

"We could split our time," Jim suggested, his mind wandering from the canyon, his eyes finding more beauty in the equally natural wonder of Laura's radiant face. "Maybe buy a place out here in Arizona, and keep my flat on in Windsor. What do you think?"

"I think we should go back to the lodge, have a hot shower, make love, and then discuss this at length over bacon, eggs over easy, hash browns and coffee," Laura replied, lighting a cigarette and vowing to herself that she *would* kick the habit, sooner rather than later.

They walked back towards the holiday lodge, as close and as much in love as any two people could be. They had shared extremes of emotional highs and lows, which had formed an inseparable bond between them. There was no question of whether they would be together or not. It was just the fine details that needed to be ironed out.

Laura felt the dull ache in her palms – that was exacerbated by the low temperature of the wintry autumnal morning – and again contemplated the medical retirement and generous gratuity that was on the table, awaiting her decision. She could put it off for another few weeks, but sooner or later would have to sign the papers or return to duty. There was no real choice. She knew what she wanted, and also knew that the job came a poor second to Jim. She had done her stint, and owed the force nothing. It had nearly cost her everything, and had no further claim on her.

Stopping, she turned to Jim, tilted her head back and kissed him gently as he lowered his mouth to meet her slightly parted lips. At that moment, Jim's idea of pond-hopping and working in public relations didn't seem a half bad way to spend the foreseeable future. It was time to move on, embrace the book of life, and start writing a new page.

Neither Laura nor Jim could possibly know that an abyss so much deeper and darker than the natural wonder behind them, and one that they had both spent so much time at the edge of, would prove impossible to walk away from. You can't run away from what and who you are. Like a slow moving storm on the horizon, events were conspiring that would involve them in as much if not more danger than they could possibly imagine.

About The Author

I write the type of original, action-packed, violent crime thrillers
that I know I would enjoy reading if they were written by such
authors as: Lee Child, David Baldacci, Harlan Coben, Michael
Connelly and their ilk.
Over twenty years in the Prison Service proved great research into
the minds of criminals, and especially into the dark world that serial
killers - of who I have met quite a few - frequent.

I live in a cottage a mile from the nearest main road in the
Yorkshire Wolds, enjoy photography, the wildlife, and of course
creating new characters to place in dilemmas that my mind dreams
up.

What makes a good read? Believable protagonists that you care
about, set in a story that stirs all of your emotions.

If you like your crime fiction fast-paced, then I believe that my
books will keep you turning the pages.

Web

www.michaelkerr.org

Facebook

www.facebook.com/MichaelKerrAuthor

RE-EMERGENCE

Ex-Marines Sam Reynolds and Chad York are at a remote pharmaceutical plant in Colorado negotiating a contract for their security company, when a deadly viral epidemic sweeps the continent, becoming a global pandemic of apocalyptic proportions.

Several months pass by, and Sam and Chad decide that the contagion has run its course. They have formed relationships with Jill Myers and Laura Willis respectively, and the four of them set out to see if any of their families have survived what has been a near extinction event for the human race.

An odyssey begins, and along with Sam's mother, a widowed gas station owner and his dog, and an orphaned teenage boy, they head west towards Carmel on the Pacific coast, in the hope of finding Jill's parents alive.

Chaos rules in what is the beginning of a new age amid a burgeoning population of indigenous fauna and animals that were released from zoos and wildlife parks when the virus struck.

The trek west is fraught with life-threatening incidents, as the group has to contend with deranged survivors in general and Willard Boyd – a homicidal psychopath who is on their trail and determined to kill them – in particular.

Some members of the group will not make it to their intended destination, as any mistake or lack of vigilance is punished swiftly and unmercifully with violence and death, which visits them in myriad forms.

To find out more, read the sample chapters that follow

CHAPTER ONE
~ EVENTS IN COLORADO ~

TOMORROW:
STANDING and gazing out of the fourth floor office window, Sam sipped strong, black coffee, savoring both the steaming liquid and the vista of the distant ice-capped Rocky Mountains shimmering in bright morning sunshine. Unbeknown to him and everyone else on the planet, total chaos was just a few days away. A near extinction event was looming on the horizon that could not be avoided.

Sam Reynolds was looking at a very lucrative deal. Krantz-Vail were having problems with security, and he had been invited – after much negotiation – to advise and assist the company in implementing a new package from the ground up.

Sam was thirty, six-foot-one, and rock solid with broad shoulders and a trim waist. Ten years in the Marine Corps had honed him into a tough fighting machine. He had seen action in many of the world's trouble spots, and done things that most mortals only read about or saw in movies and nightmares. Some of his deeds, that in service to his country had brought him citations and medals, would have warranted life imprisonment or a lethal injection, had he committed them as a civilian. Such is war. His eyes held it all, if the beholder knew how to read them. They were as pewter-gray as a winter sky; hard flints that broadcast a simple message...*Don't fuck with me. I don't take prisoners.*

After leaving the Corps, Sam had taken the plunge and sunk every dime he had into setting up shop in the highly competitive field of security and protection. A fellow ex-Marine, Chad York, came in with him as junior partner, and between them they soon built up a sound business. It was a far cry from their former occupation; fighting for life and limb in such theatres of war as Afghanistan and Iraq.

Sam had leased fourth floor offices in downtown Denver, a spitting distance from East Colfax Avenue on South Broadway. It was expensive, but what the hell, location is everything. Stenciled on the frosted glass panel of the reception office door in gold leaf Calgary script was: 'Sentinel Security Services', over a logo of a shield that bore three S's.

Most of their work came by word of mouth, and the company had quickly gained a reputation as being one of the best in the state of Colorado.

Krantz-Vail wanted a complete overhaul of their present operation, which included: mobile and static guards, CCTV, sophisticated intruder alarm systems, dog patrols...the whole nine yards.

The Krantz-Vail complex was a pharmaceutical research center; part of a giant multinational organization, headed up by its founder, Edwin Krantz, a now enfeebled but sharp-minded octogenarian billionaire who had taken over the mantle as the world's richest man; a position previously held by Microsoft chairman Bill Gates, and then by Carlos Slim Helú, a Mexican with his fingers in many pies.

Krantz lived in and worked from a penthouse suite at the company's headquarters in Chicago. He still had three passions in life; Cuban cigars, single malt whisky, and adding to his vast wealth. Advancing age and impotency had dulled his former rapacious appetite for sex with prepubescent girls, though he still enjoyed watching video of minors practicing every imaginable sex act.

"So, where's this fat cat's plant?" Chad said, pulling at his collar, not comfortable wearing a tie, which was an accessory he deemed unnecessary, even to attend weddings and funerals.

"Eighty miles west. Just south of Vail on the edge of The White River National Forest," Sam said. "Let's move out. I said we'd be there before lunch."

As they drove out of the city, they had no way of knowing that the population of Fairbanks in Alaska was being decimated by an unprecedented and lethal viral epidemic. The city was declared off limits; no one in, no one out. A strict quarantine under marshal law – a futile gesture – was in force. By car, rail, air and sea, the contagion had cast its deadly net to many other cities in North America and beyond.

The two days that Sam had planned on staying in Vail was, unbeknown to him, destined to be of a far longer duration.

It happened so fast. CNN broke the news of a national state of emergency during Sam's and Chad's second day at the facility. There was little bullshit or attempt at comforting propaganda. It was already too late to try to hoodwink or pacify viewers.

The President read a prepared statement – no doubt from a bunker deep under the White House – informing the nation that a highly infectious disease, that in most cases resulted in death within twenty-four to thirty-six hours, was out of control. The fact that everything humanly possible was being done to develop an effective vaccine was of little comfort or consolation to the millions that were already dead or dying. With immediate effect, and under threat of being shot, all unauthorized civilian movement was outlawed. CNN, who had picked up on the outbreak first, had traced its origins to Alaska and christened it the Eskimo Flu.

From the relative safety of the complex, that was over four miles from the nearest main highway, the remaining fifty-six isolated individuals could only watch news updates and become more afraid and pessimistic by the hour. Over a hundred workers had already left the plant, to live or die with their families. Those that stayed to wait it out were convinced that it would be courting almost certain death to leave. Within a week, life as they had known it was a thing of the past. Extinction was suddenly staring humankind in the face. It was a catastrophe on a par with whatever had wiped out the dinosaurs over sixty-five million years ago.

Three weeks passed, and with a self-elected working committee to make necessary decisions, a meeting was called to discuss at length what actions, as a community, they should take. The priorities were narrowed down to immediate needs. Provisions were low, and although they had their own water supply, which they boiled before using for any purpose, bottled water was the preferred choice. They viewed all outsiders as a potential health hazard, and it was decided that once in a position to enforce it, they would maintain a perimeter that they could defend.

Sam requested and was authorized to drive into Vail with a team to pick up canned goods, water, medical supplies, clothing, and protection in the shape of firearms. Sam and Chad would personally select and liberate weapons from the first gun store that they came across.

The risk of contamination was deemed both necessary and unavoidable, and so accompanied by Travis Potts, Craig Shaw, Scott Dillard and Chad, Sam drove his Jeep Cherokee down through the forest, out onto Highway 24, then picked up I-70 that led into Vail.

The city reminded them of something out of a science-fiction movie. There were bodies lying everywhere in varying stages of decomposition, and the smell of death hung in the still air. It was as if a biochemical agent like Sarin had been dropped on the town, wiping out the residents without causing any structural damage.

Sam could imagine the thousands of homes now inhabited by the dead, and knew that it would be the same all over America; all over the world.

A ragtag pack of dogs ran out from a side street, breaking Sam's rapt line of thought as they shot in front of the Jeep, to vanish around a corner apparently in a hurry to reach some unknown destination. Their haste was reminiscent of the white rabbit from Alice's Adventures in Wonderland, that was late for a very important date. They saw more dogs, cats, birds in profusion, and a lone coyote worrying a corpse. The presence of wildlife left Sam in no doubt that the Earth would adapt well to the loss of man, and flourish under new management that seemed to be unaffected.

"Stop," Scott said, pointing out of the side window. "Look. Just what the doctor ordered."

The depot was behind a chain-link fence. Halfway along was a pair of double gates that stood ajar, with a sign above them advertising the Colorado Cooler Company, and proclaiming underneath: The complete water service ~ Rocky Mountain Spring Water. Over a dozen trucks stood in the compound. Most of the cabs were empty, but the nearest truck to the gates held the cadaver of the driver, hunched behind the steering wheel; a baseball cap loose on the shrunken flesh of his head; his final load undelivered.

"Nice one, Scott," Sam said, stopping at the curb. "Pick one with a full load and drive it back to base."

Scott jogged over to the line of vehicles, skirting the one with the incumbent corpse. It was in the fifth truck that he found keys dangling from the ignition. He climbed into the cab and crossed his fingers as he turned the key. The engine spluttered a throaty wah...wah...wah of complaint, once, twice...eventually catching at the fourth attempt. He revved hard; hammer to the floor to keep it running. Checked the fuel gauge, which indicated a half full tank, then gave Sam a raised thumb, engaged first gear with the manual shift and headed for the gates with his truckload of Adam's ale.

Next stop was a large Safeway store, where Craig and Travis decided to see just how much they could pack into the back of an empty Coca-Cola transporter that was backed up to the loading dock at the rear of the building. Sam waited again, only heading off in search of a gun store when Craig signaled that the vehicle was fired-up with enough gas to get them back to the complex.

Chad grinned as they pulled up onto the sidewalk outside Budget Guns. "Hell, Sam, this is like Christmas morning. Let's go get our presents," he said, exiting the Cherokee and jogging over to the store's door.

Vernon Henton watched the thieves from the safety of his office. He had tried to call the police, repeatedly punching in 911, but the line was dead for some reason. His altered and diseased mind was unaware that the emergency services had suffered an emergency of their own; one that they had not survived. Vern's wife and two daughters had died at home ten days ago, and although Vern himself had been ill and suffered a high fever, it had passed. At some later stage he'd positioned his family in the lounge, washed of body fluids and dressed in clean clothes. His wife, June, reposed in her favorite armchair; the girls on the sofa. With the television switched on, he kissed them fondly before leaving for work each morning, presumably believing that they would enjoy the broadcast of white, hissing static that was eventually replaced by a blankness as profound as the eyes of the three corpses facing the dark screen.

Vern's malfunctioning mind refused to accept that anything was other than normal. His orderly, disciplined way of thinking would not entertain the devastating and obscene changes, that if faced would force him to acknowledge the turmoil and chaos that now reigned.

Christ knows where the staff were! It was obviously going to be down to him alone to deal with the two intruders. And he would. No one was going to rob the store on his watch.

Using forklifts, Craig and Travis loaded palettes of mainly canned food into the wagon. Rats had been feasting on much of the dried goods, fruit and vegetables. Some still fed, seemingly unconcerned that they had human company. The last two loads were of toiletries and clothing, plus quite a lot of booze and a couple of hundred assorted CDs and a selection of DVDs.

Craig pulled the roll-top door down on their consignment and went back into the warehouse for his coat, while Travis climbed up into the cab and waited for him.

The demented store manager struck from behind, and Craig fell to his knees as the meat cleaver sank into his skull. Remarkably, he regained his feet and stumbled spastically through the delivery door, crying out for help.

Jumping down from the cab, Travis ran back along the side of the transporter, catching Craig as he fell forward, dead, into his open arms.

The burly, middle-aged man who had been chasing Craig, broke into a run, his eyes wide, mouth twisted and pulled up to the right as though he had suffered a stroke.

Crazy as a shithouse rat, Travis thought as without hesitation he pushed his dead friend's body aside and brought his boot up between his would-be assailant's legs.

Vern doubled up and emitted a high-pitched wail, clutching his crotch as forks of pain blazed up into his stomach. Travis lashed out again, kicking the now kneeling man in the throat, knocking him over to lay curled on his side, whining like a whipped dog. He kept kicking, and the toe cap of his boot turned the man's head to a pulp. It was more than thirty seconds later, after all noise and movement from the man ceased, that Travis stopped his assault, to bend forward with his hands on his knees, panting heavily from his exertions. After a while he straightened up and fumbled in a pocket of his windbreaker for cigarettes and his lighter, as blood pooled around his feet from the heads of the two bodies that lay on the concrete in front of him. Lighting a cigarette with shaking hands, he looked about him in case any other homicidal maniacs were present. Stopping here had been a disaster. And shopping at Safeway had turned into a far from safe venture.

Leaving Craig and the stranger where they lay, Travis climbed back into the cab and drove off, now eager to be back at the plant, among friends.

Four blocks away, Sam and Chad entered the gun store. The smell of death had been with them since they had reached Vail; a rich, nauseous stink of corruption that had permeated throughout the town. But this was worse. In the confines of the store the air was heavy with the stench of putrefaction. The suppurating body of the owner was slumped over the glass-topped showcase counter, with the gun he'd used to shoot himself with still clenched tightly in his moldering hand.

They had both seen death in many guises, and were, to an extent, desensitized, almost detached from it. Sam noted that the guy had used a hollow point bullet, to be sure of a clean kill. The entry wound in his right temple was a neat dime-sized hole, whereas the slug's exit had left a gaping, ragged rent. A large portion of brain tissue had been blown out to congeal on the dust-covered glass; salsa for the flies that fought for a place on it.

Despite the smell, they filled their list of requirements, selecting: Remington, Mauser, Ruger and Krag rifles with scopes, several

Weatherby pump-action shotguns, and an assortment of handguns. While Sam gathered gun belts, shoulder-rigs, binoculars and a shitload of ammo, Chad went through the door behind the counter to explore the rear of the store.

"Sam. Come look at this," he called, standing in front of a locked, steel-reinforced door. Sam went back and was as curious as Chad to find out what lay behind it. Two shots from a Colt Magnum ripped the lock apart, and a sharp kick threw the door back to reveal a veritable Aladdin's cave full of awesome weaponry. There were ground-to-air missile launchers, boxes of grenades, land mines and a plethora of SMGs, including: Uzis, Heckler & Koch's and AK-47s, plus enough ammunition to start a respectable war in a small third world country.

"Christ!" Sam said, taking stock. "This guy must have been dealing with some really heavyweight dudes."

Two flame-thrower units that they found seemed excessive, but they took them anyway, and with the Cherokee fairly bristling with firearms, they drove off and headed towards the city center to carry out a quick evaluation.

Sam parked outside the main post office, and they climbed out and looked about them. Downtown was too quiet. It could have been a Sunday morning, before anyone had risen and taken to the streets. Only the still heaps that had once been people, and were now scattered like discarded mannequins, ruined the illusion. Buzzards lifted from the corpses, their flapping wings bringing movement to the still-life scene.

The silence was broken by the distant sound of engines, that slowly grew louder. Sam and Chad opened the rear doors of the Cherokee and selected shotguns, pushing cartridges into the pump-action Weatherbys as the approaching noise became a roar.

Three figures astride gleaming Harleys burst into view from a side street, spotted the Cherokee and made a beeline for the stationary vehicle and the two men. A bullet pierced the Jeep's door with a dull smack, an instant before the sound of the shot reached them. More bullets whined off the pavement; one drilling the air within an inch of Sam's head, far too close for comfort.

Like pioneers of old, Sam and Chad retreated behind the SUV, as if it was a prairie schooner, and began to return fire on the modern day warriors who were attacking them not on horseback, but on mounts of steel.

The crazed trio seemed unconcerned that they were now under fire, accelerating and continuing to shoot as they drew nearer. Sam's second shot hit the leader in the chest. He flew backwards out of the saddle, hit the concrete and bounced lifeless, his black and chrome beast carrying on rider less to mount the curb on its rear wheel and crash through a store window, engine still roaring in defiance as glass rained down on it.

Chad hit the front tire of the second bike. The rubber blew apart and the Harley flipped over to throw the rider sideways through the air, only for him to be stopped with a sickening thud as his head met the solid brick of the post office wall, to crack like an egg being broken on the side of a skillet.

The last of the three 'uneasy riders' sped by them, to be felled by a blast from Sam, who shot him in the neck, almost decapitating him; his head falling forward on to his chest to hang swinging by crimson threads of skin and muscle.

"The natives are none too friendly," Chad said, now wired in a way he had not experienced since way back when he had fought in Afghanistan.

"Okay, Rambo," Sam said. "Let's get the hell out of here. There's nothing but corpses, crazies and well fed buzzards and dogs, and I can live without being around any of them."

They headed back out of Vail to fresher air and safer climes. Their only other encounter was with an elderly man, whose streaming white hair flowed behind him as he jogged naked along the fast lane of I-70. Without breaking stride, he grinned maniacally at them and raised his middle finger in belligerent salute.

It was the same everywhere; a universal cataclysm. In Denver, Ralph Kepple, his wife, Sheila and son, Tom, had been the instruments of the city's virtual annihilation. They had flown out of Fairbanks after visiting Ralph's sister and family, just hours before the effects and implications of the infection were fully appreciated.

The Kepple family were dead within twenty hours of their return home, unconcerned at having passed a death sentence on ninety-five percent of their fellow city-dwellers.

Bobby Horton was distraught. He had woken to a living nightmare. His mother lay at the bottom of the stairs face down, her night-dress up over her ample ass, with blood leaking from that region, soaking the carpet in a large, dark irregular slick. In contrast,

277

her body was a bleached white, as though she had been drained like the sump of a car undergoing an oil change.

Bobby's father was still upstairs in bed, arched up as stiff as a board under the sheet with his mouth frozen open in a grimace, baring nicotine-stained teeth, and with his tongue poking out and up, rigid, swollen and black; eyes bulging and awash with blood, staring up to a point somewhere past the ceiling in permanent astonishment.

The phone was dead, so Bobby ran outside, stopping to lean on the gate for support as he saw the scattered bodies along the street. Drivers had been taken ill as they drove, losing control, crashing through fences and into the trees that lined the sidewalk. One car, an ageing Buick, stood less than ten feet from him with the driver's door wide open and an elderly man laying half in and half out of the vehicle. The old guy was bleeding from a gash to his forehead that had presumably been caused by his head hitting the asphalt. He was convulsing, thrashing as though suffering an epileptic fit, with his right foot drumming on the steering wheel in parody of a demented woodpecker.

Totally unequipped and unable to deal with an horrific situation that was far beyond his life experience, Bobby went back inside the house, stepping over his mother's corpse, hardly aware of his actions as he reached out to pull the sodden nightdress down over her butt, embarrassed by her nakedness. He went to his bedroom and dressed, hands shaking as he fumbled with the laces of his Nikes, his whole body feeling rubbery and out of control. He held back the screams of anguish that were rising in his throat; screams that if released, may never have stopped. Once dressed, he crossed the landing and gripped the cold brass handle of the door to his late parents' bedroom, forcing himself to enter the gloomy death chamber. Averting his eyes from his father's body, he snatched the bunch of car keys up from the nightstand and backed out, holding his breath against the coppery smell of still warm blood.

Bobby drove the Chevrolet across town to his place of work; The Denver Zoo in City Park. He had passed some bodies on the streets and in the park as he had driven in, so expected the worst. News bulletins on the car radio informed him of what was happening. He knew that most of the population was already dead, and he now had only one immediate plan.

Two of his work mates, also keepers, were lying on the staff room floor. The stench, and the sight of their contorted features overcame him, and he failed to hold back the vomit, which jetted out to splash on the upturned face of Ken Ferman, the head keeper of an enclosure called Predator Ridge. Bobby ran from the office, savagely wiping at his wet mouth and chin with the back of his hand. At just eighteen, he was facing a dilemma that he had no one to help him with or advise him on. He loved the animals he worked with, and could not bear to think of them starving in their cages and compounds. As he jogged along the walkways, it was apparent that the zoo's animals had not been affected by whatever was killing humans. He decided on his course of action. There was no choice but to release them all.

Carrying several bunches of keys, he spent the next two hours setting his charges free, leaving the more dangerous species until last. He was doing well, with only the big cats left to contend with. Most of the animals and birds he'd released had made good their escape, out into the city park and surrounding area. Some wandered the zoo grounds aimlessly, and a minority had not ventured from their enclosures, too nervous or too mentally damaged; programmed to a life of captivity and confinement, and unable to contemplate freedom.

As Bobby tried to figure out the safest way to liberate the two Bengal tigers, a previously released zebra charged. It came from behind, and as he turned, its head sideswiped his, knocking him to the ground, dazing him. The irate beast trampled him, hooves fracturing several of his ribs and rupturing his spleen, before it galloped off in the direction of Duck Lake.

Bobby could hardly move. It was an effort to snatch shallow breaths; each ragged inhalation causing sharp stabbing pains in his chest.

The hyenas broke cover from the bushes and circled him. There were five of them, all hungry and eager to devour the injured prey. Naturally cautious, they closed in slowly, slinking back as he shouted and though in great pain, waved his arms at them. But they knew that he was incapacitated. One darted forward, gripped his wrist and dragged him along the ground. His ensuing screams were incorporated with the already diverse cacophony of screeching, trumpeting and roaring from around the zoo. But there was no one to hear him, or to come to his aid.

Bobby felt himself being torn apart by the ugly, powerful, canine quadrupeds. Strong teeth bit through his ankle, splintering bones as the animal twisted and pulled against its companion, that had locked its muscular jaws around his wrist. A third tore a hole in his stomach, its broad snout crimson with blood as it wrenched his intestines from him, to create a surreal, Giger-like creation. His uncoiling guts glistened bluish-red; a living hose pipe, with hot vapor rising from their slimy surface.

At some point during the tug-of-war, with his body as the rope, Bobby ceased to scream and blacked out, taking no further active participation in the proceedings.

Later, when the hyenas had eaten their fill and quit the scene, several other species moved in to consume the remaining scraps of the keeper who had loved and cared for them, and had given them their freedom.

CHAPTER TWO
~ THE FORT ~

BACK at the plant, Travis met Sam and Chad as they parked outside the main store. He told them what had happened at the Supermarket; of the way in which Craig had wound up dead, with a meat cleaver embedded in his skull, and of how he had kicked to death the maniac who had done it. He was still shaking and in mild shock, finding it difficult to digest the episode. Sam related the incident that they had been involved in with the bikers, and knowing that they had blood on their hands went a long way to easing Travis's unfounded sense of guilt.

Sam, Chad, Travis and Scott were bombarded with questions from the others, who wanted to know what state Vail was in, and whether many people had survived the epidemic.

"We'd better hold a full meeting and tell these folks just how the land lies," Sam said to Ed Bliss, who had been the plant manager, and had subsequently formed the committee after the shit hit the fan.

"Let's say half an hour, in the canteen. I'll round everyone up and meet you there," Ed said, nervously picking at fingernails that were now short and ragged from biting, no longer carefully manicured as he had fastidiously kept them for decades.

A majority of the survivors had already started to look to Sam as a potential leader of the motley group; a position he had no intention of assuming. It was as if their knowing that he and Chad had experience of warfare and the hardship that walked hand in hand with it, in some way qualified them to deal with this apocalypse, and raised an unwarranted expectation that the two of them could somehow make everything right again. Sam was under no illusion. Nothing would *ever* be right again.

They drifted into the canteen in twos and threes, congregating at the tables, some smoking, – no longer concerned about the policy against it – many drinking coffee, others fidgeting and nervously whispering as though in a library. They were all eager to hear news of the outside world; to know what was happening away from what had now ceased to be their workplace and had become a refuge.

Sam lit a cigarette and stood up to address the expectant audience. "Firstly," he began. "I'm not going to lie to you or kid you that things aren't as bad as they really are. If Vail is representative of every other town and city, then life as we knew it is over. We can't expect help from anybody. We do know from the Internet that there are other groups out there in the same position as we're in. And like us they're having to regroup and set about building a new life. As for Vail, the only people we saw were either dead or deranged and homicidal. So we should assume rightly or wrongly that we are the only disease-free and rational survivors in this area. For the time being all outsiders should be treated as the enemy."

Sam stopped and took a mouthful of his now lukewarm coffee as he studied the sea of faces before him, trying to gauge the initial reaction to what he had told them; the overall mood it had invoked. He had already noted the strengths and weaknesses of many of them, having spent the past three weeks assessing who among them was potentially unstable, may not be able to cope adequately with such a dramatic and life-changing experience, and therefore be likely to cause problems. Putting down the now empty coffee cup, Sam continued. "This plant can be a fortress and sanctuary to us, or a prison, depending on how you look at it. We need to be very disciplined and organized, working towards the same goals as a closely knit team if we want to go forward and become a successful functioning community. Now, I'm sure that some of you have questions, so fire away"

"Uh, yeah, I got one," a big, fat guy said from the back of the room, waving his hand in the air to be seen.

Sam recognized the guy as being one of Krantz's security guards, who he'd met when they had first arrived at the plant, and who had shown undisguised resentment, probably because he thought that his position was under threat, or that new procedures and a change of job description and duties would make his job harder. He'd been right. Sam had deemed him second rate, idle, and totally unsuitable for the high standard he'd intended to implement; the porker would have had to go.

"Okay, but let's keep this get-together informal. What's your name, friend?"

"Benson...Paul Benson," he replied, his tone of voice surly.

"So what's your question, Paul?"

"I wanna know what there is to stop us all leavin' here right now, and checkin' up on our homes and families. If the flu, or whatever

282

the fuck it was is still active, then you've probably brought it back here with you."

"Good point, Paul," Sam said, thinking that the man was a moron. "The answer is simple. Anyone who wants to leave, at any time, should just go ahead and do it. All you need to ask yourself is, where would you go? And what would you do? I've told you that all we saw was death and madness. Anyone that you may meet, family or otherwise, is likely to try and kill you. And the danger of disease from the rotting corpses will be high for a few months yet, even if the epidemic *is* over."

"So what do you propose?" a rich, smooth as maple syrup female voice asked from Sam's right.

He thought that she looked striking...No, more than striking, drop dead gorgeous. She appeared to be in her late twenties. Ash-blond hair cascaded onto her shoulders, and her deep-blue eyes shone with both humor and intelligence.

"My name is Jill," she added. "Jill Myers."

Sam found it difficult to break eye contact with her as he spoke. He suddenly felt hot, flushed, and his stomach was doing back flips.

"Well, er, Jill," he said, relieved that his voice sounded calmer than he felt. "I suggest that we need to get focused and marshal our efforts. That will entail rosters and schedules for nearly everything. We need to know what people are good at; who has medical training or mechanical skills for example, to utilize all the experience and potential in this room to the best possible advantage. Hygiene, overall cleanliness, food preparation and security will all be major factors. Then there will be shopping trips, not just for food and clothing, but for more medical supplies, and any other specialist requirements. And as well as hunting for fresh meat, we should keep livestock and grow vegetables. I for one don't relish the idea of living on just canned stuff and TV dinners for any length of time. This place will have to be modified to suit us, with plenty of work and activities to keep us going forward instead of stagnating. Like it or not, we're going to have to live in a self-contained, fortified environment, and be able to cope with whatever unexpected events might come up."

Sam took his seat and looked to Ed Bliss for backup, glad to see him rise to his feet and start to address what were now his ex-staff.

"Firstly, I want to say that I think it fortuitous that Sam Reynolds and Chad York are with us at this time," he began, running his fingers fretfully through thinning hair. "Their expert knowledge of security, survival, and being able to deal with hostile environments or people, is invaluable." There was a sporadic ripple of applause from around the canteen, and Ed paused until it died away before resuming. "Being in possession of your personnel files, we should be able to place you in areas of work that will best suit you, and benefit us all. Power is no problem. We have the best industrial-size generators here that money could buy, and everything that we might possibly need is just a short drive away. Finally, for now, I am with immediate effect putting Sam and Chad in total charge of all aspects of security, with a mandate to do whatever they think is necessary to ensure the safety of all of us here at...what shall we call this place now...the Fort?"

They gathered every morning to make plans and discuss the way forward. The majority of the survivors were only too pleased to have leadership, and to be given responsibility in areas in which they were competent. Involvement gave structure and created a veneer of normality to help them adapt to what was a very abnormal existence.

At first, they had been able to contact other groups on the Internet. It was good for morale to know that there were other people with similar problems, making the best of a bad deal, and rebuilding. The nearest group to them, that they had been in touch with, was a colony, as they called themselves, near Phoenix, Arizona, many miles to the south. The near total annihilation was their common bond, and when the national grid ceased to function, the loss of communication with other select clubs of scattered survivors was a body blow.

Two incidents occurred at the Fort during the second month of what they had decided was year one of a new era. The first was a wakeup call. The second led to security becoming proactive, rather than just a protective and defensive enterprise.

Strother Cahill was the store man at the Fort. He had always kept to himself, being a quiet, introverted individual who preferred his own company, avoiding idle chitchat. Ornery and remote, Strother kept his distance from other employees, immersing himself in his work. He communicated with a nod or shake of his head, a grunt here and there, and if pressed, maybe a one syllable answer, given grudgingly. Strother was fifty-one, a stringy, gaunt looking man with short, silver-gray hair and features that reminded those of a certain age of that long gone, hell-raising actor, Lee Marvin.

Strother had seemed unperturbed by the sudden and near extinction of mankind. When asked his thoughts on the subject, he would shrug, and growl, "Shit happens." If anyone might have been considered well able to cope and adapt to what had taken place, it was him. It was therefore disturbing and shocking to everyone when Strother became the first fatality inside the Fort, by his own hand.

Chad heard the muffled explosion and headed for the rear of the building at a run. He threw open the door to the store's office, vaulted the counter and was met by the acrid smell of cordite as he entered the large warehouse. Coming to a stop, he looked towards the corpse twenty feet away, knowing immediately and exactly what had caused the thunderous report.

Sitting on a lime-green plastic contour chair, Strother had lit up a last cigarette and reflected on a disappointing life littered with unrealized dreams and thwarted ambitions. Two failed marriages and the death of his only son to leukemia, at the ripe old age of ten, had sent Strother into a slow but sure alcohol-assisted decline. He had held the M62 pineapple grenade in his right hand, under his chin, with the pin already pulled and lying at his feet, before taking a deep, final drag from the Marlboro and releasing the spring-loaded lever. His last conscious thought was of the mess he would be leaving behind for someone else to clean up.

Chad found a folded sheet of tarpaulin on the top of a packing crate. He shook it open and draped it over the headless body. Blood was still flooding from the ragged stump of the store man's neck, from which the severed arteries had sprayed scarlet, pulsing jets to paint abstract patterns on the gray concrete. Chad watched as it waned, then looking about and spotted the head. After being blown off, it had rolled across the floor to where it now lay at the end of the trail it had left, up against a photocopier. The eyes stared in fixed surprise above the remains of a face that was now an unrecognizable mulch of mangled flesh covering a skull that had suffered multiple fractures. Chad walked across to it, picked it up by hair more red than silver, and took it back to place under the tarp.

As Sam and a few others arrived, Chad was for some reason searching for the dead man's missing right hand.

"Jesus wept! What happened?" Ed Bliss said, standing frozen in his tracks, staring at the red rivulets that ran out from under Strother's makeshift shroud.

"He checked out. Offed himself with a grenade," Chad replied, stooping to pick up a finger that had marked its location with a bloody print on the carton of beakers that it had hit and fallen down in front of.

"Shit!" Sam said to Chad, regretting that they had let even the store man retain a key to the room they had utilized as an arsenal. "From now on, nobody but you and me have access to the weapons. God knows how many others might do something stupid if they get their hands on them. The last thing we need is some loose cannon running around with a fucking submachine gun or a rocket launcher."

Ed Bliss should have looked away as Chad pulled the tarp back to throw the finger in with the rest of Strother's remains, but didn't, and the sight of what was underneath it brought him to his knees, unsuccessfully attempting to hold down his lunch.

That had been the first incident. The second was even more alarming, and took place the following day as they laid Strother to rest in a grave dug in a grassy area adjacent to the parking lot.

Dave Williams was a lay preacher, and had all but finished up. "Dust to dust, ashes to—" he said, to be cut short as a small, perfectly round hole appeared in his forehead and he collapsed like a demolished building into the open grave to join Strother, with his bible still clutched in his hands.

"Move!" Sam shouted, running for the corner of the building, zigzagging as another shot split the air and a round blew flakes of brick from the wall in front of him.

Apart from Dave, they all made it back inside. Sam and Chad snatched loaded rifles from the arsenal and took the back stairs three at a time to the second floor, to try and pinpoint their assailants.

There were two men and a woman. All three were dressed in combat gear and carried hunting rifles. They walked across the parking lot to the grassy knoll, stopping at the side of the open grave to look down into it. Their laughter at the sight of Dave's crumpled body on top of Strother's sheet-wrapped corpse carried to where Sam and Chad looked out at them from an open window. One of the men unzipped his pants and proceeded to direct a thick stream of urine over the edge of the hole, on to the back of the late lay preacher's head.

"Drop the weapons, now," Sam shouted, his finger tight on the trigger of a 357 Winchester Trapper.

Two of the outsiders, whose hands were not otherwise occupied, immediately swung the barrels of their rifles up in the direction of the window, their actions met by a hail of bullets as Sam and Chad opened fire, cutting them down where they stood, and taking out their preoccupied accomplice for good measure.

Later, after throwing the bodies into the back of a pickup, they drove over a mile from the Fort, to then unload the corpses into a gulley at the side of the highway and use the flame-throwers to incinerate them, hoping that if they had been infected and were carriers of the virus, that fire would neutralize any bacteria within them.

From that day forth, all strangers were considered to be hostile, and risked being shot on sight if discovered in the proximity of the Fort. Sam and Chad selected and trained six of the other men to use the firearms, and regular external patrols were carried out. Any armed outsiders were terminated and cremated. The committee had made the decision that in these unusual and dire times, survival could only be ensured if they remained insular and, rightly or wrongly, adopted a 'judge, jury and executioner' policy.

As the weeks became months, a certain pattern developed to their post-contagion existence, and the community settled into a way of life that could not have been envisaged in their wildest dreams. Relationships blossomed, and several of the women became pregnant, which seemed to herald a new beginning. Sam and Jill Myers grew to be friends and then, with the passing of time, lovers. Chad also got involved, with a young woman called Laura Willis, who was slender, auburn-haired, with freckled, milk-white skin and jungle-cat green eyes that mesmerized him. They found by chance conversation that they had both been born and raised within three blocks of each other in Austin, Texas. Their paths had most likely crossed, but they had no recollection of ever having knowingly met.

The two couples enjoyed each other's company. They began to look forward, daring to imagine that this was just the start of what could be a bright and fulfilling new life.

If you enjoyed these sample chapters, then you can continue reading Re-Emergence in the Amazon Bookstore as either a paperback or an e-book.

Also By Michael Kerr

DI Matt Barnes Series
A REASON TO KILL
LETHAL INTENT
A NEED TO KILL
CHOSEN TO KILL
A PASSION TO KILL

The Joe Logan Series
AFTERMATH
ATONEMENT
ABSOLUTION
ALLEGIANCE

Other Crime Thrillers
DEADLY REPRISAL
DEADLY REQUITAL
BLACK ROCK BAY
A HUNGER WITHIN
THE SNAKE PIT
A DEADLY STATE OF MIND
TAKEN BY FORCE
DARK NEEDS AND EVIL DEEDS

Science Fiction / Horror
WAITING
CLOSE ENCOUNTERS OF THE STRANGE KIND
RE-EMERGENCE

Children's Fiction
Adventures in Otherworld
PART ONE – THE CHALICE OF HOPE
PART TWO – THE FAIRY CROWN